D1436107

The Stories of

BERNARD

MALAMUD

The Stories of

BERNARD

MALAMUD

CHATTO & WINDUS

THE HOGARTH PRESS
LONDON

Published in 1984 by
Chatto & Windus · The Hogarth Press
40 William IV Street
London WC2N 4DF

British Library Cataloguing in Publication Data

Malamud, Bernard
   The stories of Bernard Malamud.
   I. Title
   813'.54[F]   PS3563.A4
   ISBN 0–7011–2806–2

Printed in Great Britain by
Redwood Burn Limited, Trowbridge, Wiltshire

FOR ROBERT GIROUX

O<small>NE DAY</small> I began to write seriously: my writing had begun to impress me. Years of all sorts had gone by. The annunciation had long since tolled and the response was slow awakening. Much remained to do and become, if there was time. Some are born whole; others must seek this blessed state in a struggle to achieve order. That is no loss to speak of; ultimately such seeking becomes the subject matter of fiction. Observing, reading, thinking, one invents himself. A familiar voice asks: Who am I, and how can I say what I have to? He reads his sentences to see if the words answer the question. Thus the writer may tell his fortune. His imagination impels him to speak in several tongues though one is sufficient. At this point he, or she, may begin to write a story, a daring endeavor.

My early stories appeared in the nineteen-forties in non-commercial magazines, meaning I didn't get paid for them but was happy to have them published. "The Cost of Living" was the first story I sold. Diarmuid Russell, my agent, sent it to Pearl

Kazin at *Harper's Bazaar*, in 1949, the year my wife and I left New York City for Oregon. About three years later and a few stories in print, to my surprise, Catharine Carver, of *Partisan Review*, wanted "The Magic Barrel," a story I had asked her to read. I had written it in a carrel in the basement of the library at Oregon State, where I was allowed to teach freshman composition but not literature because I was nakedly without a Ph.D. Later, they permitted me to offer a night workshop in the short story to townspeople who, for one reason or another, wanted to take a writing class; I earned about a hundred dollars a term and got more pleasure than I had expected.

New York had lost much of its charm during World War II, and my wife and I and our infant son took off for the Pacific Northwest when I was offered a job in Corvallis, Oregon. Once there, it was a while before I had my bearings. I was overwhelmed by the beauty of Oregon, its vast skies, forests, coastal beaches; and the new life it offered, which I lived as best I could as I reflected on the old. My almost daily writing—I taught three days a week and wrote the other four—helped me make reasonable choices: what to zero in on and what to omit. On the whole I was learning much about America and holding fast to the discipline of the writing life.

Yet, almost without understanding why, I was thinking about my father's immigrant life—how he earned his meager living and what he paid for it, and about my mother's, diminished by fear and suffering—as perhaps matter for my fiction. In other words, I had them in mind as I invented the characters who became their fictional counterparts. I didn't much worry about what I was asked to teach at the college so long as I had plenty of time to work. My wife, wheeling a stroller, handed me sandwiches at lunchtime through the window of the Quonset hut I wrote and taught in, until I gave up writing on Sundays.

It was a while before I was at ease in the new culture—longer

for my New Rochelle-born wife. At first I felt displaced—one
foot in a bucket—though unafraid of—certainly enjoying—new
experience. Yet too much was tiresome. Oregon State, a former
land-grant college, had barely covered its cow tracks: Liberal
Arts was called the "Lower Division," to no one's embarrassment.
But the writing held me steady as I reacted to a more surprising
world than the one I had left in Brooklyn when my wife enticed
me across the bridge into Manhattan. I was enjoying our young
family—my son was four when my Western daughter was born.
We were making friends, some of whom became lifelong friends,
and were happy we had adventured forth.

At this time I was sharing an office with a colleague who often
wished aloud that he were a Jew. I understood the sentiment. I
was glad I was, although my father had his doubts about that.
He had sat in mourning when I married my gentile wife, but I
had thought it through and felt I knew what I was doing. After
the birth of our son my father came gently to greet my wife and
touch his grandchild. I thought of him as I began *The Assistant*
and felt I would often be writing about Jews, in celebration and
expiation, though perhaps that was having it both ways. I wanted
it both ways. I conceived of myself as a cosmopolitan man enjoying his freedom.

Before we expected it we were on our way abroad with the
happy prospect of a year in Rome. *Partisan Review* had recommended me for a Rockefeller Grant; and the college, somewhat
reluctantly, kicked in with my first sabbatical leave. Back in New
York City, in 1956, I said hello to Philip Rahv, who gazed at my
innocence and thought it was a good idea that I go abroad. We
looked up Edna and William Phillips in Paris and afterwards
moved into their hotel, the Lutèce, in Montparnasse. In Rome
we met Ralph and Fanny Ellison, who were at the American
Academy.

Before meeting Ralph I had talked to Saul Bellow one night in

Eugene, Oregon, at a lecture he gave. In 1952, after *The Natural* had appeared in a burst of imagination, I called on him at his apartment in Queens. He was about to publish *Augie March*.

That was in 1952. In 1956, after I had written *The Assistant*, Diarmuid Russell submitted it to Robert Giroux, who had bought *The Natural* for Harcourt, Brace. *The Assistant* had been to Harcourt before Giroux read it for Farrar, Straus, where he was now editor in chief. He cabled his acceptance as I sailed the high seas.

Almost from the beginning of my career as a writer I have more or less alternated writing novels with periods of work on short stories. I like the change of pace and form. I've enjoyed working in both forms—prose makes specific demands—although I confess having been longer in love with short fiction. If one begins early in life to make up and tell stories he has a better chance to be heard out if he keeps them short. "Vus hoks du mir a chinik?" (What tune are you banging on your pot?) my father once asked me when I went into a long tale about my mother's cousin.

Writing the short story, if one has that gift, is a good way to begin writing seriously. It demands form as it teaches it, although I've met some who would rather not be taught. They say that the demands of form interfere with their freedom to express themselves. But no good writer writes only as he pleases. He writes for a purpose, an idea, an effect; he writes to make himself understood and felt. I'm for freedom of thought, but one must recognize that it doesn't necessarily lead to art. Free thought may come close to self-deceit. One pays for free thought in the wrong cause if it intrudes, interferes with the logic of language and construction—if it falls like a hammer blow on the head as one is attempting to work out his fiction. Standards diluted at the start may exact a mean toll. Not many "make it" as serious writers of fiction, especially those who think of form as a catchword. Elitism in a just cause has its merits. Some in art have, by definition, to be best. There are standards in literature that a would-be writer must become familiar with—must uphold: as in the work of the finest writers of the past. The best endures in the accomplishment of the masters. One will be convinced, if he or she reads conscientiously and widely, that form as ultimate necessity is the basis of literature.

Soon I began to teach what Randall Jarrell called "imaginative writing," and most college catalogues—when these courses became popular after World War II—list as Creative Writing and teach too much of. I had gone into teaching with certain doubts —although I felt I could teach effectively—in order to support my family and get on with my writing. But being a teacher never interfered with my best concerns as a writer. I wrote steadily and happily, although it took Diarmuid Russell at least three years to sell a story. I had come to him via Maxim Lieber, who had never succeeded in selling any of my early work. "Here are some of your chickens coming home to roost" was his cheery word when he returned two or three stories. Afterwards, for one reason or another, he disappeared into Mexico, and when I last heard of him, was alive in Poland.

The doubts I speak of went with the job, for not everybody who joined my classes was a talented writer. Too many were in who should have been out. I had to teach anybody who wanted to be in my classes, though that changed when I began to teach at Bennington, where nobody frowned if I taught only six or eight people. Talent is always in short supply, although I had a handful of good writing students whom I enjoyed teaching and learning from. In essence one doesn't teach writing; he encourages talented people whom he may be able to do something for. I feel that writing courses are of limited value although they do induce some students to read fiction with care. On the whole I think such courses are overdone and overvalued. A year of them, at the most, can be helpful. After that, "creative writing" must yield to independent work with serious self-exploration going on, or the young writer will never come up with a meaningful subject matter and theme to organize his thinking around, and thus begin to provide himself with material for the long pull of a serious career. The more a writer does for himself, the better off he is. He mustn't be satisfied merely with learning tricks of the trade. Writing teaches the writer. Learning the art of the (human) sentence can keep him gainfully employed most, if not all, of his writing life.

Some writers don't need the short story to launch them into fiction, but I think it is a loss not to attempt to find out whether one can write them. I love the pleasures of the short story. One of them is the fast payoff. Whatever happens happens quickly. The writer mounts his personal Pegasus, even if it is an absent-minded nag who never made it on the race track; an ascension occurs and the ride begins. The scenery often surprises, and so do some of the people one meets. Somewhere I've said that a short story packs a self in a few pages predicating a lifetime. The drama is tense, happens fast, and is more often than not outlandish. In a few pages a good story portrays the complexity of a life while producing the surprise and effect of knowledge—not a bad payoff.

Then the writer is into the story for more than the ride. He stays with it as the terrain opens and events occur; he takes pleasure in the evolving fiction and tries to foresee its just resolution. As soon as his characters sense his confidence they show him their tricks. Before he knows it he becomes a figure in a circus with a boom-boom band. This puts him in high spirits and good form. If he's lucky, serious things may seem funny.

Much occurs in the writing that isn't expected, including some types you meet and become attached to. Before you know it you've collected two or three strangers swearing eternal love and friendship before they begin to make demands that divide and multiply. García Márquez will start a fiction with someone pushing a dream around, or running from one, and before you know it he has peopled a small country. Working alone to create stories, despite serious inconveniences, is not a bad way to live our human loneliness.

And let me say this: Literature, since it values man by describing him, tends toward morality in the same way that Robert Frost's poem is "a momentary stay against confusion." Art celebrates life and gives us our measure.

I've lived long among those I've invented.

"Good morning, professor. Are you by any chance looking for a bride, I offer only the best quality."

"I've got one, Salzman, but if she should come up with other plans I'll let you know. In the meantime, I'm hard at work on a new story."

"So enjoy," said Salzman.

Contents

The Stories of

BERNARD

MALAMUD

Take Pity

Davidov, the census-taker, opened the door without knocking, limped into the room, and sat wearily down. Out came his notebook and he was on the job. Rosen, the ex-coffee salesman, wasted, eyes despairing, sat motionless, cross-legged, on his cot. The square, clean but cold room, lit by a dim globe, was sparsely furnished: the cot, a folding chair, small table, old unpainted chests—no closets but who needed them?—and a small sink with a rough piece of green, institutional soap on its holder —you could smell it across the room. The worn black shade over the single narrow window was drawn to the ledge, surprising Davidov.

"What's the matter you don't pull the shade up?" he remarked.

Rosen ultimately sighed. "Let it stay."

"Why? Outside is light."

"Who needs light?"

"What then you need?"

"Light I don't need," replied Rosen.

Davidov, sour-faced, flipped through the closely scrawled pages of his notebook until he found a clean one. He attempted to scratch in a word with his fountain pen but it had run dry, so he fished a pencil stub out of his vest pocket and sharpened it with a cracked razor blade. Rosen paid no attention to the feathery shavings falling to the floor. He looked restless, seemed to be listening to or for something, although Davidov was convinced there was absolutely nothing to listen to. It was only when the census-taker somewhat irritably and with increasing loudness repeated a question that Rosen stirred and identified himself. He was about to furnish an address but caught himself and shrugged.

Davidov did not comment on the salesman's gesture. "So begin," he nodded.

"Who knows where to begin?" Rosen stared at the drawn shade. "Do they know here where to begin?"

"Philosophy we are not interested," said Davidov. "Start in how you met her."

"Who?" pretended Rosen.

"Her," he snapped.

"So if I got to begin, how you know about her already?" Rosen asked triumphantly.

Davidov spoke wearily, "You mentioned before."

Rosen remembered. They had questioned him upon his arrival and he now recalled blurting out her name. It was perhaps something in the air. It did not permit you to retain what you remembered. That was part of the cure, if you wanted a cure.

"Where I met her—?" Rosen murmured. "I met her where she always was—in the back room there in that hole in the wall that it was a waste of time for me I went there. Maybe I sold them a half a bag of coffee a month. This is not business."

"In business we are not interested."

"What then you are interested?" Rosen mimicked Davidov's tone.

Davidov clammed up coldly.

Rosen knew they had him where it hurt, so he went on: "The

husband was maybe forty, Axel Kalish, a Polish refugee. He worked like a blind horse when he got to America, and saved maybe two, three thousand dollars that he bought with the money this pisher grocery in a dead neighborhood where he didn't have a chance. He called my company up for credit and they sent me I should see. I recommended okay because I felt sorry. He had a wife, Eva, you know already about her, and two darling girls, one five and one three, little dolls, Fega and Surale, that I didn't want them to suffer. So right away I told him, without tricks, 'Kiddo, this is a mistake. This place is a grave. Here they will bury you if you don't get out quick!' "

Rosen sighed deeply.

"So?" Davidov had thus far written nothing, irking the ex-salesman.

"So?— Nothing. He didn't get out. After a couple months he tried to sell but nobody bought, so he stayed and starved. They never made expenses. Every day they got poorer you couldn't look in their faces. 'Don't be a damn fool,' I told him, 'go in bankruptcy.' But he couldn't stand to lose all his capital, and he was also afraid it would be hard to find a job. 'My God,' I said, 'do anything. Be a painter, a janitor, a junk man, but get out of here before everybody is a skeleton.'

"This he finally agreed with me, but before he could go in auction he dropped dead."

Davidov made a note. "How did he die?"

"On this I am not an expert," Rosen replied. "You know better than me."

"How did he die?" Davidov spoke impatiently. "Say in one word."

"From what he died?—he died, that's all."

"Answer, please, this question."

"Broke in him something. That's how."

"Broke what?"

"Broke what breaks. He was talking to me how bitter was his life, and he touched me on my sleeve to say something else, but the next minute his face got small and he fell down dead, the wife screaming, the little girls crying that it made in my heart pain. I am myself a sick man and when I saw him laying on the floor, I said to myself, 'Rosen, say goodbye, this guy is finished.' So I said it."

Rosen got up from the cot and strayed despondently around the room, avoiding the window. Davidov was occupying the only chair, so the ex-salesman was finally forced to sit on the edge of the bed again. This irritated him. He badly wanted a cigarette but disliked asking for one.

Davidov permitted him a short interval of silence, then leafed impatiently through his notebook. Rosen, to needle the census-taker, said nothing.

"So what happened?" Davidov finally demanded.

Rosen spoke with ashes in his mouth. "After the funeral—" He paused, tried to wet his lips, then went on, "He belonged to a society that they buried him, and he also left a thousand dollars insurance, but after the funeral I said to her, 'Eva, listen to me. Take the money and your children and run away from here. Let the creditors take the store. What will they get?— Nothing.'

"But she answered me, 'Where will I go, where, with my two orphans that their father left them to starve?'

" 'Go anywhere,' I said. 'Go to your relatives.'

"She laughed like laughs somebody who hasn't got no joy. 'My relatives Hitler took away from me.'

" 'What about Axel—surely an uncle somewheres?'

" 'Nobody,' she said. 'I will stay here like my Axel wanted. With the insurance I will buy new stock and fix up the store. Every week I will decorate the window, and in this way gradually will come in new customers—'

" 'Eva, my darling girl—'

" 'A millionaire I don't expect to be. All I want is I should make a little living and take care on my girls. We will live in the back here like before, and in this way I can work and watch them, too.'

" 'Eva,' I said, 'you are a nice-looking young woman, only thirty-eight years. Don't throw away your life here. Don't flush in the toilet—you should excuse me—the thousand poor dollars from your dead husband. Believe me, I know from such stores. After thirty-five years' experience I know a graveyard when I smell it. Go better someplace and find a job. You're young yet. Sometime you will meet somebody and get married.'

" 'No, Rosen, not me,' she said. 'With marriage I am finished. Nobody wants a poor widow with two children.'

" 'This I don't believe it.'

" 'I know,' she said.

"Never in my life I saw so bitter a woman's face.

" 'No,' I said. 'No.'

" 'Yes, Rosen, yes. In my whole life I never had anything. In my whole life I always suffered. I don't expect better. This is my life.'

"I said no and she said yes. What could I do? I am a man with only one kidney, and worse than that, that I won't mention it. When I talked she didn't listen, so I stopped to talk. Who can argue with a widow?"

The ex-salesman glanced up at Davidov but the census-taker did not reply. "What happened then?" he asked.

"What happened?" mocked Rosen. "Happened what happens."

Davidov's face grew red.

"What happened, happened," Rosen said hastily. "She ordered from the wholesalers all kinds goods that she paid for them cash. All week she opened boxes and packed on the shelves cans, jars, packages. Also she cleaned, and she washed, and she mopped with oil the floor. With tissue paper she made new decorations in the window, everything should look nice—but who came in? Nobody except a few poor customers from the tenement around the corner. And when they came? When was closed the supermarkets and they needed some little item that they forgot to buy, like a quart milk, fifteen cents' cheese, a small can sardines for lunch. In a few months was again dusty the cans on the shelves, and her money was gone. Credit she couldn't get except from me, and from me she got because I paid out of my pocket the company. This she didn't know. She worked, she dressed clean, she waited that the store should get better. Little by little the shelves got empty, but where was the profit? They ate it up. When I looked on the little girls I knew what she didn't tell me. Their faces were white, they were thin, they were hungry. She kept the little food that was left, on the shelves. One night I brought in a nice piece of sirloin, but I could see from her eyes that she didn't like that I did it. So what else could I do? I have a heart and I am human."

Here the ex-salesman wept.

Davidov pretended not to see though once he peeked.

Rosen blew his nose, then went on more calmly, "When the children were sleeping we sat in the dark there, in the back, and not once in four hours opened the door should come in a customer. 'Eva, for Godsakes, *run away*,' I said.

" 'I have no place to go,' she said.

" 'I will give you where you can go, and please don't say to me no. I am a bachelor, this you know. I got whatever I need and more besides. Let me help you and the children. Money don't interest me. Interests me good health, but I can't buy it. I'll tell you what I will do. Let this place go to the creditors and move into a two-family house that I own, which the top floor is now empty. Rent will cost you nothing. In the meantime you can go and find a job. I will also pay the downstairs lady to take care of the girls—God bless them—until you will come home. With your wages you will buy the food, if you need clothes, and also save a little. This you can use when you get married someday. What do you say?'

"She didn't answer me. She only looked on me in such a way, with such burning eyes, like I was small and ugly. For the first time I thought to myself, 'Rosen, this woman don't like you.'

" 'Thank you very kindly, my friend Mr. Rosen,' she answered me, 'but charity we are not needing. I got yet a paying business, and it will get better when times are better. Now is bad times. When comes again good times will get better the business.'

" 'Who charity?' I cried to her. 'What charity? Speaks to you your husband's a friend.'

" 'Mr. Rosen, my husband didn't have no friends.'

" 'Can't you see that I want to help the children?'

" 'The children have their mother.'

" 'Eva, what's the matter with you?' I said. 'Why do you make sound bad something that I mean it should be good?'

"This she didn't answer. I felt sick in my stomach, and was coming also a headache so I left.

"All night I didn't sleep, and then all of a sudden I figured out a reason why she was worried. She was worried I would ask for some kind of payment except cash. She got the wrong man. Anyway, this made me think of something that I didn't think about before. I thought now to ask her to marry me. What did she have to lose? I could take care of myself without any trouble to them. Fega and Surale would have a father he could give them for the movies, or sometime to buy a little doll to play with, and when I died, would go to them my investments and insurance policies.

"The next day I spoke to her.

" 'For myself, Eva, I don't want a thing. Absolutely not a thing. For you and your girls—everything. I am not a strong man, Eva. In fact, I am sick. I tell you this you should understand I don't expect to live long. But even for a few years would be nice to have a little family.'

"She was with her back to me and didn't speak.

"When she turned around again her face was white but the mouth was like iron.

" 'No, Mr. Rosen.'

" 'Why not, tell me?'

" 'I had enough with sick men.' She began to cry. 'Please, Mr. Rosen. Go home.'

"I didn't have strength I should argue with her, so I went home. I went home but hurt me in my mind. All day long and all night I felt bad. My back pained me where was missing my kidney. Also too much smoking. I tried to understand this woman but I couldn't. Why should somebody that her two children were starving always say no to a man that he wanted to help her? What did I do to her bad? Am I maybe a murderer she should hate me so much? All that I felt in my heart was pity for her and the children, but I couldn't convince her. Then I went back and begged her she should let me help them, and once more she told me no.

" 'Eva,' I said, 'I don't blame you that you don't want a sick man. So come with me to a marriage broker and we will find you a strong, healthy husband that he will support you and your girls. I will give the dowry.'

"She screamed, 'On this I don't need your help, Rosen!'

"I didn't say no more. What more could I say? All day long, from early in the morning till late in the night she worked like an animal. All day she mopped, she washed with soap and a brush the shelves, the few cans she polished, but the store was still rotten. The little girls I was afraid to look at. I could see in their faces their bones. They were tired, they were weak. Little Surale held with her hand all the time the dress of Fega. Once when I saw them in the street I gave them some cakes, but when I tried the next day to give them something else, the mother shouldn't know, Fega answered me, 'We can't take, Momma says today is a fast day.'

"I went inside. I made my voice soft. 'Eva, on my bended knees, I am a man with nothing in this world. Allow me that I should have a little pleasure before I die. Allow me that I should help you to stock up once more the store.'

"So what did she do? She cried, it was terrible to see. And after she cried, what did she say? She told me to go away and I shouldn't come back. I felt like to pick up a chair and break her head.

"In my house I was too weak to eat. For two days I took in my mouth nothing except maybe a spoon of chicken noodle soup, or maybe a glass tea without sugar. This wasn't good for me. My health felt bad.

"Then I made up a scheme that I was a friend of Axel's who lived in Jersey. I said I owed Axel seven hundred dollars that he lent me this money fifteen years ago, before he got married. I said I did not have the whole money now, but I would send her every week twenty dollars till it was paid up the debt. I put inside the letter two tens and gave it to a friend of mine, also a salesman, he should mail it in Newark so she wouldn't be suspicious who wrote the letters."

To Rosen's surprise Davidov had stopped writing. The book was full, so he tossed it onto the table, yawned, yet listened amiably. His curiosity had died.

Rosen got up and fingered the notebook. He tried to read the small distorted handwriting but could not make out a single word.

"It's not English and it's not Yiddish," he said. "Could it be in Hebrew?"

"No," answered Davidov. "It's an old-fashioned language they don't use it nowadays."

"Oh?" Rosen returned to the cot. He saw no purpose in going on now that it was not required, but he felt he had to.

"Came back all the letters," he said dully. "The first she opened it, then pasted back again the envelope, but the rest she didn't even open."

" 'Here,' I said to myself, 'is a very strange thing—a person that you can never give her anything. —*But I will give.'*

"I went then to my lawyer and we made out a will that everything I had—all my investments, my two houses that I owned, also furniture, my car, the checking account—every cent would go to her, and when she died, the rest would be left for the two girls. The same with my insurance. They would be my beneficiaries. Then I signed and went home. In the kitchen I turned on the gas and put my head in the stove.

"Let her say now no."

Davidov, scratching his stubbled cheek, nodded. This was the part he already knew. He got up and, before Rosen could cry no, idly raised the window shade.

It was twilight in space but a woman stood before the window. Rosen with a bound was off his cot to see.

It was Eva, staring at him with haunted, beseeching eyes. She raised her arms to him.

Infuriated, the ex-salesman shook his fist.

"Whore, bastard, bitch," he shouted at her. "Go 'way from here. Go home to your children."

Davidov made no move to hinder him as Rosen rammed down the window shade.

The First Seven Years

FELD, the shoemaker, was annoyed that his helper, Sobel, was so insensitive to his reverie that he wouldn't for a minute cease his fanatic pounding at the other bench. He gave him a look, but Sobel's bald head was bent over the last as he worked, and he didn't notice. The shoemaker shrugged and continued to peer through the partly frosted window at the nearsighted haze of falling February snow. Neither the shifting white blur outside, nor the sudden deep remembrance of the snowy Polish village where he had wasted his youth, could turn his thoughts from Max the college boy (a constant visitor in the mind since early that morning when Feld saw him trudging through the snowdrifts on his way to school), whom he so much respected because of the sacrifices he had made throughout the years—in winter or direst heat—to further his education. An old wish returned to haunt the shoemaker: that he had had a son instead of a daughter, but this blew away in the snow, for Feld, if anything, was a practical man. Yet he could not help but contrast the diligence of the boy, who was a peddler's son, with Miriam's unconcern for an education. True, she was always with a book in her hand, yet when the opportunity arose for a college education, she had said no she would rather find a job. He had begged her to go, pointing out how many fathers could not afford to send their children to college, but she said she wanted to be independent. As for education, what was it, she asked, but books, which Sobel, who diligently read the classics, would as usual advise her on. Her answer greatly grieved her father.

A figure emerged from the snow and the door opened. At the counter the man withdrew from a wet paper bag a pair of battered shoes for repair. Who he was the shoemaker for a moment had no idea, then his heart trembled as he realized, before he had thoroughly discerned the face, that Max himself was standing there, embarrassedly explaining what he wanted done to his old shoes. Though Feld listened eagerly, he couldn't hear a word, for the opportunity that had burst upon him was deafening.

He couldn't exactly recall when the thought had occurred to him, because it was clear he had more than once considered suggesting to the boy that he go out with Miriam. But he had not dared speak, for if Max said no, how would he face him again? Or suppose Miriam, who harped so often on independence, blew up in anger and shouted at him for his meddling? Still, the chance was too good to let by: all it meant was an introduction. They might long ago have become friends had they happened to meet somewhere, therefore was it not his duty—an obligation— to bring them together, nothing more, a harmless connivance to replace an accidental encounter in the subway, let's say, or a mutual friend's introduction in the street? Just let him once see and talk to her and he would for sure be interested. As for Miriam, what possible harm for a working girl in an office, who met only loudmouthed salesmen and illiterate shipping clerks, to make the acquaintance of a fine scholarly boy? Maybe he would awaken in her a desire to go to college; if not—the shoemaker's mind at last came to grips with the truth—let her marry an educated man and live a better life.

When Max finished describing what he wanted done to his shoes, Feld marked them, both with enormous holes in the soles which he pretended not to notice, with large white-chalk X's and the rubber heels, thinned to the nails, he marked with O's, though it troubled him he might have mixed up the letters. Max inquired the price, and the shoemaker cleared his throat and asked the boy, above Sobel's insistent hammering, would he please step through the side door there into the hall. Though surprised, Max did as the shoemaker requested, and Feld went in after him. For a minute they were both silent, because Sobel had stopped banging, and it seemed they understood neither was to say anything until the noise began again. When it did, loudly, the shoemaker quickly told Max why he had asked to talk to him.

"Ever since you went to high school," he said, in the dimly lit hallway, "I watched you in the morning go to the subway to school, and I said always to myself, this is a fine boy that he wants so much an education."

"Thanks," Max said, nervously alert. He was tall and grotesquely thin, with sharply cut features, particularly a beak-like nose. He was wearing a loose, long, slushy overcoat that hung down to his ankles, looking like a rug draped over his bony shoulders, and a soggy old brown hat, as battered as the shoes he had brought in.

"I am a businessman," the shoemaker abruptly said to conceal his embarrassment, "so I will explain you right away why I talk to you. I have a girl, my daughter Miriam—she is nineteen—a very nice girl and also so pretty that everybody looks on her when she passes by in the street. She is smart, always with a book, and I thought to myself that a boy like you, an educated boy—I thought maybe you will be interested sometime to meet a girl like this." He laughed a bit when he had finished and was tempted to say more but had the good sense not to.

Max stared down like a hawk. For an uncomfortable second he was silent, then he asked, "Did you say nineteen?"

"Yes."

"Would it be all right to inquire if you have a picture of her?"

"Just a minute." The shoemaker went into the store and hastily returned with a snapshot that Max held up to the light.

"She's all right," he said.

Feld waited.

"And is she sensible—not the flighty kind?"

"She is very sensible."

After another short pause, Max said it was okay with him if he met her.

"Here is my telephone," said the shoemaker, hurriedly handing him a slip of paper. "Call her up. She comes home from work six o'clock."

Max folded the paper and tucked it away into his worn leather wallet.

"About the shoes," he said. "How much did you say they will cost me?"

"Don't worry about the price."

"I just like to have an idea."

"A dollar—dollar fifty. A dollar fifty," the shoemaker said.

At once he felt bad, for he usually charged $2.25 for this kind of job. Either he should have asked the regular price or done the work for nothing.

Later, as he entered the store, he was startled by a violent clanging and looked up to see Sobel pounding upon the naked last. It broke, the iron striking the floor and jumping with a thump against the wall, but before the enraged shoemaker could cry out, the assistant had torn his hat and coat off the hook and rushed out into the snow.

:　　　:　　　:

So Feld, who had looked forward to anticipating how it would go with his daughter and Max, instead had a great worry on his mind. Without his temperamental helper he was a lost man, especially as it was years now since he had carried the store alone. The shoemaker had for an age suffered from a heart condition that threatened collapse if he dared exert himself. Five years ago, after an attack, it had appeared as though he would have either to sacrifice his business on the auction block and live on a pittance thereafter, or put himself at the mercy of some unscrupulous employee who would in the end probably ruin him. But just at the moment of his darkest despair, this Polish refugee, Sobel, had appeared one night out of the street and begged for work. He was a stocky man, poorly dressed, with a bald head that had once been blond, a severely plain face, and soft blue eyes prone to tears over the sad books he read, a young man but old—no one would have guessed thirty. Though he confessed he knew nothing of shoemaking, he said he was apt and would work for very little if Feld taught him the trade. Thinking that with, after all, a landsman, he would have less to fear than from a complete stranger, Feld took him on and within six weeks the refugee rebuilt as good a shoe as he, and not long thereafter expertly ran the business for the thoroughly relieved shoemaker.

Feld could trust him with anything and did, frequently going home after an hour or two at the store, leaving all the money in the till, knowing Sobel would guard every cent of it. The amazing thing was that he demanded so little. His wants were few; in money he wasn't interested—in nothing but books, it seemed —which he one by one lent to Miriam, together with his profuse, queer written comments, manufactured during his lonely rooming house evenings, thick pads of commentary which the shoemaker peered at and twitched his shoulders over as his daughter, from her fourteenth year, read page by sanctified page, as if the word of God were inscribed on them. To protect Sobel, Feld himself had to see that he received more than he asked for. Yet his conscience bothered him for not insisting that the assistant accept a better wage than he was getting, though Feld had honestly told him he could earn a handsome salary if he worked elsewhere, or maybe opened a place of his own. But the assistant answered, somewhat ungraciously, that he was not interested in going elsewhere, and though Feld frequently asked himself, What keeps him here? why does he stay? he finally answered it that the man, no doubt because of his terrible experiences as a refugee, was afraid of the world.

After the incident with the broken last, angered by Sobel's behavior, the shoemaker decided to let him stew for a week in the rooming house, although his own strength was taxed dangerously and the business suffered. However, after several sharp nagging warnings from both his wife and daughter, he went finally in search of Sobel, as he had once before, quite recently, when over some fancied slight—Feld had merely asked him not to give Miriam so many books to read because her eyes were strained and red—the assistant had left the place in a huff, an incident which, as usual, came to nothing, for he had returned after the shoemaker had talked to him, and taken his seat at the bench. But this time, after Feld had plodded through the snow to Sobel's house—he had thought of sending Miriam but the idea became repugnant to him—the burly landlady at the door informed him in a nasal voice that Sobel was not at home, and though Feld knew this was a nasty lie, for where had the refugee to go? still for some reason he was not completely sure of—it may have been the cold and his fatigue—he decided not to insist on seeing him. Instead he went home and hired a new helper.

Thus he settled the matter, though not entirely to his satisfaction, for he had much more to do than before, and so, for example, could no longer lie late in bed mornings because he had to get up to open the store for the new assistant, a speechless, dark man with an irritating rasp as he worked, whom he would not trust with the key as he had Sobel. Furthermore, this one, though able to do a fair repair job, knew nothing of grades of leather or prices, so Feld had to make his own purchases; and every night at closing time it was necessary to count the money in the till and lock up. However, he was not dissatisfied, for he lived much in his thoughts of Max and Miriam. The college boy had called her, and they had arranged a meeting for this coming Friday night. The shoemaker would personally have preferred Saturday, which he felt would make it a date of the first magnitude, but he learned Friday was Miriam's choice, so he said nothing. The day of the week did not matter. What mattered was the aftermath. Would they like each other and want to be friends? He sighed at all the time that would have to go by before he knew for sure. Often he was tempted to talk to Miriam about the boy, to ask whether she thought she would like his type—he had told her only that he considered Max a nice boy and had suggested he call her—but the one time he tried she snapped at him—justly—how should she know?

At last Friday came. Feld was not feeling particularly well so he stayed in bed, and Mrs. Feld thought it better to remain in the bedroom with him when Max called. Miriam received the boy, and her parents could hear their voices, his throaty one, as they talked. Just before leaving, Miriam brought Max to the bedroom door and he stood there a minute, a tall, slightly hunched figure wearing a thick, droopy suit, and apparently at ease as he greeted the shoemaker and his wife, which was surely a good sign. And Miriam, although she had worked all day, looked fresh and pretty. She was a large-framed girl with a well-shaped body, and she had a fine open face and soft hair. They made, Feld thought, a first-class couple.

Miriam returned after 11:30. Her mother was already asleep, but the shoemaker got out of bed and after locating his bathrobe went into the kitchen, where Miriam, to his surprise, sat at the table, reading.

"So where did you go?" Feld asked pleasantly.

"For a walk," she said, not looking up.

"I advised him," Feld said, clearing his throat, "he shouldn't spend so much money."

"I didn't care."

The shoemaker boiled up some water for tea and sat down at the table with a cupful and a thick slice of lemon.

"So how," he sighed after a sip, "did you enjoy?"

"It was all right."

He was silent. She must have sensed his disappointment, for she added, "You can't really tell much the first time."

"You will see him again?"

Turning a page, she said that Max had asked for another date.

"For when?"

"Saturday."

"So what did you say?"

"What did I say?" she asked, delaying for a moment—"I said yes."

Afterwards she inquired about Sobel, and Feld, without exactly knowing why, said the assistant had got another job. Miriam said nothing more and went on reading. The shoemaker's conscience did not trouble him; he was satisfied with the Saturday date.

During the week, by placing here and there a deft question, he managed to get from Miriam some information about Max. It surprised him to learn that the boy was not studying to be either a doctor or lawyer but was taking a business course leading to a degree in accountancy. Feld was a little disappointed because he thought of accountants as bookkeepers and would have preferred "a higher profession." However, it was not long before he had investigated the subject and discovered that Certified Public Accountants were highly respected people, so he was thoroughly content as Saturday approached. But because Saturday was a

busy day, he was much in the store and therefore did not see
Max when he came to call for Miriam. From his wife he learned
there had been nothing especially revealing about their greeting.
Max had rung the bell and Miriam had got her coat and left with
him—nothing more. Feld did not probe, for his wife was not
particularly observant. Instead, he waited up for Miriam with a
newspaper on his lap, which he scarcely looked at so lost was he
in thinking of the future. He awoke to find her in the room with
him, tiredly removing her hat. Greeting her, he was suddenly
inexplicably afraid to ask anything about the evening. But since
she volunteered nothing he was at last forced to inquire how she
had enjoyed herself. Miriam began something noncommittal, but
apparently changed her mind, for she said after a minute, "I was
bored."

When Feld had sufficiently recovered from his anguished disappointment to ask why, she answered without hesitation, "Because he's nothing more than a materialist."

"What means this word?"

"He has no soul. He's only interested in things."

He considered her statement for a long time, then asked, "Will
you see him again?"

"He didn't ask."

"Suppose he will ask you?"

"I won't see him."

He did not argue; however, as the days went by he hoped
increasingly she would change her mind. He wished the boy
would telephone, because he was sure there was more to him
than Miriam, with her inexperienced eye, could discern. But
Max didn't call. As a matter of fact he took a different route to
school, no longer passing the shoemaker's store, and Feld was
deeply hurt.

Then one afternoon Max came in and asked for his shoes. The
shoemaker took them down from the shelf where he had placed

them, apart from the other pairs. He had done the work himself and the soles and heels were well built and firm. The shoes had been highly polished and somehow looked better than new. Max's Adam's apple went up once when he saw them, and his eyes had little lights in them.

"How much?" he asked, without directly looking at the shoemaker.

"Like I told you before," Feld answered sadly. "One dollar fifty cents."

Max handed him two crumpled bills and received in return a newly minted silver half dollar.

He left. Miriam had not been mentioned. That night the shoemaker discovered that his new assistant had been all the while stealing from him, and he suffered a heart attack.

:   :   :

Though the attack was very mild, he lay in bed for three weeks. Miriam spoke of going for Sobel, but sick as he was Feld rose in wrath against the idea. Yet in his heart he knew there was no other way, and the first weary day back in the shop thoroughly convinced him, so that night after supper he dragged himself to Sobel's rooming house.

He toiled up the stairs, though he knew it was bad for him, and at the top knocked at the door. Sobel opened it and the shoemaker entered. The room was a small, poor one, with a single window facing the street. It contained a narrow cot, a low table, and several stacks of books piled haphazardly around on the floor along the wall, which made him think how queer Sobel was, to be uneducated and read so much. He had once asked him, Sobel, why you read so much? and the assistant could not answer him. Did you ever study in a college someplace? he had asked, but Sobel shook his head. He read, he said, to know. But to know what, the shoemaker demanded, and to know, why?

Sobel never explained, which proved he read so much because he was queer.

Feld sat down to recover his breath. The assistant was resting on his bed with his heavy back to the wall. His shirt and trousers were clean, and his stubby fingers, away from the shoemaker's bench, were strangely pallid. His face was thin and pale, as if he had been shut in this room since the day he had bolted from the store.

"So when you will come back to work?" Feld asked him.

To his surprise, Sobel burst out, "Never."

Jumping up, he strode over to the window that looked out upon the miserable street. "Why should I come back?" he cried.

"I will raise your wages."

"Who cares for your wages!"

The shoemaker, knowing he didn't care, was at a loss what else to say.

"What do you want from me, Sobel?"

"Nothing."

"I always treated you like you was my son."

Sobel vehemently denied it. "So why you look for strange boys in the street they should go out with Miriam? Why you don't think of me?"

The shoemaker's hands and feet turned freezing cold. His voice became so hoarse he couldn't speak. At last he cleared his throat and croaked, "So what has my daughter got to do with a shoemaker thirty-five years old who works for me?"

"Why do you think I worked so long for you?" Sobel cried out. "For the stingy wages I sacrificed five years of my life so you could have to eat and drink and where to sleep?"

"Then for what?" shouted the shoemaker.

"For Miriam," he blurted—"for her."

The shoemaker, after a time, managed to say, "I pay wages in cash, Sobel," and lapsed into silence. Though he was seething with excitement, his mind was coldly clear, and he had to admit to himself he had sensed all along that Sobel felt this way. He had never so much as thought it consciously, but he had felt it and was afraid.

"Miriam knows?" he muttered hoarsely.

"She knows."

"You told her?"

"No."

"Then how does she know?"

"How does she know?" Sobel said. "Because she knows. She knows who I am and what is in my heart."

Feld had a sudden insight. In some devious way, with his books and commentary, Sobel had given Miriam to understand that he loved her. The shoemaker felt a terrible anger at him for his deceit.

"Sobel, you are crazy," he said bitterly. "She will never marry a man so old and ugly like you."

Sobel turned black with rage. He cursed the shoemaker, but then, though he trembled to hold it in, his eyes filled with tears and he broke into deep sobs. With his back to Feld, he stood at the window, fists clenched, and his shoulders shook with his choked sobbing.

Watching him, the shoemaker's anger diminished. His teeth were on edge with pity for the man, and his eyes grew moist. How strange and sad that a refugee, a grown man, bald and old with his miseries, who had by the skin of his teeth escaped Hitler's incinerators, should fall in love, when he had got to America, with a girl less than half his age. Day after day, for five years he had sat at his bench, cutting and hammering away, waiting for the girl to become a woman, unable to ease his heart with speech, knowing no protest but desperation.

"Ugly I didn't mean," he said half aloud.

Then he realized that what he had called ugly was not Sobel

but Miriam's life if she married him. He felt for his daughter a strange and gripping sorrow, as if she were already Sobel's bride, the wife, after all, of a shoemaker, and had in her life no more than her mother had had. And all his dreams for her—why he had slaved and destroyed his heart with anxiety and labor—all these dreams of a better life were dead.

The room was quiet. Sobel was standing by the window reading, and it was curious that when he read he looked young.

"She is only nineteen," Feld said brokenly. "This is too young yet to get married. Don't ask her for two years more, till she is twenty-one, then you can talk to her."

Sobel didn't answer. Feld rose and left. He went slowly down the stairs but once outside, though it was an icy night and the crisp falling snow whitened the street, he walked with a stronger stride.

But the next morning, when the shoemaker arrived, heavy-hearted, to open the store, he saw he needn't have come, for his assistant was already seated at the last, pounding leather for his love.

The Mourners

KESSLER, formerly an egg candler, lived alone on social
security. Though past sixty-five, he might have found well-paying
work with more than one butter and egg wholesaler, for he
sorted and graded with speed and accuracy, but he was a quar-
relsome type and considered a troublemaker, so the wholesalers
did without him. Therefore, after a time he retired, living with
few wants on his old-age pension. Kessler inhabited a small
cheap flat on the top floor of a decrepit tenement on the East
Side. Perhaps because he lived above so many stairs, no one
bothered to visit him. He was much alone, as he had been most
of his life. At one time he'd had a family, but unable to stand his
wife or children, always in his way, he had after some years
walked out on them. He never saw them thereafter because he
never sought them, and they did not seek him. Thirty years had
passed. He had no idea where they were, nor did he think much
about it.

In the tenement, although he had lived there ten years, he was
more or less unknown. The tenants on both sides of his flat on
the fifth floor, an Italian family of three middle-aged sons and

their wizened mother, and a sullen, childless German couple named Hoffman, never said hello to him, nor did he greet any of them on the way up or down the narrow wooden stairs. Others of the house recognized Kessler when they passed him in the street, but they thought he lived elsewhere on the block. Ignace, the small, bent-back janitor, knew him best, for they had several times played two-handed pinochle; but Ignace, usually the loser because he lacked skill at cards, had stopped going up after a time. He complained to his wife that he couldn't stand the stink there, that the filthy flat with its junky furniture made him sick. The janitor had spread the word about Kessler to the others on the floor, and they shunned him as a dirty old man. Kessler understood this but had contempt for them all.

One day Ignace and Kessler began a quarrel over the way the egg candler piled oily bags overflowing with garbage into the dumbwaiter, instead of using a pail. One word shot off another, and they were soon calling each other savage names, when Kessler slammed the door in the janitor's face. Ignace ran down five flights of stairs and loudly cursed out the old man to his impassive wife. It happened that Gruber, the landlord, a fat man with a consistently worried face, who wore yards of baggy clothes, was in the building, making a check of plumbing repairs, and to him the enraged Ignace related the trouble he was having with Kessler. He described, holding his nose, the smell in Kessler's flat, and called him the dirtiest person he ever saw. Gruber knew his janitor was exaggerating, but he felt burdened by financial worries which shot his blood pressure up to astonishing heights, so he settled it quickly by saying, "Give him notice." None of the tenants in the house had held a written lease since the war, and Gruber felt confident, in case somebody asked questions, that he could easily justify his dismissal of Kessler as an undesirable tenant. It had occurred to him that Ignace could then slap a cheap coat of paint on the walls, and the flat would be let to someone for five dollars more than the old man was paying.

That night after supper, Ignace victoriously ascended the stairs and knocked on Kessler's door. The egg candler opened it, and seeing who stood there, immediately slammed it shut. Ignace shouted through the door, "Mr. Gruber says to give notice. We don't want you around here. Your dirt stinks the whole house." There was silence, but Ignace waited, relishing what he had said. Although after five minutes he still heard no sound, the janitor stayed there, picturing the old Jew trembling behind the locked door. He spoke again, "You got two weeks' notice till the first, then you better move out or Mr. Gruber and myself will throw you out." Ignace watched as the door slowly opened. To his surprise he found himself frightened at the old man's appearance. He looked, in the act of opening the door, like a corpse adjusting his coffin lid. But if he appeared dead, his voice was alive. It rose terrifyingly harsh from his throat, and he sprayed curses over all the years of Ignace's life. His eyes were reddened, his cheeks sunken, and his wisp of beard moved agitatedly. He seemed to be losing weight as he shouted. The janitor no longer had any heart for the matter, but he could not bear so many insults all at once, so he cried out, "You dirty old bum, you better get out and don't make so much trouble." To this the enraged Kessler swore they would first have to kill him and drag him out dead.

On the morning of the first of December, Ignace found in his letter box a soiled folded paper containing Kessler's twenty-five dollars. He showed it to Gruber that evening when the landlord came to collect the rent money. Gruber, after a minute of absently contemplating the money, frowned disgustedly.

"I thought I told you to give notice."

"Yes, Mr. Gruber," Ignace agreed. "I gave him."

"That's a helluva chutzpah," said Gruber. "Gimme the keys."

Ignace brought the ring of passkeys, and Gruber, breathing heavily, began the lumbering climb up the long avenue of stairs.

Although he rested on each landing, the fatigue of climbing, and his profuse flowing perspiration, heightened his irritation.

Arriving at the top floor he banged his fist on Kessler's door. "Gruber, the landlord. Open up here."

There was no answer, no movement within, so Gruber inserted his key into the lock and twisted. Kessler had barricaded the door with a chest and some chairs. Gruber had to put his shoulder to the door and shove before he could step into the hallway of the badly lit two-and-a-half-room flat. The old man, his face drained of blood, was standing in the kitchen doorway.

"I warned you to scram outa here," Gruber said loudly. "Move out or I'll telephone the city marshal."

"Mr. Gruber—" began Kessler.

"Don't bother me with your lousy excuses, just beat it." He gazed around. "It looks like a junk shop and it smells like a toilet. It'll take me a month to clean up here."

"This smell is only cabbage that I am cooking for my supper. Wait, I'll open a window and it will go away."

"When you go away, it'll go away." Gruber took out his bulky wallet, counted out twelve dollars, added fifty cents, and plunked the money on top of the chest. "You got two more weeks till the fifteenth, then you gotta be out or I will get a dispossess. Don't talk back talk. Get outa here and go somewhere that they don't know you and maybe you'll get a place."

"No, Mr. Gruber," Kessler cried passionately. "I didn't do nothing, and I will stay here."

"Don't monkey with my blood pressure," said Gruber. "If you're not out by the fifteenth, I will personally throw you on your bony ass."

Then he left and walked heavily down the stairs.

The fifteenth came and Ignace found the twelve-fifty in his letter box. He telephoned Gruber and told him.

"I'll get a dispossess," Gruber shouted. He instructed the janitor to write out a note saying to Kessler that his money was refused, and to stick it under his door. This Ignace did. Kessler returned the money to the letter box, but again Ignace wrote a note and slipped it, with the money, under the old man's door.

After another day Kessler received a copy of his eviction notice. It said to appear in court on Friday at 10 a.m. to show cause why he should not be evicted for continued neglect and destruction of rental property. The official notice filled Kessler with great fright because he had never in his life been to court. He did not appear on the day he had been ordered to.

That same afternoon the marshal came with two brawny assistants. Ignace opened Kessler's lock for them and as they pushed their way into the flat, the janitor hastily ran down the stairs to hide in the cellar. Despite Kessler's wailing and carrying on, the two assistants methodically removed his meager furniture and set it out on the sidewalk. After that they got Kessler out, though they had to break open the bathroom door because the old man had locked himself in there. He shouted, struggled, pleaded with his neighbors to help him, but they looked on in a silent group outside the door. The two assistants, holding the old man tightly by the arms and skinny legs, carried him, kicking and moaning, down the stairs. They sat him in the street on a chair amid his junk. Upstairs, the marshal bolted the door with a lock Ignace had supplied, signed a paper which he handed to the janitor's wife, and then drove off in an automobile with his assistants.

Kessler sat on a split chair on the sidewalk. It was raining and the rain soon turned to sleet, but he still sat there. People passing by skirted the pile of his belongings. They stared at Kessler and he stared at nothing. He wore no hat or coat, and the snow fell on him, making him look like a piece of his dispossessed goods. Soon the wizened Italian woman from the top floor returned to the house with two of her sons, each carrying a loaded shopping bag. When she recognized Kessler sitting amid his furniture, she began to shriek. She shrieked in Italian at Kessler although he paid no attention to her. She stood on the stoop, shrunken, gesticulating with thin arms, her loose mouth working angrily. Her sons tried to calm her, but still she shrieked. Several of the neighbors came down to see who was making the racket. Finally, the two sons, unable to think what else to do, set down their shopping bags, lifted Kessler out of the chair, and carried him up the stairs. Hoffman, Kessler's other neighbor, working with a small triangular file, cut open the padlock, and Kessler was carried into the flat from which he had been evicted. Ignace screeched at everybody, calling them filthy names, but the three men went downstairs and hauled up Kessler's chairs, his broken table, chest, and ancient metal bed. They piled all the furniture into the bedroom. Kessler sat on the edge of the bed and wept. After a while, after the old Italian woman had sent in a soup plate full of hot macaroni seasoned with tomato sauce and grated cheese, they left.

Ignace phoned Gruber. The landlord was eating and the food turned to lumps in his throat. "I'll throw them all out, the bastards," he yelled. He put on his hat, got into his car, and drove through the slush to the tenement. All the time he was thinking of his worries: high repair costs; it was hard to keep the place together; maybe the building would someday collapse. He had read of such things. All of a sudden the front of the building parted from the rest and fell like a breaking wave into the street. Gruber cursed the old man for taking him from his supper. When he got to the house, he snatched Ignace's keys and ascended the sagging stairs. Ignace tried to follow, but Gruber told him to stay the hell in his hole. When the landlord was not looking, Ignace crept up after him.

Gruber turned the key and let himself into Kessler's dark flat. He pulled the light chain and found the old man sitting limply on the side of the bed. On the floor at his feet lay a plate of stiffened macaroni.

"What do you think you're doing here?" Gruber thundered.

The old man sat motionless.

"Don't you know it's against the law? This is trespassing and you're breaking the law. Answer me."

Kessler remained mute.

Gruber mopped his brow with a large yellowed handkerchief.

"Listen, my friend, you're gonna make lots of trouble for yourself. If they catch you in here you might go to the workhouse. I'm only trying to advise you."

To his surprise Kessler looked at him with wet, brimming eyes.

"What did I did to you?" he bitterly wept. "Who throws out of his house a man that he lived there ten years and pays every month on time his rent? What did I do, tell me? Who hurts a man without a reason? Are you Hitler or a Jew?" He was hitting his chest with his fist.

Gruber removed his hat. He listened carefully, at first at a loss what to say, but then answered: "Listen, Kessler, it's not personal. I own this house and it's falling apart. My bills are sky high. If the tenants don't take care they have to go. You don't take care and you fight with my janitor, so you have to go. Leave in the morning, and I won't say another word. But if you don't leave the flat, you'll get the heave-ho again. I'll call the marshal."

"Mr. Gruber," said Kessler, "I won't go. Kill me if you want it, but I won't go."

Ignace hurried away from the door as Gruber left in anger. The next morning, after a restless night of worries, the landlord set out to drive to the city marshal's office. On the way he stopped at a candy store for a pack of cigarettes and there decided once more to speak to Kessler. A thought had occurred to him: he would offer to get the old man into a public home.

He drove to the tenement and knocked on Ignace's door.

"Is the old gink still up there?"

"I don't know if so, Mr. Gruber." The janitor was ill at ease.

"What do you mean you don't know?"

"I didn't see him go out. Before, I looked in his keyhole but nothing moves."

"So why didn't you open the door with your key?"

"I was afraid," Ignace answered nervously.

"What are you afraid?"

Ignace wouldn't say.

A fright went through Gruber but he didn't show it. He grabbed the keys and walked ponderously up the stairs, hurrying every so often.

No one answered his knock. As he unlocked the door he broke into heavy sweat.

But the old man was there, alive, sitting without shoes on the bedroom floor.

"Listen, Kessler," said the landlord, relieved although his head pounded. "I got an idea that, if you do it the way I say, your troubles are over."

He explained his proposal to Kessler, but the egg candler was not listening. His eyes were downcast, and his body swayed slowly sideways. As the landlord talked on, the old man was thinking of what had whirled through his mind as he had sat out on the sidewalk in the falling snow. He had thought through his miserable life, remembering how, as a young man, he had abandoned his family, walking out on his wife and three innocent children, without even in some way attempting to provide for them; without, in all the intervening years—so God help him— once trying to discover if they were alive or dead. How, in so short a life, could a man do so much wrong? This thought smote him to the heart and he recalled the past without end and moaned and tore at his flesh with his nails.

Gruber was frightened at the extent of Kessler's suffering. Maybe I should let him stay, he thought. Then as he watched the old man, he realized he was bunched up there on the floor engaged in an act of mourning. There he sat, white from fasting, rocking back and forth, his beard dwindled to a shade of itself.

Something's wrong here—Gruber tried to imagine what and found it all oppressive. He felt he ought to run out, get away, but then saw himself fall and go tumbling down the five flights of stairs; he groaned at the broken picture of himself lying at the bottom. Only he was still there in Kessler's bedroom, listening to the old man praying. Somebody's dead, Gruber muttered. He figured Kessler had got bad news, yet instinctively he knew he hadn't. Then it struck him with a terrible force that the mourner was mourning him: it was *he* who was dead.

The landlord was agonized. Sweating brutally, he felt an enormous constricted weight in him that forced itself up until his head was at the point of bursting. For a full minute he awaited a stroke; but the feeling painfully passed, leaving him miserable.

When after a while, he gazed around the room, it was clean, drenched in daylight, and fragrant. Gruber then suffered unbearable remorse for the way he had treated the old man. With a cry of shame he pulled the sheet off Kessler's bed, and wrapping it around himself, sank to the floor and became a mourner.

Idiots First

THE THICK ticking of the tin clock stopped. Mendel, dozing in the dark, awoke in fright. The pain returned as he listened. He drew on his cold embittered clothing, and wasted minutes sitting at the edge of the bed.

"Isaac," he ultimately sighed.

In the kitchen, Isaac, his astonished mouth open, held six peanuts in his palm. He placed each on the table. "One . . . two . . . nine."

He gathered each peanut and appeared in the doorway. Mendel, in loose hat and long overcoat, still sat on the bed. Isaac watched with small eyes and ears, thick hair graying the sides of his head.

"Schlaf," he nasally said.

"No," muttered Mendel. As if stifling he rose. "Come, Isaac."

He wound his old watch though the sight of the stopped mechanism nauseated him.

Isaac wanted to hold it to his ear.

"No, it's late." Mendel put the watch carefully away. In the drawer he found the little paper bag of crumpled ones and fives and slipped it into his overcoat pocket. He helped Isaac on with his coat.

Isaac looked at one dark window, then at the other. Mendel stared at both blank windows.

They went slowly down the darkly lit stairs, Mendel first, Isaac watching the moving shadows on the wall. To one long shadow he offered a peanut.

"Hungrig."

In the vestibule the old man gazed through the thin glass. The November night was cold and bleak. Opening the door, he cautiously thrust his head out. Though he saw nothing he quickly shut the door.

"Ginzburg, that he came to see me yesterday," he whispered in Isaac's ear.

Isaac sucked air.

"You know who I mean?"

Isaac combed his chin with his fingers.

"That's the one, with the black whiskers. Don't talk to him or go with him if he asks you."

Isaac moaned.

"Young people he don't bother so much," Mendel said in afterthought.

It was suppertime and the street was empty, but the store windows dimly lit their way to the corner. They crossed the deserted street and went on. Isaac, with a happy cry, pointed to the three golden balls. Mendel smiled but was exhausted when they got to the pawnshop.

The pawnbroker, a red-bearded man with black horn-rimmed glasses, was eating a whitefish at the rear of the store. He craned his head, saw them, and settled back to sip his tea.

In five minutes he came forward, patting his shapeless lips with a large white handkerchief.

Mendel, breathing heavily, handed him the worn gold watch.

The pawnbroker, raising his glasses, screwed in his eyepiece. He turned the watch over once. "Eight dollars."

The dying man wet his cracked lips. "I must have thirty-five."

"So go to Rothschild."

"Cost me myself sixty."

"In 1905." The pawnbroker handed back the watch. It had stopped ticking. Mendel wound it slowly. It ticked hollowly.

"Isaac must go to my uncle that he lives in California."

"It's a free country," said the pawnbroker.

Isaac, watching a banjo, snickered.

"What's the matter with him?" the pawnbroker asked.

"So let be eight dollars," muttered Mendel, "but where will I get the rest till tonight?"

"How much for my hat and coat?" he asked.

"No sale." The pawnbroker went behind the cage and wrote out a ticket. He locked the watch in a small drawer but Mendel still heard it ticking.

In the street he slipped the eight dollars into the paper bag, then searched in his pockets for a scrap of writing. Finding it, he strained to read the address by the light of the street lamp.

As they trudged to the subway, Mendel pointed to the sprinkled sky.

"Isaac, look how many stars are tonight."

"Eggs," said Isaac.

"First we will go to Mr. Fishbein, after we will eat."

They got off the train in upper Manhattan and had to walk several blocks before they located Fishbein's house.

"A regular palace," Mendel murmured, looking forward to a moment's warmth.

Isaac stared uneasily at the heavy door of the house.

Mendel rang. The servant, a man with long sideburns, came to the door and said Mr. and Mrs. Fishbein were dining and could see no one.

"He should eat in peace but we will wait till he finishes."

"Come back tomorrow morning. Tomorrow morning Mr. Fishbein will talk to you. He don't do business or charity at this time of the night."

"Charity I am not interested—"

"Come back tomorrow."

"Tell him it's life or death—"

"Whose life or death?"

"So if not his, then mine."

"Don't be such a big smart aleck."

"Look me in my face," said Mendel, "and tell me if I got time till tomorrow morning?"

The servant stared at him, then at Isaac, and reluctantly let them in.

The foyer was a vast high-ceilinged room with many oil paintings on the walls, voluminous silken draperies, a thick flowered rug on the floor, and a marble staircase.

Mr. Fishbein, a paunchy bald-headed man with hairy nostrils and small patent-leather feet, ran lightly down the stairs, a large napkin tucked under a tuxedo coat button. He stopped on the fifth step from the bottom and examined his visitors.

"Who comes on Friday night to a man that he has guests to spoil him his supper?"

"Excuse me that I bother you, Mr. Fishbein," Mendel said. "If I didn't come now I couldn't come tomorrow."

"Without more preliminaries, please state your business. I'm a hungry man."

"Hungrig," wailed Isaac.

Fishbein adjusted his pince-nez. "What's the matter with him?"

"This is my son Isaac. He is like this all his life."

Isaac mewled.

"I am sending him to California."

"Mr. Fishbein don't contribute to personal pleasure trips."

"I am a sick man and he must go tonight on the train to my Uncle Leo."

"I never give to unorganized charity," Fishbein said, "but if you are hungry I will invite you downstairs in my kitchen. We having tonight chicken with stuffed derma."

"All I ask is thirty-five dollars for the train to my uncle in California. I have already the rest."

"Who is your uncle? How old a man?"

"Eighty-one years, a long life to him."

Fishbein burst into laughter. "Eighty-one years and you are sending him this halfwit."

Mendel, flailing both arms, cried, "Please, without names."

Fishbein politely conceded.

"Where is open the door there we go in the house," the sick man said. "If you will kindly give me thirty-five dollars, God will bless you. What is thirty-five dollars to Mr. Fishbein? Nothing. To me, for my boy, is everything."

Fishbein drew himself up to his tallest height.

"Private contributions I don't make—only to institutions. This is my fixed policy."

Mendel sank to his creaking knees on the rug.

"Please, Mr. Fishbein, if not thirty-five, give maybe twenty."

"Levinson!" Fishbein angrily called.

The servant with the long sideburns appeared at the top of the stairs.

"Show this party where is the door—unless he wishes to partake food before leaving the premises."

"For what I got chicken won't cure it," Mendel said.

"This way if you please," said Levinson, descending.

Isaac assisted his father up.

"Take him to an institution," Fishbein advised over the marble balustrade. He ran quickly up the stairs and they were at once outside, buffeted by winds.

The walk to the subway was tedious. The wind blew mournfully. Mendel, breathless, glanced furtively at shadows. Isaac, clutching his peanuts in his frozen fist, clung to his father's side. They entered a small park to rest for a minute on a stone bench under a leafless two-branched tree. The thick right branch was raised, the thin left one hung down. A very pale moon rose slowly. So did a stranger as they approached the bench.

"Gut yuntif," he said hoarsely.

Mendel, drained of blood, waved his wasted arms. Isaac yowled sickly. Then a bell chimed and it was only ten. Mendel let out a piercing anguished cry as the bearded stranger disappeared into the bushes. A policeman came running and, though he beat the bushes with his nightstick, could turn up nothing. Mendel and Isaac hurried out of the little park. When Mendel glanced back the dead tree had its thin arm raised, the thick one down. He moaned.

They boarded a trolley, stopping at the home of a former friend, but he had died years ago. On the same block they went into a cafeteria and ordered two fried eggs for Isaac. The tables were crowded except where a heavyset man sat eating soup with kasha. After one look at him they left in haste, although Isaac wept.

Mendel had another address on a slip of paper but the house was too far away, in Queens, so they stood in a doorway shivering.

What can I do, he frantically thought, in one short hour?

He remembered the furniture in the house. It was junk but might bring a few dollars. "Come, Isaac." They went once more to the pawnbroker's to talk to him, but the shop was dark and an iron gate—rings and gold watches glinting through it—was drawn tight across his place of business.

They huddled behind a telephone pole, both freezing. Isaac whimpered.

"See the big moon, Isaac. The whole sky is white."

He pointed but Isaac wouldn't look.

Mendel dreamed for a minute of the sky lit up, long sheets of light in all directions. Under the sky, in California, sat Uncle Leo drinking tea with lemon. Mendel felt warm but woke up cold.

Across the street stood an ancient brick synagogue.

He pounded on the huge door but no one appeared. He waited till he had breath and desperately knocked again. At last there were footsteps within, and the synagogue door creaked open on its massive brass hinges.

A darkly dressed sexton, holding a dripping candle, glared at them.

"Who knocks this time of night with so much noise on the synagogue door?"

Mendel told the sexton his troubles. "Please, I would like to speak to the rabbi."

"The rabbi is an old man. He sleeps now. His wife won't let you see him. Go home and come back tomorrow."

"To tomorrow I said goodbye already. I am a dying man."

Though the sexton seemed doubtful he pointed to an old wooden house next door. "In there he lives." He disappeared into the synagogue with his lit candle casting shadows around him.

Mendel, with Isaac clutching his sleeve, went up the wooden steps and rang the bell. After five minutes a big-faced, gray-haired, bulky woman came out on the porch with a torn robe thrown over her nightdress. She emphatically said the rabbi was sleeping and could not be waked.

But as she was insisting, the rabbi himself tottered to the door. He listened a minute and said, "Who wants to see me let them come in."

They entered a cluttered room. The rabbi was an old skinny man with bent shoulders and a wisp of white beard. He wore a flannel nightgown and black skullcap; his feet were bare.

"Vey is mir," his wife muttered. "Put on shoes or tomorrow comes sure pneumonia." She was a woman with a big belly, years younger than her husband. Staring at Isaac, she turned away.

Mendel apologetically related his errand. "All I need is thirty-five dollars."

"Thirty-five?" said the rabbi's wife. "Why not thirty-five thousand? Who has so much money? My husband is a poor rabbi. The doctors take away every penny."

"Dear friend," said the rabbi, "if I had I would give you."

"I got already seventy," Mendel said, heavy-hearted. "All I need more is thirty-five."

"God will give you," said the rabbi.

"In the grave," said Mendel. "I need tonight. Come, Isaac."

"Wait," called the rabbi.

He hurried inside, came out with a fur-lined caftan, and handed it to Mendel.

"Yascha," shrieked his wife, "not your new coat!"

"I got my old one. Who needs two coats for one old body?"

"Yascha, I am screaming—"

"Who can go among poor people, tell me, in a new coat?"

"Yascha," she cried, "what can this man do with your coat? He needs tonight the money. The pawnbrokers are asleep."

"So let him wake them up."

"No." She grabbed the coat from Mendel.

He held onto a sleeve, wrestling her for the coat. Her I know, Mendel thought. "Shylock," he muttered. Her eyes glittered.

The rabbi groaned and tottered dizzily. His wife cried out as Mendel yanked the coat from her hands.

"Run," cried the rabbi.

"Run, Isaac."

They ran out of the house and down the steps.

"Stop, you thief," called the rabbi's wife.

The rabbi pressed both hands to his temples and fell to the floor. "Help!" his wife wept. "Heart attack! Help!"

But Mendel and Isaac ran through the streets with the rabbi's new fur-lined caftan. After them noiselessly ran Ginzburg.

It was very late when Mendel bought the train ticket in the only booth open.

There was no time to stop for a sandwich so Isaac ate his peanuts and they hurried to the train in the vast deserted station.

"So in the morning," Mendel gasped as they ran, "there comes a man that he sells sandwiches and coffee. Eat but get change. When reaches California the train, will be waiting for you on the station Uncle Leo. If you don't recognize him he will recognize you. Tell him I send best regards."

But when they arrived at the gate to the platform it was shut, the light out.

"Too late," said the uniformed ticket collector, a bulky, bearded man with hairy nostrils and a fishy smell.

He pointed to the station clock. "Already past twelve."

"But I see standing there still the train," Mendel said, hopping in his grief.

"It just left—in one more minute."

"A minute is enough. Just open the gate."

"Too late I told you."

Mendel socked his bony chest with both hands. "With my whole heart I beg you this little favor."

"Favors you had enough already. For you the train is gone. You shoulda been dead already at midnight. I told you that yesterday. This is the best I can do."

"Ginzburg!" Mendel shrank from him.

"Who else?" The voice was metallic, eyes glittered, the expression amused.

"For myself," the old man begged, "I don't ask a thing. But what will happen to my boy?"

Ginzburg shrugged slightly. "What will happen happens. This isn't my responsibility. I got enough to think about without worrying about somebody on one cylinder."

"What then is your responsibility?"

"To create conditions. To make happen what happens. I ain't in the anthropomorphic business."

"Whichever business you in, where is your pity?"

"This ain't my commodity. The law is the law."

"Which law is this?"

"The cosmic, universal law, goddamn it, the one I got to follow myself."

"What kind of a law is it?" cried Mendel. "For God's sake, don't you understand what I went through in my life with this poor boy? Look at him. For thirty-nine years, since the day he was born, I wait for him to grow up, but he don't. Do you understand what this means in a father's heart? Why don't you let him go to his uncle?" His voice had risen and he was shouting.

Isaac mewled loudly.

"Better calm down or you'll hurt somebody's feelings," Ginzburg said, with a wink toward Isaac.

"All my life," Mendel cried, his body trembling, "what did I have? I was poor. I suffered from my health. When I worked I worked too hard. When I didn't work was worse. My wife died a young woman. But I didn't ask from anybody nothing. Now I ask a small favor. Be so kind, Mr. Ginzburg."

The ticket collector was picking his teeth with a matchstick.

"You ain't the only one, my friend, some got it worse than you. That's how it goes."

"You dog you." Mendel lunged at Ginzburg's throat and began to choke. "You bastard, don't you understand what it means human?"

They struggled nose to nose. Ginzburg, though his astonished eyes bulged, began to laugh. "You pipsqueak nothing. I'll freeze you to pieces."

His eyes lit in rage, and Mendel felt an unbearable cold like an icy dagger invading his body, all of his parts shriveling.

Now I die without helping Isaac.

A crowd gathered. Isaac yelped in fright.

Clinging to Ginzburg in his last agony, Mendel saw reflected in the ticket collector's eyes the depth of his terror. Ginzburg, staring at himself in Mendel's eyes, saw mirrored in them the extent of his own awful wrath. He beheld a shimmering, starry, blinding light that produced darkness.

Ginzburg looked astounded. "Who, me?"

His grip on the squirming old man loosened, and Mendel, his heart barely beating, slumped to the ground.

"Go," Ginzburg muttered, "take him to the train."

"Let pass," he commanded a guard.

The crowd parted. Isaac helped his father up and they tottered down the steps to the platform where the train waited, lit and ready to go.

Mendel found Isaac a coach seat and hastily embraced him. "Help Uncle Leo, Isaakl. Also remember your father and mother."

"Be nice to him," he said to the conductor. "Show him where everything is."

He waited on the platform until the train began slowly to move. Isaac sat at the edge of his seat, his face strained in the direction of his journey. When the train was gone, Mendel ascended the stairs to see what had become of Ginzburg.

The Last Mohican

 FIDELMAN, a self-confessed failure as a painter, came to
Italy to prepare a critical study of Giotto, the opening chapter of
which he had carried across the ocean in a new pigskin-leather
briefcase, now gripped in his perspiring hand. Also new were his
gum-soled oxblood shoes, a tweed suit he had on despite the late-
September sun slanting hot in the Roman sky, although there
was a lighter one in his bag; and a dacron shirt and set of cotton-
dacron underwear, good for quick and easy washing for the
traveler. His suitcase, a bulky, two-strapped affair which embarrassed him slightly, he had borrowed from his sister Bessie. He
planned, if he had any money left at the end of the year, to buy a
new one in Florence. Although he had been in not much of a
mood when he had left the U.S.A., Fidelman revived in Naples,
and at the moment, as he stood in front of the Rome railroad
station, after twenty minutes still absorbed in his first sight of the
Eternal City, he was conscious of a certain exaltation that de-
volved on him after he had discovered that directly across the
many-vehicled piazza stood the remains of the Baths of Diocletian. Fidelman remembered having read that Michelangelo

had had a hand in converting the baths into a church and convent, the latter ultimately changed into the museum that presently was there. "Imagine," he muttered. "Imagine all that history."

In the midst of his imagining, Fidelman experienced the sensation of suddenly seeing himself as he was, to the pinpoint, outside and in, not without bittersweet pleasure; and as the well-known image of his face rose before him he was taken by the depth of pure feeling in his eyes, slightly magnified by glasses, and the sensitivity of his elongated nostrils and often tremulous lips, nose divided from lips by a mustache of recent vintage that looked, Fidelman thought, as if it had been sculptured there, adding to his dignified appearance although he was a little on the short side. But almost at the same moment, this unexpectedly intense sense of his being—it was more than appearance—faded, exaltation having gone where exaltation goes, and Fidelman became aware that there was an exterior source to the strange, almost tri-dimensional reflection of himself he had felt as well as seen. Behind him, a short distance to the right, he had noticed a stranger—give a skeleton a couple of pounds—loitering near a bronze statue on a stone pedestal of the heavy-dugged Etruscan wolf suckling the infants Romulus and Remus, the man contemplating Fidelman already acquisitively so as to suggest to the traveler that he had been mirrored (lock, stock, barrel) in the other's gaze for some time, perhaps since he had stepped off the train. Casually studying him, though pretending no, Fidelman beheld a person of about his own height, oddly dressed in brown knickers and black, knee-length woolen socks drawn up over slightly bowed, broomstick legs, these grounded in small, porous, pointed shoes. His yellowed shirt was open at the gaunt throat, both sleeves rolled up over skinny, hairy arms. The stranger's high forehead was bronzed, his black hair thick behind small ears, the dark, close-shaven beard tight on the face; his experienced nose was weighted at the tip, and the soft brown eyes, above all, *wanted*. Though his expression suggested humility, he all but licked his lips as he approached the ex-painter.

"Shalom," he greeted Fidelman.

"Shalom," the other hesitantly replied, uttering the word—so far as he recalled—for the first time in his life. My God, he thought, a handout for sure. My first hello in Rome and it has to be a schnorrer.

The stranger extended a smiling hand. "Susskind," he said, "Shimon Susskind."

"Arthur Fidelman." Transferring his briefcase to under his left arm while standing astride the big suitcase, he shook hands with Susskind. A blue-smocked porter came by, glanced at Fidelman's bag, looked at him, then walked away.

Whether he knew it or not Susskind was rubbing his palms contemplatively together.

"Parla italiano?"

"Not with ease, although I read it fluently. You might say I need practice."

"Yiddish?"

"I express myself best in English."

"Let it be English then." Susskind spoke with a slight British intonation. "I knew you were Jewish," he said, "the minute my eyes saw you."

Fidelman chose to ignore the remark. "Where did you pick up your knowledge of English?"

"In Israel."

Israel interested Fidelman. "You live there?"

"Once, not now," Susskind answered vaguely. He seemed suddenly bored.

"How so?"

Susskind twitched a shoulder. "Too much heavy labor for a man of my modest health. Also I couldn't stand the suspense."

Fidelman nodded.

"Furthermore, the desert air makes me constipated. In Rome I am lighthearted."

"A Jewish refugee from Israel, no less," Fidelman said good-humoredly.

"I'm always running," Susskind answered mirthlessly. If he was lighthearted, he had yet to show it.

"Where else from, if I may ask?"

"Where else but Germany, Hungary, Poland? Where not?"

"Ah, that's so long ago." Fidelman then noticed the gray in the man's hair. "Well, I'd better be going," he said. He picked up his bag as two porters hovered uncertainly nearby.

But Susskind offered certain services. "You got a hotel?"

"All picked and reserved."

"How long are you staying?"

What business is it of his? However, Fidelman courteously replied, "Two weeks in Rome, the rest of the year in Florence, with a few side trips to Siena, Assisi, Padua, and maybe also Venice."

"You wish a guide in Rome?"

"Are you a guide?"

"Why not?"

"No," said Fidelman. "I'll look as I go along to museums, libraries, et cetera."

This caught Susskind's attention. "What are you, a professor?"

Fidelman couldn't help blushing. "Not exactly, really just a student."

"From which institution?"

He coughed a little. "By that I mean a professional student, you might say. Call me Trofimov, from Chekhov. If there's something to learn I want to learn it."

"You have some kind of a project?" the other persisted. "A grant?"

"No grant. My money is hard-earned. I worked and saved a long time to take a year in Italy. I made certain sacrifices. As for a project, I'm writing on the painter Giotto. He was one of the most important—"

"You don't have to tell me about Giotto," Susskind interrupted with a little smile.

"You've studied his work?"

"Who doesn't know Giotto?"

"That's interesting to me," said Fidelman, secretly irritated. "How do you happen to know him?"

"How do you mean?"

"I've given a good deal of time and study to his work."

"So I know him too."

I'd better get this over with before it begins to amount to something, Fidelman thought. He set down his bag and fished with a finger in his leather coin purse. The two porters watched with interest, one taking a sandwich out of his pocket, unwrapping the newspaper, and beginning to eat.

"This is for yourself," Fidelman said.

Susskind hardly glanced at the coin as he let it drop into his pants pocket. The porters then left.

The refugee had an odd way of standing motionless, like a cigar store Indian about to burst into flight. "In your luggage," he said vaguely, "would you maybe have a suit you can't use? I could use a suit."

At last he comes to the point. Fidelman, though annoyed, controlled himself. "All I have is a change from the one you now see me wearing. Don't get the wrong idea about me, Mr. Susskind. I'm not rich. In fact, I'm poor. Don't let a few new clothes deceive you. I owe my sister money for them."

Susskind glanced down at his shabby, baggy knickers. "I haven't had a suit for years. The one I was wearing when I ran away from Germany fell apart. One day I was walking around naked."

"Isn't there a welfare organization that could help you out—

some group in the Jewish community interested in refugees?"

"The Jewish organizations wish to give me what they wish, not what I wish," Susskind replied bitterly. "The only thing they offer me is a ticket back to Israel."

"Why don't you take it?"

"I told you already, here I feel free."

"Freedom is a relative term."

"Don't tell me about freedom."

He knows all about that, too, Fidelman thought. "So you feel free," he said, "but how do you live?"

Susskind coughed, a brutal cough.

Fidelman was about to say something more on the subject of freedom but left it unsaid. Jesus, I'll be saddled with him all day if I don't watch out.

"I'd better be getting off to the hotel." He bent again for his bag.

Susskind touched him on the shoulder and when Fidelman exasperatedly straightened up, the half dollar he had given the man was staring him in the eye.

"On this we both lose money."

"How do you mean?"

"Today the lira sells six twenty-three on the dollar, but for specie they only give you five hundred."

"In that case, give it here and I'll let you have a dollar." From his wallet Fidelman quickly extracted a crisp bill and handed it to the refugee.

"Not more?" Susskind sighed.

"Not more," the student answered emphatically.

"Maybe you would like to see Diocletian's bath? There are some enjoyable Roman coffins inside. I will guide you for another dollar."

"No thanks." Fidelman said goodbye and, lifting the suitcase, lugged it to the curb. A porter appeared and the student, after some hesitation, let him carry it toward the line of small dark-green taxis in the piazza. The porter offered to carry the brief-case too, but Fidelman wouldn't part with it. He gave the cab driver the address of the hotel, and the taxi took off with a lurch. Fidelman at last relaxed. Susskind, he noticed, had disappeared. Gone with his breeze, he thought. But on the way to the hotel he had an uneasy feeling that the refugee, crouched low, might be clinging to the little tire on the back of the cab; he didn't look out to see.

:　　　:　　　:

Fidelman had reserved a room in an inexpensive hotel not far from the station, with its very convenient bus terminal. Then, as was his habit, he got himself quickly and tightly organized. He was always concerned with not wasting time, as if it were his only wealth—not true, of course, though Fidelman admitted he was ambitious—and he soon arranged a schedule that made the most of his working hours. Mornings he usually visited the Italian libraries, searching their catalogues and archives, read in poor light, and made profuse notes. He napped for an hour after lunch, then at four, when the churches and museums were re-opening, hurried off to them with lists of frescoes and paintings he must see. He was anxious to get to Florence, at the same time a little unhappy at all he would not have time to take in in Rome. Fidelman promised himself to return again if he could afford it, perhaps in the spring, and look at anything he pleased.

After dark he managed to unwind and relax. He ate as the Romans did, late, enjoyed a half liter of white wine and smoked a cigarette. Afterwards he liked to wander—especially in the old sections near the Tiber. He had read that here, under his feet, were the ruins of ancient Rome. It was an inspiring business, he, Arthur Fidelman, after all born a Bronx boy, walking around in all this history. History was mysterious, the remembrance of things unknown, in a way burdensome, in a way a sensuous experience. It uplifted and depressed, why he did not know, except that it excited his thoughts more than he thought good for him. This kind of excitement was all right up to a point, perfect maybe for a creative artist, but less so for a critic. A critic, he thought, should live on beans. He walked for miles along the winding river, gazing at the star-strewn skies. Once, after a couple of days in the Vatican Museum, he saw flights of angels— gold, blue, white—intermingled in the sky. "My God, I got to stop using my eyes so much," Fidelman said to himself. But back in his room he sometimes wrote till morning.

Late one night, about a week after his arrival in Rome, as Fidelman was writing notes on the Byzantine-style mosaics he had seen during the day, there was a knock on the door, and though the student, immersed in his work, was not conscious he had said "Avanti," he must have, for the door opened, and instead of an angel, in came Susskind in his shirt and baggy knickers.

Fidelman, who had all but forgotten the refugee, certainly never thought of him, half rose in astonishment. "Susskind," he exclaimed, "how did you get in here?"

Susskind for a moment stood motionless, then answered with a weary smile, "I'll tell you the truth, I know the desk clerk."

"But how did you know where I live?"

"I saw you walking in the street so I followed you."

"You mean you saw me accidentally?"

"How else? Did you leave me your address?"

Fidelman resumed his seat. "What can I do for you, Susskind?" He spoke grimly.

The refugee cleared his throat. "Professor, the days are warm but the nights are cold. You see how I go around naked." He held forth bluish arms, goosefleshed. "I came to ask you to reconsider about giving away your old suit."

"And who says it's an old suit?" Despite himself, Fidelman's voice thickened.

"One suit is new, so the other is old."

"Not precisely. I am afraid I have no suit for you, Susskind. The one I presently have hanging in the closet is a little more than a year old and I can't afford to give it away. Besides, it's gabardine, more like a summer suit."

"On me it will be for all seasons."

After a moment's reflection, Fidelman drew out his billfold and counted four single dollars. These he handed to Susskind.

"Buy yourself a warm sweater."

Susskind also counted the money. "If four," he said, "why not five?"

Fidelman flushed. The man's warped nerve. "Because I happen to have four available," he answered. "That's twenty-five hundred lire. You should be able to buy a warm sweater and have something left over besides."

"I need a suit," Susskind said. "The days are warm but the nights are cold." He rubbed his arms. "What else I need I won't tell you."

"At least roll down your sleeves if you're so cold."

"That won't help me."

"Listen, Susskind," Fidelman said gently, "I would gladly give you the suit if I could afford to, but I can't. I have barely enough money to squeeze out a year for myself here. I've already told you I am indebted to my sister. Why don't you try to get yourself a job somewhere, no matter how menial? I'm sure that in a short while you'll work yourself up into a decent position."

"A job, he says," Susskind muttered gloomily. "Do you know what it means to get a job in Italy? Who will give me a job?"

"Who gives anybody a job? They have to go out and look for it."

"You don't understand, professor. I am an Israeli citizen and this means I can only work for an Israeli company. How many

Israeli companies are there here?—maybe two, El Al and Zim, and even if they had a job, they wouldn't give it to me because I have lost my passport. I would be better off now if I were stateless. A stateless person shows his laissez-passer and sometimes he can find a small job."

"But if you lost your passport why didn't you put in for a duplicate?"

"I did, but did they give it to me?"

"Why not?"

"Why not? They say I sold it."

"Had they reason to think that?"

"I swear to you somebody stole it from me."

"Under such circumstances," Fidelman asked, "how do you live?"

"How do I live?" He chomped with his teeth. "I eat air."

"Seriously?"

"Seriously, on air. I also peddle," he confessed, "but to peddle you need a license, and that the Italians won't give me. When they caught me peddling I was interned for six months in a work camp."

"Didn't they attempt to deport you?"

"They did, but I sold my mother's old wedding ring that I kept in my pocket so many years. The Italians are a humane people. They took the money and let me go, but they told me not to peddle any more."

"So what do you do now?"

"I peddle. What should I do, beg?—I peddle. But last spring I got sick and gave my little money away to the doctors. I still have a bad cough." He coughed fruitily. "Now I have no capital to buy stock with. Listen, professor, maybe we can go in partnership together? Lend me twenty thousand lire and I will buy ladies' nylon stockings. After I sell them I will return you your money."

"I have no funds to invest, Susskind."

"You will get it back, with interest."

"I honestly am sorry for you," Fidelman said, "but why don't you at least do something practical? Why don't you go to the Joint Distribution Committee, for instance, and ask them to assist you? That's their business."

"I already told you why. They wish me to go back, but I wish to stay here."

"I still think going back would be the best thing for you."

"No," cried Susskind angrily.

"If that's your decision, freely made, then why pick on me? Am I responsible for you then, Susskind?"

"Who else?" Susskind loudly replied.

"Lower your voice, please, people are sleeping around here," said Fidelman, beginning to perspire. "Why should I be?"

"You know what responsibility means?"

"I think so."

"Then you are responsible. Because you are a man. Because you are a Jew, aren't you?"

"Yes, goddamn it, but I'm not the only one in the whole wide world. Without prejudice, I refuse the obligation. I am a single individual and can't take on everybody's personal burden. I have the weight of my own to contend with."

He reached for his billfold and plucked out another dollar.

"This makes five. It's more than I can afford, but take it and after this please leave me alone. I have made my contribution."

Susskind stood there, oddly motionless, an impassioned statue, and for a moment Fidelman wondered if he would stay all night, but at last the refugee thrust forth a stiff arm, took the fifth dollar, and departed.

Early the next morning Fidelman moved out of the hotel into another, less convenient for him, but far away from Shimon Susskind and his endless demands.

:   :   :

This was Tuesday. On Wednesday, after a busy morning in the library, Fidelman entered a nearby trattoria and ordered a plate of spaghetti with tomato sauce. He was reading his *Messaggero*, anticipating the coming of the food, for he was unusually hungry, when he sensed a presence at the table. He looked up, expecting the waiter, but beheld instead Susskind standing there, alas, unchanged.

Is there no escape from him? thought Fidelman, severely vexed. Is this why I came to Rome?

"Shalom, professor," Susskind said, keeping his eyes off the table. "I was passing and saw you sitting here alone, so I came in to say shalom."

"Susskind," Fidelman said in anger, "have you been following me again?"

"How could I follow you?" asked the astonished Susskind. "Do I know where you live now?"

Though Fidelman blushed a little, he told himself he owed nobody an explanation. So he had found out he had moved—good.

"My feet are tired. Can I sit five minutes?"

"Sit."

Susskind drew out a chair. The spaghetti arrived, steaming hot. Fidelman sprinkled it with cheese and wound his fork into several tender strands. One of the strings of spaghetti seemed to stretch for miles, so he stopped at a certain point and swallowed the forkful. Having foolishly neglected to cut the long spaghetti string he was left sucking it, seemingly endlessly. This embarrassed him.

Susskind watched with rapt attention.

Fidelman at last reached the end of the long spaghetti, patted his mouth with a napkin, and paused in his eating.

"Would you care for a plateful?"

Susskind, eyes hungry, hesitated. "Thanks," he said.

"Thanks yes or thanks no?"

"Thanks no." The eyes looked away.

Fidelman resumed eating, carefully winding his fork; he had had not too much practice with this sort of thing and was soon involved in the same dilemma with the spaghetti. Seeing Susskind still watching him, he became tense.

"We are not Italians, professor," the refugee said. "Cut it in small pieces with your knife. Then you will swallow it easier."

"I'll handle it as I please," Fidelman responded testily. "This is my business. You attend to yours."

"My business," Susskind sighed, "don't exist. This morning I had to let a wonderful chance get away from me. I had a chance to buy ladies' stockings at three hundred lire if I had money to buy half a gross. I could easily sell them for five hundred a pair. We would have made a nice profit."

"The news doesn't interest me."

"So if not ladies' stockings, I can also get sweaters, scarves, men's socks, also cheap leather goods, ceramics—whatever would interest you."

"What interests me is what you did with the money I gave you for a sweater."

"It's getting cold, professor," Susskind said worriedly. "Soon comes the November rains, and in winter the tramontana. I thought I ought to save your money to buy a couple of kilos of chestnuts and a bag of charcoal for my burner. If you sit all day on a busy street corner you can sometimes make a thousand lire. Italians like hot chestnuts. But if I do this I will need some warm clothes, maybe a suit."

"A suit," Fidelman remarked sarcastically, "why not an over-coat?"

"I have a coat, poor that it is, but now I need a suit. How can anybody come in company without a suit?"

Fidelman's hand trembled as he laid down his fork. "To my mind you are utterly irresponsible and I won't be saddled with you. I have the right to choose my own problems and the right to my privacy."

"Don't get excited, professor, it's bad for your digestion. Eat in peace." Susskind got up and left the trattoria.

Fidelman hadn't the appetite to finish his spaghetti. He paid the bill, waited ten minutes, then departed, glancing around from time to time to see if he was being followed. He headed down the sloping street to a small piazza where he saw a couple of cabs. Not that he could afford one, but he wanted to make sure Susskind didn't tail him back to his new hotel. He would warn the clerk at the desk never to allow anybody of the refugee's name or description even to make inquiries about him.

Susskind, however, stepped out from behind a plashing fountain at the center of the little piazza. Modestly addressing the speechless Fidelman, he said, "I don't wish to take only, professor. If I had something to give you, I would gladly give it to you."

"Thanks," snapped Fidelman, "just give me some peace of mind."

"That you have to find yourself," Susskind answered.

In the taxi Fidelman decided to leave for Florence the next day, rather than at the end of the week, and once and for all be done with the pest.

That night, after returning to his room from an unpleasurable walk in the Trastevere—he had a headache from too much wine at supper—Fidelman found his door ajar and at once recalled that he had forgotten to lock it, although he had as usual left the key with the desk clerk. He was at first frightened, but when he tried the armadio in which he kept his clothes and suitcase, it was shut tight. Hastily unlocking it, he was relieved to see his blue gabardine suit—a one-button-jacket affair, the trousers a little frayed at the cuffs, but all in good shape and usable for years to come—hanging amid some shirts the maid had pressed for him;

and when he examined the contents of the suitcase he found nothing missing, including, thank God, his passport and traveler's checks. Gazing around the room, Fidelman saw all in place. Satisfied, he picked up a book and read ten pages before he thought of his briefcase. He jumped to his feet and began to search everywhere, remembering distinctly that it had been on the night table as he had lain on the bed that afternoon, rereading his chapter. He searched under the bed and behind the night table, then again throughout the room, even on top of and behind the armadio. Fidelman hopelessly opened every drawer, no matter how small, but found neither the briefcase nor, what was worse, the chapter in it.

With a groan he sank down on the bed, insulting himself for not having made a copy of the manuscript, because he had more than once warned himself that something like this might happen to it. But he hadn't because there were some revisions he had contemplated making, and he had planned to retype the entire chapter before beginning the next. He thought now of complaining to the owner of the hotel, who lived on the floor below, but it was already past midnight and he realized nothing could be done until morning. Who could have taken it? The maid or the hall porter? It seemed unlikely they would risk their jobs to steal a piece of leather goods that would bring them only a few thousand lire in a pawnshop. Possibly a sneak thief? He would ask tomorrow if other persons on the floor were missing something. He somehow doubted it. If a thief, he would then and there have ditched the chapter and stuffed the briefcase with Fidelman's oxblood shoes, left by the bed, and the fifteen-dollar R. H. Macy sweater that lay in full view of the desk. But if not the maid or porter or a sneak thief, then who? Though Fidelman had not the slightest shred of evidence to support his suspicions, he could think of only one person—Susskind. This thought stung him. But if Susskind, why? Out of pique, perhaps, that he had not been given the suit he had coveted, nor was able to pry it out of the armadio? Try as he would, Fidelman could think of no one else and no other reason. Somehow the peddler had followed him home (he suspected their meeting at the fountain) and had got into his room while he was out to supper.

Fidelman's sleep that night was wretched. He dreamed of pursuing the refugee in the Jewish catacombs under the ancient Appian Way, threatening him with a blow on the presumptuous head with a seven-flamed candelabrum he clutched in his hand; while Susskind, clever ghost, who knew the ins and outs of all the crypts and alleys, eluded him at every turn. Then Fidelman's candles all blew out, leaving him sightless and alone in the cemeterial dark; but when the student arose in the morning and wearily drew up the blinds, the yellow Italian sun winked him cheerfully in both bleary eyes.

:　　　　:　　　　:

Fidelman postponed going to Florence. He reported his loss to the Questura, and though the police were polite and eager to help, they could do nothing for him. On the form on which the inspector noted the complaint, he listed the briefcase as worth ten thousand lire, and for "valore del manuscritto" he drew a line. Fidelman, after giving the matter a good deal of thought, did not report Susskind, first, because he had absolutely no proof, for the desk clerk swore he had seen no stranger around in knickers; second, because he was afraid of the consequences for the refugee if he was written down "suspected thief" as well as "unlicensed peddler" and inveterate refugee. He tried instead to rewrite the chapter, which he felt sure he knew by heart, but when he sat down at the desk, there were important thoughts, whole paragraphs, even pages, that went blank in the mind. He considered sending to America for his notes for the chapter, but they were in a barrel in his sister's attic in Levittown, among many notes for other projects. The thought of Bessie, a mother of five, poking around in his things, and the work entailed in sorting the cards, then getting them packaged and mailed to him across the ocean, wearied Fidelman unspeakably; he was certain she would send the wrong ones. He laid down his pen and went into the street, seeking Susskind. He searched for him in neighborhoods where he had seen him before, and though Fidelman spent hours looking, literally days, Susskind never appeared; or if he perhaps did, the sight of Fidelman caused him to vanish. And when the student inquired about him at the Israeli consulate, the clerk, a new man on the job, said he had no record of such a person or his lost passport; on the other hand, he was known at the Joint Distribution Committee, but by name and address only, an impossibility, Fidelman thought. They gave him a number to go to but the place had long since been torn down to make way for an apartment house.

Time went without work, without accomplishment. To put an end to this appalling waste Fidelman tried to force himself back into his routine of research and picture viewing. He moved out of the hotel, which he now could not stand for the harm it had done him (leaving a telephone number and urging he be called if the slightest clue turned up), and he took a room in a small pensione near the stazione and here had breakfast and supper rather than go out. He was much concerned with expenditures and carefully recorded them in a notebook he had acquired for the purpose. Nights, instead of wandering in the city, feasting himself upon its beauty and mystery, he kept his eyes glued to paper, sitting steadfastly at his desk in an attempt to re-create his initial chapter, because he was lost without a beginning. He had tried writing the second chapter from notes in his possession, but it had come to nothing. Always Fidelman needed something solid behind him before he could advance, some worthwhile accomplishment upon which to build another. He worked late, but his mood, or inspiration, or whatever it was, had deserted him, leaving him with growing anxiety, almost disorientation; of not knowing—it seemed to him for the first time in months—what he must do next, a feeling that was torture. Therefore he again took up his search for the refugee. He thought now that once he had settled it, knew that the man had or hadn't stolen his chapter— whether he recovered it or not seemed at the moment immaterial —just the knowing of it would ease his mind and again he would *feel* like working, the crucial element.

Daily he combed the crowded streets, searching for Susskind wherever people peddled. On successive Sunday mornings he took the long ride to the Porta Portese market and hunted for hours among the piles of secondhand goods and junk lining the back streets, hoping his briefcase would magically appear, though it never did. He visited the open market at Piazza Fontanella Borghese, and observed the ambulant vendors at Piazza Dante. He looked among fruit and vegetable stalls set up in the streets, whenever he chanced upon them, and dawdled on busy street corners after dark, among beggars and fly-by-night peddlers. After the first cold snap at the end of October, when the chestnut sellers appeared throughout the city, huddled over pails of glowing coals, he sought in their faces the missing Susskind. Where in all of modern and ancient Rome was he? The man lived in the open air—he had to appear somewhere. Sometimes when riding in a bus or tram, Fidelman thought he had glimpsed somebody in a crowd, dressed in the refugee's clothes, and he invariably got off to run after whoever it was—once a man standing in front of the Banco di Santo Spirito, gone when Fidelman breathlessly arrived; and another time he overtook a person in knickers, but this one wore a monocle. Sir Ian Susskind?

In November it rained. Fidelman wore a blue beret with his trench coat and a pair of black Italian shoes, smaller, despite their pointed toes, than his burly oxbloods which overheated his feet and whose color he detested. But instead of visiting museums he frequented movie houses, sitting in the cheapest seats and regretting the cost. He was, at odd hours in certain streets, several times accosted by prostitutes, some heartbreakingly pretty, one a slender, unhappy-looking girl with bags under her eyes whom he desired mightily, but Fidelman feared for his health. He had got to know the face of Rome and spoke Italian fairly fluently, but his heart was burdened, and in his blood raged a murderous hatred of the bandy-legged refugee—although there were times when he bethought himself he might be wrong—so Fidelman more than once cursed him to perdition.

:   :   :

One Friday night, as the first star glowed over the Tiber, Fidelman, walking aimlessly along the left riverbank, came upon a synagogue and wandered in among a crowd of Sephardim with Italianate faces. One by one they paused before a sink in an antechamber to dip their hands under a flowing faucet, then in the house of worship touched with loose fingers their brows, mouths, and breasts as they bowed to the Ark, Fidelman doing likewise. Where in the world am I? Three rabbis rose from a bench and the service began, a long prayer, sometimes chanted, sometimes accompanied by invisible organ music, but no Susskind anywhere. Fidelman sat at a desk-like pew in the last row, where he could inspect the congregants yet keep an eye on the door. The synagogue was unheated and the cold rose like an exudation from the marble floor. The student's freezing nose burned like a lit candle. He got up to go, but the beadle, a stout man in a high hat and short caftan, wearing a long thick silver chain around his neck, fixed the student with his powerful left eye.

"From New York?" he inquired, slowly approaching.

Half the congregation turned to see who.

"State, not city," answered Fidelman, nursing an active guilt for the attention he was attracting. Then, taking advantage of a pause, he whispered, "Do you happen to know a man named Susskind? He wears knickers."

"A relative?" The beadle gazed at him sadly.

"Not exactly."

"My own son—killed in the Ardeatine Caves." Tears stood forth in his eyes.

"Ah, for that I'm sorry."

But the beadle had exhausted the subject. He wiped his wet lids with pudgy fingers and the curious Sephardim turned back to their prayer books.

"Which Susskind?" the beadle wanted to know.

"Shimon."

He scratched his ear. "Look in the ghetto."

"I looked."

"Look again."

The beadle walked slowly away and Fidelman sneaked out.

The ghetto lay behind the synagogue for several crooked, well-packed blocks, encompassing aristocratic palazzi ruined by age and unbearable numbers, their discolored façades strung with lines of withered wet wash, the fountains in the piazzas, dirt-laden, dry. And dark stone tenements, built partly on centuries-old ghetto walls, inclined toward one another across narrow, cobblestoned streets. In and among the impoverished houses were the wholesale establishments of wealthy Jews, dark holes ending in jeweled interiors, silks and silver of all colors. In the mazed streets wandered the present-day poor, Fidelman among them, oppressed by history, although, he joked to himself, it added years to his life.

A white moon shone upon the ghetto, lighting it like dark day. Once he thought he saw a ghost he knew by sight, and hastily followed him through a thick stone passage to a blank wall where shone in white letters under a tiny electric bulb: VIETATO URINARE. Here was a smell but no Susskind.

For thirty lire the student bought a dwarfed, blackened banana from a street vendor (not S) on a bicycle, and stopped to eat. A crowd of ragazzi gathered to watch.

"Anybody here know Susskind, a refugee wearing knickers?" Fidelman announced, stooping to point the banana where the pants went beneath the knees. He also made his legs a trifle bowed but nobody noticed.

There was no response until he had finished his fruit, then a thin-faced boy with brown liquescent eyes out of Murillo piped: "He sometimes works in the Cimitero Verano, the Jewish section."

There too? thought Fidelman. "Works in the cemetery?" he inquired. "With a shovel?"

"He prays for the dead," the boy answered, "for a small fee."

Fidelman bought him a quick banana and the others dispersed.

In the cemetery, deserted on the Sabbath—he should have come Sunday—Fidelman went among the graves, reading legends carved on tombstones, many topped with small brass candelabra, whilst withered yellow chrysanthemums lay on the stone tablets of other graves, dropped stealthily, Fidelman imagined, on All Souls' Day—a festival in another part of the cemetery—by renegade sons and daughters unable to bear the sight of their dead bereft of flowers, while the crypts of the goyim were lit and in bloom. Many were burial places, he read on the stained stones, of those who, for one reason or another, had died in the late large war, including an empty place, it said under a six-pointed star engraved upon a marble slab that lay on the ground, for "My beloved father / Betrayed by the damned Fascists / Murdered at Auschwitz by the barbarous Nazis / O *Crime Orribile*." But no Susskind.

:   :   :

Three months had gone by since Fidelman's arrival in Rome. Should he, he many times asked himself, leave the city and this foolish search? Why not off to Florence, and there amid the art splendors of the world, be inspired to resume his work? But the loss of his first chapter was like a spell cast over him. There were times he scorned it as a man-made thing, like all such, replaceable; other times he feared it was not the chapter per se, but that his volatile curiosity had become somehow entangled with Susskind's strange personality— Had he repaid generosity by stealing a man's life work? Was he so distorted? To satisfy himself, to know man, Fidelman had to know, though at what a cost in precious time and effort. Sometimes he smiled wryly at all this; ridiculous, the chapter grieved him for itself only—the precious thing he had created, then lost—especially when he got to thinking of the long diligent labor, how painstakingly he had built each idea, how cleverly mastered problems of order, form, how impressive the finished product, Giotto reborn! It broke the heart. What else, if after months he was here, still seeking?

And Fidelman was unchangingly convinced that Susskind had taken it, or why would he still be hiding? He sighed much and gained weight. Mulling over his frustrated career, on the backs of envelopes containing unanswered letters from his sister Bessie he aimlessly sketched little angels flying. Once, studying his minuscule drawings, it occurred to him that he might someday return to painting, but the thought was more painful than Fidelman could bear.

One bright morning in mid-December, after a good night's sleep, his first in weeks, he vowed he would have another look at the Navicella and then be off to Florence. Shortly before noon he visited the porch of St. Peter's, trying, from his remembrance of Giotto's sketch, to see the mosaic as it had been before its many restorations. He hazarded a note or two in shaky handwriting, then left the church and was walking down the sweeping flight of stairs, when he beheld at the bottom—his heart misgave him, was he still seeing pictures, a sneaky apostle added to the over-loaded boatful?—ecco Susskind! The refugee, in beret and long green G.I. raincoat, from under whose skirts showed his black-stockinged, rooster's ankles—indicating knickers going on above though hidden—was selling black and white rosaries to all who would buy. He had several strands of beads in one hand, while in the palm of the other a few gilded medallions glinted in the winter sun. Despite his outer clothing, Susskind looked, it must be said, unchanged, not a pound more of meat or muscle, the face though aged, ageless. Gazing at him, the student ground his teeth in remembrance. He was tempted quickly to hide, and un-observed observe the thief; but his impatience, after the long un-happy search, was too much for him. With controlled trepidation he approached Susskind on his left as the refugee was busily engaged on the right, urging a sale of beads upon a woman drenched in black.

"Beads, rosaries, say your prayers with holy beads."

"Greetings, Susskind," Fidelman said, coming shakily down the stairs, dissembling the Unified Man, all peace and content-ment. "One looks for you everywhere and finds you here. Wie gehts?"

Susskind, though his eyes flickered, showed no surprise to speak of. For a moment his expression seemed to say he had no idea who this was, had forgotten Fidelman's existence, but then at last remembered—somebody long ago from another country, whom you smiled on, then forgot.

"Still here?" he perhaps ironically joked.

"Still." Fidelman was embarrassed at his voice slipping.

"Rome holds you?"

"Rome," faltered Fidelman, "—the air." He breathed deep and exhaled with emotion.

Noticing the refugee was not truly attentive, his eyes roving upon potential customers, Fidelman, girding himself, remarked, "By the way, Susskind, you didn't happen to notice—did you?—the briefcase I was carrying with me around the time we met in September?"

"Briefcase—what kind?" This he said absently, his eyes on the church doors.

"Pigskin. I had in it"—here Fidelman's voice could be heard cracking—"a chapter of critical work on Giotto I was writing. You know, I'm sure, the Trecento painter?"

"Who doesn't know Giotto?"

"Do you happen to recall whether you saw, if, that is—" He stopped, at a loss for words other than accusatory.

"Excuse me—business." Susskind broke away and bounced up the steps two at a time. A man he approached shied away. He had beads, didn't need others.

Fidelman had followed the refugee. "Reward," he muttered up close to his ear. "Fifteen thousand for the chapter, and who has it can keep the brand-new briefcase. That's his business, no questions asked. Fair enough?"

Susskind spied a lady tourist, including camera and guide book. "Beads—holy beads." He held up both hands but she was just a Lutheran, passing through.

"Slow today," Susskind complained as they walked down the stairs, "but maybe it's the items. Everybody has the same. If I had some big ceramics of the Holy Mother, they go like hot cakes—a good investment for somebody with a little cash."

"Use the reward for that," Fidelman cagily whispered, "buy Holy Mothers."

If he heard, Susskind gave no sign. At the sight of a family of nine emerging from the main portal above, the refugee, calling addio over his shoulder, fairly flew up the steps. But Fidelman uttered no response. I'll get the rat yet. He went off to hide behind a high fountain in the square. But the flying spume raised by the wind wet him, so he retreated behind a massive column and peeked out at short intervals to keep the peddler in sight.

At two o'clock, when St. Peter's closed to visitors, Susskind dumped his goods into his raincoat pockets and locked up shop. Fidelman followed him all the way home, indeed the ghetto, although along a street he had not consciously been on before, which led into an alley where the refugee pulled open a left-handed door and, without transition, was "home." Fidelman, sneaking up close, caught a dim glimpse of an overgrown closet containing bed and table. He found no address on wall or door, nor, to his surprise, any door lock. This for a moment depressed him. It meant Susskind had nothing worth stealing. Of his own, that is. The student promised himself to return tomorrow, when the occupant was elsewhere.

Return he did, in the morning, while the entrepreneur was out selling religious articles, glanced around once, and was quickly inside. He shivered—a pitch-black freezing cave. Fidelman scratched up a thick match and confirmed bed and table, also a rickety chair, but no heat or light except a drippy candle stub in a saucer on the table. He lit the yellow candle and searched all over the place. In the table drawer a few eating implements plus safety razor, though where he shaved was a mystery, probably a public toilet. On a shelf above the thin-blanketed bed stood half a flask of red wine, part of a package of spaghetti, and a hard panino. Also an unexpected little fish bowl with a bony goldfish swimming around in arctic seas. The fish, reflecting the candle flame, gulped repeatedly, threshing its frigid tail as Fidelman watched. He loves pets, thought the student. Under the bed he found a chamber pot, but nowhere a briefcase with a fine critical chapter in it. The place was not more than an icebox someone probably had lent the refugee to come in out of the rain. Alas, Fidelman sighed. Back in the pensione, it took a hot-water bottle two hours to thaw him out; but from the visit he never fully recovered.

:   :   :

In this latest dream of Fidelman's he was spending the day in a cemetery all crowded with tombstones, when up out of an empty grave rose this long-nosed brown shade, Virgilio Susskind, beckoning.

Fidelman hurried over.

"Have you read Tolstoy?"

"Sparingly."

"Why is art?" asked the shade, drifting off.

Fidelman, willy-nilly, followed, and the ghost, as it vanished, led him up steps going through the ghetto and into a marble synagogue.

The student, left alone, for no reason he could think of lay down upon the stone floor, his shoulders keeping strangely warm as he stared at the sunlit vault above. The fresco therein revealed this saint in fading blue, the sky flowing from his head, handing an old knight in a thin red robe his gold cloak. Nearby stood a humble horse and two stone hills.

Giotto. San Francesco dona le vesti al cavaliere povero.

Fidelman awoke running. He stuffed his blue gabardine into a paper bag, caught a bus, and knocked early on Susskind's heavy portal.

"Avanti." The refugee, already garbed in beret and raincoat (probably his pajamas), was standing at the table, lighting the candle with a flaming sheet of paper. To Fidelman the paper looked like the underside of a typewritten page. Despite himself, the student recalled in letters of fire his entire chapter.

"Here, Susskind," he said in a trembling voice, offering the bundle, "I bring you my suit. Wear it in good health."

The refugee glanced at it without expression. "What do you wish for it?"

"Nothing at all." Fidelman laid the bag on the table, called goodbye, and left.

He soon heard footsteps clattering after him across the cob-
blestones.

"Excuse me, I kept this under my mattress for you." Susskind
thrust at him the pigskin briefcase.

Fidelman savagely opened it, searching frenziedly in each
compartment, but the bag was empty. The refugee was already in
flight. With a bellow the student started after him. "You bastard,
you burned my chapter!"

"Have mercy," cried Susskind, "I did you a favor."

"I'll do you one and cut your throat."

"The words were there but the spirit was missing."

In a towering rage, Fidelman forced a burst of speed, but the
refugee, light as the wind in his marvelous knickers, his green
coattails flying, rapidly gained ground.

The ghetto Jews, framed in amazement in their medieval windows, stared at the wild pursuit. But in the middle of it, Fidelman, stout and short of breath, moved by all he had lately
learned, had a triumphant insight.

"Susskind, come back," he shouted, half sobbing. "The suit is
yours. All is forgiven."

He came to a dead halt but the refugee ran on. When last seen
he was still running.

Black Is

My Favorite Color

CHARITY QUIETNESS sits in the toilet eating her two hard-boiled eggs while I'm having my ham sandwich and coffee in the kitchen. That's how it goes, only don't get the idea of ghettoes. If there's a ghetto I'm the one that's in it. She's my cleaning woman from Father Divine and comes in once a week to my small three-room apartment on my day off from the liquor store. "Peace," she says to me, "Father reached on down and took me right up in Heaven." She's a small person with a flat body, frizzy hair, and a quiet face that the light shines out of, and Mama had such eyes before she died. The first time Charity Quietness came in to clean, a little more than a year and a half, I made the mistake to ask her to sit down at the kitchen table with me and eat her lunch. I was still feeling not so hot after Ornita left, but I'm the kind of a man—Nat Lime, forty-four, a bachelor with a daily growing bald spot on the back of my head, and I could lose frankly fifteen pounds—who enjoys company so long as he has it. So she cooked up her two hard-boiled eggs and sat down and took a small bite out of one of them. But after a minute she stopped chewing and she got up and carried the eggs in a cup to the bathroom, and since then she eats there. I said to her more than once, "Okay, Charity Quietness, so have it your way, eat the eggs in the kitchen by yourself and I'll eat when you're done," but she smiles absentminded, and eats in the toilet. It's my fate with colored people.

Although black is still my favorite color you wouldn't know it from my luck except in short quantities, even though I do all right in the liquor store business in Harlem, on Eighth Avenue between 110th and 111th. I speak with respect. A large part of my life I've had dealings with Negro people, most on a business basis but sometimes for friendly reasons with genuine feeling on both sides. I'm drawn to them. At this time of my life I should have one or two good colored friends, but the fault isn't necessarily mine. If they knew what was in my heart toward them, but how can you tell that to anybody nowadays? I've tried more than once but the language of the heart either is a dead language or else nobody understands it the way you speak it. Very few. What I'm saying is, personally for me there's only one human color and that's the color of blood. I like a black person if not because he's black, then because I'm white. It comes to the same thing. If I wasn't white my first choice would be black. I'm satisfied to be white because I have no other choice. Anyway, I got an eye for color. I appreciate. Who wants everybody to be the same? Maybe it's like some kind of a talent. Nat Lime might be a liquor dealer in Harlem, but once in the jungle in New Guinea in the Second World War, I got the idea, when I shot at a running Jap and missed him, that I had some kind of a talent, though maybe it's the kind where you have a good idea now and then, but in the end what do they come to? After all, it's a strange world.

Where Charity Quietness eats her eggs makes me think about Buster Wilson when we were both boys in the Williamsburg section of Brooklyn. There was this long block of run-down dirty frame houses in the middle of a not-so-hot white neighborhood full of pushcarts. The Negro houses looked to me like they had been born and died there, dead not long after the beginning of the world. I lived on the next street. My father was a cutter with arthritis in both hands, big red knuckles and fingers so swollen he didn't cut, and my mother was the one who went to work. She sold paper bags from a secondhand pushcart on Ellery Street. We didn't starve but nobody ate chicken unless we were sick, or the chicken was. This was my first acquaintance with a lot of black people and I used to poke around on their poor block. I think I thought, brother, if there can be like this, what can't there be? I mean I caught an early idea what life was about. Anyway, I met Buster Wilson there. He used to play marbles by himself. I sat on the curb across the street, watching him shoot one marble lefty and the other one righty. The hand that won picked up the marbles. It wasn't so much of a game but he didn't ask me to come over. My idea was to be friendly, only he never encouraged, he discouraged. Why did I pick him out for a friend? Maybe because I had no others then, we were new in the neighborhood, from Manhattan. Also I liked his type. Buster did everything alone. He was a skinny kid and his brothers' clothes hung on him like worn-out potato sacks. He was a beanpole boy, about twelve, and I was then ten. His arms and legs were burnt-out matchsticks. He always wore a brown wool sweater, one arm half unraveled, the other went down to the wrist. His long and narrow head had a white part cut straight in the short woolly hair, maybe with a ruler there, by his father, a barber but too drunk to stay a barber. In those days though I had little myself I was old enough to know who was better off, and the whole block of colored houses made me feel bad in the daylight. But I went there as much as I could because the street was full of life. In the night it looked different, it's hard to tell a cripple in the dark. Sometimes I was afraid to walk by the houses when they were dark and quiet. I was afraid there were people looking at me that

I couldn't see. I liked it better when they had parties at night and everybody had a good time. The musicians played their banjos and saxophones and the houses shook with the music and laughing. The young girls, with their pretty dresses and ribbons in their hair, caught me in my throat when I saw them through the windows.

But with the parties came drinking and fights. Sundays were bad days after the Saturday night parties. I remember once that Buster's father, also long and loose, always wearing a dirty gray Homburg hat, chased another black man in the street with a half-inch chisel. The other one, maybe five feet high, lost his shoe and when they wrestled on the ground he was already bleeding through his suit, a thick red blood smearing the sidewalk. I was frightened by the blood and wanted to pour it back in the man who was bleeding from the chisel. On another time Buster's father was playing in a crap game with two big bouncy red dice, in the back of an alley between two middle houses. Then about six men started fist-fighting there, and they ran out of the alley and hit each other in the street. The neighbors, including children, came out and watched, everybody afraid but nobody moving to do anything. I saw the same thing near my store in Harlem, years later, a big crowd watching two men in the street, their breaths hanging in the air on a winter night, murdering each other with switch knives, but nobody moved to call a cop. I didn't either. Anyway, I was just a young kid but I still remember how the cops drove up in a police paddy wagon and broke up the fight by hitting everybody they could hit with big nightsticks. This was in the days before La Guardia. Most of the fighters were knocked out cold, only one or two got away. Buster's father started to run back in his house but a cop ran after him and cracked him on his Homburg hat with a club, right on the front porch. Then the Negro men were lifted up by the cops, one at the arms and the other at the feet, and they heaved them in the paddy wagon.

Buster's father hit the back of the wagon and fell, with his nose spouting very red blood, on top of three other men. I personally couldn't stand it, I was scared of the human race so I ran home, but I remember Buster watching without any expression in his eyes. I stole an extra fifteen cents from my mother's pocketbook and I ran back and asked Buster if he wanted to go to the movies, I would pay. He said yes. This was the first time he talked to me.

So we went more than once to the movies. But we never got to be friends. Maybe because it was a one-way proposition—from me to him. Which includes my invitations to go with me, my (poor mother's) movie money, Hershey chocolate bars, watermelon slices, even my best Nick Carter and Merriwell books that I spent hours picking up in the junk shops, and that he never gave me back. Once, he let me go in his house to get a match so we could smoke some butts we found, but it smelled so heavy, so impossible, I died till I got out of there. What I saw in the way of furniture I won't mention—the best was falling apart in pieces. Maybe we went to the movies all together five or six matinees that spring and in the summertime, but when the shows were over he usually walked home by himself.

"Why don't you wait for me, Buster?" I said. "We're both going in the same direction."

But he was walking ahead and didn't hear me. Anyway he didn't answer.

One day when I wasn't expecting it he hit me in the teeth. I felt like crying but not because of the pain. I spit blood and said, "What did you hit me for? What did I do to you?"

"Because you a Jew bastard. Take your Jew movies and your Jew candy and shove them up your Jew ass."

And he ran away.

I thought to myself how was I to know he didn't like the movies. When I was a man I thought, you can't force it.

Years later, in the prime of my life, I met Mrs. Ornita Harris. She was standing by herself under an open umbrella at the bus stop, crosstown 110th, and I picked up her green glove that she had dropped on the wet sidewalk. It was in the end of November. Before I could ask her was it hers, she grabbed the glove out of my hand, closed her umbrella, and stepped in the bus. I got on right after her. I was annoyed so I said, "If you'll pardon me, Miss, there's no law that you have to say thanks, but at least don't make a criminal out of me."

"Well, I'm sorry," she said, "but I don't like white men trying to do me favors."

I tipped my hat and that was that. In ten minutes I got off the bus but she was already gone.

Who expected to see her again, but I did. She came into my store about a week later for a bottle of Scotch.

"I would offer you a discount," I told her, "but I know you don't like a certain kind of a favor and I'm not looking for a slap in the face."

Then she recognized me and got a little embarrassed.

"I'm sorry I misunderstood you that day."

"So mistakes happen."

The result was she took the discount. I gave her a dollar off.

She used to come in every two weeks for a fifth of Haig & Haig. Sometimes I waited on her, sometimes my helpers, Jimmy or Mason, also colored, but I said to give the discount. They both looked at me but I had nothing to be ashamed. In the spring when she came in we used to talk once in a while. She was a slim woman, dark, but not the most dark, about thirty years I would say, also well built, with a combination nice legs and a good-size bosom that I like. Her face was pretty, with big eyes and high cheekbones, but lips a little thick and nose a little broad. Sometimes she didn't feel like talking, she paid for the bottle, less discount, and walked out. Her eyes were tired and she didn't look to me like a happy woman.

I found out her husband was once a window cleaner on the
big buildings, but one day his safety belt broke and he fell fifteen
stories. After the funeral she got a job as a manicurist in a Times
Square barber shop. I told her I was a bachelor and lived with
my mother in a small three-room apartment on West Eighty-
third near Broadway. My mother had cancer, and Ornita said
she was very sorry.

One night in July we went out together. How that happened
I'm still not so sure. I guess I asked her and she didn't say no.
Where do you go out with a Negro woman? We went to the
Village. We had a good dinner and walked in Washington
Square Park. It was a hot night. Nobody was surprised when they
saw us, nobody looked at us like we were against the law. If they
looked maybe they saw my new lightweight suit that I bought
yesterday and my shiny bald spot when we walked under a lamp,
also how pretty she was for a man my type. We went in a movie
on West Eighth Street. I didn't want to go in but she said she had
heard about the picture. We went in like strangers and we came
out like strangers. I wondered what was in her mind and I
thought to myself, whatever is in there it's not a certain white
man that I know. All night long we went together like we were
chained. After the movie she wouldn't let me take her back to
Harlem. When I put her in a taxi she asked me, "Why did we
bother?"

For the steak, I thought of saying. Instead I said, "You're
worth the bother."

"Thanks anyway."

Kiddo, I thought to myself after the taxi left, you just found
out what's what, now the best thing is forget her.

It's easy to say. In August we went out the second time. That
was the night she wore a purple dress and I thought to myself,
my God, what colors. Who paints that picture paints a master-
piece. Everybody looked at us but I had pleasure. That night
when she took off her dress it was in a furnished room I had the

sense to rent a few days before. With my sick mother, I couldn't ask her to come to my apartment, and she didn't want me to go home with her where she lived with her brother's family on West 115th near Lenox Avenue. Under her purple dress she wore a black slip, and when she took that off she had white underwear. When she took off the white underwear she was black again. But I know where the next white was, if you want to call it white. And that was the night I think I fell in love with her, the first time in my life, though I have liked one or two nice girls I used to go with when I was a boy. It was a serious proposition. I'm the kind of a man when I think of love I'm thinking of marriage. I guess that's why I am a bachelor.

That same week I had a holdup in my place, two big men— both black—with revolvers. One got excited when I rang open the cash register so he could take the money, and he hit me over the ear with his gun. I stayed in the hospital a couple of weeks. Otherwise I was insured. Ornita came to see me. She sat on a chair without talking much. Finally I saw she was uncomfortable so I suggested she ought to go home.

"I'm sorry it happened," she said.

"Don't talk like it's your fault."

When I got out of the hospital my mother was dead. She was a wonderful person. My father died when I was thirteen and all by herself she kept the family alive and together. I sat shiva for a week and remembered how she sold paper bags on her pushcart. I remembered her life and what she tried to teach me. Nathan, she said, if you ever forget you are a Jew a goy will remind you. Mama, I said, rest in peace on this subject. But if I do something you don't like, remember, on earth it's harder than where you are. Then when my week of mourning was finished, one night I said, "Ornita, let's get married. We're both honest people and if you love me like I love you it won't be such a bad time. If you don't like New York I'll sell out here and we'll move someplace else. Maybe to San Francisco where nobody knows us. I was there for a week in the Second War and I saw white and colored living together."

"Nat," she answered me, "I like you but I'd be afraid. My husband woulda killed me."

"Your husband is dead."

"Not in my memory."

"In that case I'll wait."

"Do you know what it'd be like—I mean the life we could expect?"

"Ornita," I said, "I'm the kind of a man, if he picks his own way of life he's satisfied."

"What about children? Were you looking forward to half-Jewish polka dots?"

"I was looking forward to children."

"I can't," she said.

Can't is can't. I saw she was afraid and the best thing was not to push. Sometimes when we met she was so nervous that whatever we did she couldn't enjoy it. At the same time I still thought I had a chance. We were together more and more. I got rid of my furnished room and she came to my apartment—I gave away Mama's bed and bought a new one. She stayed with me all day on Sundays. When she wasn't so nervous she was affectionate, and if I know what love is, I had it. We went out a couple of times a week, the same way—usually I met her in Times Square and sent her home in a taxi, but I talked more about marriage and she talked less against it. One night she told me she was still trying to convince herself but she was almost convinced. I took an inventory of my liquor stock so I could put the store up for sale.

Ornita knew what I was doing. One day she quit her job, the next she took it back. She also went away a week to visit her sister in Philadelphia for a little rest. She came back tired but said maybe. Maybe is maybe so I'll wait. The way she said it, it was closer to yes. That was the winter two years ago. When she was in Philadelphia I called up a friend of mine from the army, now a CPA, and told him I would appreciate an invitation for an evening. He knew why. His wife said yes right away. When Ornita came back we went there. The wife made a fine dinner. It wasn't a bad time and they told us to come again. Ornita had a few drinks. She looked relaxed, wonderful. Later, because of a twenty-four-hour taxi strike I had to take her home on the subway. When we got to the 116th Street station she told me to go back on the train, and she would walk the couple of blocks to her house. I didn't like a woman walking alone on the streets at that time of the night. She said she never had any trouble but I insisted nothing doing. I said I would walk to her stoop with her and when she went upstairs I would go to the subway.

On the way there, on 115th in the middle of the block before Lenox, we were stopped by three men—maybe they were boys. One had a black hat with a half-inch brim, one a green cloth hat, and the third wore a black leather cap. The green hat was wearing a short coat and the other two had long ones. It was under a streetlight but the leather cap snapped a six-inch switchblade open in the light.

"What you doin' with this white son of a bitch?" he said to Ornita.

"I'm minding my own business," she answered him, "and I wish you would too."

"Boys," I said, "we're all brothers. I'm a reliable merchant in the neighborhood. This young lady is my dear friend. We don't want any trouble. Please let us pass."

"You talk like a Jew landlord," said the green hat. "Fifty a week for a single room."

·"No charge fo' the rats," said the half-inch brim.

"Believe me, I'm no landlord. My store is Nathan's Liquors

between Hundred Tenth and Eleventh. I also have two colored clerks, Mason and Jimmy, and they will tell you I pay good wages as well as I give discounts to certain customers."

"Shut your mouth, Jewboy," said the leather cap, and he moved the knife back and forth in front of my coat button. "No more black pussy for you."

"Speak with respect about this lady, please."

I got slapped on my mouth.

"That ain't no lady," said the long face in the half-inch brim, "that's black pussy. She deserve to have evvy bit of her hair shave off. How you like to have evvy bit of your hair shave off, black pussy?"

"Please leave me and this gentleman alone or I'm gonna scream long and loud. That's my house three doors down."

They slapped her. I never heard such a scream. Like her husband was falling fifteen stories.

I hit the one that slapped her and the next I knew I was laying in the gutter with a pain in my head. I thought, goodbye, Nat, they'll stab me for sure, but all they did was take my wallet and run in three directions.

Ornita walked back with me to the subway and she wouldn't let me go home with her again.

"Just get home safely."

She looked terrible. Her face was gray and I still remembered her scream. It was a terrible winter night, very cold February, and it took me an hour and ten minutes to get home. I felt bad for leaving her but what could I do?

We had a date downtown the next night but she didn't show up, the first time.

In the morning I called her in her place of business.

"For God's sake, Ornita, if we got married and moved away we wouldn't have the kind of trouble that we had. We wouldn't come in that neighborhood any more."

"Yes, we would. I have family there and don't want to move anyplace else. The truth of it is I can't marry you, Nat. I got troubles enough of my own."

"I coulda sworn you love me."

"Maybe I do but I can't marry you."

"For God's sake, why?"

"I got enough trouble of my own."

I went that night in a cab to her brother's house to see her. He was a quiet man with a thin mustache. "She gone," he said, "left for a long visit to some close relatives in the South. She said to tell you she appreciate your intentions but didn't think it will work out."

"Thank you kindly," I said.

Don't ask me how I got home.

Once, on Eighth Avenue, a couple of blocks from my store, I saw a blind man with a white cane tapping on the sidewalk. I figured we were going in the same direction so I took his arm.

"I can tell you're white," he said.

A heavy colored woman with a full shopping bag rushed after us.

"Never mind," she said, "I know where he live."

She pushed me with her shoulder and I hurt my leg on the fire hydrant.

That's how it is. I give my heart and they kick me in my teeth.

"Charity Quietness—you hear me?—come out of that goddamn toilet!"

My Son the Murderer

HE WAKES feeling his father is in the hallway, listening. He listens to him sleep and dream. Listening to him get up and fumble for his pants. He won't put on his shoes. To him not going to the kitchen to eat. Staring with shut eyes in the mirror. Sitting an hour on the toilet. Flipping the pages of a book he can't read. To his anguish, loneliness. The father stands in the hall. The son hears him listen.

My son the stranger, he won't tell me anything.

I open the door and see my father in the hall. Why are you standing there, why don't you go to work?

On account of I took my vacation in the winter instead of the summer like I usually do.

What the hell for if you spend it in this dark smelly hallway, watching my every move? Guessing what you can't see. Why are you always spying on me?

My father goes to the bedroom and after a while sneaks out in the hallway again, listening.

I hear him sometimes in his room but he don't talk to me and I don't know what's what. It's a terrible feeling for a father. Maybe someday he will write me a letter, My dear father . . .

My dear son Harry, open up your door. My son the prisoner.

My wife leaves in the morning to stay with my married daughter, who is expecting her fourth child. The mother cooks and cleans for her and takes care of the three children. My daughter is having a bad pregnancy, with high blood pressure, and lays in bed most of the time. This is what the doctor advised her. My wife is gone all day. She worries something is wrong with Harry. Since he graduated college last summer he is alone, nervous, in his own thoughts. If you talk to him, half the time he yells if he answers you. He reads the papers, smokes, he stays in his room. Or once in a while he goes for a walk in the street.

How was the walk, Harry?

A walk.

My wife advised him to go look for work, and a couple of times he went, but when he got some kind of an offer he didn't take the job.

It's not that I don't want to work. It's that I feel bad.

So why do you feel bad?

I feel what I feel. I feel what is.

Is it your health, sonny? Maybe you ought to go to a doctor?

I asked you not to call me by that name any more. It's not my health. Whatever it is I don't want to talk about it. The work wasn't the kind I want.

So take something temporary in the meantime, my wife said to him.

He starts to yell. Everything's temporary. Why should I add more to what's temporary? My gut feels temporary. The goddamn world is temporary. On top of that I don't want temporary work. I want the opposite of temporary, but where is it? Where do you find it?

My father listens in the kitchen.

My temporary son.

She says I'll feel better if I work. I say I won't. I'm twenty-two since December, a college graduate, and you know where you can stick that. At night I watch the news programs. I watch the war from day to day. It's a big burning war on a small screen. It rains bombs and the flames roar higher. Sometimes I lean over and touch the war with the flat of my hand. I wait for my hand to die.

My son with the dead hand.

I expect to be drafted any day but it doesn't bother me the way it used to. I won't go. I'll go to Canada or somewhere I can go.

The way he is frightens my wife and she is glad to go to my daughter's house early in the morning to take care of the three children. I stay with him in the house but he don't talk to me.

You ought to call up Harry and talk to him, my wife says to my daughter.

I will sometime but don't forget there's nine years' difference between our ages. I think he thinks of me as another mother around and one is enough. I used to like him when he was a little boy but now it's hard to deal with a person who won't reciprocate to you.

She's got high blood pressure. I think she's afraid to call.

I took two weeks off from my work. I'm a clerk at the stamp window in the post office. I told the superintendent I wasn't feeling so good, which is no lie, and he said I should take sick leave. I said I wasn't that sick, I only needed a little vacation. But I told my friend Moe Berkman I was staying out because Harry has me worried.

I understand what you mean, Leo. I got my own worries and anxieties about my kids. If you got two girls growing up you got hostages to fortune. Still in all we got to live. Why don't you come to poker on this Friday night? We got a nice game going. Don't deprive yourself of a good form of relaxation.

I'll see how I feel by Friday how everything is coming along. I can't promise you.

Try to come. These things, if you give them time, all will pass away. If it looks better to you, come on over. Even if it don't look so good, come on over anyway because it might relieve your tension and worry that you're under. It's not so good for your heart at your age if you carry that much worry around.

It's the worst kind of worry. If I worry about myself I know what the worry is. What I mean, there's no mystery. I can say to myself, Leo you're a big fool, stop worrying about nothing—over what, a few bucks? Over my health that has always stood up pretty good although I have my ups and downs? Over that I'm now close to sixty and not getting any younger? Everybody that don't die by age fifty-nine gets to be sixty. You can't beat time when it runs along with you. But if the worry is about somebody else, that's the worst kind. That's the real worry because if he won't tell you, you can't get inside of the other person and find out why. You don't know where's the switch to turn off. All you do is worry more.

So I wait out in the hall.

Harry, don't worry so much about the war.

Please don't tell me what to worry about or what not to worry about.

Harry, your father loves you. When you were a little boy, every night when I came home you used to run to me. I picked you up and lifted you up to the ceiling. You liked to touch it with your small hand.

I don't want to hear about that any more. It's the very thing I don't want to hear. I don't want to hear about when I was a child.

Harry, we live like strangers. All I'm saying is I remember better days. I remember when we weren't afraid to show we loved each other.

He says nothing.

Let me cook you an egg.

An egg is the last thing in the world I want.

So what do you want?

He put his coat on. He pulled his hat off the clothes tree and went down into the street.

Harry walked along Ocean Parkway in his long overcoat and creased brown hat. His father was following him and it filled him with rage.

He walked at a fast pace up the broad avenue. In the old days there was a bridle path at the side of the walk where the concrete bicycle path is now. And there were fewer trees, their black branches cutting the sunless sky. At the corner of Avenue X, just about where you can smell Coney Island, he crossed the street and began to walk home. He pretended not to see his father cross over, though he was infuriated. The father crossed over and followed his son home. When he got to the house he figured Harry was upstairs already. He was in his room with the door shut. Whatever he did in his room he was already doing.

Leo took out his small key and opened the mailbox. There were three letters. He looked to see if one of them was, by any chance, from his son to him. My dear father, let me explain myself. The reason I act as I do . . . There was no such letter. One of the letters was from the Post Office Clerks Benevolent Society, which he slipped into his coat pocket. The other two letters were for Harry. One was from the draft board. He brought it up to his son's room, knocked on the door, and waited.

He waited for a while.

To the boy's grunt he said, There is a draft-board letter here for you. He turned the knob and entered the room. His son was lying on his bed with his eyes shut.

Leave it on the table.

Do you want me to open it for you, Harry?

No, I don't want you to open it. Leave it on the table. I know what's in it.

Did you write them another letter?

That's my goddamn business.

The father left it on the table.

The other letter to his son he took into the kitchen, shut the door, and boiled up some water in a pot. He thought he would read it quickly and seal it carefully with a little paste, then go downstairs and put it back in the mailbox. His wife would take it out with her key when she returned from their daughter's house and bring it up to Harry.

The father read the letter. It was a short letter from a girl. The girl said Harry had borrowed two of her books more than six months ago and since she valued them highly she would like him to send them back to her. Could he do that as soon as possible so that she wouldn't have to write again?

As Leo was reading the girl's letter Harry came into the kitchen and when he saw the surprised and guilty look on his father's face, he tore the letter out of his hands.

I ought to murder you the way you spy on me.

Leo turned away, looking out of the small kitchen window into the dark apartment-house courtyard. His face burned, he felt sick.

Harry read the letter at a glance and tore it up. He then tore up the envelope marked personal.

If you do this again don't be surprised if I kill you. I'm sick of you spying on me.

Harry, you are talking to your father.

He left the house.

Leo went into his room and looked around. He looked in the dresser drawers and found nothing unusual. On the desk by the window was a paper Harry had written on. It said: Dear Edith, why don't you go fuck yourself? If you write me another stupid letter I'll murder you.

The father got his hat and coat and left the house. He ran

slowly for a while, running then walking until he saw Harry on the other side of the street. He followed him, half a block behind.

He followed Harry to Coney Island Avenue and was in time to see him board a trolleybus going to the Island. Leo had to wait for the next one. He thought of taking a taxi and following the trolleybus, but no taxi came by. The next bus came fifteen minutes later and he took it all the way to the Island. It was February and Coney Island was wet, cold, and deserted. There were few cars on Surf Avenue and few people on the streets. It felt like snow. Leo walked on the boardwalk amid snow flurries, looking for his son. The gray sunless beaches were empty. The hot-dog stands, shooting galleries, and bathhouses were shuttered up. The gunmetal ocean, moving like melted lead, looked freezing. A wind blew in off the water and worked its way into his clothes so that he shivered as he walked. The wind white-capped the leaden waves and the slow surf broke on the empty beaches with a quiet roar.

He walked in the blow almost to Sea Gate, searching for his son, and then walked back again. On his way toward Brighton Beach he saw a man on the shore standing in the foaming surf. Leo hurried down the boardwalk stairs and onto the ribbed-sand beach. The man on the roaring shore was Harry, standing in water to the tops of his shoes.

Leo ran to his son. Harry, it was a mistake, excuse me, I'm sorry I opened your letter.

Harry did not move. He stood in the water, his eyes on the swelling leaden waves.

Harry, I'm frightened. Tell me what's the matter. My son, have mercy on me.

I'm frightened of the world, Harry thought. It fills me with fright.

He said nothing.

A blast of wind lifted his father's hat and carried it away over the beach. It looked as though it was going to be blown into the surf, but then the wind blew it toward the boardwalk, rolling like a wheel along the wet sand. Leo chased after his hat. He chased it one way, then another, then toward the water. The wind blew the hat against his legs and he caught it. By now he was crying. Breathless, he wiped his eyes with icy fingers and returned to his son at the edge of the water.

He is a lonely man. This is the type he is. He will always be lonely.

My son who made himself into a lonely man.

Harry, what can I say to you? All I can say to you is who says life is easy? Since when? It wasn't for me and it isn't for you. It's life, that's the way it is—what more can I say? But if a person don't want to live what can he do if he's dead? Nothing is nothing, it's better to live.

Come home, Harry, he said. It's cold here. You'll catch a cold with your feet in the water.

Harry stood motionless in the water and after a while his father left. As he was leaving, the wind plucked his hat off his head and sent it rolling along the shore. He watched it go.

My father listens in the hallway. He follows me in the street. We meet at the edge of the water.

He runs after his hat.

My son stands with his feet in the ocean.

The German Refugee

OSKAR GASSNER sits in his cotton-mesh undershirt and summer bathrobe at the window of his stuffy, hot, dark hotel room on West Tenth Street as I cautiously knock. Outside, across the sky, a late-June green twilight fades in darkness. The refugee fumbles for the light and stares at me, hiding despair but not pain.

I was in those days a poor student and would brashly attempt to teach anybody anything for a buck an hour, although I have since learned better. Mostly I gave English lessons to recently arrived refugees. The college sent me, I had acquired a little experience. Already a few of my students were trying their broken English, theirs and mine, in the American marketplace. I was then just twenty, on my way into my senior year in college, a skinny, life-hungry kid, eating himself waiting for the next world war to start. It was a miserable cheat. Here I was panting to get going, and across the ocean Adolf Hitler, in black boots and a square mustache, was tearing up and spitting at all the flowers. Will I ever forget what went on with Danzig that summer?

Times were still hard from the Depression but I made a

little living from the poor refugees. They were all over uptown Broadway in 1939. I had four I tutored—Karl Otto Alp, the former film star; Wolfgang Novak, once a brilliant economist; Friedrich Wilhelm Wolff, who had taught medieval history at Heidelberg; and after the night I met him in his disordered cheap hotel room, Oskar Gassner, the Berlin critic and journalist, at one time on the *Acht Uhr Abendblatt*. They were accomplished men. I had my nerve associating with them, but that's what a world crisis does for people, they get educated.

Oskar was maybe fifty, his thick hair turning gray. He had a big face and heavy hands. His shoulders sagged. His eyes, too, were heavy, a clouded blue; and as he stared at me after I had identified myself, doubt spread in them like underwater currents. It was as if, on seeing me, he had again been defeated. I had to wait until he came to. I stayed at the door in silence. In such cases I would rather be elsewhere, but I had to make a living. Finally he opened the door and I entered. Rather, he released it and I was in. "Bitte"—he offered me a seat and didn't know where to sit himself. He would attempt to say something and then stop, as though it could not possibly be said. The room was cluttered with clothing, boxes of books he had managed to get out of Germany, and some paintings. Oskar sat on a box and attempted to fan himself with his meaty hand. "Zis heat," he muttered, forcing his mind to the deed. "Impozzible. I do not know such heat." It was bad enough for me but terrible for him. He had difficulty breathing. He tried to speak, lifted a hand, and let it drop. He breathed as though he was fighting a war; and maybe he won because after ten minutes we sat and slowly talked.

Like most educated Germans Oskar had at one time studied English. Although he was certain he couldn't say a word he managed to put together a fairly decent, if sometimes comical English sentence. He misplaced consonants, mixed up nouns and verbs, and mangled idioms, yet we were able at once to communicate. We conversed in English, with an occasional assist by me in pidgin-German or Yiddish, what he called "Jiddish." He had been to America before, last year for a short visit. He had come a month before Kristallnacht, when the Nazis shattered the Jewish store windows and burnt all the synagogues, to see if he could find a job for himself; he had no relatives in America and getting a job would permit him quickly to enter the country. He had been promised something, not in journalism, but with the help of a foundation, as a lecturer. Then he returned to Berlin, and after a frightening delay of six months was permitted to emigrate. He had sold whatever he could, managed to get some paintings, gifts of Bauhaus friends, and some boxes of books out by bribing two Dutch border guards; he had said goodbye to his wife and left the accursed country. He gazed at me with cloudy eyes. "We parted amicably," he said in German, "my wife was gentile. Her mother was an appalling anti-Semite. They returned to live in Stettin." I asked no questions. Gentile is gentile, Germany is Germany.

His new job was in the Institute for Public Studies, in New York. He was to give a lecture a week in the fall term and during next spring, a course, in English translation, in "The Literature of the Weimar Republic." He had never taught before and was afraid to. He was in that way to be introduced to the public, but the thought of giving the lecture in English just about paralyzed him. He didn't see how he could do it. "How is it pozzible? I cannot say two words. I cannot pronounziate. I will make a fool of myself." His melancholy deepened. Already in the two months since his arrival, and a round of diminishingly expensive hotel rooms, he had had two English tutors, and I was the third. The others had given him up, he said, because his progress was so poor, and he thought he also depressed them. He asked me whether I felt I could do something for him, or should he go to a speech specialist, someone, say, who charged five dollars an hour, and beg his assistance? "You could try him," I said, "and then come back to me." In those days I figured what I knew, I knew. At that he managed a smile. Still, I wanted him to make up his mind or it would be no confidence down the line. He said, after a while, he would stay with me. If he went to the five-dollar professor it might help his tongue but not his appetite. He would have no money left to eat with. The Institute had paid him in advance for the summer, but it was only three hundred dollars and all he had.

He looked at me dully. "Ich weiss nicht, wie ich weiter machen soll."

I figured it was time to move past the first step. Either we did that quickly or it would be like drilling rock for a long time.

"Let's stand at the mirror," I said.

He rose with a sigh and stood there beside me, I thin, elongated, red-headed, praying for success, his and mine; Oskar uneasy, fearful, finding it hard to face either of us in the faded round glass above his dresser.

"Please," I said to him, "could you say 'right'?"

"Ghight," he gargled.

"No—right. You put your tongue here." I showed him where as he tensely watched the mirror. I tensely watched him. "The tip of it curls behind the ridge on top, like this."

He placed his tongue where I showed him.

"Please," I said, "now say right."

Oskar's tongue fluttered. "Rright."

"That's good. Now say 'treasure'—that's harder."

"Tgheasure."

"The tongue goes up in front, not in the back of the mouth. Look."

He tried, his brow wet, eyes straining, "Trreasure."

"That's it."

"A miracle," Oskar murmured.

I said if he had done that he could do the rest.

We went for a bus ride up Fifth Avenue and then walked for a while around Central Park Lake. He had put on his German hat, with its hatband bow at the back, a broad-lapeled wool suit, a necktie twice as wide as the one I was wearing, and walked with a small-footed waddle. The night wasn't bad, it had got a bit cooler. There were a few large stars in the sky and they made me sad.

"Do you sink I will succezz?"

"Why not?" I asked.

Later he bought me a bottle of beer.

: : :

To many of these people, articulate as they were, the great loss was the loss of language—that they could not say what was in them to say. You have some subtle thought and it comes out like a piece of broken bottle. They could, of course, manage to communicate, but just to communicate was frustrating. As Karl Otto Alp, the ex-film star who became a buyer for Macy's, put it years later, "I felt like a child, or worse, often like a moron. I am left with myself unexpressed. What I know, indeed, what I am, becomes to me a burden. My tongue hangs useless." The same with Oskar it figures. There was a terrible sense of useless tongue, and I think the reason for his trouble with his other tutors was that to keep from drowning in things unsaid he wanted to swallow the ocean in a gulp: today he would learn English and tomorrow wow them with an impeccable Fourth of July speech, followed by a successful lecture at the Institute for Public Studies.

We performed our lessons slowly, step by step, everything in its place. After Oskar moved to a two-room apartment in a house on West Eighty-fifth Street, near the Drive, we met three times a week at four-thirty, worked an hour and a half, then, since it was too hot to cook, had supper at the Seventy-second Street Automat and conversed on my time. The lessons we divided into three parts: diction exercises and reading aloud; then grammar, because Oskar felt the necessity of it, and composition correction; with conversation, as I said, thrown in at supper. So far as I could see he was coming along. None of these exercises was giving him as much trouble as they apparently had in the past. He seemed to be learning and his mood lightened. There were moments of elation as he heard his accent flying off. For instance when sink became think. He stopped calling himself "hopelezz," and I became his "bezt teacher," a little joke I liked.

Neither of us said much about the lecture he had to give early in October, and I kept my fingers crossed. It was somehow to come out of what we were doing daily, I think I felt, but exactly how, I had no idea; and to tell the truth, though I didn't say so to Oskar, the lecture frightened me. That and the ten more to follow during the fall term. Later, when I learned that he had been attempting, with the help of the dictionary, to write in English and had produced "a complete disahster," I suggested maybe he ought to stick to German and we could afterwards both try to put it into passable English. I was cheating when I said that because my German is meager, enough to read simple stuff but certainly not good enough for serious translation; anyway, the idea was to get Oskar into production and worry about translating later. He sweated with it, from enervating morning to exhausted night, but no matter what language he tried, though he had been a professional writer for a generation and knew his subject cold, the lecture refused to move past page one.

It was a sticky, hot July, and the heat didn't help at all.

:   :   :

I had met Oskar at the end of June, and by the seventeenth of July we were no longer doing lessons. They had foundered on the "impozzible" lecture. He had worked on it each day in frenzy and growing despair. After writing more than a hundred opening pages he furiously flung his pen against the wall, shouting he could not longer write in that filthy tongue. He cursed the German language. He hated the damned country and the damned people. After that, what was bad became worse. When he gave up attempting to write the lecture, he stopped making progress in English. He seemed to forget what he already knew. His tongue thickened and the accent returned in all its fruitiness. The little he had to say was in handcuffed and tortured English. The only German I heard him speak was in a whisper to himself. I doubt he knew he was talking it. That ended our formal work together, though I did drop in every other day or so to sit with him. For hours he sat motionless in a large green velour armchair, hot enough to broil in, and through tall windows stared at the colorless sky above Eighty-fifth Street with a wet depressed eye.

Then once he said to me, "If I do not this legture prepare, I will take my life."

"Let's begin, Oskar," I said. "You dictate and I'll write. The ideas count, not the spelling."

He didn't answer so I stopped talking.

He had plunged into an involved melancholy. We sat for hours, often in profound silence. This was alarming to me, though I had already had some experience with such depression. Wolfgang Novak, the economist, though English came more easily to him, was another. His problems arose mainly, I think, from physical illness. And he felt a greater sense of the lost country than Oskar. Sometimes in the early evening I persuaded Oskar to come with me for a short walk on the Drive. The tail end of sunsets over the Palisades seemed to appeal to him. At least he looked. He would put on full regalia—hat, suit coat, tie, no matter how hot or what I suggested—and we went slowly down the stairs, I wondering whether he would make it to the bottom.

We walked slowly uptown, stopping to sit on a bench and watch night rise above the Hudson. When we returned to his room, if I sensed he had loosened up a bit, we listened to music on the radio; but if I tried to sneak in a news broadcast, he said to me, "Please, I cannot more stand of world misery." I shut off the radio. He was right, it was a time of no good news. I squeezed my brain. What could I tell him? Was it good news to be alive? Who could argue the point? Sometimes I read aloud to him—I remember he liked the first part of *Life on the Mississippi*. We still went to the Automat once or twice a week, he perhaps out of habit, because he didn't feel like going anywhere —I to get him out of his room. Oskar ate little, he toyed with a spoon. His eyes looked as though they had been squirted with a dark dye.

Once after a momentary cooling rainstorm we sat on newspapers on a wet bench overlooking the river and Oskar at last began to talk. In tormented English he conveyed his intense and everlasting hatred of the Nazis for destroying his career, uprooting his life, and flinging him like a piece of bleeding meat to the hawks. He cursed them thickly, the German nation, an inhuman, conscienceless, merciless people. "They are pigs mazquerading as peacogs," he said. "I feel certain that my wife, in her heart, was a Jew hater." It was a terrible bitterness, and eloquence beyond the words he spoke. He became silent again. I wanted to hear more about his wife but decided not to ask.

Afterwards in the dark, Oskar confessed that he had attempted suicide during his first week in America. He was living, at the end of May, in a small hotel, and had one night filled himself with barbiturates; but his phone had fallen off the table and the hotel operator had sent up the elevator boy, who found him unconscious and called the police. He was revived in the hospital.

"I did not mean to do it," he said, "it was a mistage."

"Don't ever think of it," I said, "it's total defeat."

"I don't," he said wearily, "because it is so arduouz to come bag to life."

"Please, for any reason whatever."

Afterwards when we were walking, he surprised me by saying, "Maybe we ought to try now the legture onze more."

We trudged back to the house and he sat at his hot desk, I trying to read as he slowly began to reconstruct the first page of his lecture. He wrote, of course, in German.

:   :   :

He got nowhere. We were back to sitting in silence in the heat. Sometimes, after a few minutes, I had to take off before his mood overcame mine. One afternoon I came unwillingly up the stairs —there were times I felt momentary surges of irritation with him—and was frightened to find Oskar's door ajar. When I knocked no one answered. As I stood there, chilled down the spine, I realized I was thinking about the possibility of his attempting suicide again. "Oskar?" I went into the apartment, looked into both rooms and the bathroom, but he wasn't there. I thought he might have drifted out to get something from a store and took the opportunity to look quickly around. There was nothing startling in the medicine chest, no pills but aspirin, no iodine. Thinking, for some reason, of a gun, I searched his desk drawer. In it I found a thin-paper airmail letter from Germany. Even if I had wanted to, I couldn't read the handwriting, but as I held it in my hand I did make out a sentence: "Ich bin dir siebenundzwanzig Jahre treu gewesen." There was no gun in the drawer. I shut it and stopped looking. It had occurred to me if you want to kill yourself all you need is a straight pin. When Oskar returned he said he had been sitting in the public library, unable to read.

Now we are once more enacting the changeless scene, curtain

rising on two speechless characters in a furnished apartment, I in a straight-back chair, Oskar in the velour armchair that smothered rather than supported him, his flesh gray, the big gray face unfocused, sagging. I reached over to switch on the radio but he barely looked at me in a way that begged no. I then got up to leave but Oskar, clearing his throat, thickly asked me to stay. I stayed, thinking, was there more to this than I could see into? His problems, God knows, were real enough, but could there be something more than a refugee's displacement, alienation, financial insecurity, being in a strange land without friends or a speakable tongue? My speculation was the old one: not all drown in this ocean, why does he? After a while I shaped the thought and asked him was there something below the surface, invisible? I was full of this thing from college, and wondered if there mightn't be some unknown quantity in his depression that a psychiatrist maybe might help him with, enough to get him started on his lecture.

He meditated on this and after a few minutes haltingly said he had been psychoanalyzed in Vienna as a young man. "Just the jusual drek," he said, "fears and fantazies that afterwaards no longer bothered me."

"They don't now?"

"Not."

"You've written many articles and lectures before," I said. "What I can't understand, though I know how hard the situation is, is why you can never get past page one."

He half lifted his hand. "It is a paralyzis of my will. The whole legture is clear in my mind, but the minute I write down a single word—or in English or in German—I have a terrible fear I will not be able to write the negst. As though someone has thrown a stone at a window and the whole house—the whole idea zmashes. This repeats, until I am dezperate."

He said the fear grew as he worked that he would die before

he completed the lecture, or if not that, he would write it so disgracefully he would wish for death. The fear immobilized him.

"I have lozt faith. I do not—not longer possezz my former value of myself. In my life there has been too much illusion."

I tried to believe what I was saying: "Have confidence, the feeling will pass."

"Confidenze I have not. For this and alzo whatever elze I have lozt I thank the Nazis."

:   :   :

It was by then mid-August and things were growing steadily worse wherever one looked. The Poles were mobilizing for war. Oskar hardly moved. I was full of worries though I pretended calm weather.

He sat in his massive armchair, breathing like a wounded animal.

"Who can write aboud Walt Whitman in such terrible times?"

"Why don't you change the subject?"

"It mages no differenze what is the subject. It is all uzelezz."

I came every day, as a friend, neglecting my other students and therefore my livelihood. I had a panicky feeling that if things went on as they were going they would end in Oskar's suicide; and I felt a frenzied desire to prevent that. What's more, I was sometimes afraid I was myself becoming melancholy, a new talent, call it, of taking less pleasure in my little pleasures. And the heat continued, oppressive, relentless. We thought of escape into the country, but neither of us had the money. One day I bought Oskar a secondhand electric fan—wondering why we hadn't thought of that before—and he sat in the breeze for hours each day, until after a week, shortly after the Soviet-Nazi non-aggression pact was signed, the motor gave out. He could not sleep at night and sat at his desk with a wet towel on his head, still attempting to write the lecture. He wrote reams on a treadmill, it came out nothing. When he slept in exhaustion he had fantastic frightening dreams of the Nazis inflicting torture, sometimes forcing him to look upon the corpses of those they had slain. In one dream he told me about he had gone back to Germany to visit his wife. She wasn't home and he had been directed to a cemetery. There, though the tombstone read another name, her blood seeped out of the earth above her shallow grave. He groaned aloud at the memory.

Afterwards he told me something about her. They had met as students, lived together, and were married at twenty-three. It wasn't a very happy marriage. She had turned into a sickly woman, unable to have children. "Something was wrong with her interior strugture."

Though I asked no questions, Oskar said, "I offered her to come with me here, but she refused this."

"For what reason?"

"She did not think I wished her to come."

"Did you?" I asked.

"Not," he said.

He explained he had lived with her for almost twenty-seven years under difficult circumstances. She had been ambivalent about their Jewish friends and his relatives, though outwardly she seemed not a prejudiced person. But her mother was always a dreadful anti-Semite.

"I have nothing to blame myzelf," Oskar said.

He took to his bed. I took to the New York Public Library. I read some of the German poets he was trying to write about, in English translation. Then I read *Leaves of Grass* and wrote down what I thought one or two of them had got from Whitman. One day, toward the end of August, I brought Oskar what I had written. It was in good part guessing, but my idea wasn't to do the lecture for him. He lay on his back, motionless, and listened sadly to what I had written. Then he said, no, it wasn't the love of death they had got from Whitman—that ran through German poetry—but it was most of all his feeling for Bruder-mensch, his humanity.

"But this does not grow long on German earth," he said, "and is soon deztroyed."

I said I was sorry I had got it wrong, but he thanked me anyway.

I left, defeated, and as I was going down the stairs, heard the sound of sobbing. I will quit this, I thought, it has got to be too much for me. I can't drown with him.

I stayed home the next day, tasting a new kind of private misery too old for somebody my age, but that same night Oskar called me on the phone, blessing me wildly for having read those notes to him. He had got up to write me a letter to say what I had missed, and it ended in his having written half the lecture. He had slept all day and tonight intended to finish it up.

"I thank you," he said, "for much, alzo including your faith in me."

"Thank God," I said, not telling him I had just about lost it.

:   :   :

Oskar completed his lecture—wrote and rewrote it—during the first week in September. The Nazis had invaded Poland, and though we were greatly troubled, there was some sense of re-lease; maybe the brave Poles would beat them. It took another week to translate the lecture, but here we had the assistance of Friedrich Wilhelm Wolff, the historian, a gentle, erudite man, who liked translating and promised his help with future lectures. We then had about two weeks to work on Oskar's delivery. The weather had changed, and so, slowly, had he. He had awakened from defeat, battered, after a wearying battle. He had lost close to twenty pounds. His complexion was still gray; when I looked at his face I expected to see scars, but it had lost its flabby unfocused quality. His blue eyes had returned to life and he walked with quick steps, as though to pick up a few for all the steps he hadn't taken during those long hot days he had lain in his room.

We went back to our former routine, meeting three late afternoons a week for diction, grammar, and the other exercises. I taught him the phonetic alphabet and transcribed lists of words he was mispronouncing. He worked many hours trying to fit each sound in place, holding a matchstick between his teeth to keep his jaws apart as he exercised his tongue. All this can be a dreadfully boring business unless you think you have a future. Looking at him, I realized what's meant when somebody is called "another man."

The lecture, which I now knew by heart, went off well. The director of the Institute had invited a number of prominent people. Oskar was the first refugee they had employed, and there was a move to make the public cognizant of what was then a new ingredient in American life. Two reporters had come with a lady photographer. The auditorium of the Institute was crowded. I sat in the last row, promising to put up my hand if he couldn't be heard, but it wasn't necessary. Oskar, in a blue suit, his hair cut, was of course nervous, but you couldn't see it unless you studied him. When he stepped up to the lectern, spread out his manuscript, and spoke his first English sentence in public, my heart hesitated; only he and I, of everybody there, had any idea of the anguish he had been through. His enunciation wasn't at all bad —a few *s*'s for *th*'s, and he once said bag for back, but otherwise he did all right. He read poetry well—in both languages—and though Walt Whitman, in his mouth, sounded a little as though he had come to the shores of Long Island as a German immigrant, still the poetry read as poetry:

And I know the Spirit of God is the brother of my own,
And that all the men ever born are also my brothers,
and the women my sisters and lovers,
And that the kelson of creation is love . . .

Oskar read it as though he believed it. Warsaw had fallen, but the verses were somehow protective. I sat back conscious of two things: how easy it is to hide the deepest wounds; and the pride I felt in the job I had done.

:   :   :

Two days later I came up the stairs into Oskar's apartment to find a crowd there. The refugee, his face beet-red, lips bluish, a trace of froth in the corners of his mouth, lay on the floor in his limp pajamas, two firemen on their knees working over him with an inhalator. The windows were open and the air stank.

A policeman asked me who I was and I couldn't answer.

"No, oh no."

I said no but it was unchangeably yes. He had taken his life—gas—I hadn't even thought of the stove in the kitchen.

"Why?" I asked myself. "Why did he do it?" Maybe it was the fate of Poland on top of everything else, but the only answer anyone could come up with was Oskar's scribbled note that he wasn't well, and had left Martin Goldberg all his possessions. I am Martin Goldberg.

I was sick for a week, had no desire either to inherit or investigate, but I thought I ought to look through his things before the court impounded them, so I spent a morning sitting in the depths of Oskar's armchair, trying to read his correspondence. I had found in the top drawer a thin packet of letters from his wife and an airmail letter of recent date from his mother-in-law.

She writes in a tight script it takes me hours to decipher, that her daughter, after Oskar abandons her, against her own mother's fervent pleas and anguish, is converted to Judaism by a vengeful rabbi. One night the Brown Shirts appear, and though the mother wildly waves her bronze crucifix in their faces, they drag Frau Gassner, together with the other Jews, out of the apartment house, and transport them in lorries to a small border town in conquered Poland. There, it is rumored, she is shot in the head and topples into an open ditch with the naked Jewish men, their wives and children, some Polish soldiers, and a handful of gypsies.

The Maid's Shoes

THE MAID had left her name with the porter's wife. She said she was looking for steady work and would take anything but preferred not to work for an old woman. Still, if she had to she would. She was forty-five and looked older. Her face was worn but her hair was black, and her eyes and lips were pretty. She had few good teeth. When she laughed she was embarrassed around the mouth. Although it was cold in early October, that year in Rome, and the chestnut vendors were already bent over their pans of glowing charcoals, the maid wore only a threadbare black cotton dress which had a split down the left side, where about two inches of seam had opened on the hip, exposing her underwear. She had sewn the seam several times but this was one of the times it was open again. Her heavy but well-formed legs were bare and she wore house slippers as she talked to the portinaia; she had done a single day's washing for a signora down the street and carried her shoes in a paper bag. There were three comparatively new apartment houses on the hilly street and she left her name in each.

The portinaia, a dumpy woman wearing a brown tweed skirt

she had got from an English family that had once lived in the building, said she would remember the maid but then she forgot; she forgot until an American professor moved into a furnished apartment on the fifth floor and asked her to help him find a maid. The portinaia brought him a girl from the neighborhood, a girl of sixteen, recently from Umbria, who came with her aunt. But the professor, Orlando Krantz, did not like the way the aunt played up certain qualities of the girl, so he sent her away. He told the portinaia he was looking for an older woman, someone he wouldn't have to worry about. Then the portinaia thought of the maid who had left her name and address, and she went to her house on the Via Appia Antica near the catacombs and told her an American was looking for a maid, mezzo servizio; she would give him her name if the maid agreed to make it worth her while. The maid, whose name was Rosa, shrugged her shoulders and looked stiffly down the street. She said she had nothing to offer the portinaia.

"Look at what I'm wearing," she said. "Look at this junk pile, can you call it a house? I live here with my son and his bitch of a wife who counts every spoonful of soup in my mouth. They treat me like dirt and dirt is all I have to my name."

"In that case I can do nothing for you," the portinaia said. "I have myself and my husband to think of." But she returned from the bus stop and said she would recommend the maid to the American professor if she gave her five thousand lire the first time she was paid.

"How much will he pay?" the maid asked the portinaia.

"I would ask for eighteen thousand a month. Tell him you have to spend two hundred lire a day for carfare."

"That's almost right," Rosa said. "It will cost me forty one way and forty back. But if he pays me eighteen thousand I'll give you five if you sign that's all I owe you."

"I will sign," said the portinaia, and she recommended the maid to the American professor.

The Maid's Shoes

Orlando Krantz was a nervous man of sixty. He had mild gray eyes, a broad mouth, and a pointed clefted chin. His round head was bald and he had a bit of a belly, although the rest of him was quite thin. He was a somewhat odd-looking man but an authority in law, the portinaia told Rosa. The professor sat at a table in his study, writing all day, yet was up every half hour on some pretext or other to look nervously around. He worried how things were going and often came out of his study to see. He would watch Rosa working, then went in and wrote. In a half hour he would come out, ostensibly to wash his hands in the bathroom or drink a glass of cold water, but he was really passing by to see what she was doing. She was doing what she had to. Rosa worked quickly, especially when he was watching. She seemed, he thought, to be unhappy, but that was none of his business. Their lives, he knew, were full of troubles, often sordid; it was best to be detached.

This was the professor's second year in Italy; he had spent the first in Milan, and the second was in Rome. He had rented a large three-bedroom apartment, one of which he used as a study. His wife and daughter, who had returned for a visit to the States in August, would have the other bedrooms; they were due back before not too long. When the ladies returned, he had told Rosa, he would put her on full time. There was a maid's room where she could sleep; indeed, which she already used as her own though she was in the apartment only from nine till four. Rosa agreed to a full-time arrangement because it would mean all her meals in and no rent to pay her son and his dog-faced wife.

While they were waiting for Mrs. Krantz and the daughter to arrive, Rosa did the marketing and cooking. She made the professor's breakfast when she came in, and his lunch at one. She offered to stay later than four, to prepare his supper, which he ate at six, but he preferred to take that meal out. After shopping she cleaned the house, thoroughly mopping the marble floors with a wet rag she pushed around with a stick, though the floors did not look particularly dusty to him. She also washed and ironed his laundry. She was a good worker, her slippers clip-clopping as she hurried from one room to the next, and she frequently finished up about an hour or so before she was due to go home; so she retired to the maid's room and there read *Tempo* or *Epoca*, or sometimes a love story in photographs, with the words printed in italics under each picture. Often she pulled her bed down and lay in it under blankets, to keep warm. The weather had turned rainy, and now the apartment was uncomfortably cold. The custom of the condominium in this apartment house was not to heat until the fifteenth of November, and if it was cold before then, as it was now, the people of the house had to do the best they could. The cold disturbed the professor, who wrote with his gloves and hat on, and increased his nervousness so that he was out to look at her more often. He wore a heavy blue bathrobe over his clothes; sometimes the bathrobe belt was wrapped around a hot-water bottle he had placed against the lower part of his back, under the suit coat. Sometimes he sat on the hot-water bag as he wrote, a sight that caused Rosa, when she once saw this, to smile behind her hand. If he left the hot-water bag in the dining room after lunch, Rosa asked if she might use it. As a rule he allowed her to, and then she did her work with the rubber bag pressed against her stomach with her elbow. She said she had trouble with her liver. That was why the professor did not mind her going to the maid's room to lie down before leaving, after she had finished her work.

Once after Rosa had gone home, smelling tobacco smoke in the corridor near her room, the professor entered it to investigate. The room was not more than an elongated cubicle with a narrow bed that lifted sideways against the wall; there was also a small green cabinet, and an adjoining tiny bathroom containing a toilet and a sitz bath fed by a cold-water tap. She often did the laundry on a washboard in the sitz bath, but never, so far as he knew, had bathed in it. The day before her daughter-in-law's name day she had asked permission to take a hot bath in his tub in the big bathroom, and though he had hesitated a moment, the professor finally said yes. In her room, he opened a drawer at the bottom of the cabinet and found a hoard of cigarette butts in it, the butts he had left in ashtrays. He noticed, too, that she had collected his old newspapers and magazines from the waste-baskets. She also saved cord, paper bags, and rubber bands; also pencil stubs he had thrown away. After he found that out, he occasionally gave her some meat left over from lunch, and cheese that had gone dry, to take with her. For this she brought him flowers. She also brought a dirty egg or two her daughter-in-law's hen had laid, but he thanked her and said the yolks were too strong for his taste. He noticed that she needed a pair of shoes, for those she put on to go home in were split in two places, and she wore the same black dress with the tear in it every day, which embarrassed him when he had to speak to her; however, he thought he would refer these matters to his wife when she arrived.

As jobs went, Rosa knew she had a good one. The professor paid well and promptly, and he never ordered her around in the haughty manner of some of her Italian employers. This one was nervous and fussy but not a bad sort. His main fault was his silence. Though he could speak a better than passable Italian, he preferred, when not at work, to sit in an armchair in the living room, reading. Only two souls in the whole apartment, you would think they would want to say something to each other once in a while. Sometimes when she served him a cup of coffee as he read, she tried to get in a word about her troubles. She wanted to tell him about her long, impoverished widowhood, how badly her son had turned out, and what her miserable daughter-in-law was like to live with. But though he listened courteously; although they shared the same roof, and even the same hot-water bottle and bathtub, they almost never shared speech. He said no more to her than a crow would, and clearly showed he preferred to be left alone. So she left him alone and was lonely in the apartment. Working for foreigners had its advantages, she thought, but it also had disadvantages.

After a while the professor noticed that the telephone was ringing regularly for Rosa each afternoon during the time she usually was resting in her room. In the following week, instead of staying in the house until four, after her telephone call she asked permission to leave. At first she said her liver was bothering her, but later she stopped giving excuses. Although he did not much approve of this sort of thing, suspecting she would take advantage of him if he was too liberal in granting favors, he informed her that, until his wife arrived, she might leave at three on two afternoons of the week, provided that all her duties were fully discharged. He knew that everything was done before she left but thought he ought to say it. She listened meekly—her eyes aglow, lips twitching—and meekly agreed. He presumed, when he happened to think about it afterwards, that Rosa had a good spot here, by any standard, and she ought soon to show it in her face, change her unhappy expression for one less so. However, this did not happen, for when he chanced to observe her, even on days when she was leaving early, she seemed sadly preoccupied, sighed much, as if something on her heart was weighing her down.

He never asked what, preferring not to become involved in whatever it was. These people had endless troubles, and if you let yourself get involved in them you got endlessly involved. He knew of one woman, the wife of a colleague, who had said to her maid: "Lucrezia, I am sympathetic to your condition but I don't want to hear about it." This, the professor reflected, was basically good policy. It kept employer-employee relationships where they belonged—on an objective level. He was, after all, leaving Italy in April and would never in his life see Rosa again. It would do her a lot more good if, say, he sent her a small check at Christmas, than if he needlessly immersed himself in her miseries now. The professor knew he was nervous and often impatient, and he was sometimes sorry for his nature; but he was what he was and preferred to stay aloof from what did not closely and personally concern him.

But Rosa would not have it so. One morning she knocked on his study door, and when he said avanti, she went in embarrassedly, so that even before she began to speak he was himself embarrassed.

"Professore," Rosa said, unhappily, "please excuse me for bothering your work, but I have to talk to somebody."

"I happen to be very busy," he said, growing a little angry. "Can it wait a while?"

"It'll take only a minute. Your troubles hang on all your life but it doesn't take long to tell them."

"Is it your liver complaint?" he asked.

"No. I need your advice. You're an educated man and I'm no more than an ignorant peasant."

"What kind of advice?" he asked impatiently.

"Call it anything you like. The fact is I have to speak to somebody. I can't talk to my son, even if it were possible in this case. When I open my mouth he roars like a bull. And my daughter-in-law isn't worth wasting my breath on. Sometimes, on the roof, when we're hanging the wash, I say a few words to the portinaia, but she isn't a sympathetic person so I have to come to you, I'll tell you why."

Before he could say how he felt about hearing her confidences, Rosa had launched into a story about this middle-aged government worker in the tax bureau, whom she had happened to meet in the neighborhood. He was married, had four children, and sometimes worked as a carpenter after leaving his office at two o'clock each day. His name was Armando; it was he who telephoned her every afternoon. They had met recently on a bus, and he had, after two or three meetings, seeing that her shoes weren't fit to wear, urged her to let him buy her a new pair. She had told him not to be foolish. One could see he had very little, and it was enough that he took her to the movies twice a week. She had said that, yet every time they met he talked about the shoes he wanted to buy her.

"I'm only human," Rosa frankly told the professor, "and I need the shoes badly, but you know how these things go. If I put on his shoes they may carry me to his bed. That's why I thought I would ask you if I ought to take them."

The professor's face and bald head were flushed. "I don't see how I can possibly advise you—"

"You're the educated one," she said.

"However," he went on, "since the situation is still essentially hypothetical, I will go so far as to say you ought to tell this generous gentleman that his responsibilities should be to his family. He would do well not to offer you gifts, as you will do, not to accept them. If you don't, he can't possibly make any claims upon you or your person. This is all I care to say. Since you have requested advice, I've given it, but I won't say any more."

Rosa sighed. "The truth of it is I could use a pair of shoes. Mine look as though they've been chewed by goats. I haven't had a new pair in six years."

But the professor had nothing more to add.

After Rosa had gone for the day, in thinking about her problem, he decided to buy her a pair of shoes. He was concerned that she might be expecting something of the sort, had planned, so to speak, to have it work out this way. But since this was conjecture only, evidence entirely lacking, he would assume, until proof to the contrary became available, that she had no ulterior motive in asking his advice. He considered giving her five thousand lire to make the purchase of the shoes herself and relieve him of the trouble, but he was doubtful, for there was no guarantee she would use the money for the agreed purpose. Suppose she came in the next day, saying she had had a liver attack that had necessitated calling the doctor, who had charged three thousand lire for his visit; therefore would the professor, in view of these unhappy circumstances, supply an additional three thousand for the shoes? That would never do, so the next morning, when the maid was at the grocer's, the professor slipped into her room and quickly traced on paper the outline of her miserable shoe—a task but he accomplished it quickly. That evening, in a store on the same piazza as the restaurant where he liked to eat, he bought Rosa a pair of brown shoes for fifty-five hundred lire, slightly more than he had planned to spend; but they were a solid pair of ties, walking shoes with a medium heel, a practical gift.

He gave them to Rosa the next day, a Wednesday. He felt embarrassed to be doing that, because he realized that despite his warnings to her, he had permitted himself to meddle in her affairs; but he considered giving her the shoes a psychologically proper move in more ways than one. In presenting her with them he said, "Rosa, I have perhaps a solution to suggest in the matter you discussed with me. Here are a pair of new shoes for you. Tell your friend you must refuse his. And when you do, perhaps it would be advisable also to inform him that you intend to see him a little less frequently from now on."

Rosa was overjoyed at the professor's kindness. She attempted to kiss his hand but he thrust it behind him and retired to his study. On Thursday, when he opened the apartment door to her ring, she was wearing his shoes. She carried a large paper bag from which she offered the professor three small oranges still on a branch with green leaves. He said she needn't have brought them, but Rosa, smiling half hiddenly in order not to show her teeth, said that she wanted him to see how grateful she was.

Later she requested permission to leave at three so she could show Armando her new shoes.

He said dryly, "You may go at that hour if your work is done."

She thanked him profusely. Hastening through her tasks, she left shortly after three, but not before the professor, in his hat, gloves, and bathrobe, standing at his open study door as he was inspecting the corridor floor she had just mopped, saw her hurrying out of the apartment, wearing a pair of dressy black needle-point pumps. This angered him; and when Rosa appeared the next morning, though she begged him not to when he said she had made a fool of him and he was firing her to teach her a lesson, the professor did. She wept, pleading for another chance, but he would not change his mind. So she desolately wrapped up the odds and ends in her room in a newspaper and left, still crying. Afterwards he was upset and very nervous. He could not stand the cold that day and he could not work.

A week later, the morning the heat was turned on, Rosa appeared at the apartment door, and begged to have her job back. She was distraught, said her son had hit her, and gently touched her puffed black-and-blue lip. With tears in her eyes, although she didn't cry, Rosa explained it was no fault of hers that she had accepted both pairs of shoes. Armando had given her his pair first; had, out of jealousy of a possible rival, forced her to take them. Then when the professor had kindly offered his pair of shoes, she had wanted to refuse them but was afraid of angering him and losing her job. This was God's truth, so help her St. Peter. She would, she promised, find Armando, whom she had not seen in a week, and return his shoes if the professor would take her back. If he didn't, she would throw herself into the Tiber. He, though he didn't care for talk of this kind, felt a certain sympathy for her. He was disappointed in himself at the way he had handled her. It would have been better to have said a few appropriate words on the subject of honesty and then philosophically dropped the matter. In firing her he had only made things difficult for them both, because, in the meantime, he had tried two other maids and found them unsuitable. One stole, the other was lazy. As a result the house was a mess, impossible for him to work in, although the portinaia came up for an hour each morning to clean. It was his good fortune that Rosa had appeared at the door just then. When she removed her coat, he noticed with satisfaction that the tear in her dress had finally been mended.

She went grimly to work, dusting, polishing, cleaning everything in sight. She unmade beds, then made them, swept under them, mopped, polished head- and footboards, adorned the beds with newly pressed spreads. Though she had just got her job back and worked with her usual efficiency, she worked, he observed, in sadness, frequently sighing, attempting a smile only when his eye was on her. This is their nature, he thought; they have hard lives. To spare her further blows by her son he gave her permission to live in. He offered extra money to buy meat for her supper but she refused it, saying pasta would do. Pasta and green salad was all she ate at night. Occasionally she boiled an artichoke left over from lunch and ate it with oil and vinegar. He invited her to drink the white wine in the cupboard and take fruit. Once in a while she did, always telling what and how much, though he repeatedly asked her not to. The apartment was nicely in order. Though the phone rang, as usual, daily at three, only seldom did she leave the house after she had talked to Armando.

Then one dismal morning Rosa came to the professor and in her distraught way confessed she was pregnant. Her face was lit in despair; her white underwear shone through her black dress.

He felt annoyance, disgust, blaming himself for having re-employed her.

"You must leave at once," he said, trying to keep his voice from trembling.

"I can't," she said. "My son will kill me. In God's name, help me, professore."

He was infuriated by her stupidity. "Your sexual adventures are none of my responsibility.

"Was it this Armando?" he asked almost savagely.

She nodded.

"Have you informed him?"

"He says he can't believe it." She tried to smile but couldn't.

"I'll convince him," he said. "Do you have his telephone number?"

She told it to him. He called Armando at his office, identified himself, and asked the government clerk to come at once to the apartment. "You have a grave responsibility to Rosa."

"I have a grave responsibility to my family," Armando answered.

"You might have considered them before this."

"All right, I'll come over tomorrow after work. It's impossible today. I have a carpentering contract to finish up."

"She'll expect you," the professor said.

When he hung up he felt less angry, although still more emotional than he cared to feel. "Are you quite sure of your condition?" he asked her, "that you are pregnant?"

"Yes." She was crying now. "Tomorrow is my son's birthday. What a beautiful present it will be for him to find out his mother's a whore. He'll break my bones, if not with his hands, then with his teeth."

"It hardly seems likely you can conceive, considering your age."

"My mother gave birth at fifty."

"Isn't there a possibility you are mistaken?"

"I don't know. It's never been this way before. After all, I've been a widow—"

"Well, you'd better find out."

"Yes, I want to," Rosa said. "I want to see the midwife in my neighborhood but I haven't got a single lira. I spent all I had left when I wasn't working, and I had to borrow carfare to get here. Armando can't help me just now. He has to pay for his wife's teeth this week. She has very bad teeth, poor thing. That's why I came to you. Could you advance me two thousand of my pay so I can be examined by the midwife?"

After a minute he counted two one-thousand-lire notes out of his wallet. "Go to her now," he said. He was about to add that if she was pregnant, not to come back, but he was afraid she might do something desperate, or lie to him so she could go on working. He didn't want her around any more. When he thought of his wife and daughter arriving amid this mess, he felt sick with nervousness. He wanted to get rid of the maid as soon as possible.

The next day Rosa came in at twelve instead of nine. Her dark face was pale. "Excuse me for being late," she murmured. "I was praying at my husband's grave."

"That's all right," the professor said. "But did you go to the midwife?"

"Not yet."

"Why not?" Though angry he spoke calmly.

She stared at the floor.

"Please answer my question."

"I was going to say I lost the two thousand lire on the bus, but after being at my husband's grave I'll tell you the truth. After all, it's bound to come out."

This is terrible, he thought, it's unending. "What did you do with the money?"

"That's what I mean," Rosa sighed. "I bought my son a present. Not that he deserves it, but it was his birthday." She burst into tears.

He stared at her a minute, then said, "Please come with me."

The professor left the apartment in his bathrobe, and Rosa

followed. Opening the elevator door he stepped inside, holding the door for her. She entered the elevator.

They stopped two floors below. He got out and nearsightedly scanned the names on the brass plates above the bells. Finding the one he wanted, he pressed the button. A maid opened the door and let them in. She seemed frightened by Rosa's expression.

"Is the doctor in?" the professor asked the doctor's maid.

"I will see."

"Please ask him if he'll see me for a minute. I live in the building, two flights up."

"Sì, signore." She glanced again at Rosa, then went inside.

The Italian doctor came out, a short middle-aged man with a beard. The professor had once or twice passed him in the cortile of the apartment house. The doctor was buttoning his shirt cuff.

"I am sorry to trouble you, sir," said the professor. "This is my maid, who has been having some difficulty. She would like to determine whether she is pregnant. Can you assist her?"

The doctor looked at him, then at the maid, who had a handkerchief to her eyes.

"Let her come into my office."

"Thank you," said the professor. The doctor nodded.

The professor went up to his apartment. In a half hour the phone rang.

"Pronto."

It was the doctor. "She is not pregnant," he said. "She is frightened. She also has trouble with her liver."

"Can you be certain, doctor?"

"Yes."

"Thank you," said the professor. "If you write her a prescription, please have it charged to me, and also send me your bill."

"I will," said the doctor and hung up.

Rosa came into the apartment. "The doctor told you?" the professor said. "You aren't pregnant."

The Maid's Shoes

"It's the Virgin's blessing," said Rosa.

Speaking quietly, he then told her she would have to go. "I'm sorry, Rosa, but I simply cannot be constantly caught up in this sort of thing. It upsets me and I can't work."

She turned her head away.

The doorbell rang. It was Armando, a small thin man in a long gray overcoat. He was wearing a rakish black Borsalino and a slight mustache. He had dark, worried eyes. He tipped his hat to them.

Rosa told him she was leaving the apartment.

"Then let me help you get your things," Armando said. He followed her to the maid's room and they wrapped Rosa's things in newspaper.

When they came out of the room, Armando carrying a shopping bag, Rosa holding a shoe box wrapped in a newspaper, the professor handed Rosa the remainder of her month's wages.

"I'm sorry," he said, "but I have my wife and daughter to think of. They'll be here in a few days."

She answered nothing. Armando, smoking a cigarette butt, gently opened the door for her and they left together.

Later the professor inspected the maid's room and saw that Rosa had taken all her belongings but the shoes he had given her. When his wife arrived in the apartment, shortly before Thanksgiving, she gave the shoes to the portinaia, who wore them a week, then gave them to her daughter-in-law.

The Magic Barrel

NOT LONG AGO there lived in uptown New York, in a small, almost meager room, though crowded with books, Leo Finkle, a rabbinical student at the Yeshiva University. Finkle, after six years of study, was to be ordained in June and had been advised by an acquaintance that he might find it easier to win himself a congregation if he were married. Since he had no present prospects of marriage, after two tormented days of turning it over in his mind, he called in Pinye Salzman, a marriage broker whose two-line advertisement he had read in the *Forward*.

The matchmaker appeared one night out of the dark fourth-floor hallway of the graystone rooming house where Finkle lived, grasping a black, strapped portfolio that had been worn thin with use. Salzman, who had been long in the business, was of slight but dignified build, wearing an old hat, and an overcoat too short and tight for him. He smelled frankly of fish, which he loved to eat, and although he was missing a few teeth, his presence was not displeasing, because of an amiable manner curiously contrasted with mournful eyes. His voice, his lips, his wisp of beard, his bony fingers were animated, but give him a moment of repose and his mild blue eyes revealed a depth of sadness, a characteristic that put Leo a little at ease although the situation, for him, was inherently tense.

He at once informed Salzman why he had asked him to come, explaining that but for his parents, who had married comparatively late in life, he was alone in the world. He had for six years devoted himself almost entirely to his studies, as a result of which, understandably, he had found himself without time for social life and the company of young women. Therefore he thought it the better part of trial and error—of embarrassing fumbling—to call in an experienced person to advise him on these matters. He remarked in passing that the function of the marriage broker was ancient and honorable, highly approved in the Jewish community, because it made practical the necessary without hindering joy. Moreover, his own parents had been brought together by a matchmaker. They had made, if not a financially profitable marriage—since neither had possessed any worldly goods to speak of—at least a successful one in the sense of their everlasting devotion to each other. Salzman listened in embarrassed surprise, sensing a sort of apology. Later, however, he experienced a glow of pride in his work, an emotion that had left him years ago, and he heartily approved of Finkle.

The two went to their business. Leo had led Salzman to the only clear place in the room, a table near a window that overlooked the lamp-lit city. He seated himself at the matchmaker's side but facing him, attempting by an act of will to suppress the unpleasant tickle in his throat. Salzman eagerly unstrapped his portfolio and removed a loose rubber band from a thin packet of much-handled cards. As he flipped through them, a gesture and sound that physically hurt Leo, the student pretended not to see and gazed steadfastly out the window. Although it was still February, winter was on its last legs, signs of which he had for the first time in years begun to notice. He now observed the round white moon, moving high in the sky through a cloud menagerie, and watched with half-open mouth as it penetrated a huge hen, and dropped out of her like an egg laying itself. Salzman, though pretending through eyeglasses he had just slipped on to be engaged in scanning the writing on the cards, stole occasional glances at the young man's distinguished face, noting with pleasure the long, severe scholar's nose, brown eyes heavy with learning, sensitive yet ascetic lips, and a certain almost hollow quality of the dark cheeks. He gazed around at shelves upon shelves of books and let out a soft, contented sigh.

When Leo's eyes fell upon the cards, he counted six spread out in Salzman's hand.

"So few?" he asked in disappointment.

"You wouldn't believe me how much cards I got in my office," Salzman replied. "The drawers are already filled to the top, so I keep them now in a barrel, but is every girl good for a new rabbi?"

Leo blushed at this, regretting all he had revealed of himself in a curriculum vitae he had sent to Salzman. He had thought it best to acquaint him with his strict standards and specifications, but in having done so, felt he had told the marriage broker more than was absolutely necessary.

He hesitantly inquired, "Do you keep photographs of your clients on file?"

"First comes family, amount of dowry, also what kind promises," Salzman replied, unbuttoning his tight coat and settling himself in the chair. "After comes pictures, rabbi."

"Call me Mr. Finkle. I'm not yet a rabbi."

Salzman said he would, but instead called him doctor, which he changed to rabbi when Leo was not listening too attentively.

Salzman adjusted his horn-rimmed spectacles, gently cleared his throat, and read in an eager voice the contents of the top card:

"Sophie P. Twenty-four years. Widow one year. No children. Educated high school and two years college. Father promises eight thousand dollars. Has wonderful wholesale business. Also real estate. On the mother's side comes teachers, also one actor. Well known on Second Avenue."

Leo gazed up in surprise. "Did you say a widow?"

"A widow don't mean spoiled, rabbi. She lived with her husband maybe four months. He was a sick boy she made a mistake to marry him."

"Marrying a widow has never entered my mind."

"This is because you have no experience. A widow, especially if she is young and healthy like this girl, is a wonderful person to marry. She will be thankful to you the rest of her life. Believe me, if I was looking now for a bride, I would marry a widow."

Leo reflected, then shook his head.

Salzman hunched his shoulders in an almost imperceptible gesture of disappointment. He placed the card down on the wooden table and began to read another:

"Lily H. High school teacher. Regular. Not a substitute. Has savings and new Dodge car. Lived in Paris one year. Father is successful dentist thirty-five years. Interested in professional man. Well-Americanized family. Wonderful opportunity.

"I know her personally," said Salzman. "I wish you could see this girl. She is a doll. Also very intelligent. All day you could talk to her about books and theyater and what not. She also knows current events."

"I don't believe you mentioned her age?"

"Her age?" Salzman said, raising his brows. "Her age is thirty-two years."

Leo said after a while, "I'm afraid that seems a little too old."

Salzman let out a laugh. "So how old are you, rabbi?"

"Twenty-seven."

"So what is the difference, tell me, between twenty-seven and thirty-two? My own wife is seven years older than me. So what did I suffer?— Nothing. If Rothschild's a daughter wants to marry you, would you say on account her age, no?"

"Yes," Leo said dryly.

Salzman shook off the no in the yes. "Five years don't mean a thing. I give you my word that when you will live with her for one week you will forget her age. What does it mean five years— that she lived more and knows more than somebody who is younger? On this girl, God bless her, years are not wasted. Each one that it comes makes better the bargain."

"What subject does she teach in high school?"

"Languages. If you heard the way she speaks French, you will think it is music. I am in the business twenty-five years, and I recommend her with my whole heart. Believe me, I know what I'm talking, rabbi."

"What's on the next card?" Leo said abruptly.

Salzman reluctantly turned up the third card:

"Ruth K. Nineteen years. Honor student. Father offers thirteen thousand cash to the right bridegroom. He is a medical doctor. Stomach specialist with marvelous practice. Brother-in-law owns own garment business. Particular people."

Salzman looked as if he had read his trump card.

"Did you say nineteen?" Leo asked with interest.

"On the dot."

"Is she attractive?" He blushed. "Pretty?"

Salzman kissed his fingertips. "A little doll. On this I give you my word. Let me call the father tonight and you will see what means pretty."

But Leo was troubled. "You're sure she's that young?"

"This I am positive. The father will show you the birth certificate."

"Are you positive there isn't something wrong with her?" Leo insisted.

"Who says there is wrong?"

"I don't understand why an American girl her age should go to a marriage broker."

A smile spread over Salzman's face.

"So for the same reason you went, she comes."

Leo flushed. "I am pressed for time."

Salzman, realizing he had been tactless, quickly explained. "The father came, not her. He wants she should have the best, so he looks around himself. When we will locate the right boy he will introduce him and encourage. This makes a better marriage than if a young girl without experience takes for herself. I don't have to tell you this."

"But don't you think this young girl believes in love?" Leo spoke uneasily.

Salzman was about to guffaw but caught himself and said soberly, "Love comes with the right person, not before."

Leo parted dry lips but did not speak. Noticing that Salzman had snatched a glance at the next card, he cleverly asked, "How is her health?"

"Perfect," Salzman said, breathing with difficulty. "Of course, she is a little lame on her right foot from an auto accident that it happened to her when she was twelve years, but nobody notices on account she is so brilliant and also beautiful."

Leo got up heavily and went to the window. He felt curiously bitter and upbraided himself for having called in the marriage broker. Finally, he shook his head.

"Why not?" Salzman persisted, the pitch of his voice rising.

"Because I detest stomach specialists."

"So what do you care what is his business? After you marry her do you need him? Who says he must come every Friday night in your house?"

Ashamed of the way the talk was going, Leo dismissed Salzman, who went home with heavy, melancholy eyes.

Though he had felt only relief at the marriage broker's departure, Leo was in low spirits the next day. He explained it as arising from Salzman's failure to produce a suitable bride for him. He did not care for his type of clientele. But when Leo found himself hesitating whether to seek out another match-maker, one more polished than Pinye, he wondered if it could be—his protestations to the contrary, and although he honored his father and mother—that he did not, in essence, care for the matchmaking institution? This thought he quickly put out of mind yet found himself still upset. All day he ran around in the woods—missed an important appointment, forgot to give out his laundry, walked out of a Broadway cafeteria without paying and had to run back with the ticket in his hand; had even not recognized his landlady in the street when she passed with a friend and courteously called out, "A good evening to you, Doctor Finkle." By nightfall, however, he had regained sufficient calm to sink his nose into a book and there found peace from his thoughts.

Almost at once there came a knock on the door. Before Leo could say enter, Salzman, commercial cupid, was standing in the room. His face was gray and meager, his expression hungry, and he looked as if he would expire on his feet. Yet the marriage broker managed, by some trick of the muscles, to display a broad smile.

"So good evening. I am invited?"

Leo nodded, disturbed to see him again, yet unwilling to ask the man to leave.

Beaming still, Salzman laid his portfolio on the table. "Rabbi, I got for you tonight good news."

"I've asked you not to call me rabbi. I'm still a student."

"Your worries are finished. I have for you a first-class bride."

"Leave me in peace concerning this subject." Leo pretended lack of interest.

"The world will dance at your wedding."

"Please, Mr. Salzman, no more."

"But first must come back my strength," Salzman said weakly. He fumbled with the portfolio straps and took out of the leather case an oily paper bag, from which he extracted a hard, seeded roll and a small smoked whitefish. With a quick motion of his hand he stripped the fish out of its skin and began ravenously to chew. "All day in a rush," he muttered.

Leo watched him eat.

"A sliced tomato you have maybe?" Salzman hesitantly inquired.

"No."

The marriage broker shut his eyes and ate. When he had finished he carefully cleaned up the crumbs and rolled up the remains of the fish, in the paper bag. His spectacled eyes roamed the room until he discovered, amid some piles of books, a one-burner gas stove. Lifting his hat he humbly asked, "A glass tea you got, rabbi?"

Conscience-stricken, Leo rose and brewed the tea. He served it with a chunk of lemon and two cubes of lump sugar, delighting Salzman.

After he had drunk his tea, Salzman's strength and good spirits were restored.

"So tell me, rabbi," he said amiably, "you considered some more the three clients I mentioned yesterday?"

"There was no need to consider."

"Why not?"

"None of them suits me."

"What then suits you?"

Leo let it pass because he could give only a confused answer.

Without waiting for a reply, Salzman asked, "You remember this girl I talked to you—the high school teacher?"

"Age thirty-two?"

But, surprisingly, Salzman's face lit in a smile. "Age twenty-nine."

Leo shot him a look. "Reduced from thirty-two?"

"A mistake," Salzman avowed. "I talked today with the dentist. He took me to his safety deposit box and showed me the birth certificate. She was twenty-nine years last August. They made her a party in the mountains where she went for her vacation. When her father spoke to me the first time I forgot to write the age and I told you thirty-two, but now I remember this was a different client, a widow."

"The same one you told me about, I thought she was twenty-four?"

"A different. Am I responsible that the world is filled with widows?"

"No, but I'm not interested in them, nor, for that matter, in schoolteachers."

Salzman pulled his clasped hands to his breast. Looking at the ceiling he devoutly exclaimed, "Yiddishe kinder, what can I say to somebody that he is not interested in high school teachers? So what then you are interested?"

Leo flushed but controlled himself.

"In what else will you be interested," Salzman went on, "if you not interested in this fine girl that she speaks four languages and has personally in the bank ten thousand dollars? Also her father guarantees further twelve thousand. Also she has a new car, wonderful clothes, talks on all subjects, and she will give you a first-class home and children. How near do we come in our life to paradise?"

"If she's so wonderful, why wasn't she married ten years ago?"

"Why?" said Salzman with a heavy laugh. "—Why? Because she is *partikiler*. This is why. She wants the *best*."

Leo was silent, amused at how he had entangled himself. But Salzman had aroused his interest in Lily H., and he began seriously to consider calling on her. When the marriage broker observed how intently Leo's mind was at work on the facts he had supplied, he felt certain they would soon come to an agreement.

:　　　:　　　:

Late Saturday afternoon, conscious of Salzman, Leo Finkle walked with Lily Hirschorn along Riverside Drive. He walked briskly and erectly, wearing with distinction the black fedora he had that morning taken with trepidation out of the dusty hat box on his closet shelf, and the heavy black Saturday coat he had thoroughly whisked clean. Leo also owned a walking stick, a present from a distant relative, but quickly put temptation aside and did not use it. Lily, petite and not unpretty, had on something signifying the approach of spring. She was au courant, animatedly, with all sorts of subjects, and he weighed her words and found her surprisingly sound—score another for Salzman, whom he uneasily sensed to be somewhere around, hiding perhaps high in a tree along the street, flashing the lady signals with a pocket mirror; or perhaps a cloven-hoofed Pan, piping nuptial ditties as he danced his invisible way before them, strewing wild buds on the walk and purple grapes in their path, symbolizing fruit of a union, though there was of course still none.

Lily startled Leo by remarking, "I was thinking of Mr. Salzman, a curious figure, wouldn't you say?"

Not certain what to answer, he nodded.

She bravely went on, blushing, "I for one am grateful for his introducing us. Aren't you?"

He courteously replied, "I am."

"I mean," she said with a little laugh—and it was all in good taste, or at least gave the effect of being not in bad—"do you mind that we came together so?"

He was not displeased with her honesty, recognizing that she meant to set the relationship aright, and understanding that it took a certain amount of experience in life, and courage, to want to do it quite that way. One had to have some sort of past to make that kind of beginning.

He said that he did not mind. Salzman's function was traditional and honorable—valuable for what it might achieve, which, he pointed out, was frequently nothing.

Lily agreed with a sigh. They walked on for a while and she

said after a long silence, again with a nervous laugh, "Would you mind if I asked you something a little bit personal? Frankly, I find the subject fascinating." Although Leo shrugged, she went on half embarrassedly, "How was it that you came to your calling? I mean, was it a sudden passionate inspiration?"

Leo, after a time, slowly replied, "I was always interested in the Law."

"You saw revealed in it the presence of the Highest?"

He nodded and changed the subject. "I understand that you spent a little time in Paris, Miss Hirschorn?"

"Oh, did Mr. Salzman tell you, Rabbi Finkle?" Leo winced but she went on, "It was ages ago and almost forgotten. I remember I had to return for my sister's wedding."

And Lily would not be put off. "When," she asked in a slightly trembly voice, "did you become enamored of God?"

He stared at her. Then it came to him that she was talking not about Leo Finkle but a total stranger, some mystical figure, perhaps even passionate prophet that Salzman had dreamed up for her—no relation to the living or dead. Leo trembled with rage and weakness. The trickster had obviously sold her a bill of goods, just as he had him, who'd expected to become acquainted with a young lady of twenty-nine, only to behold, the moment he had laid eyes upon her strained and anxious face, a woman past thirty-five and aging rapidly. Only his self-control had kept him this long in her presence.

"I am not," he said gravely, "a talented religious person," and in seeking words to go on, found himself possessed by shame and fear. "I think," he said in a strained manner, "that I came to God not because I loved Him but because I did not."

This confession he spoke harshly because its unexpectedness shook him.

Lily wilted. Leo saw a profusion of loaves of bread go flying like ducks high over his head, not unlike the winged loaves by which he had counted himself to sleep last night. Mercifully, then, it snowed, which he would not put past Salzman's machinations.

:   :   :

He was infuriated with the marriage broker and swore he would throw him out of the room the moment he reappeared. But Salzman did not come that night, and when Leo's anger had subsided, an unaccountable despair grew in its place. At first he thought this was caused by his disappointment in Lily, but before long it became evident that he had involved himself with Salzman without a true knowledge of his own intent. He gradually realized—with an emptiness that seized him with six hands—that he had called in the broker to find him a bride because he was incapable of doing it himself. This terrifying insight he had derived as a result of his meeting and conversation with Lily Hirschorn. Her probing questions had somehow irritated him into revealing—to himself more than her—the true nature of his relationship to God, and from that it had come upon him, with shocking force, that apart from his parents, he had never loved anyone. Or perhaps it went the other way, that he did not love God so well as he might, because he had not loved man. It seemed to Leo that his whole life stood starkly revealed and he saw himself for the first time as he truly was—unloved and loveless. This bitter but somehow not fully unexpected revelation brought him to a point of panic, controlled only by extraordinary effort. He covered his face with his hands and cried.

The week that followed was the worst of his life. He did not eat and lost weight. His beard darkened and grew ragged. He stopped attending seminars and almost never opened a book. He seriously considered leaving the Yeshiva, although he was deeply troubled at the thought of the loss of all his years of study—saw them like pages torn from a book, strewn over the city—and at the devastating effect of this decision upon his parents. But he had lived without knowledge of himself, and never in the Five Books and all the Commentaries—mea culpa—had the truth been revealed to him. He did not know where to turn, and in all this desolating loneliness there was no *to whom*, although he often thought of Lily but not once could bring himself to go downstairs and make the call. He became touchy and irritable, especially with his landlady, who asked him all manner of personal questions; on the other hand, sensing his own disagreeableness, he waylaid her on the stairs and apologized abjectly, until, mortified, she ran from him. Out of this, however, he drew the consolation that he was a Jew and that a Jew suffered. But gradually, as the long and terrible week drew to a close, he regained his composure and some idea of purpose in life: to go on as planned. Although he was imperfect, the ideal was not. As for his quest of a bride, the thought of continuing afflicted him with anxiety and heartburn, yet perhaps with this new knowledge of himself he would be more successful than in the past. Perhaps love would now come to him and a bride to that love. And for this sanctified seeking who needed a Salzman?

The marriage broker, a skeleton with haunted eyes, returned that very night. He looked, withal, the picture of frustrated expectancy—as if he had steadfastly waited the week at Miss Lily Hirschorn's side for a telephone call that never came.

Casually coughing, Salzman came immediately to the point: "So how did you like her?"

Leo's anger rose and he could not refrain from chiding the matchmaker: "Why did you lie to me, Salzman?"

Salzman's pale face went dead white, the world had snowed on him.

"Did you not state that she was twenty-nine?" Leo insisted.

"I give you my word—"

"She was thirty-five, if a day. *At least* thirty-five."

"Of this don't be too sure. Her father told me—"

"Never mind. The worst of it is that you lied to her."

"How did I lie to her, tell me?"

"You told her things about me that weren't true. You made me out to be more, consequently less than I am. She had in mind a totally different person, a sort of semi-mystical Wonder Rabbi."

"All I said, you was a religious man."

"I can imagine."

Salzman sighed. "This is my weakness that I have," he confessed. "My wife says to me I shouldn't be a salesman, but when I have two fine people that they would be wonderful to be married, I am so happy that I talk too much." He smiled wanly. "This is why Salzman is a poor man."

Leo's anger left him. "Well, Salzman, I'm afraid that's all."

The marriage broker fastened hungry eyes on him.

"You don't want any more a bride?"

"I do," said Leo, "but I have decided to seek her in another way. I am no longer interested in an arranged marriage. To be frank, I now admit the necessity of premarital love. That is, I want to be in love with the one I marry."

"Love?" said Salzman, astounded. After a moment he remarked, "For us, our love is our life, not for the ladies. In the ghetto they—"

"I know, I know," said Leo. "I've thought of it often. Love, I have said to myself, should be a product of living and worship rather than its own end. Yet for myself I find it necessary to establish the level of my need and fulfill it."

Salzman shrugged but answered, "Listen, rabbi, if you want love, this I can find for you also. I have such beautiful clients that you will love them the minute your eyes will see them."

Leo smiled unhappily. "I'm afraid you don't understand."

But Salzman hastily unstrapped his portfolio and withdrew a manila packet from it.

"Pictures," he said, quickly laying the envelope on the table.

Leo called after him to take the pictures away, but as if on the wings of the wind, Salzman had disappeared.

March came. Leo had returned to his regular routine. Although he felt not quite himself yet—lacked energy—he was making plans for a more active social life. Of course it would cost something, but he was an expert in cutting corners; and when there were no corners left he would make circles rounder. All the while Salzman's pictures had lain on the table, gathering dust. Occasionally as Leo sat studying, or enjoying a cup of tea, his eyes fell on the manila envelope, but he never opened it.

The days went by and no social life to speak of developed with a member of the opposite sex—it was difficult, given the circumstances of his situation. One morning Leo toiled up the stairs to his room and stared out the window at the city. Although the day was bright his view of it was dark. For some time he watched the people in the street below hurrying along and then turned with a heavy heart to his little room. On the table was the packet. With a sudden relentless gesture he tore it open. For a half hour he stood by the table in a state of excitement, examining the photographs of the ladies Salzman had included. Finally, with a deep sigh he put them down. There were six, of varying degrees of attractiveness, but look at them long enough and they all became Lily Hirschorn: all past their prime, all starved behind bright smiles, not a true personality in the lot. Life, despite their frantic yoohooings, had passed them by; they were pictures in a briefcase that stank of fish. After a while, however, as Leo attempted to return the photographs into the envelope, he found in it another, a snapshot of the type taken by a machine for a quarter. He gazed at it a moment and let out a low cry.

Her face deeply moved him. Why, he could at first not say. It gave him the impression of youth—spring flowers, yet age—a sense of having been used to the bone, wasted; this came from the eyes, which were hauntingly familiar, yet absolutely strange. He had a vivid impression that he had met her before, but try as he might he could not place her although he could almost recall her name, as if he had read it in her own handwriting. No, this couldn't be; he would have remembered her. It was not, he affirmed, that she had an extraordinary beauty—no, though her face was attractive enough; it was that *something* about her moved him. Feature for feature, even some of the ladies of the photographs could do better; but she leaped forth to his heart— had *lived*, or wanted to—more than just wanted, perhaps regretted how she had lived—had somehow deeply suffered: it could be seen in the depths of those reluctant eyes, and from the way the light enclosed and shone from her, and within her, opening realms of possibility: this was her own. Her he desired. His head ached and eyes narrowed with the intensity of his gazing, then as if an obscure fog had blown up in the mind, he experienced fear of her and was aware that he had received an impression, somehow, of evil. He shuddered, saying softly, it is thus with us all. Leo brewed some tea in a small pot and sat sipping it without sugar, to calm himself. But before he had finished drinking, again with excitement he examined the face and found it good: good for Leo Finkle. Only such a one could understand him and help him seek whatever he was seeking. She might, perhaps, love him. How she had happened to be among the discards in Salzman's barrel he could never guess, but he knew he must urgently go find her.

Leo rushed downstairs, grabbed up the Bronx telephone book, and searched for Salzman's home address. He was not listed, nor was his office. Neither was he in the Manhattan book. But Leo remembered having written down the address on a slip of paper after he had read Salzman's advertisement in the "personals" column of the *Forward*. He ran up to his room and tore through his papers, without luck. It was exasperating. Just when he needed the matchmaker he was nowhere to be found. Fortunately Leo remembered to look in his wallet. There on a card he found his name written and a Bronx address. No phone number was listed, the reason—Leo now recalled—he had originally communicated with Salzman by letter. He got on his coat, put a hat on over his skullcap and hurried to the subway station. All the way to the far end of the Bronx he sat on the edge of his seat. He was more than once tempted to take out the picture and see if the girl's face was as he remembered, but he refrained, allowing the snapshot to remain in his inside coat pocket, content to have her so close. When the train pulled into the station he was waiting at the door and bolted out. He quickly located the street Salzman had advertised.

The building he sought was less than a block from the subway, but it was not an office building, nor even a loft, nor a store in which one could rent office space. It was a very old tenement house. Leo found Salzman's name in pencil on a soiled tag under the bell and climbed three dark flights to his apartment. When he knocked, the door was opened by a thin, asthmatic, gray-haired woman, in felt slippers.

"Yes?" she said, expecting nothing. She listened without listening. He could have sworn he had seen her, too, before but knew it was an illusion.

"Salzman—does he live here? Pinye Salzman," he said, "the matchmaker?"

She stared at him a long minute. "Of course."

He felt embarrassed. "Is he in?"

"No." Her mouth, though left open, offered nothing more.

"The matter is urgent. Can you tell me where his office is?"

"In the air." She pointed upward.

"You mean he has no office?" Leo asked.

"In his socks."

He peered into the apartment. It was sunless and dingy, one large room divided by a half-open curtain, beyond which he could see a sagging metal bed. The near side of the room was crowded with rickety chairs, old bureaus, a three-legged table, racks of cooking utensils, and all the apparatus of a kitchen. But there was no sign of Salzman or his magic barrel, probably also a figment of the imagination. An odor of frying fish made Leo weak to the knees.

"Where is he?" he insisted. "I've got to see your husband."

At length she answered, "So who knows where he is? Every time he thinks a new thought he runs to a different place. Go home, he will find you."

"Tell him Leo Finkle."

She gave no sign she had heard.

He walked downstairs, depressed.

But Salzman, breathless, stood waiting at his door.

Leo was astounded and overjoyed. "How did you get here before me?"

"I rushed."

"Come inside."

They entered. Leo fixed tea, and a sardine sandwich for Salzman. As they were drinking he reached behind him for the packet of pictures and handed them to the marriage broker.

Salzman put down his glass and said expectantly, "You found somebody you like?"

"Not among these."

The marriage broker turned away.

"Here is the one I want." Leo held forth the snapshot.

Salzman slipped on his glasses and took the picture into his trembling hand. He turned ghastly and let out a groan.

"What's the matter?" cried Leo.

"Excuse me. Was an accident this picture. She isn't for you."

Salzman frantically shoved the manila packet into his portfolio. He thrust the snapshot into his pocket and fled down the stairs.

Leo, after momentary paralysis, gave chase and cornered the

marriage broker in the vestibule. The landlady made hysterical outcries but neither of them listened.

"Give me back the picture, Salzman."

"No." The pain in his eyes was terrible.

"Tell me who she is then."

"This I can't tell you. Excuse me."

He made to depart, but Leo, forgetting himself, seized the matchmaker by his tight coat and shook him frenziedly.

"Please," sighed Salzman. "*Please.*"

Leo ashamedly let him go. "Tell me who she is," he begged. "It's very important for me to know."

"She is not for you. She is a wild one—wild, without shame. This is not a bride for a rabbi."

"What do you mean wild?"

"Like an animal. Like a dog. For her to be poor was a sin. This is why to me she is dead now."

"In God's name, what do you mean?"

"Her I can't introduce to you," Salzman cried.

"Why are you so excited?"

"Why, he asks," Salzman said, bursting into tears. "This is my baby, my Stella, she should burn in hell."

:   :   :

Leo hurried up to bed and hid under the covers. Under the covers he thought his life through. Although he soon fell asleep he could not sleep her out of his mind. He woke, beating his breast. Though he prayed to be rid of her, his prayers went unanswered. Through days of torment he endlessly struggled not to love her; fearing success, he escaped it. He then concluded to convert her to goodness, himself to God. The idea alternately nauseated and exalted him.

He perhaps did not know that he had come to a final decision until he encountered Salzman in a Broadway cafeteria. He was sitting alone at a rear table, sucking the bony remains of a fish.

The marriage broker appeared haggard, and transparent to the point of vanishing.

Salzman looked up at first without recognizing him. Leo had grown a pointed beard and his eyes were weighted with wisdom.

"Salzman," he said, "love has at last come to my heart."

"Who can love from a picture?" mocked the marriage broker.

"It is not impossible."

"If you can love her, then you can love anybody. Let me show you some new clients that they just sent me their photographs. One is a little doll."

"Just her I want," Leo murmured.

"Don't be a fool, doctor. Don't bother with her."

"Put me in touch with her, Salzman," Leo said humbly. "Perhaps I can be of service."

Salzman had stopped eating and Leo understood with emotion that it was now arranged.

Leaving the cafeteria, he was, however, afflicted by a tormenting suspicion that Salzman had planned it all to happen this way.

:　　　:　　　:

Leo was informed by letter that she would meet him on a certain corner, and she was there one spring night, waiting under a street lamp. He appeared, carrying a small bouquet of violets and rosebuds. Stella stood by the lamppost, smoking. She wore white with red shoes, which fitted his expectations, although in a troubled moment he had imagined the dress red, and only the shoes white. She waited uneasily and shyly. From afar he saw that her eyes—clearly her father's—were filled with desperate innocence. He pictured, in her, his own redemption. Violins and lit candles revolved in the sky. Leo ran forward with flowers outthrust.

Around the corner, Salzman, leaning against a wall, chanted prayers for the dead.

The Jewbird

THE WINDOW was open so the skinny bird flew in. Flappity-flap with its frazzled black wings. That's how it goes. It's open, you're in. Closed, you're out and that's your fate. The bird wearily flapped through the open kitchen window of Harry Cohen's top-floor apartment on First Avenue near the lower East River. On a rod on the wall hung an escaped canary cage, its door wide open, but this black-type longbeaked bird—its ruffled head and small dull eyes, crossed a little, making it look like a dissipated crow—landed if not smack on Cohen's thick lamb chop, at least on the table, close by. The frozen-foods salesman was sitting at supper with his wife and young son on a hot August evening a year ago. Cohen, a heavy man with hairy chest and beefy shorts; Edie, in skinny yellow shorts and red halter; and their ten-year-old Morris (after her father)—Maurie, they called him, a nice kid though not overly bright—were all in the city after two weeks out, because Cohen's mother was dying. They had been enjoying Kingston, New York, but drove back when Mama got sick in her flat in the Bronx.

"Right on the table," said Cohen, putting down his beer glass and swatting at the bird. "Son of a bitch."

"Harry, take care with your language," Edie said, looking at Maurie, who watched every move.

The bird cawed hoarsely and with a flap of its bedraggled wings—feathers tufted this way and that—rose heavily to the top of the open kitchen door, where it perched staring down.

"Gevalt, a pogrom!"

"It's a talking bird," said Edie in astonishment.

"In Jewish," said Maurie.

"Wise guy," muttered Cohen. He gnawed on his chop, then put down the bone. "So if you can talk, say what's your business. What do you want here?"

"If you can't spare a lamb chop," said the bird, "I'll settle for a piece of herring with a crust of bread. You can't live on your nerve forever."

"This ain't a restaurant," Cohen replied. "All I'm asking is what brings you to this address?"

"The window was open," the bird sighed; adding after a moment, "I'm running. I'm flying but I'm also running."

"From whom?" asked Edie with interest.

"Anti-Semeets."

"Anti-Semites?" they all said.

"That's from who."

"What kind of anti-Semites bother a bird?" Edie asked.

"Any kind," said the bird, "also including eagles, vultures, and hawks. And once in a while some crows will take your eyes out."

"But aren't you a crow?"

"Me? I'm a Jewbird."

Cohen laughed heartily. "What do you mean by that?"

The bird began dovening. He prayed without Book or tallith, but with passion. Edie bowed her head though not Cohen. And

Maurie rocked back and forth with the prayers, looking up with one wide-open eye.

When the prayer was done Cohen remarked, "No hat, no phylacteries?"

"I'm an old radical."

"You're sure you're not some kind of a ghost or dybbuk?"

"Not a dybbuk," answered the bird, "though one of my relatives had such an experience once. It's all over now, thanks God. They freed her from a former lover, a crazy jealous man. She's now the mother of two wonderful children."

"Birds?" Cohen asked slyly.

"Why not?"

"What kind of birds?"

"Like me. Jewbirds."

Cohen tipped back in his chair and guffawed. "That's a big laugh. I heard of a Jewfish but not a Jewbird."

"We're once removed." The bird rested on one skinny leg, then on the other. "Please, could you spare maybe a piece of herring with a small crust of bread?"

Edie got up from the table.

"What are you doing?" Cohen asked her.

"I'll clear the dishes."

Cohen turned to the bird. "So what's your name, if you don't mind saying?"

"Call me Schwartz."

"He might be an old Jew changed into a bird by somebody," said Edie, removing a plate.

"Are you?" asked Harry, lighting a cigar.

"Who knows?" answered Schwartz. "Does God tell us everything?"

Maurie got up on his chair. "What kind of herring?" he asked the bird in excitement.

"Get down, Maurie, or you'll fall," ordered Cohen.

"If you haven't got matjes, I'll take schmaltz," said Schwartz.

"All we have is marinated, with slices of onion—in a jar," said Edie.

"If you'll open for me the jar I'll eat marinated. Do you have also, if you don't mind, a piece of rye bread—the spitz?"

Edie thought she had.

"Feed him out on the balcony," Cohen said. He spoke to the bird. "After that take off."

Schwartz closed both bird eyes. "I'm tired and it's a long way."

"Which direction are you headed, north or south?"

Schwartz, barely lifting his wings, shrugged.

"You don't know where you're going?"

"Where there's charity I'll go."

"Let him stay, papa," said Maurie. "He's only a bird."

"So stay the night," Cohen said, "but not longer."

In the morning Cohen ordered the bird out of the house but Maurie cried, so Schwartz stayed for a while. Maurie was still on vacation from school and his friends were away. He was lonely and Edie enjoyed the fun he had playing with the bird.

"He's no trouble at all," she told Cohen, "and besides his appetite is very small."

"What'll you do when he makes dirty?"

"He flies across the street in a tree when he makes dirty, and if nobody passes below, who notices?"

"So all right," said Cohen, "but I'm dead set against it. I warn you he ain't gonna stay here long."

"What have you got against the poor bird?"

"Poor bird, my ass. He's a foxy bastard. He thinks he's a Jew."

"What difference does it make what he thinks?"

"A Jewbird, what a chutzpah. One false move and he's out on his drumsticks."

At Cohen's insistence Schwartz lived out on the balcony in a new wooden birdhouse Edie had bought him.

"With many thanks," said Schwartz, "though I would rather have a human roof over my head. You know how it is at my age. I like the warm, the windows, the smell of cooking. I would also be glad to see once in a while the *Jewish Morning Journal* and have now and then a schnapps because it helps my breathing, thanks God. But whatever you give me, you won't hear complaints."

However, when Cohen brought home a bird feeder full of dried corn, Schwartz said, "Impossible."

Cohen was annoyed. "What's the matter, crosseyes, is your life getting too good for you? Are you forgetting what it means to be migratory? I'll bet a helluva lot of crows you happen to be acquainted with, Jews or otherwise, would give their eyeteeth to eat this corn."

Schwartz did not answer. What can you say to a grubber yung?

"Not for my digestion," he later explained to Edie. "Cramps. Herring is better even if it makes you thirsty. At least rainwater don't cost anything." He laughed sadly in breathy caws.

And herring, thanks to Edie, who knew where to shop, was what Schwartz got, with an occasional piece of potato pancake, and even a bit of soupmeat when Cohen wasn't looking.

When school began in September, before Cohen would once again suggest giving the bird the boot, Edie prevailed on him to wait a little while until Maurie adjusted.

"To deprive him right now might hurt his school work, and you know what trouble we had last year."

"So okay, but sooner or later the bird goes. That I promise you."

Schwartz, though nobody had asked him, took on full responsibility for Maurie's performance in school. In return for favors granted, when he was let in for an hour or two at night, he spent most of his time overseeing the boy's lessons. He sat on top of the dresser near Maurie's desk as he laboriously wrote out his homework. Maurie was a restless type and Schwartz gently kept him to his studies. He also listened to him practice his screechy violin, taking a few minutes off now and then to rest his ears in the bathroom. And they afterwards played dominoes. The boy was an indifferent checkers player and it was impossible to teach him chess. When he was sick, Schwartz read him comic books though he personally disliked them. But Maurie's work improved in school and even his violin teacher admitted his playing was better. Edie gave Schwartz credit for these improvements though the bird pooh-poohed them.

Yet he was proud there was nothing lower than C minuses on Maurie's report card, and on Edie's insistence celebrated with a little schnapps.

"If he keeps up like this," Cohen said, "I'll get him in an Ivy League college for sure."

"Oh, I hope so," sighed Edie.

But Schwartz shook his head. "He's a good boy—you don't have to worry. He won't be a shicker or a wife beater, God forbid, but a scholar he'll never be, if you know what I mean, although maybe a good mechanic. It's no disgrace in these times."

"If I was you," Cohen said, angered, "I'd keep my big snoot out of other people's private business."

"Harry, please," said Edie.

"My goddamn patience is wearing out. That crosseyes butts into everything."

Though he wasn't exactly a welcome guest in the house, Schwartz gained a few ounces although he did not improve in appearance. He looked bedraggled as ever, his feathers unkempt, as though he had just flown out of a snowstorm. He spent, he admitted, little time taking care of himself. Too much to think about. "Also outside plumbing," he told Edie. Still there was more glow to his eyes so that though Cohen went on calling him crosseyes he said it less emphatically.

Liking his situation, Schwartz tried tactfully to stay out of Cohen's way, but one night when Edie was at the movies and Maurie was taking a hot shower, the frozen-foods salesman began a quarrel with the bird.

"For Christ sake, why don't you wash yourself sometimes? Why must you always stink like a dead fish?"

"Mr. Cohen, if you'll pardon me, if somebody eats garlic he will smell from garlic. I eat herring three times a day. Feed me flowers and I will smell like flowers."

"Who's obligated to feed you anything at all? You're lucky to get herring."

"Excuse me, I'm not complaining," said the bird. "You're complaining."

"What's more," said Cohen, "even from out on the balcony I can hear you snoring away like a pig. It keeps me awake nights."

"Snoring," said Schwartz, "isn't a crime, thanks God."

"All in all you are a goddamn pest and freeloader. Next thing you'll want to sleep in bed next to my wife."

"Mr. Cohen," said Schwartz, "on this rest assured. A bird is a bird."

"So you say, but how do I know you're a bird and not some kind of a goddamn devil?"

"If I was a devil you would know already. And I don't mean because your son's good marks."

"Shut up, you bastard bird," shouted Cohen.

"Grubber yung," cawed Schwartz, rising to the tips of his talons, his long wings outstretched.

Cohen was about to lunge for the bird's scrawny neck but Maurie came out of the bathroom, and for the rest of the evening until Schwartz's bedtime on the balcony, there was pretend peace.

But the quarrel had deeply disturbed Schwartz and he slept badly. His snoring woke him, and awake, he was fearful of what would become of him. Wanting to stay out of Cohen's way, he kept to the birdhouse as much as possible. Cramped by it, he paced back and forth on the balcony ledge, or sat on the bird-house roof, staring into space. In the evenings, while overseeing Maurie's lessons, he often fell asleep. Awakening, he nervously hopped around exploring the four corners of the room. He spent much time in Maurie's closet, and carefully examined his bureau drawers when they were left open. And once when he found a large paper bag on the floor, Schwartz poked his way into it to investigate what possibilities were. The boy was amused to see the bird in the paper bag.

"He wants to build a nest," he said to his mother.

Edie, sensing Schwartz's unhappiness, spoke to him quietly.

"Maybe if you did some of the things my husband wants you, you would get along better with him."

"Give me a for instance," Schwartz said.

"Like take a bath, for instance."

"I'm too old for baths," said the bird. "My feathers fall out without baths."

"He says you have a bad smell."

"Everybody smells. Some people smell because of their thoughts or because who they are. My bad smell comes from the food I eat. What does his come from?"

"I better not ask him or it might make him mad," said Edie.

In late November Schwartz froze on the balcony in the fog and cold, and especially on rainy days he woke with stiff joints and could barely move his wings. Already he felt twinges of rheumatism. He would have liked to spend more time in the warm house, particularly when Maurie was in school and Cohen at work. But though Edie was goodhearted and might have sneaked him in in the morning, just to thaw out, he was afraid to ask her. In the meantime Cohen, who had been reading articles about the migration of birds, came out on the balcony one night after work when Edie was in the kitchen preparing pot roast, and peeking into the birdhouse, warned Schwartz to be on his way soon if he knew what was good for him. "Time to hit the flyways."

"Mr. Cohen, why do you hate me so much?" asked the bird. "What did I do to you?"

"Because you're an A-number-one troublemaker, that's why. What's more, whoever heard of a Jewbird? Now scat or it's open war."

But Schwartz stubbornly refused to depart so Cohen embarked on a campaign of harassing him, meanwhile hiding it from Edie and Maurie. Maurie hated violence and Cohen didn't want to leave a bad impression. He thought maybe if he played dirty tricks on the bird he would fly off without being physically kicked out. The vacation was over, let him make his easy living off the fat of somebody else's land. Cohen worried about the effect of the bird's departure on Maurie's schooling but decided to take the chance, first, because the boy now seemed to have the knack of studying—give the black bird-bastard credit—and second, because Schwartz was driving him bats by being there always, even in his dreams.

The frozen-foods salesman began his campaign against the bird by mixing watery cat food with the herring slices in Schwartz's dish. He also blew up and popped numerous paper bags outside the birdhouse as the bird slept, and when he had got Schwartz good and nervous, though not enough to leave, he brought a full-grown cat into the house, supposedly a gift for little Maurie, who had always wanted a pussy. The cat never stopped springing up at Schwartz whenever he saw him, one day managing to claw out several of his tail feathers. And even at lesson time, when the cat was usually excluded from Maurie's room, though somehow or other he quickly found his way in at the end of the lesson, Schwartz was desperately fearful of his life and flew from pinnacle to pinnacle—light fixture to clothes tree to door top—in order to elude the beast's wet jaws.

Once when the bird complained to Edie how hazardous his existence was, she said, "Be patient, Mr. Schwartz. When the cat gets to know you better he won't try to catch you any more."

"When he stops trying we will both be in Paradise," Schwartz answered. "Do me a favor and get rid of him. He makes my whole life worry. I'm losing feathers like a tree loses leaves."

"I'm awfully sorry but Maurie likes the pussy and sleeps with it."

What could Schwartz do? He worried but came to no decision, being afraid to leave. So he ate the herring garnished with cat food, tried hard not to hear the paper bags bursting like fire-crackers outside the birdhouse at night, and lived terror-stricken, closer to the ceiling than the floor, as the cat, his tail flicking, endlessly watched him.

Weeks went by. Then on the day after Cohen's mother had died in her flat in the Bronx, when Maurie came home with a zero on an arithmetic test, Cohen, enraged, waited until Edie had taken the boy to his violin lesson, then openly attacked the bird. He chased him with a broom on the balcony and Schwartz frantically flew back and forth, finally escaping into his bird-house. Cohen triumphantly reached in, and grabbing both skinny legs, dragged the bird out, cawing loudly, his wings wildly beating. He whirled the bird around and around his head. But Schwartz, as he moved in circles, managed to swoop down and catch Cohen's nose in his beak, and hung on for dear life. Cohen cried out in great pain, punched at the bird with his fist, and tugging at its legs with all his might, pulled his nose free. Again he swung the yawking Schwartz around until the bird grew dizzy, then with a furious heave, flung him into the night. Schwartz sank like a stone into the street. Cohen then tossed the birdhouse and feeder after him, listening at the ledge until they crashed on the sidewalk below. For a full hour, broom in hand, his heart palpitating and nose throbbing with pain, Cohen waited for Schwartz to return, but the brokenhearted bird didn't.

That's the end of that dirty bastard, the salesman thought and went in. Edie and Maurie had come home.

"Look," said Cohen, pointing to his bloody nose swollen three times its size, "what that sonofabitchy bird did. It's a permanent scar."

"Where is he now?" Edie asked, frightened.

"I threw him out and he flew away. Good riddance."

Nobody said no, though Edie touched a handkerchief to her eyes and Maurie rapidly tried the nine-times table and found he knew approximately half.

In the spring when the winter's snow had melted, the boy, moved by a memory, wandered in the neighborhood, looking for Schwartz. He found a dead black bird in a small lot by the river, his two wings broken, neck twisted, and both bird-eyes plucked clean.

"Who did it to you, Mr. Schwartz?" Maurie wept.

"Anti-Semeets," Edie said later.

The Letter

AT THE GATE stands Teddy holding his letter.

: : :

On Sunday afternoons Newman sat with his father on a white bench in the open ward. The son had brought a pineapple tart but the old man wouldn't eat it.

Twice during the two and a half hours he spent in the ward with his father, Newman said, "Do you want me to come back next Sunday or don't you? Do you want to have next Sunday off?"

The old man said nothing. Nothing meant yes or it meant no. If you pressed him to say which he wept.

"All right, I'll see you next Sunday. But if you want a week off sometime, let me know. I want a Sunday off myself."

His father said nothing. Then his mouth moved and after a while he said, "Your mother didn't talk to me like that. She didn't like to leave any dead chickens in the bathtub. When is she coming to see me here?"

"Pa, she's been dead since before you got sick and tried to take your life. Try to keep that in your memory."

"Don't ask me to believe that one," his father said, and Newman got up to go to the station where he took the Long Island Rail Road train to New York City.

He said, "Get better, pa," when he left, and his father answered, "Don't tell me that, I am better."

Sundays after he left his father in Ward 12 of Building B and walked across the hospital grounds, that spring and dry summer, at the arched iron-barred gate between brick posts under a towering oak that shadowed the raw red brick wall, he met Teddy standing there with his letter in his hand. Newman could have got out through the main entrance of Building B of the hospital complex, but this way to the railroad station was shorter. The gate was open to visitors on Sundays only.

Teddy was a stout soft man in loose gray institutional clothes and canvas slippers. He was fifty or more and maybe so was his letter. He held it as he always held it, as though he had held it always, a thick squarish finger-soiled blue envelope with unsealed flap. Inside were four sheets of cream paper with nothing written on them. After he had looked at the paper the first time, Newman had handed the envelope back to Teddy, and the green-uniformed guard had let him out the gate. Sometimes there were other patients standing by the gate who wanted to walk out with Newman but the guard said they couldn't.

"What about mailing my letter," Teddy said on Sundays.

He handed Newman the finger-smudged envelope. It was easier to take, then hand back, than to refuse to take it.

The mailbox hung on a short cement pole just outside the iron gate on the other side of the road, a few feet from the oak tree. Teddy would throw a right jab in its direction. Once it had been painted red and was now painted blue. There was also a mailbox in the doctor's office in each ward. Newman had reminded him, but Teddy said he didn't want the doctor reading his letter.

"You bring it to the office and so they read it."

"That's his job," Newman answered.

"Not on my head," said Teddy. "Why don't you mail it? It won't do you any good if you don't."

"There's nothing in it to mail."

"That's what you say."

His heavy head was set on a short sunburned neck, the coarse grizzled hair cropped an inch from the skull. One of his eyes was a fleshy gray, the other was walleyed. He stared beyond Newman when he talked to him, sometimes through his shoulder. And Newman noticed he never so much as glanced at the blue envelope when it was momentarily out of his hand, when Newman was holding it. Once in a while he pointed a short finger at something but said nothing. When he said nothing he rose a little on the balls of his toes. The guard did not interfere when Teddy handed Newman the letter every Sunday.

Newman gave it back.

"It's your mistake," said Teddy. Then he said, "I got my walking privileges. I'm almost sane. I fought in Guadalcanal."

Newman said he knew that.

"Where did you fight?"

"Nowhere yet."

"Why don't you mail my letter out?"

"It's for your own good the doctor reads it."

"That's a hot one." Teddy stared at the mailbox through Newman's shoulder.

"The letter isn't addressed to anybody and there's no stamp on it."

"Put one on. They won't let me buy one three or three ones."

"It's eight cents now. I'll put one on if you address the envelope."

"Not me," said Teddy.

Newman no longer asked why.

"It's not that kind of a letter."

He asked what kind it was.

"Blue with white paper inside of it."

"Saying what?"

"Shame on you," said Teddy.

Newman left on the four o'clock train. The ride home was not so bad as the ride there, though Sundays were murderous.

Teddy holds his letter.

"No luck?"

"No luck," said Newman.

"It's off your noodle."

He handed the envelope to Newman anyway and after a while Newman gave it back.

Teddy stared at his shoulder.

:　　　:　　　:

Ralph holds the finger-soiled blue envelope.

:　　　:　　　:

On Sunday a tall lean grim old man, clean-shaven, faded-eyed, wearing a worn-thin World War I overseas cap on his yellowed white head, stood at the gate with Teddy. He looked eighty.

The guard in the green uniform told him to step back, he was blocking the gate.

"Step back, Ralph, you're in the way of the gate."

"Why don't you stick it in the box on your way out?" Ralph asked in a gravelly old man's voice, handing the letter to Newman.

Newman wouldn't take it. "Who are you?"

Teddy and Ralph said nothing.

"It's his father," the guard at the gate said.

"Whose?"

"Teddy."

"My God," said Newman. "Are they both in here?"

"That's right," said the guard.

"Was he just admitted or has he been here all the while?"

"He just got his walking privileges returned again. They were revoked about a year."

"I got them back after five years," Ralph said.

"One year."

"Five."

"It's astonishing anyway," Newman said. "Neither one of you resembles the other."

"Who do you resemble?" asked Ralph.

Newman couldn't say.

"What war were you in?" Ralph asked.

"No war at all."

"That settles your pickle. Why don't you mail my letter?"

Teddy stood by sullenly. He rose on his toes and threw a short right and left at the mailbox.

"I thought it was Teddy's letter."

"He told me to mail it for him. He fought at Iwo Jima. We fought two wars. I fought in the Marne and the Argonne Forest. I had both my lungs gassed with mustard gas. The wind changed and the Huns were gassed. That's not all that were."

"Tough turd," said Teddy.

"Mail it anyway for the poor kid," said Ralph. His tall body trembled. He was an angular man with deep-set bluish eyes and craggy features that looked as though they had been hacked out of a tree.

"I told your son I would if he wrote something on the paper," Newman said.

"What do you want it to say?"

"Anything he wants it to. Isn't there somebody he wants to communicate with? If he doesn't want to write it he could tell me what to say and I'll write it out."

"Tough turd," said Teddy.

"He wants to communicate to me," said Ralph.

"It's not a bad idea," Newman said. "Why doesn't he write a few words to you? Or you could write a few words to him."

"A Bronx cheer on you."

"It's my letter," Teddy said.

"I don't care who writes it," said Newman. "I could write a message for you wishing him luck. I could say you hope he gets out of here soon."

"A Bronx cheer to that."

"Not in my letter," Teddy said.

"Not in mine either," said Ralph grimly. "Why don't you mail it like it is? I bet you're afraid to."

"No I'm not."

"I'll bet you are."

"No I'm not."

"I have my bets going."

"There's nothing to mail. There's nothing in the letter. It's a blank."

"What makes you think so?" asked Ralph. "There's a whole letter in there. Plenty of news."

"I'd better be going," Newman said, "or I'll miss my train."

The guard opened the gate to let him out. Then he shut the gate.

Teddy turned away and stared over the oak tree into the summer sun with his gray eye and his walleyed one.

Ralph trembled at the gate.

"Who do you come here to see on Sundays?" he called to Newman.

"My father."

"What war was he in?"

"The war in his head."

"Has he got his walking privileges?"

"No, they won't give him any."

"What I mean, he's crazy?"

"That's right," said Newman, walking away.

"So are you," said Ralph. "Why don't you come back here and hang around with the rest of us?"

In Retirement

HE HAD lately taken to studying his old Greek grammar of fifty years ago. He read in Bulfinch and wanted to reread the *Odyssey* in Greek. His life had changed. He slept less these days and in the morning got up to stare at the sky over Gramercy Park. He watched the clouds until they took shapes he could reflect on. He liked strange, haunted vessels, and he liked to watch mythological birds and animals. He had noticed that if he contemplated these forms in the clouds, could keep his mind on them for a while, there might be a diminution of his morning depression. Dr. Morris was sixty-six, a physician, retired for two years. He had shut down his practice in Queens and moved to Manhattan. He had retired himself after a heart attack, not too serious but serious enough. It was his first attack and he hoped his last, though in the end he hoped to go quickly. His wife was dead and his daughter lived in Scotland. He wrote her twice a month and heard from her twice a month. And though he had a few friends he visited, and kept up with medical journals, and liked museums and theater, generally he contended with loneliness. And he was concerned about the future; the future was by old age possessed.

After a light breakfast he would dress warmly and go out for a walk around the Square. That was the easy part of the walk. He took this walk even when it was very cold, or nasty rainy, or had snowed several inches and he had to proceed very carefully. After the Square he crossed the street and went down Irving Place, a tall figure with a cape and cane, and picked up his *Times*. If the weather was not too bad he continued on to Fourteenth Street, around to Park Avenue South, up Park and along East Twentieth back to the narrow, tall, white stone apartment building he lived in. Rarely, lately, had he gone in another direction though when on the long walk, he stopped at least once on the way, perhaps in front of a mid-block store, perhaps at a street corner; and asked himself where else he might go. This was the difficult part of the walk. What was difficult was that it made no difference which way he went. He now wished he had not retired. He had become more conscious of his age since his retirement, although sixty-six was not eighty. Still it was old. He experienced moments of anguish.

One morning after his rectangular long walk in the rain, he found a letter on the rubber mat under the line of mailboxes in the lobby. It was a narrow, deep lobby with false green marble columns and several bulky chairs where few people ever sat. Dr. Morris had seen a young woman with long hair, in a white raincoat and maroon shoulder bag, carrying a plastic bubble umbrella, hurry down the vestibule steps and leave the house as he was about to enter. In fact he held the door open for her and got a breath of her bold perfume. He did not remember seeing her before and felt a momentary confusion as to who she might be. He later imagined her taking the letter out of her box, reading it hastily, then stuffing it into the maroon cloth purse she carried over her shoulder; but she had stuffed in the envelope and not the letter.

That had fallen to the floor. He imagined this as he bent to retrieve it. It was a folded sheet of heavy white writing paper, written on in black ink in a masculine hand. The doctor unfolded and glanced at it without making out the salutation or any of its contents. He would have to put on his reading glasses, and he thought Flaherty, the doorman and elevator man, might see him if the elevator should suddenly descend. Of course Flaherty might think the doctor was reading his own mail, except that he never read it, such as it was, in the lobby. He did not want the man thinking he was reading someone else's letter. He also thought of handing him the letter and describing the young woman who had dropped it. Perhaps he could return it to her? But for some reason not at once clear to him the doctor slipped it into his pocket to take upstairs to read. His arm began to tremble and he felt his heart racing at a rate that bothered him.

After the doctor had got his own mail out of the box—nothing more than the few medical circulars he held in his hand—Flaherty took him up to the fifteenth floor. Flaherty spelled the night man at 8 a.m. and was himself relieved at 4 p.m. He was a slender man of sixty with sparse white hair on his half-bald head, who had lost part of his jaw under the left ear after two bone operations. He would be out for a few months; then return, the lower part of the left side of his face partially caved in; still it was not a bad face to look at. Although the doorman never spoke of his ailment, the doctor knew he was not done with cancer of the jaw, but of course he kept this to himself; and he sensed when the man was concealing pain.

This morning, though preoccupied, he asked, "How is it going, Mr. Flaherty?"

"Not too tough."

"Not a bad day." He said this, thinking not of the rain but of the letter in his pocket.

"Fine and dandy," Flaherty quipped. On the whole he moved and talked animatedly, and was careful to align the elevator with the floor before letting passengers off. Sometimes the doctor wished he could say more to him than he usually did; but not this morning.

He stood by the large double window of his living room over-looking the Square, in the dull rainy-day February light, in pleasurable excitement reading the letter he had found, the kind he had anticipated it might be. It was a letter written by a father to his daughter, addressed to "Dear Evelyn." What it expressed after an irresolute start was the father's dissatisfaction with his daughter's way of life. And it ended with an exhortatory para-graph of advice: "You have slept around long enough. I don't understand what you get out of that type of behavior any more. I think you have tried everything there is to try. You claim you are a serious person but let men use you for what they can get. There is no true payoff to you unless it is very temporary, and the real payoff to them is that they have got themselves an easy lay. I know how they think about this and how they talk about it in the lavatory the next day. Now I want to urge you once and for all that you ought to be more serious about your life. You have experimented long enough. I honestly and sincerely and urgently advise you to look around for a man of steady habits and good character who will marry you and treat you like the person I believe you want to be. I don't want to think of you any more as a drifting semi-prostitute. Please follow this advice, the age of twenty-nine is no longer sixteen." The letter was signed, "Your Father," and under his signature, another sentence, in neat small handwriting, was appended: "Your sex life fills me full of fear. Mother."

The doctor put the letter away in a drawer. His excitement had left him and he felt ashamed of having read it. He was sympathetic to the father, and at the same time sympathetic to the young woman, though perhaps less so to her. After a while he tried to study his Greek grammar but could not concentrate. The letter remained in his mind like a billboard sign as he was reading the *Times*, and he was conscious of it throughout the day, as though it had aroused in him some sort of expectation he could not define. Sentences from it would replay themselves in his thoughts. He reveried the young woman as he had imagined her after reading what the father had written, and as the woman— was she Evelyn?—he had seen coming out of the house. He could not be certain the letter was hers. Perhaps it was not; still he thought of it as belonging to her, the woman he had held the door for whose perfume still lingered in his senses.

That night, thoughts of her kept him from falling asleep. "I'm too old for this nonsense." He got up to read and was able to concentrate, but when his head lay once more on the pillow, a long freight train of thoughts provocative of her rumbled by drawn by a long black locomotive. He pictured Evelyn, the drifting semi-prostitute, in bed with various lovers, engaged in various acts of sex. Once she lay alone, erotically naked, her maroon cloth purse drawn close to her nude body. He also thought of her as an ordinary girl with many fewer lovers than her father seemed to think. This was probably closer to the truth. He wondered if he could be useful to her in some way. He felt a fright he could not explain but managed to dispel it by promising himself to burn the letter in the morning. The freight train, with its many cars, clattered along in the foggy distance. When the doctor awoke at 10 a.m. on a sunny winter's morning, there was no awareness, light or heavy, of his morning depression.

But he did not burn the letter. He reread it several times during the day, each time returning it to his desk drawer and locking it there. Then he unlocked the drawer to read it again. As the day passed he was aware of an insistent hunger in himself. He recalled memories, experienced longing, intense desires he had not felt in years. The doctor was concerned by this change in him, this disturbance. He tried to blot the letter out of his mind but could not. Yet he would still not burn it, as though if he did, he had shut the door on certain possibilities in his life, other ways to go, whatever that might mean. He was astonished —even thought of it as affronted, that this was happening to him at his age. He had seen it in others, former patients, but had not expected it in himself.

The hunger he felt, a hunger for pleasure, disruption of habit, renewal of feeling, yet a fear of it, continued to grow in him like a dead tree come to life and spreading its branches. He felt as though he was hungry for exotic experience, which, if he was to have it, might make him ravenously hungry. He did not want that to happen. He recalled mythological figures: Sisyphus, Midas, who for one reason or another had been eternally cursed. He thought of Tithonus, his youth gone, become a grasshopper living forever. The doctor felt he was caught in an overwhelming emotion, a fearful dark wind.

When Flaherty left for the day at 4 p.m. and Silvio, who had tight curly black hair, was on duty, Dr. Morris came down and sat in the lobby, pretending to read his newspaper. As soon as the elevator went up he approached the letter boxes and scanned the name plates for an Evelyn, whoever she might be. He found no Evelyns, though there was an E. Gordon and an E. Commings. He suspected one of them might be she. He knew that single women often preferred not to reveal their first names in order to keep cranks at a distance, conceal themselves from potential annoyers. He casually asked Silvio if Miss Gordon or Miss Commings was named Evelyn, but Silvio said he didn't know, although probably Mr. Flaherty would because he distributed the mail. "Too many peoples in this house," Silvio shrugged. The doctor remarked he was just curious, a lame remark but all he could think of. He went out for an aimless short stroll and when he returned said nothing more to Silvio. They rode silently up in the elevator, the doctor standing tall, almost stiff. That night he slept badly. When he fell deeply asleep a moment his dreams were erotic. He woke feeling desire and repulsion and lay mourning himself. He felt powerless to be other than he was.

He was up before five and was uselessly in the lobby before seven. He felt he must find out, settle who she was. In the lobby, Richard, the night man who had brought him down, returned to a pornographic paperback he was reading; the mail, as Dr. Morris knew, hadn't come. He knew it would not arrive until after eight, but hadn't the patience to wait in his apartment. So he left the building, bought the *Times* on Irving Place, continued on his walk, and because it was a pleasant morning, not too cold, sat on a bench in Union Square Park. He stared at the newspaper but could not read it. He watched some sparrows pecking at dead grass. He was an older man, true enough, but had lived long enough to know that age often meant little in man-woman relationships. He was still vigorous and bodies are bodies. The doctor was back in the lobby at eight-thirty, an act of restraint. Flaherty had received the mail sack and was alphabetizing the first-class letters on a long table before distributing them into the boxes. He did not look well today. He moved slowly. His misshapen face was gray, the mouth slack; one heard his breathing; his eyes harbored pain.

"Nothin for you yet," he said to the doctor, not looking up.

"I'll wait this morning," said Dr. Morris. "I should be hearing from my daughter."

"Nothin yet, but you might hit the lucky number in this last bundle." He removed the string.

As he was alphabetizing the last bundle of letters the elevator buzzed and Flaherty had to go up for a call.

The doctor pretended to be absorbed in his *Times*. When the elevator door shut he sat momentarily still, then went to the table and hastily riffled through the C pile of letters. E. Commings was Ernest Commings. He shuffled through the G's, watch-

ing the metal arrow as it showed the elevator descending. In the
G pile there were two letters addressed to Evelyn Gordon. One
was from her mother. The other, also handwritten, was from a
Lee Bradley. Almost against the will the doctor removed this
letter and slipped it into his suit pocket. His body was hot. He
was sitting in the chair turning the page of his newspaper when
the elevator door opened.

"Nothin at all for you," Flaherty said after a moment.

"Thank you," said Dr. Morris. "I think I'll go up."

In his apartment the doctor, conscious of his whisperous
breathing, placed the letter on the kitchen table and sat looking
at it, waiting for a tea kettle to boil. The kettle whistled as
it boiled but still he sat with the unopened letter before him.
For a while he sat there with dulled thoughts. Soon he fantasied
Lee Bradley describing the sexual pleasure he had had with Evelyn Gordon. He fantasied the lovers' acts they engaged in.
Then though he audibly told himself not to, he steamed open
the flap of the envelope and had to place it flat on the table so he
could read it. His heart beat in anticipation of what he might
read. But to his surprise the letter was a bore, an egoistic account
of some stupid business deal this Bradley was concocting. Only
the last sentences came surprisingly to life. "Be in your bed when
I get there tonight. Be wearing only your white panties."

The doctor didn't know whom he was more disgusted with,
this fool or himself. In truth, himself. Slipping the sheet of paper
into the envelope, he resealed it with a thin layer of paste he had
rubbed carefully on the flap with his fingertip. Later in the day
he tucked the letter into his inside pocket and pressed the elevator button for Silvio. The doctor left the building and afterwards returned with a copy of the *Post* he seemed to be involved
with until Silvio had to take up two women who had come into
the lobby; then the doctor slipped the letter into Evelyn Gordon's
box and went out for a breath of air.

He was sitting near the table in the lobby when the young woman he had held the door open for came in shortly after 6 p.m. He was aware of her perfume almost at once. Silvio was not around at that moment; he had gone down to the basement to eat a sandwich. She inserted a small key into Evelyn Gordon's mailbox and stood before the open box, smoking, as she read Bradley's letter. She was wearing a light-blue pants suit with a brown knit sweater-coat. Her tail of black hair was tied with a brown silk scarf. Her face, though a little heavy, was pretty, her intense eyes blue, the lids lightly eye-shadowed. Her body, he thought, was finely proportioned. She had not noticed him but he was more than half in love with her.

He observed her many mornings. He would come down later now, at nine, and spend some time going through the medical circulars he had got out of his box, sitting on a throne-like wooden chair near a tall unlit lamp in the rear of the lobby. He would watch people as they left for work or shopping in the morning. Evelyn appeared at about half past nine and stood smoking in front of her box, absorbed in the morning's mail. When spring came she wore brightly colored skirts with pastel blouses, or light slim pants suits. Sometimes she wore mini-dresses. Her figure was exquisite. She received many letters and read most of them with apparent pleasure, some with what seemed suppressed excitement. A few she gave short shrift to, scanned these and stuffed them into her bag. He imagined they were from her father, or mother. He thought that most of her letters came from lovers, past and present, and he felt a sort of sadness that there was none from him in her mailbox. He would write to her.

He thought it through carefully. Some women needed an older man; it stabilized their lives. Sometimes a difference of as many as thirty or even thirty-five years offered no serious disadvantages. A younger woman inspired an older man to remain virile.

And despite the heart incident his health was good, in some ways better than before. A woman like Evelyn, probably at odds with herself, could benefit from a steadying relationship with an older man, someone who would respect and love her and help her to respect and love herself; who would demand less from her in certain ways than some young men awash in their egoism; who would awake in her a stronger sense of well-being, and if things went quite well, perhaps even love for a particular man.

"I am a retired physician, a widower," he wrote to Evelyn Gordon. "I write you with some hesitation and circumspection, although needless to say with high regard, because I am old enough to be your father. I have observed you often in this building and as we passed each other in nearby streets; I have grown to admire you. I wonder if you will permit me to make your acquaintance? Would you care to have dinner with me and perhaps enjoy a film or performance of a play? I do not think my company will disappoint you. If you are so inclined—so kind, certainly—to consider this request tolerantly, I will be obliged if you place a note to that effect in my mailbox. I am respectfully yours, Simon Morris, M.D."

He did not go down to mail his letter. He thought he would keep it to the last moment. Then he had a fright about it that woke him out of momentary sleep. He dreamed he had written and sealed the letter and then remembered he had appended another sentence: "Be wearing your white panties." When he woke he wanted to tear open the envelope to see whether he had included Bradley's remark. But when he was thoroughly waked up, he knew he had not. He bathed and shaved early and for a while observed the cloud formations out the window. At close to nine Dr. Morris descended to the lobby. He would wait till Flaherty answered a buzz, and when he was gone, drop his letter into her box; but Flaherty that morning seemed to have no calls to answer. The doctor had forgotten it was Saturday. He did not know it was till he got his *Times* and sat with it in the lobby, pretending to be waiting for the mail delivery. The mail sack arrived late on Saturdays. At last he heard a prolonged buzz, and Flaherty, who had been on his knees polishing the brass door knob, got up on one foot, then rose on both legs and walked slowly to the elevator. His asymmetric face was gray. Shortly before ten o'clock the doctor slipped his letter into Evelyn Gordon's mailbox. He decided to withdraw to his apartment, then thought he would rather wait where he usually waited while she collected her mail. She had never noticed him there.

The mail sack was dropped in the vestibule at ten-after, and Flaherty alphabetized the first bundle before he responded to another call. The doctor read his paper in the dark rear of the lobby, because he was really not reading it. He was anticipating Evelyn's coming. He had on a new green suit, blue striped shirt, and a pink tie. He wore a new hat. He waited with anticipation and love.

When the elevator door opened, Evelyn walked out in an elegant slit black skirt, pretty sandals, her hair tied with a red scarf. A sharp-featured man with puffed sideburns and carefully combed medium-long hair, in a turn-of-the-century haircut, followed her out of the elevator. He was shorter than she by half a head. Flaherty handed her two letters, which she dropped into the black patent-leather pouch she was carrying. The doctor thought—hoped—she would walk past the mailboxes without stopping; but she saw the white of his letter through the slot and stopped to remove it. She tore open the envelope, pulled out the single sheet of handwritten paper, read it with immediate intense concentration. The doctor raised his newspaper to his eyes, although he could still watch over the top of it. He watched in fear.

How mad I was not to anticipate she might come down with a man.

When she had finished reading the letter, she handed it to her companion—possibly Bradley—who read it, grinned broadly, and said something inaudible as he handed it back to her.

Evelyn Gordon quietly ripped the letter into small bits, and turning, flung the pieces in the doctor's direction. The fragments came at him like a blast of wind-driven snow. He thought he would sit forever on his wooden throne in the swirling snowstorm.

The old doctor sat in his chair, the floor around him littered with his torn-up letter.

Flaherty swept it up with his little broom into a metal container. He handed the doctor a thin envelope stamped with foreign stamps.

"Here's a letter from your daughter that's just come."

The doctor pressed the bridge of his nose. He wiped his eyes with his fingers.

"There's no setting aside old age," he remarked after a while.

"No, sir," said Flaherty.

"Or death."

"They move up on you."

The doctor tried to say something splendidly kind, but could not say it.

Flaherty took him up to the fifteenth floor in his elevator.

The Loan

THE SWEET, the heady smell of Lieb's white bread drew customers in droves long before the loaves were baked. Alert behind the counter, Bessie, Lieb's second wife, discerned a stranger among them, a frail, gnarled man with a hard hat who hung, disjoined, at the edge of the crowd. Though the stranger looked harmless enough among the aggressive purchasers of baked goods, she was at once concerned. Her glance questioned him but he signaled with a deprecatory nod of his hatted head that he would wait—glad to (forever)—though his face glittered with misery. If suffering had marked him, he no longer sought to conceal the sign; the shining was his own—him—now. So he frightened Bessie.

She made quick hash of the customers, and when they, after her annihilating service, were gone, she returned him her stare.

He tipped his hat. "Pardon me—Kobotsky. Is Lieb the baker here?"

"Who Kobotsky?"

"An old friend"—frightening her further.

"From where?"

The Loan

"From long ago."

"What do you want to see him?"

The question insulted, so Kobotsky was reluctant to say.

As if drawn into the shop by the magic of a voice the baker, shirtless, appeared from the rear. His pink fleshy arms had been deep in dough. For a hat he wore jauntily a flour-covered brown paper sack. His peering glasses were dusty with flour, and the inquisitive face white with it, so that he resembled a paunchy ghost; but the ghost, through the glasses, was Kobotsky, not he.

"Kobotsky," the baker cried almost with a sob, for it was so many years gone Kobotsky reminded him of, when they were both at least young, and circumstances were—ah, different. Unable, for sentimental reasons, to refrain from smarting tears, he jabbed them away with a thrust of the hand.

Kobotsky removed his hat—he had grown all but bald where Lieb was gray—and patted his flushed forehead with an immaculate handkerchief.

Lieb sprang forward with a stool. "Sit, Kobotsky."

"Not here," Bessie murmured.

"Customers," she explained to Kobotsky. "Soon comes the supper rush."

"Better in the back," nodded Kobotsky.

So that was where they went, happier for the privacy. But it happened that no customers came so Bessie went in to hear.

Kobotsky sat enthroned on a tall stool in a corner of the room, stoop-shouldered, his black coat and hat on, the stiff, gray-veined hands drooping over thin thighs. Lieb, peering through full moons, eased his bones on a flour sack. Bessie lent an attentive ear, but the visitor was dumb. Embarrassed, Lieb did the talking: ah, of old times. The world was new. We were, Kobotsky, young. Do you remember how both together, immigrants out of steerage, we registered in night school?

"Haben, hatte, gehabt." He cackled at the sound of it.

No word from the gaunt one on the stool. Bessie fluttered around an impatient duster. She shot a glance into the shop: empty.

Lieb, acting the life of the party, recited, to cheer his friend: " 'Come,' said the wind to the trees one day, 'Come over the meadow with me and play.' Remember, Kobotsky?"

Bessie sniffed aloud. "Lieb, the bread!"

The baker bounced up, strode over to the gas oven, and pulled one of the tiered doors down. Just in time he yanked out the trays of brown breads in hot pans, and set them on the tin-top worktable.

Bessie clucked at the narrow escape.

Lieb peered into the shop. "Customers," he said triumphantly. Flushed, she went in. Kobotsky, with wetted lips, watched her go. Lieb set to work molding the risen dough in a huge bowl into two trays of pans. Soon the bread was baking, but Bessie was back.

The honey odor of the new loaves distracted Kobotsky. He breathed the fragrance as if this were the first air he was tasting, and even beat his fist against his chest at the delicious smell.

"Oh, my God," he all but wept. "Wonderful."

"With tears," Lieb said humbly, pointing to the large bowl of dough.

Kobotsky nodded.

For thirty years, the baker explained, he was never with a penny to his name. One day, out of misery, he had wept into the dough. Thereafter his bread was such it brought customers in from everywhere.

"My cakes they don't like so much, but my bread and rolls they run miles to buy."

:   :   :

Kobotsky blew his nose, then peeked into the shop: three customers.

The Loan

"Lieb"—a whisper.

Despite himself the baker stiffened.

The visitor's eyes swept back to Bessie out front, then under raised brows, questioned the baker.

Lieb, however, remained mute.

Kobotsky coughed clear his throat. "Lieb, I need two hundred dollars." His voice broke.

Lieb slowly sank onto the sack. He knew—had known. From the minute of Kobotsky's appearance he had weighed in his thoughts the possibility of this against the remembrance of the lost and bitter hundred, fifteen years ago. Kobotsky swore he had repaid it, Lieb said no. Afterwards a broken friendship. It took years to blot out of the system the memoried outrage.

Kobotsky bowed his head.

At least admit you were wrong, Lieb thought, waiting a cruelly long time.

Kobotsky stared at his crippled hands. Once a cutter of furs, driven by arthritis out of the business.

Lieb gazed too. The bottom of a truss bit into his belly. Both eyes were cloudy with cataracts. Though the doctor swore he would see after the operation, he feared otherwise.

He sighed. The wrong was in the past. Forgiven: forgiven at the dim sight of him.

"For myself, positively, but she"—Lieb nodded toward the shop—"is a second wife. Everything is in her name." He held up empty hands.

Kobotsky's eyes were shut.

"But I will ask her—" Lieb looked doubtful.

"My wife needs—"

The baker raised a palm. "Don't speak."

"Tell her—"

"Leave it to me."

He seized the broom and circled the room, raising clouds of white dust.

When Bessie, breathless, got back she threw one look at them, and with tightened lips waited adamant.

Lieb hastily scoured the pots in the iron sink, stored the bread pans under the table, and stacked the fragrant loaves. He put one eye to the slot of the oven: baking, all baking.

Facing Bessie, he broke into a sweat so hot it momentarily stunned him.

Kobotsky squirmed atop the stool.

"Bessie," said the baker at last, "this is my old friend."

She nodded gravely.

Kobotsky lifted his hat.

"His mother—God bless her—gave me many times a plate hot soup. Also when I came to this country, for years I ate at his table. His wife is a very fine person—Dora—you will someday meet her—"

Kobotsky softly groaned.

"So why I didn't meet her yet?" Bessie said, after a dozen years still jealous of the first wife's prerogatives.

"You will."

"Why didn't I?"

"Lieb—" pleaded Kobotsky.

"Because I didn't see her myself fifteen years," Lieb admitted.

"Why not?" she pounced.

Lieb paused. "A mistake."

Kobotsky turned away.

"My fault," said Lieb.

"Because you never go anyplace," Bessie spat out. "Because you live always in the shop. Because it means nothing to you to have friends."

Lieb solemnly agreed.

"Now she is sick," he announced. "The doctor must operate. This will cost two hundred dollars. I promised Kobotsky—"

Bessie screamed.

Hat in hand, Kobotsky got off the stool.

Pressing a palm to her bosom, Bessie lifted her arm to her eyes. She tottered. They both ran forward to steady her but she did not fall. Kobotsky retreated quickly to the stool and Lieb returned to the sink.

Bessie, her face like the inside of a loaf, quietly addressed the visitor. "I have pity for your wife but we can't help you. I am sorry, Mr. Kobotsky, we are poor people, we don't have the money."

"A mistake," Lieb cried, enraged.

Bessie strode over to the shelf and tore out a bill box. She dumped its contents on the table, the papers flying everywhere.

"Bills," she shouted.

Kobotsky hunched his shoulders.

"Bessie, we have in the bank—"

"No—"

"I saw the bankbook."

"So what if you saved a few dollars, so have you got life insurance?"

He made no answer.

"Can you get?" she taunted.

The front door banged. It banged often. The shop was crowded with customers clamoring for bread. Bessie stomped out to wait on them.

:   :   :

In the rear the wounded stirred. Kobotsky, with bony fingers, buttoned his overcoat.

"Sit," sighed the baker.

"Lieb, I am sorry—"

Kobotsky sat, his face lit with sadness.

When Bessie finally was rid of the rush, Lieb went into the shop. He spoke to her quietly, almost in a whisper, and she answered as quietly, but it took only a minute to start them quarreling.

Kobotsky slipped off the stool. He went to the sink, wet half his handkerchief, and held it to his dry eyes. Folding the damp handkerchief, he thrust it into his overcoat pocket, then took out a small penknife and quickly pared his fingernails.

As he entered the shop, Lieb was pleading with Bessie, reciting the embittered hours of his toil, the enduring drudgery. And now that he had a penny to his name, what was there to live for if he could not share it with a dear friend? But Bessie had her back to him.

"Please," Kobotsky said, "don't fight. I will go away now."

Lieb gazed at him in exasperation. Bessie stayed with head averted.

"Yes," Kobotsky sighed, "the money I wanted for Dora, but she is not sick, Lieb, she is dead."

"Ai," Lieb cried, wringing his hands.

Bessie faced the visitor, pallid.

"Not now," he spoke kindly, "five years ago."

Lieb groaned.

"The money I need for a stone on her grave. She never had a stone. Next Sunday is five years that she is dead and every year I promise her, 'Dora, this year I will give you your stone,' and every year I gave her nothing."

The grave, to his everlasting shame, lay uncovered before all eyes. He had long ago paid a fifty-dollar deposit for a headstone with her name on it in clearly chiseled letters, but had never got the rest of the money. If there wasn't one thing to do with it there was always another: first an operation; the second year he couldn't work, imprisoned again by arthritis; the third a widowed sister lost her only son and the little Kobotsky earned had to help support her; the fourth incapacitated by boils that made him ashamed to walk out into the street. This year he was at least working, but only for just enough to eat and sleep, so Dora still lay without a stone, and for aught he knew he would someday return to the cemetery and find her grave gone.

Tears sprang into the baker's eyes. One gaze at Bessie's face—and the odd looseness of her neck and shoulders—told him that she too was moved. Ah, he had won out. She would now say yes, give the money, and they would then all sit down at the table and eat together.

:⠀⠀⠀⠀:⠀⠀⠀⠀:

But Bessie, though weeping, shook her head, and before they could guess what, had blurted out the story of her afflictions: how the Bolsheviki came when she was a little girl and dragged her beloved father into the snowy fields without his shoes; the shots scattered the blackbirds in the trees and the snow oozed blood; how, when she was married a year, her husband, a sweet and gentle man, an educated accountant—rare in those days and that place—died of typhus in Warsaw; and how she, abandoned in her grief, years later found sanctuary in the home of an older brother in Germany, who sacrificed his own chances to send her, before the war, to America, and himself ended, with wife and daughter, in one of Hitler's incinerators.

"So I came to America and met here a poor baker, a poor man—who was always in his life poor—without a cent and without enjoyment, and I married him, God knows why, and with my both hands, working day and night, I fixed up for him his piece of business and we make now, after twelve years, a little living. But Lieb is not a healthy man, also with eyes that he needs an operation, and this is not yet everything. Suppose, God forbid, that he died, what will I do alone by myself? Where will I go, where, and who will take care of me if I have nothing?"

The baker, who had often heard this tale, munched, as he listened, chunks of bread.

When she had finished he tossed the shell of a loaf away. Kobotsky, at the end of the story, held his hands over his ears.

Tears streaming from her eyes, Bessie raised her head and suspiciously sniffed the air. Screeching suddenly, she ran into the rear and with a cry wrenched open the oven door. A cloud of smoke billowed out at her. The loaves in the trays were blackened bricks—charred corpses.

Kobotsky and the baker embraced and sighed over their lost youth. They pressed mouths together and parted forever.

The Cost of Living

W INTER had fled the city streets but Sam Tomashev-
sky's face, when he stumbled into the back room of his grocery
store, was a blizzard. Sura, sitting at the round table eating bread
and a salted tomato, looked up in fright, and the tomato turned a
deeper red. She gulped the bite she had bitten and with pudgy fist
socked her chest to make it go down. The gesture already was
one of mourning, for she knew from the wordless sight of him
there was trouble.

"My God," Sam croaked.

She screamed, making him shudder, and he fell wearily into a
chair. Sura was standing, enraged and frightened.

"Speak, for God's sake."

"Next door," Sam muttered.

"What happened next door?"—upping her voice.

"Comes a store!"

"What kind of a store?" The cry was piercing.

He waved his arms in rage. "A grocery comes next door."

"Oi." She bit her knuckle and sank down moaning. It could
not have been worse.

They had, all winter, been haunted by the empty store. An Italian shoemaker had owned it for years, and then a streamlined shoe-repair shop had opened up next block where they had two men in red smocks hammering away in the window and everyone stopped to look. Pellegrino's business had slackened off as if someone was shutting a faucet, and one day he had looked at his workbench, and when everything stopped jumping, it loomed up ugly and empty. All morning he had sat motionless, but in the afternoon he put down the hammer he had been clutching and got his jacket and an old darkened Panama hat a customer had never called for when he used to do hat cleaning and blocking; then he went into the neighborhood, asking among his former customers for work they might want done. He collected two pairs of shoes, a man's brown and white ones for summertime and a pair of ladies' dancing slippers. At the same time, Sam found his own soles and heels had been worn paper thin for being so many hours on his feet—he could feel the cold floorboards under him as he walked—and that made three pairs all together, which was what Mr. Pellegrino had that week—and another pair the week after. When the time came for him to pay next month's rent he sold everything to a junkman and bought candy to peddle with in the streets, but after a while no one saw the shoemaker any more, a stocky man with round eyeglasses and a bristling mustache, wearing a summer hat in wintertime.

When they tore up the counters and other fixtures and moved them out, when the store was empty except for the sink glowing in the rear, Sam would occasionally stand there at night, everyone on the block but him closed, peering into the window exuding darkness. Often while gazing through the dusty plate glass, which gave him back the image of a grocer gazing out, he felt as he had when he was a boy in Kamenets-Podolski and going—the three of them—to the river; they would, as they passed, swoop a frightened glance into a tall wooden house, eerily narrow, topped by a strange double-steepled roof, where there had once been a ghastly murder and now the place was haunted. Returning late, at times in early moonlight, they walked a distance away, speechless, listening to the ravenous silence of the house, room after room fallen into deeper stillness, and in the midmost a pit of churning quiet from which, if you thought about it, evil erupted. And so it seemed in the dark recesses of the empty store, where so many shoes had been leathered and hammered into life, and so many people had left something of themselves in the coming and going, that even in emptiness the store contained some memory of their presences, unspoken echoes in declining tiers, and that in a sense was what was so frightening. Afterwards when Sam went by the store, even in daylight he was afraid to look, and quickly walked past, as they had the haunted house when he was a boy.

But whenever he shut his eyes the empty store was stuck in his mind, a long black hole eternally revolving so that while he slept he was not asleep but within, revolving: what if it should happen to me? What if after twenty-seven years of toil (he should years ago have got out), what if after all of that, your own store, a place of business . . . after all the years, the years, the thousands of cans he had wiped off and packed away, the milk cases dragged in like rocks from the street before dawn in freeze or heat; insults, petty thievery, doling of credit to the impoverished by the poor; the peeling ceiling, fly-specked shelves, puffed cans, dirt, swollen veins, the back-breaking sixteen-hour day like a heavy hand slapping, upon awaking, the skull, pushing the head down to bend the body's bones; the hours; the work, the years, my God, and where is my life now? Who will save me now, and where will I go, where? Often he had thought these thoughts, subdued after months; and the garish FOR RENT sign had yellowed and fallen in the window so how could anyone know the place was to let? But they did. Today when he had all but laid the ghost of fear, a streamer in red cracked him across the eyes: National Grocery Will Open Another of Its Bargain Price Stores On These Premises, and the woe went into him and his heart bled.

At last Sam raised his head and told her, "I will go to the landlord next door."

Sura looked at him through puffy eyelids. "So what will you say?"

"I will talk to him."

Ordinarily she would have said, "Sam, don't be a fool," but she let him go.

Averting his head from the glare of the new red sign in the window, he entered the hall next door. As he labored up the steps the bleak light of the skylight fell on him and grew heavier as he ascended. He went unwillingly, not knowing what he would say to the landlord. Reaching the top floor, he paused before the door at the jabbering in Italian of a woman bewailing her fate. Sam already had one foot on the top stair, ready to descend, when he heard the coffee advertisement and realized it had been a radio play. Now the radio was off, the hallway oppressively silent. He listened and at first heard no voices inside, so he knocked without allowing himself to think any more. He was a little frightened and lived in suspense until the slow heavy steps of the landlord, who was also the barber across the street, reached the door, and it was—after some impatient fumbling with the lock—opened.

When the barber saw Sam in the hall he was disturbed, and Sam at once knew why he had not been in the grocery store even once in the past two weeks. However, the barber, becoming cordial, invited Sam to step into the kitchen where his wife and a stranger were seated at the table eating from piled-high plates of spaghetti.

"Thanks," said Sam shyly. "I just ate."

The barber came out into the hall, shutting the door behind

him. He glanced vaguely down the stairway and turned to Sam. His movements were unresolved. Since the death of his son in the war he had become absentminded; and sometimes when he walked one had the impression he was dragging something.

"Is it true?" Sam asked in embarrassment, "What it says downstairs on the sign?"

"Sam," the barber began heavily. He stopped to wipe his mouth with a paper napkin he held in his hand and said, "Sam, you know this store I had no rent for it for seven months?"

"I know."

"I can't afford. I was waiting for maybe a liquor store or a hardware, but I don't have no offers from them. Last month this chain store make me an offer and then I wait five weeks for something else. I had to take it, I couldn't help myself."

Shadows thickened in the darkness. In a sense Pellegrino was present, standing with them at the top of the stairs.

"When will they move in?" Sam sighed.

"Not till May."

The grocer was too faint to say anything. They stared at each other, not knowing what to suggest. But the barber forced a laugh and said the chain store wouldn't hurt Sam's business.

"Why not?"

"Because you carry different brands of goods and when the customers want those brands they go to you."

"Why should they go to me if my prices are higher?"

"A chain store brings more customers and they might like things that you got."

Sam felt ashamed. He did not doubt the barber's sincerity, but his stock was meager and he could not imagine chain store customers interested in what he had to sell.

Holding Sam by the arm, the barber told him in confidential tones of a friend who had a meat store next to an A & P supermarket and was making out very well.

Sam tried hard to believe he would make out well but couldn't.

"So did you sign with them the lease yet?" he asked.

"Friday," said the barber.

"Friday?" Sam had a wild hope. "Maybe," he said, trying to hold it down, "maybe I could find you, before Friday, a new tenant?"

"What kind of a tenant?"

"A tenant," Sam said.

"What kind of store is he interested?"

Sam tried to think. "A shoe store," he said.

"Shoemaker?"

"No, a shoe store where they sell shoes."

The barber pondered it. At last he said if Sam could get a tenant he wouldn't sign the lease with the chain store.

As Sam descended the stairs the light from the top-floor bulb diminished on his shoulders but not the heaviness, for he had no one in mind to take the store.

However, before Friday he thought of two people. One was the red-haired salesman for a wholesale grocery jobber, who had lately been recounting his investments in new stores; but when Sam spoke to him on the phone he said he was only interested in high-income grocery stores, which was no solution to the problem. The other man he hesitated to call, because he didn't like him. That was I. Kaufman, a former dry-goods merchant, with a wart under his left eyebrow. Kaufman had made some fortunate real estate deals and had become quite wealthy. Years ago he and Sam had stores next to one another on Marcy Avenue in Williamsburg. Sam took him for a lout and was not above saying so, for which Sura often ridiculed him, seeing how Kaufman had prospered, and where Sam was. Yet they stayed on comparatively good terms, perhaps because the grocer never asked for favors. When Kaufman happened to be around in the Buick, he usually dropped in, which Sam increasingly disliked, for Kaufman gave advice without stint and Sura sandpapered it in when he had left.

Despite qualms he telephoned him. Kaufman was pontifically surprised and said yes he would see what he could do. On Friday morning the barber took the red sign out of the window so as not to prejudice a possible deal. When Kaufman marched in with his cane that forenoon, Sam, who for once, at Sura's request, had dispensed with his apron, explained to him they had thought of the empty store next door as perfect for a shoe store because the neighborhood had none and the rent was reasonable. And since Kaufman was always investing in one project or another they thought he might be interested in this. The barber came over from across the street and unlocked the door. Kaufman clomped into the empty store, appraised the structure of the place, tested the floor, peered through the barred window into the back yard, and squinting, totaled with moving lips how much shelving was necessary and at what cost. Then he asked the barber how much rent and the barber named a modest figure.

Kaufman nodded sagely and said nothing to either of them there, but in the grocery store he vehemently berated Sam for wasting his time.

"I didn't want to make you ashamed in front of the goy," he said in anger, even his wart red, "but who do you think, if he is in his right mind, will open a shoe store in this stinky neighborhood?"

Before departing, he gave good advice the way a tube bloops toothpaste, and ended by saying to Sam, "If a chain store grocery comes in you're finished. Get out of here before the birds pick the meat out of your bones."

Then he drove off in his Buick. Sura was about to begin a commentary, but Sam pounded his fist on the table and that ended it. That evening the barber pasted the red sign back on the window, for he had signed the lease.

Lying awake nights, Sam knew what was going on inside the store, though he never went near it. He could see carpenters sawing the sweet-smelling pine that willingly yielded to the sharp blade and became in tiers the shelves rising almost to the ceiling. The painters arrived, a long man and a short one he was positive he knew, their faces covered with paint drops. They thickly calcimined the ceiling and painted everything in bright colors, impractical for a grocery but pleasing to the eye. Electricians appeared with fluorescent lamps which obliterated the yellow darkness of globed bulbs; and then the fixture men hauled down from their vans the long marble-top counters and gleaming enameled three-windowed refrigerator, for cooking, medium, and best butter; and a case for frozen foods, creamy white, the latest thing. As he was admiring it all, he turned to see if anyone was watching him, and when he had reassured himself, and turned again to look through the window, it had been whitened so he could see nothing more. He had to get up then to smoke a cigarette and was tempted to put on his pants and go in slippers quietly down the stairs to see if the window was really soaped up. That it might be kept him there, so he returned to bed, and being still unable to sleep he worked until he had polished, with a bit of rag, a small hole in the center of the white window, and enlarged that till he could make out everything clearly. The store was assembled now, spic-and-span, roomy, ready to receive the goods; it was a pleasure to come in. He whispered to himself this would be good if it was mine, but then the alarm banged in his ear and he had to get up and drag in the milk cases. At 8 a.m. three enormous trucks rolled down the block and six young men in white duck jackets jumped off and packed the store in seven hours. All day Sam's heart beat so hard he sometimes fondled it with his hand as though trying to calm a bird that wanted to fly off.

When the chain store opened in the middle of May, with a horseshoe wreath of roses in the window, Sura counted up that night and proclaimed they were ten dollars short; which wasn't so bad, Sam said, till she reminded him ten times six was sixty. She openly wept, sobbing they must do *something*, driving Sam to a thorough wiping of the shelves with wet cloths she handed him, oiling the floor, and washing, inside and out, the front window, which she redecorated with white tissue paper from the five-and-ten. Then she told him to call the wholesaler, who read off this week's specials; and when they were delivered, Sam packed three cases of cans in a towering pyramid in the window. Only no one seemed to buy. They were fifty dollars short the next week and Sam thought, if it stays like this we can exist, and he cut the price of beer, lettering with black crayon on wrapping paper a sign for the window that beer was reduced in price, thus selling fully five cases more that day, though Sura nagged what was the good of it if they made no profit—lost on paper bags—and the customers who came in for beer went next door for bread and canned goods? Yet Sam still hoped, but the next week they were seventy-two behind, and in two weeks a clean hundred. The chain store, with a manager and two clerks, was busy all day, but with Sam there was never, any more, anything resembling a rush. Then he discovered that they carried, next door, every brand he had and many he hadn't, and he felt for the barber a furious anger.

That summer, usually better for his business, was bad, and the fall was worse. The store was so silent it got to be a piercing pleasure when someone opened the door. They sat long hours under the unshaded bulb in the rear, reading and rereading the newspaper, and looking up hopefully when anyone passed by in the street, though trying not to look when they could tell he was going next door. Sam now kept open an hour longer, till midnight, although that wearied him greatly, but he was able, during the extra hour, to pick up a dollar or two among the housewives who had run out of milk, or needed a last-minute loaf of bread for school sandwiches. To cut expenses he put out one of the two lights in the window and a lamp in the store. He had the phone removed, bought his paper bags from peddlers, shaved every second day and, although he would not admit it, ate less. Then in an unexpected burst of optimism he ordered eighteen cases of goods from the jobber and filled the empty sections of his shelves with low-priced items clearly marked, but as Sura said, who saw them if nobody came in? People he had seen every day for ten, fifteen, even twenty years disappeared as if they had moved or died. Sometimes when he was delivering a small order somewhere he saw a former customer who either quickly crossed the street, or ducked the other way and walked around the block. The barber, too, avoided him and he avoided the barber. Sam schemed to give short weight on loose items but couldn't bring himself to. He considered canvassing the neighborhood from house to house for orders he would personally deliver but then remembered Mr. Pellegrino and gave up the idea. Sura, who had all their married life nagged him, now sat silent in the back. When Sam counted the receipts for the first week in December he knew he could no longer hope. The wind blew outside and the store was cold. He offered it for sale but no one would take it.

One morning Sura got up and slowly ripped her cheeks with her fingernails. Sam went across the street for a haircut. He had formerly had his hair cut once a month, but now it had grown ten weeks and was thickly pelted at the back of the neck. The barber cut it with his eyes shut. Then Sam called an auctioneer, who moved in with two lively assistants and a red auction flag that flapped and furled in the icy breeze as though it were a holiday. The money they got was not a quarter of the sum needed to pay the creditors. Sam and Sura closed the store and moved away. So long as he lived he would not return to the old neighborhood, afraid his store was standing empty, and he dreaded to look through the window.

Man in the Drawer

A SOFT SHALOM I thought I heard but considering the Slavic cast of the driver's face it seemed unlikely. He had been eyeing me in his rearview mirror since I had stepped into the taxi and, to tell the truth, I had momentary apprehensions. I'm forty-seven and have recently lost weight but not, I confess, nervousness. It's my American clothes, I thought at first. One is a recognizable stranger. Unless he had been tailing me to begin with, but how could that be if it was a passing cab I had hailed myself?

The taxi driver sat in his shirt sleeves on a cool June day, not more than 50° Fahrenheit. He was a man in his thirties who looked as if what he ate didn't fully feed him—in afterthought a discontented type, his face on the tired side, not bad-looking—now that I'd studied him a little, though the head seemed pressed a bit flat by somebody's heavy hand even though protected by a mat of healthy hair. His face, as I said, veered toward Slavic: broad cheekbones, small firm chin, but he sported a longish nose and a distinctive larynx on a slender hairy neck; a mixed type, it appeared. At any rate, the shalom had seemed to alter his appearance, even the probing eyes. He was dissatisfied for certain this fine June day—his job, fate, appearance—whatever. And a sort of indigenous sadness hung on or around him, coming God knows from where; nor did he seem to mind if who he was, was immediately apparent; not everybody could do that or wanted to. This one showed himself as is. Not too prosperous, I would say, yet no underground man. He sat firm in his seat, all of him driving, a touch frantically. I have an experienced eye for details.

"Israeli?" he asked in a whisper.

"Amerikansky." I know no Russian, just a few polite words.

He dug into his shirt pocket for a thin pack of cigarettes and swung his arm over the seat, the Volga swerving to avoid a truck making a turn.

"Take care!"

I was thrown sideways—no apologies. Extracting a Bulgarian cigarette I wasn't eager to smoke—too strong—I handed him his pack. I was considering offering my prosperous American cigarettes in return but didn't want to affront him.

"Feliks Levitansky," he said. "How do you do? I am taxi driver." His accent was strong, verging on fruity, but redeemed by fluency of tongue.

"Ah, you speak English? I sort of thought so."

"My profession is translator—English, French." He shrugged sideways.

"Howard Harvitz is my name. I'm here for a short vacation, about three weeks. My wife died not so long ago, and I'm traveling partly to relieve my mind."

My voice caught, but then I went on to say that if I could manage to dig up some material for a magazine article or two, so much the better.

In sympathy Levitansky raised both hands from the wheel.

"Watch out, for God's sake!"

"Horovitz?" he asked.

I spelled it for him. "Frankly, it was Harris after I entered college but I changed it back recently. My father had it legally done after I graduated from high school. He was a doctor, a practical sort."

"You don't look to me Jewish."

"If not why did you say shalom?"

"Sometimes you say." After a minute he asked, "For which reason?"

"For which reason what?"

"Why you changed back your name?"

"I had a crisis in my life."

"Existential? Economic?"

"To tell the truth I changed it back after my wife died."

"What is the significance?"

"The significance is I am closer to myself."

The driver popped a match with his thumbnail and lit his cigarette.

"I am marginal Jew," he said, "although my father—Avrahm Isaakovich Levitansky—was Jewish. Because my mother was gentile woman I was given choice, but she insisted me to register for internal passport with notation of Jewish nationality in respect for my father. I did so."

"You don't say!"

"My father died in my childhood. I was rised—raised?—to respect Jewish people and religion, but I went my own way. I am atheist. This is almost inevitable."

"You mean Soviet life?"

Levitansky smoked without replying as I grew embarrassed by my question. I looked around to see if I knew where we were. In afterthought he asked, "To which destination?"

I said, still on the former subject, that I had been not much a Jew myself. "My mother and father were totally assimilated."

"By their choice?"

"Of course by their choice."

"Do you wish," he then asked, "to visit Central Synagogue on Arkhipova Street? Very interesting experience."

"Not just now," I said, "but take me to the Chekhov Museum on Sadovaya Kudrinskaya."

At that the driver, sighing, seemed to take heart.

: : :

Rose, I said to myself.

I blew my nose. After her death I had planned to visit the Soviet Union but couldn't get myself to move. I'm a slow man after a blow, though I confess I've never been one for making his mind up in a hurry about important things. Eight months later, when I was more or less packing, I felt that some of the relief I was looking for derived, in addition to what was still on my mind, from the necessity of making an unexpected serious personal decision. Out of loneliness I had begun to see my former wife, Lillian, in the spring; and before long, since she had remained unmarried and attractive, to my surprise there was some hesitant talk of remarriage; these things slip from one sentence to another before you know it. If we did get married we could turn the Russian trip into a sort of honeymoon—I won't say second because we hadn't had much of a first. In the end, since our lives had been so frankly complicated—hard on each other—I found it hard to make up my mind, though Lillian, I give her credit, seemed to be willing to take the chance. My feelings were so difficult to assess I decided to decide nothing for sure. Lillian, who is a forthright type with a mind like a lawyer's, asked me if I was cooling to the idea, and I told her that since the death of my wife I had been examining my life and needed more time to see where I stood. "Still?" she said, meaning the self-searching, and implying forever. All I could answer was "Still," and then in anger, "Forever." I warned myself: Beware of further complicated entanglements.

Well, that almost killed it. It wasn't a particularly happy evening, though it had its moments. I had once been very much in love with Lillian. I figured then that a change of scene for me, maybe a month abroad, might be helpful. I had for a long time wanted to visit the U.S.S.R., and taking the time to be alone and, I hoped, at ease to think things through, might give the trip additional value.

So I was surprised, once my visa was granted—though not too surprised—that my anticipation was by now blunted and I was experiencing some uneasiness. I blamed it on a dread of traveling that sometimes hits me before I move. Will I get there? Will the plane be hijacked? Maybe a war breaks out and I'm surrounded by artillery. To be frank, though I've resisted the idea, I consider myself an anxious man, which, when I try to explain it to myself, means being this minute halfway into the next. I sit still in a hurry, worry uselessly about the future, and carry the burden of an overripe conscience.

I realized that what troubled me most about going into Soviet Russia were those stories in the papers of some tourist or casual traveler in this or that Soviet city who is, without warning, grabbed by the secret police on charges of "spying," "illegal economic activity," "hooliganism," or whatnot. This poor guy, like somebody from Sudbury, Mass., is held incommunicado until he confesses, and is then sentenced to a prison camp in the wilds of Siberia. After I got my visa I sometimes had fantasies of a stranger shoving a fat envelope of papers into my hand, and then arresting me as I was stupidly reading them—of course for spying. What would I do in that case? I think I would pitch the envelope into the street, shouting, "Don't pull that one on me, I can't read Russian," and walk away with whatever dignity I had, hoping that would freeze them in their tracks. A man in danger, if he's walking away from it, seems indifferent, innocent. At least to himself; then in my mind I hear footsteps coming after me, and since my reveries tend to be rational, two husky KGB men grab me, shove my arms up my back, and make the arrest. Not for littering the streets, as I hope might be the case, but for "attempting to dispose of certain incriminating documents," a fact it's hard to deny.

I see H. Harvitz yelling, squirming, kicking right and left, till his mouth is shut by somebody's stinking palm and he is dragged by force—not to mention a blackjack whack on the skull—into the inevitable black Zis I've read about and see on movie screens.

The cold war is a frightening business. I've sometimes wished spying had reached such a pitch of perfection that both the U.S.S.R. and the U.S.A. knew everything there is to know about the other, and having sensibly exchanged this information by trading computers that keep facts up to date, let each other alone thereafter. That ruins the spying business; there's that much more sanity in the world, and for a man like me the thought of a trip to the Soviet Union is pure pleasure.

Right away at the Kiev airport I had a sort of scare, after flying in from Paris on a mid-June afternoon. A customs official confiscated from my suitcase five copies of *Visible Secrets*, a poetry anthology for high school students I had edited some years ago, which I had brought along to give away to Russians I met who might be interested in American poetry. I was asked to sign a document the official had written out in Cyrillic, except that *Visible Secrets* was printed in English, "secrets" underlined. The uniformed customs officer, a heavyset man with a layer of limp hair on a smallish head, red stars on his shoulders, said that the paper I was required to sign stated I understood it was not permitted to bring five copies of a foreign book into the Soviet Union; but I would get my property back at the Moscow airport when I left the country. I worried that I oughtn't to sign but was urged to by my Intourist guide, a bleached blonde with wobbly heels whose looks and good humor kept me calm, though my clothes were frankly steaming. She said it was a matter of no great consequence and advised me to write my signature quickly, because it was delaying our departure to the Dniepro Hotel.

At that point I asked what would happen if I parted with the books, no longer claimed them as my property. The Intouristka inquired of the customs man, who answered calmly, earnestly, and at great length.

"He says," she said, "that the Soviet Union will not take away from a foreign visitor his legal property."

Since I had only four days in the city and time was going faster than usual, I reluctantly signed the paper plus four carbons —one for each book—or five mysterious government departments?—and was given a copy which I filed in my billfold.

Despite this incident—it had its comic quality—my stay in Kiev, in spite of the loneliness I usually experience my first few days in a strange city, went quickly and interestingly. In the mornings I was driven around in a private car on guided tours of the hilly, broad-avenued, green-leaved city, whose colors were reminiscent of a subdued Rome. But in the afternoons I wandered around alone. I would start by taking a bus or streetcar, riding a few kilometers, then getting off to walk in this or that neighborhood. Once I strayed into a peasants' market where collective farmers and country folk in beards and boots out of a nineteenth-century Russian novel sold their produce to city people. I thought I must write about this to Rose—I meant of course Lillian. Another time, in a deserted street when I happened to think of the customs receipt in my billfold, I turned in my tracks to see if I was being followed. I wasn't but enjoyed the adventure.

An experience I liked less was getting lost one late afternoon several kilometers above a boathouse on the Dnieper. I was walking along the riverbank liking the boats and island beaches and, before I knew it, had come a good distance from the hotel and was eager to get back because I was hungry. I didn't feel like retracing my route on foot—much too much tourism in three days—so I thought of a cab, and since none was around, maybe an autobus that might be going in the general direction I had come from. I tried approaching a few passers-by whom I addressed in English or pidgin-German, and occasionally trying "Pardonnez-moi"; but the effect was apparently to embarrass them. One young woman ran a few awkward steps from me before she began to walk again.

Though frustrated, irritated, I spoke to two men passing by, one of whom, the minute he heard my first few words, walked on quickly, his eyes aimed straight ahead, the other indicating by gestures he was deaf and dumb. On impulse I tried him in halting Yiddish that my grandfather had taught me when I was a child, and was then directed, in an undertone in the same language, to a nearby bus stop.

As I was unlocking the door to my room, thinking this was a story I would be telling friends all winter, my phone was ringing. It was a woman's voice. I understood "Gospodin Garvitz" and one or two other words as she spoke at length in musical Russian. Her voice had the lilt of a singer's. Though I couldn't get the gist of her remarks, I had this sudden vivid reverie, you might call it, of me walking with a pretty Russian girl in a white birchwood near Yasnaya Polyana, and coming out of the trees, sincerely talking, into a meadow that sloped to the water; then rowing her around in a small lovely lake. It was a peaceful business. I even had thoughts: wouldn't it be something if I got myself engaged to a Russian girl? That was the general picture, but when the caller was done talking, whatever I had to say I said in English and she slowly hung up.

After breakfast the next morning, she, or somebody who sounded like her—I was aware of the contralto quality—called again.

"If you understand English," I said, "or maybe a little German or French—even Yiddish if you happen to know it—we'd get along fine. But not in Russian, I'm sorry to say. Nyet Russki. I'd be glad to meet you for lunch or whatever you like; so if you get the drift of my remarks why don't you say da? Then dial the English interpreter on extension 37. She could explain to me what's what and we can meet at your convenience."

I had the impression she was listening with both ears, but after a while the phone hung silent in my hand. I wondered where she had got my name, and was someone testing me to find out whether I did or didn't speak Russian. I honestly did not.

Afterwards I wrote a short letter to Lillian, telling her I would be leaving for Moscow via Aeroflot, tomorrow at 4 p.m., and I intended to stay there for two weeks, with a break of maybe three or four days in Leningrad, at the Astoria Hotel. I wrote down the exact dates and later airmailed the letter in a street box some distance from the hotel, whatever good that did. I hoped Lillian would get it in time to reach me by return mail before I left the Soviet Union. To tell the truth I was uneasy all day.

But by the next morning my mood had shifted, and as I was standing at the railing in a park above the Dnieper, looking at the buildings going up across the river in what had once been steppeland, I experienced a curious sense of relief. The vast construction I beheld—it was as though two or three scattered small cities were rising out of the earth—astonished me. This sort of thing was going on all over Russia—halfway around the world— and when I considered what it meant in terms of sheer labor, capital goods, plain morale, I was then and there convinced that the Soviet Union would never willingly provoke a war, nuclear or otherwise, with the United States. Neither would America, in its right mind, with the Soviet Union.

For the first time since I had come to Russia I felt secure and safe, and I enjoyed there, at the breezy railing above the Dnieper, a rare few minutes of euphoria.

:   :   :

Why is it that the most interesting architecture is from Czarist times? I asked myself, and if I'm not mistaken Levitansky quivered, no doubt coincidental. Unless I had spoken aloud to myself, which I sometimes do; I decided I hadn't. We were on our way to the museum, hitting a fast eighty kilometers, because traffic was sparse.

"What do you think of my country, the Union of Soviet Socialist Republics?" the driver inquired, turning his head to see where I was.

"I would appreciate it if you kept your eyes on the road."

"Don't be nervous, I drive now for years."

Then I answered that I was impressed by much I had seen. Obviously it was a great country.

Levitansky's round face appeared in the mirror smiling pleasantly, his teeth eroded. The smile seemed to have come from within the mouth. Now that he had revealed his half-Jewish antecedents I had the impression he looked more Jewish than Slavic, and more dissatisfied than I had previously thought. That I got from the restless eyes.

"Also our system—Communism?"

I answered carefully, not wanting to give offense. "I'll be honest with you. I've seen some unusual things—even inspiring— but my personal taste is for a lot more individual freedom than people seem to have here. America has its serious faults, God knows, but at least we're privileged to criticize—if you know what I mean. My father used to say, 'You can't beat the Bill of Rights.' It's an open society, which means freedom of choice, at least in theory."

"Communism is altogether better political system," Levitansky replied candidly, "although it is not in present stage totally realized. In present stage"—he swallowed, reflected, did not finish the thought. Instead he said, "Our Revolution was magnificent and holy event. I love early Soviet history, excitement of

Communist idealism, and magnificent victory over bourgeois and imperialist forces. Overnight was lifted up—uplifted—the whole suffering masses. Pasternak called this 'splendid surgery.' Evgeny Zamyatin—maybe you know his books?—spoke thus: 'The Revolution consumes the earth with fire, but then is born a new life.' Many of our poets said similar things."

I didn't argue, each to his own revolution.

"You told before," said Levitansky, glancing at me again in the mirror, "that you wish to write articles about your visit. Political or not political?"

"What I have in mind is something on the literary museums of Moscow for an American travel magazine. That's the sort of thing I do. I'm a free-lance writer." I laughed apologetically. It's strange how stresses shift when you're in another country.

Levitansky politely joined in the laugh, stopping in midcourse. "I wish to be certain, what is free-lance writer?"

I told him. "I also edit a bit. I've done anthologies of poetry and essays, both for high school kids."

"We have here free-lance. I am writer also," Levitansky said solemnly.

"You don't say? You mean as translator?"

"Translation is my profession but I am also original writer."

"Then you do three things to earn a living—write, translate, and drive this cab?"

"The taxi is not my true work."

"Are you translating anything in particular now?"

The driver cleared his throat. "In present time I have no translation project."

"What sort of thing do you write?"

"I write stories."

"Is that so? What kind, if I might ask?"

"I will tell you what kind—little ones—short stories, imagined from life."

"Have you published any?"

He seemed about to turn around to look me in the eye but reached instead into his shirt pocket. I offered my American pack. He shook out a cigarette and lit it, exhaling slowly.

"A few pieces although not recently. To tell the truth"—he sighed—"I write presently for the drawer. You know this expression? Like Isaac Babel, 'I am master of the genre of silence.'"

"I've heard it," I said, not knowing what else to say.

"The mice should read and criticize," Levitansky said bitterly. "This what they don't eat and make their drops—droppings— on. It is perfect criticism."

"I'm sorry about that."

"We arrive now to Chekhov Museum."

I leaned forward to pay him and made the impulsive mistake of adding a one-ruble tip. His face flared. "I am Soviet citizen." He forcibly returned the ruble.

"Call it a thoughtless error," I apologized. "No harm meant."

"Hiroshima! Nagasaki!" he taunted as the Volga took off in a burst of smoke. "Aggressor against the suffering poor people of Vietnam!"

"That's none of my doing," I called after him.

:   :   :

An hour and a half later, after I had signed the guest book and was leaving the museum, I saw a man standing, smoking, under a linden tree across the street. Nearby was a parked taxi. We stared at each other—I wasn't certain at first who it was, but Levitansky nodded amiably to me, calling "Welcome! Welcome!" He waved an arm, smiling open-mouthed. He had combed his thick hair and was wearing a loose dark suit coat over a tieless white shirt, and baggy pants. His socks, striped red-white-and-blue, you could see through his sandals.

I am forgiven, I thought. "Welcome to you," I said, crossing the street.

"How did you enjoy Chekhov Museum?"

"I did indeed. I've made a lot of notes. You know what they have there? They have one of his black fedoras, also his pince-nez that you see in pictures of him. Awfully moving."

Levitansky wiped an eye—to my surprise. He seemed not quite the same man, modified. It's funny, you hear a few personal facts from a stranger and he changes as he speaks. The taxi driver is now a writer, even if part-time. Anyway, that's my dominant impression.

"Excuse me my former anger," Levitansky explained. "Now is not for me the best of times. 'It was the best of times, it was the worst of times,' " he said, smiling sadly.

"So long as you pardon my unintentional blunder. Are you perhaps free to drive me to the Metropole, or are you here by coincidence?"

I looked around to see if anyone was coming out of the museum.

"If you wish to engage me I will drive you, but at first I wish to show you something—how do you say?—of interest."

He reached through the open front window of the taxi and brought forth a flat package wrapped in brown paper tied with red string.

"Stories which I wrote."

"I don't read Russian," I said.

"My wife has translated some of them. She is not by her profession a translator, although her English is advanced and sensitive. She had been for two years in England for Soviet Purchasing Commission. We became acquainted in university. I prefer not to translate my stories because I do not translate so well Russian into English, although I do it beautifully the opposite. Also I will not force myself—it is like self-imitation. Perhaps the stories appear a little awkward in English—also my wife admits this—but you can read and form opinion."

Though he offered the package hesitantly, he offered it as if it was a bouquet of spring flowers. Can it be some sort of trick? I asked myself. Are they testing me because I signed that damned document in the Kiev airport, five copies no less?

Levitansky seemed to know my thought. "It is purely stories."

He bit the string in two, and laying the package on the fender of the Volga, unpeeled the wrapping. There were the stories, clipped separately, typed on long sheets of thin blue paper. I took one Levitansky handed me and scanned the top page—it seemed a story—then I flipped through the other pages and handed the manuscript back. "I'm not much a critic of stories."

"I don't seek critic. I seek for reader with literary experience and taste. If you have redacted books of poems and also essays, you will be able to judge literary quality of my stories. Please, I request you will read them."

After a long minute I heard myself say, "Well, I might at that." I didn't recognize the voice and wasn't sure why I had said what I had. You might say I spoke apart from myself, with reluctance that either he wasn't aware of or chose to ignore.

"If you respect—if you approve my stories, perhaps you will be able to arrange for publication in Paris or either London?" His larynx wobbled.

I stared at the man. "I don't happen to be going to Paris, and I'll be in London only between planes to the U.S.A."

"In this event, perhaps you will show to your publisher, and he will publish my work in America?" Levitansky was now visibly uneasy.

"In America?" I said, raising my voice in disbelief.

For the first time he gazed around before replying.

"If you will be so kind to show them to publisher of your books—he is reliable publisher?—perhaps he will wish to bring out volume of my stories? I will make contract whatever he will like. Money, if I could get, is not an idea."

"Whatever volume are you talking about?"

He said that from thirty stories he had written he had chosen eighteen, of which these were a sample. "Unfortunately more are not now translated. My wife is biochemist assistant and works long hours in laboratory. I am sure your publisher will enjoy to read these. It will depend on your opinion."

Either this man has a fantastic imagination, or he's out of his right mind. "I wouldn't want to get myself involved in smuggling a Russian manuscript out of Russia."

"I have informed you that my manuscript is of made-up stories."

"That may be but it's still a chancy enterprise. I'd be taking chances I have no desire to take, to be frank."

"At least if you will read," he sighed.

I took the stories again and thumbed slowly through each. What I was looking for I couldn't say: maybe a booby trap? Should I or shouldn't I? Why should I?

He handed me the wrapping paper and I rolled up the stories in it. The quicker I read them, the quicker I've read them. I stepped into the cab.

"As I said, I'm at the Metropole. Come by tonight about nine o'clock and I'll give you my opinion for what it's worth. But I'm afraid I'll have to limit it to that, Mr. Levitansky, without further obligation or expectations, or it's no deal. My room number is 538."

"Tonight?—so soon?" he said, scratching both palms. "You must read with care so you will realize the art."

"Tomorrow night, then, same time. I'd rather not have them in my room longer than that."

Levitansky agreed. Whistling through eroded teeth, he drove me carefully to the Metropole.

:　　　:　　　:

That night, sipping vodka from a drinking glass, I read Levitansky's stories. They were simply and strongly written—I had almost expected it—and not badly translated; in fact the translation read much better than I had been led to think, although there were of course some gaffes—odd constructions, illfitting stiff words, some indicated by question marks and taken, I suppose, from a thesaurus. And the stories, short tales dealing—somewhat to my surprise—mostly with Moscow Jews, were good, artistically done, really moving. The situations they revealed weren't exactly news to me: I'm a careful reader of the *Times*. But the stories weren't written to complain. What they had to say was achieved as form, no telling the dancer from the dance. I poured myself another glass of the potato potion—I was beginning to feel high, occasionally wondering why I was putting so much away—relaxing, I guess. I then reread the stories with admiration for Levitansky. I had the feeling he was no ordinary man. I felt excited, then depressed, as if I had been let in on a secret I didn't want to know.

It's a hard life here for a fiction writer, I thought.

Afterwards, having the stories around made me uneasy. In one of them a Russian writer burns his stories in the kitchen sink. Obviously nobody had burned these. I thought to myself, if I'm caught with them in my possession, considering what they indicate about conditions here, there's no question I'll be up to my hips in trouble. I wish I had insisted that Levitansky come back for them tonight.

There was a solid rap on the door. I felt I had risen a few inches out of my chair. It was, after a while, only Levitansky.

"Out of the question," I said, thrusting the stories at him. "Absolutely out of the question!"

:   :   :

The next night we sat facing each other over glasses of cognac in the writer's small, book-crowded study. He was dignified, at first haughty, wounded, hardly masking his impatience. I wasn't myself exactly comfortable.

I had come out of courtesy and other considerations, I guess; principally a dissatisfaction I couldn't define.

Levitansky, the taxi driver rattling around in his Volga-Pegasus, amateur trying to palm off a half-ass ms., had faded in my mind, and I saw him now as a serious Soviet writer with publishing problems. There are many others. What can I do for him? I thought. Why should I?

"I didn't express what I really felt last night," I apologized. "You caught me by surprise, I'm sorry to say."

Levitansky was scratching each hand with the blunt fingers of the other. "How did you acquire my address?"

I reached into my pocket for a wad of folded brown wrapping paper. "It's on this—Novo Ostapovskaya Street, 488, Flat 59. I took a cab."

"I had forgotten this."

Maybe, I thought.

Still, I had practically had to put my foot in the door to get in. Levitansky's wife had answered my uncertain knock, her eyes immediately worried, an expression I took to be the one she lived with. The eyes, astonished to behold a stranger, became outright uneasy once I inquired in English for her husband. I felt, as in Kiev, that my native tongue had become my enemy.

"Have you not the wrong apartment?"

"I hope not. Not if Gospodin Levitansky lives here. I came to see him about his—ah—manuscript."

Her eyes darkened as her face paled. Ten seconds later I was in the flat, the door locked behind me.

"Levitansky!" she summoned him. It had a reluctant quality: Come but don't come.

He appeared in apparently the same shirt, pants, tricolor socks. There was at first pretend-boredom in a tense, tired face. He could not, however, conceal excitement, his lit eyes roving over my face.

"Oh ho," Levitansky said.

My God, I thought, has he been expecting me?

"I came to talk to you for a few minutes, if you don't mind," I said. "I want to say what I think of the stories you kindly let me read."

He curtly spoke in Russian to his wife and she snapped an answer back. "I wish to introduce my wife, Irina Filipovna Levitansky, biochemist. She is patient although not a saint."

She smiled tentatively, an attractive woman about twenty-eight, a little on the hefty side, in house slippers and plain dress. The edge of her slip hung below her skirt.

There was a touch of British in her accent. "I am pleased to be acquainted." If so one hardly noticed. She stepped into black pumps and slipped a bracelet on her wrist, a lit cigarette dangling from the corner of her mouth. Her legs and arms were shapely, her brown hair cut short. I had the impression of tight lips in a pale face.

"I will go to Kovalevsky, next door," she said.

"Not on my account, I hope? All I have to say—"

"Our neighbors in the next flat." Levitansky grimaced. "Also thin walls." He knocked a knuckle on a hollow wall.

I indicated my dismay.

"Please, not long," Irina said, "because I am afraid."

Surely not of me? Agent Howard Harvitz, C.I.A.—a comical thought.

Their small square living room wasn't unattractive but Levitansky signaled the study inside. He offered sweet cognac in whiskey tumblers, then sat facing me at the edge of his chair, repressed energy all but visible. I had the momentary sense his chair was about to move, fly off.

If it does he flies alone.

"What I came to say," I told him, "is that I like your stories and am sorry I didn't say so last night. I like the primary, close-to-the-bone quality of the writing. The stories impress me as strong if simply wrought; I appreciate your feeling for people and at the same time the objectivity with which you render them. It's sort of Chekhovian in quality, but more compressed, sinewy, direct, if you know what I mean. For instance, that story about the old father coming to see his son who ducks out on him. I can't comment on your style, having only read the stories in translation."

"Chekhovian," Levitansky admitted, smiling through his worn teeth, "is fine compliment. Mayakovsky, our early Soviet poet, described him 'the strong and gay artist of the world.' I wish it was possible for Levitansky to be so gay in life and art." He seemed to be staring at the drawn shade in the room, though maybe no place in particular, then said, perhaps heartening himself, "In Russian is magnificent my style—precise, economy, including wit. The style may be difficult to translate in English because is less rich language."

"I've heard that said. In fairness I should add I have some reservations about the stories, yet who hasn't on any given piece of imaginative work?"

"I have myself reservations."

The admission made, I skipped the criticism. I had been wondering about a picture on his bookcase and then asked who it was. "It's a face I've seen before. The eyes are poetic, you might say."

"So is the voice. This is picture of Boris Pasternak as young man. On the wall yonder is Mayakovsky. He was also remarkable poet, wild, joyful, neurasthenic, a lover of the Revolution. He spoke: 'This is *my* Revolution.' To him was it 'a holy washerwoman who cleaned off all the filth from the earth.' Unfortunately he was later disillusioned and also shot himself."

"I have read that."

"He wrote: 'I wish to be understood by my country—but if no, I will fly through Russia like a slanting rainstorm.' "

"Have you by chance read *Dr. Zhivago*?"

"I have read," the writer sighed, and then began to declaim in Russian—I guessed some lines from a poem.

"It is to Marina Tsvetayeva, Soviet poetess, good friend of Pasternak." Levitansky fiddled with the pack of cigarettes on the table. "The end of her life was unfortunate."

"Is there no picture of Osip Mandelstam?" I hesitated as I spoke the name.

He reacted as though he had just met me. "You know Mandelstam?"

"Just a few poems in an anthology."

"Our best poet—he is holy—gone with so many others. My wife does not hang his photograph."

"I guess why I really came," I said after a minute, "is I wanted to express my sympathy and respect."

Levitansky popped a match with his thumbnail. His hand trembled as he shook the flame out without lighting the cigarette.

Embarrassed for him, I pretended to be looking elsewhere. "It's a small room. Does your son sleep here?"

"Don't confuse my story of writer, which you have read, with life of author. My wife and I are married eight years, but without children."

"Might I ask whether the experience you describe in that same story—the interview with the editor—was true?"

"Not true although truth," the writer said impatiently. "I write from imagination. I am not interested to repeat contents of diaries or total memory."

"On that I go along."

"Also, which is not in story, I have submitted to Soviet journals sketches and tales many many times but only few have been published, although not my best. Some people, but only few, know my work through samizdat, which is passing from one to another the manuscript."

"Did you submit any of the Jewish stories?"

"Please, stories are stories, they have not nationality."

"I mean by that those about Jews."

"Some I have submitted but they were not accepted."

I said, "After reading the stories you gave me, I wondered how it is you write so well about Jews? You call yourself marginal —that was your word—yet you write with authority. Not that one can't, I suppose, but it's surprising when one does."

"Imagination makes authority. When I write about Jews comes out stories, so I write about Jews. Is not important that I am half-Jew. What is important is observation, feeling, also art. In the past I have observed my Jewish father. Also I study, sometimes, Jews in the synagogue. I sit on the bench for strangers. The gabbai watches me with dark eyes and I watch him. But whatever I write, whether is about Jews, Galicians, or Georgians, must be work of invention, or for me it does not live."

"I'm not much of a synagogue-goer myself," I told him, "but I like to drop in once in a while to be refreshed by the language and images of a time and place where God was. That may be strange because I had no religious education to speak of."

"I am atheist."

"I understand what you mean by imagination—as for instance that prayer-shawl story. But am I right"—I lowered my voice— "that you are saying something about the condition of Jews in this country?"

"I do not make propaganda," Levitansky said sternly. "I am not Israeli spokesman. I am Soviet artist."

"I didn't mean you weren't but there's a strong sympathy for Jews, and ideas are born in life. One senses an awareness of injustice."

"Whatever is the injustice, the product must be art."

"Well, I respect your philosophy."

"Please do not respect so much," the writer said irritably. "We have in this country a quotation: 'It is impossible to make out of apology a fur coat.' The idea is similar. I appreciate your respect but need now practical assistance.

"Listen at first to me," Levitansky went on, slapping the table with his palm. "I am in desperate situation. I have written for years but little is published. In the past, one, two editors who were friends told me, private, that my stories are excellent but I violate social realism. This what you call objectivity they called it excessive naturalism and sentiment. It is hard to listen to such nonsense. They advise me swim but not to use my legs. They have warned me; also they have made excuses for me which I do not like them. Even they say I am crazy, although I explained them I submit my stories *because* Soviet Union is great country. A great country does not fear what artist writes. A great country breathes into its lungs work of writers, painters, musicians, and becomes more strong. That I told to them but they replied I am not sufficient realist. This is the reason I am not invited to be member of Writers Union. Without this is impossible to publish." He smiled sourly. "They have demanded me to stop submitting to journals my work, so I have stopped."

"I'm sorry about that," I said. "I don't myself believe any good comes from exiling poets."

"I cannot continue any more in this fashion," Levitansky said, laying his hand on his heart. "I feel I am locked in drawer with my stories. Now I must get out or I suffocate. It becomes for me each day more difficult to write. It is not easy to request a stranger for such important personal favor. My wife advised me not. She is angry, also frightened, but it is impossible to go on in this way. I know in my bones I am important Soviet writer. I must have audience. I wish to see my books to be read by Soviet people. I wish to have in minds different than my own and my wife acknowledgment of my art. I wish them to know my work is related to Russian writers of the past as well as modern. I am in tradition of Chekhov, Gorky, Isaac Babel. I know if book of my stories will be published, it will make for me favorable reputation. This is reason why you must help me—it is necessary for my interior liberty."

His confession came in an agitated burst. I use the word advisedly because that's partly what upset me. I have never cared for confessions such as are meant to involve unwilling people in others' personal problems. Russians are past masters of the art—you can see it in their novels.

"I appreciate the honor of your request," I said, "but all I am is a passing tourist. That's a pretty tenuous relationship between us."

"I do not ask tourist—I ask human being—man," Levitansky said passionately. "Also you are free-lance writer. You know now what I am and what is on my heart. You sit in my house. Who else can I ask? I would prefer to publish in Europe my stories, maybe with Mondadori or Einaudi in Italy, but if this is impossible to you I will publish in America. Someday my work will be read in my own country, maybe after I am dead. This is terrible irony but my generation lives on such ironies. Since I am not now ambitious to die it will be great relief to me to know that at least in one language is alive my art. Mandelstam wrote: 'I will be enclosed in some alien speech.' Better so than nothing."

"You say I know who you are, but do you know who I am?" I asked him. "I'm a plain person, not very imaginative, though I don't write a bad article. My whole life, for some reason, has been without much real adventure, except I was divorced once and remarried happily to a woman whose death I am still mourning. Now I'm here more or less on a vacation, not to jeopardize myself by taking chances of an unknown sort. What's more—and this is the main thing I came to tell you—I wouldn't at all be surprised if I am already under suspicion and would do you more harm than good."

I told Levitansky about the airport incident in Kiev. "I signed a document I couldn't even read, which was a foolish thing to do."

"In Kiev this happened?"

"That's right."

He laughed dismally. "It would not happen to you if you entered through Moscow. In the Ukraine—what is your word?—they are rubes, country people."

"That might be—nevertheless I signed the paper."

"Do you have copy?"

"Not with me. In my desk drawer in the hotel."

"I am certain this is receipt for your books which officials will return to you when you depart from Soviet Union."

"That's what I'd be afraid of."

"Why afraid?" he asked. "Are you afraid to receive back umbrella which you have lost?"

"I'd be afraid one thing might lead to another—more questions, other searches. It would be stupid to have your manuscript in my suitcase, in Russian, no less, that I can't even read. Suppose they accuse me of being some kind of courier transferring stolen documents?"

The thought raised me to my feet. I realized the tension in the room was thick as steam, mostly mine.

Levitansky rose, embittered. "There is no question of spying. I do not think I have presented myself as traitor to my country."

"I didn't say anything of the sort. All I'm saying is I don't want to get into trouble with the Soviet authorities. Nobody can blame me for that. In other words the enterprise isn't for me."

"I have made at one time inquirings," Levitansky insisted. "You will have nothing to fear for tourist who has been a few weeks in U.S.S.R. under guidance of Intourist, and does not speak Russian. They sometimes ask questions to political people, also bourgeois journalists who have made bad impression. I would deliver to you the manuscript in the last instant. It is typed on less than one hundred fifty sheets thin paper and will make small package, weightless. If it should look to you like trouble, you can leave it in dustbin. My name will not be anywhere and if they find it and track—trace to me the stories, I will answer /I threw them out myself. They won't believe this, but what other can I say? It will make no difference anyway. If I stop my writing I may as well be dead. No harm will come to you."

"I'd rather not, if you don't mind."

With what I guess was a curse of despair, Levitansky reached for the portrait on his bookcase and flung it against the wall. Pasternak struck Mayakovsky, splattering him with glass, shattering himself, and both pictures crashed to the floor.

"Free-lance writer," he shouted, "go to hell to America! Tell to Negroes about Bill of Rights! Tell them they are free although you keep them slaves! Talk to sacrificed Vietnamese people that you respect them!"

Irina Filipovna entered the room on the run. "Feliks," she entreated, "Kovalevsky hears every word!

"Please," she begged me, "please go away. Leave poor Levitansky alone. I beg you from my miserable heart."

I left in a hurry. The next day I flew to Leningrad.

:   :   :

Three days later, after a tense visit to Leningrad, I was sitting loosely in a beat-up taxi with a cheerful Intouristka, a half hour after my arrival at the Moscow airport. We were driving to the Ukraine Hotel, where I was assigned for my remaining days in the Soviet Union. I would have preferred the Metropole again because it is so conveniently located and I was used to it, but on second thought, better some place where a certain party wouldn't know I lived. The Volga we were riding in seemed somehow familiar, but if so it was safely in the hands of a small stranger with a large wool cap, a man wearing sunglasses, who paid me no particular attention.

I had had a rather special several minutes in Leningrad on my first day. On a white summer's evening, shortly after I had unpacked in my room at the Astoria, I discovered the Winter Palace and Hermitage after a walk along Nevsky Prospekt. Chancing on Palace Square, vast, deserted at the moment, I felt an unexpected intense emotion thinking of the revolutionary events that had occurred on this spot. My God, I thought, why should I feel myself part of Russian history? It's a contagious business, what happens to men. On the Palace Bridge I gazed at the ice-blue Neva, in the distance the golden steeple of the cathedral built by Peter the Great gleaming under masses of wind-driven clouds in patches of green sky. It's the Soviet Union but it's still Russia.

The next day I woke up anxious. In the street I was approached twice by strangers speaking English; I think my suede shoes attracted them. The first, tight-eyed and badly dressed, wanted to sell me blackmarket rubles. "Nyet," I said, tipping my straw hat and hurrying on. The second, a tall, bearded boy of about nineteen, with a left-sided tuft longer than the right, wearing a home-knitted green pullover, offered to buy jazz records, "youth clothes," and American cigarettes. "Sorry, nothing for sale." I escaped him too, except that green sweater followed me for a kilometer along one of the canals. I broke into a run. When I looked back he had disappeared. I slept badly—it stayed light too long past midnight; and in the morning inquired about the possibility of an immediate flight to Helsinki. I was informed I couldn't book one for a week. I decided to return to Moscow a day before I had planned to, mostly to see what they had in the Dostoevsky Museum.

I had been thinking about Levitansky. How much of a writer was he really? I had read three of eighteen stories he wanted to publish. Suppose he had showed me the best and the others were mediocre or thereabouts? Was it worth taking a chance for that kind of book? I thought, the best thing for my peace of mind is to forget the guy. Before checking out of the Astoria I received a chatty letter from Lillian, forwarded from Moscow, apparently not in response to my recent one to her but written earlier. Should I marry her? Did I dare? The phone rang piercingly, but when I picked up the receiver no one answered. On the plane to Moscow I had visions of a crash; there must be many nobody ever reads of.

:   :   :

In my room on the twelfth floor of the Ukraine I relaxed in a green plastic-covered armchair. There was also a single low bed and a utilitarian pinewood desk, an apple-green telephone plunked on it for instant use. I'll be home in a week, I thought. Now I'd better shave and see if anything is left in the way of a concert or opera ticket for tonight. I'm in a mood for music.

The electric plug in the bathroom didn't work, so I put away my shaver and was lathering up when I jumped to a single explosive knock on the door. I opened it slowly and there stood Levitansky with a brown paper packet in his hand.

Is this son of a bitch out to compromise me?

"How did you happen to find out where I was only twenty minutes after I got back, Mr. Levitansky?"

"How I found you?" the writer shrugged. He seemed deathly tired, the face longer, leaner, resembling a hungry fox on his last unsteady legs, but still in business.

"My brother-in-law was chauffeur for you from the airport. He heard the girl inquire your name. We have spoke of you. Dmitri—this is my wife's brother—informed me you have registered at the Ukraine. I inquired downstairs your room number and it was granted to me."

"However it happened," I said firmly, "I want you to know I

haven't changed my mind. I don't want to get more involved. I thought it all through while I was in Leningrad and that's my decision."

"I may come in?"

"Please, but for obvious reasons I'd appreciate a short visit."

Levitansky sat, thin knees pressed together in the armchair, his parcel awkwardly on his lap. If he was happy he had found me, it did nothing for his expression.

I finished shaving, put on a fresh white shirt, and sat down on the bed. "Sorry I have nothing to offer in the way of an aperitif but I could call downstairs?"

Levitansky twiddled his fingers no. He was dressed without change down to his socks. Did his wife wash out the same pair each night, or were all his socks tricolored?

"To speak frankly," I said, "I have to protest this constant tension you've whipped up in and around me. Nobody in his right mind can expect a complete stranger visiting the Soviet Union to pull his chestnuts out of the fire. It's your country that's hindering you as a writer, not me or the United States of America. Since you live here what can you do but live with it?"

"I love my country," Levitansky said.

"Nobody denies it. That holds for me, though love for country—let's face it—is a mixed bag. Nationality isn't soul as I'm sure you agree. But what I'm also saying is there are things about his country one might not like that he has to make his peace with. I'm assuming you're not thinking of counter-revolution. So if you're up against a wall you can't climb, or dig under, or outflank, at least stop banging your head against it, not to mention mine. Do what you can. It's amazing, for instance, what can be said in a fairy tale."

"I have written already my fairy tales," he said moodily. "Now is the time for truth without disguises. I will make my peace to this point where it interferes with my interior liberty; and then

I must stop to make my peace. My brother-in-law has also told to me, 'You must write acceptable stories, others can do it, so why cannot you?' And I have answered to him, 'Yes, but must be acceptable to *me!*' "

"In that case, aren't you up against the impossible? If you permit me to say it, are those Jews in your stories, if they can't have their matzos and prayer books, any freer in their religious lives than you are as a writer? What I mean is, one has to face up to the nature of his society."

"I have faced up. Do you face up to yours?" he asked with a flash of scorn.

"My own problem is not that I can't express myself but that I don't. In my own mind Vietnam is a demoralizing mistake, yet I've never really opposed it except to sign petitions and vote for congressmen who say they're against the war. My first wife used to criticize me. She said I wrote the wrong things and was involved in everything but useful action. My second wife knew it but made me think she didn't. Maybe I'm just waking up to the fact that the U.S. government has for years been mucking up my self-respect."

Levitansky's larynx moved up like a flag on a pole, then sank.

He tried again, saying, "The Soviet Union preservates for us the great victories of our Revolution. Because of this I have remained for years at peace with the State. Communism is still to me inspirational ideal although this historical period is spoiled by leaders with impoverished view of humanity. They have pissed on Revolution."

"Stalin?"

"Him especially, but also others. Even so I have obeyed Party directives, and when I could not longer obey I wrote for drawer. I said to myself, 'Levitansky, history changes every minute and also Communism will change.' I believed if the State restricts two, three generations of artists, what is this against development of true socialist society—maybe best society of world history? So what does it mean if some of us are sacrificed to Party purpose? The aesthetic mode is not in necessity greater than politics—than needs of Revolution. Then in fifty years more will be secure the State, and all Soviet artists will say whatever they wish. This is what I tried to think, but do not longer think so. I do not believe more in partiinost, which is guided thought, an expression which is to me ridiculous. I do not think Revolution is fulfilled in country of unpublished novelists, poets, playwriters, who hide in drawers whole libraries of literature that will never be printed or if so, it will be printed after they stink in their graves. I think now the State will never be secure—never! It is not in the nature of politics, or human condition, to be finished with Revolution. Evgeny Zamyatin told: 'There is no final revolution. Revolutions are infinite!' "

"I guess that's along my own line of thinking," I said, hoping for reasons of personal safety to forestall Levitansky's ultimate confession—which he, with brooding eyes, was already relentlessly making—lest in the end it imprison me in his will and history.

"I have learned from writing my stories," the writer was saying, "that imagination is enemy of the State. I have learned from my writing that I am not free man. I ask for your help, not to harm my country, which still has magnificent socialistic possibilities, but in order to help me escape its worst errors. I do not wish to defame Russia. My purpose in my work is to show its true heart. So have done our writers from Pushkin to Pasternak and also, in his own way, Solzhenitsyn. If you believe in democratic humanism you must help artist to be free. Is not true?"

I got up, I think to shake myself out of his question. "What exactly is my responsibility to you, Levitansky?" I tried to contain the exasperation I felt.

"We are members of mankind. If I am drowning you must assist to save me."

"In unknown waters if I can't swim?"

"If not, throw to me rope."

"I'm a visitor here. I've told you I may be suspect. For all I know you yourself might be a Soviet agent out to get me, or the room may be bugged, and then where are we? Mr. Levitansky, please, I don't want to hear or argue any more. I'll just plead personal inability and ask you to leave."

"Bugged?"

"By a listening device planted in this room."

Levitansky turned gray. He sat a moment in meditation, then rose wearily from the chair.

"I withdraw now request for your assistance. I accept your word that you are not capable. I do not wish to make criticism of you. All I wish to say, Gospodin Garvitz, is it requires more to change a man's character than to change his name."

Levitansky left the room, leaving in his wake faint fumes of cognac. He had also passed gas.

"Come back!" I called, not too loudly, but if he heard through the door he didn't answer. Good riddance, I thought. Not that I don't sympathize with him but look what he's done to *my* interior liberty. Who has to come thousands of miles to Russia to get entangled in this kind of mess? It's a helluva way to spend a vacation.

The writer had gone but not his sneaky manuscript. It was lying on my bed.

"That's his baby, not mine." Angered, I knotted my tie and slipped on my coat, then via the English-language number, called for a cab.

A half hour later I was in the taxi, riding back and forth along Novo Ostapovskaya Street until I spotted the apartment house I thought it might be. It wasn't, it was another like it. I paid the driver and walked till I thought I had located it. After going up the stairs I was sure I had. When I knocked on Levitansky's door, the writer, looking older, distant—as if he'd been away on a trip and had just returned; or maybe simply interrupted at his work, his thoughts still in his words on the page, his pen in hand— stared at me. Very blankly.

"Levitansky, my heart breaks for you, I swear, but I am not, at this time of my life, considering my condition and recent experiences, in much of a mood to embark on a dangerous adventure. Please accept deepest regrets."

I thrust the manuscript into his hand and went down the stairs. Hurrying out of the building, I was, to my horror, unable to avoid Irina Levitansky coming in. Her eyes lit in fright as she recognized me an instant before I hit her full force and sent her sprawling along the walk.

"Oh, my God, what have I done? I beg your pardon!" I helped the dazed, hurt woman to her feet, brushed off her soiled skirt, and futilely, her pink blouse, split and torn on her lacerated arm and shoulder. I stopped dead when I felt myself experiencing erotic sensation.

Irina Filipovna held a handkerchief to her bloody nostril and wept a little. We sat on a stone bench, a girl of ten and her little brother watching us. Irina said something to them in Russian and they moved off.

"I was frightened of you also as you are of us," she said. "I trust you now because Levitansky does. But I will not urge you to take the manuscript. The responsibility is for you to decide."

"It's not a responsibility I want."

She said as though to herself, "Maybe I will leave Levitansky. He is wretched so much it is no longer a marriage. He drinks. Also he does not earn a living. My brother Dmitri allows him to drive the taxi two, three hours of the day, to my brother's disadvantage. Except for a ruble or two from this, I support him. Levitansky does not longer receive translation commissions. Also a neighbor in the house—I am sure Kovalevsky—has denounced him to the police for delinquency and parasitism. There will be a hearing. Levitansky says he will burn his manuscripts."

I said I had just returned the package of stories.

"He will not," she said. "But even if he burns, he will write more. If they take him away in prison he will write on toilet paper. When he comes out, he will write on newspaper margins. He sits this minute at his table. He is a magnificent writer. I cannot ask him not to write, but now I must decide if this is the condition I wish for myself for the rest of my life."

Irina sat in silence, an attractive woman with shapely legs and feet, in a soiled skirt and torn blouse. I left her on the stone bench, her handkerchief squeezed in her fist.

That night—July 2, I was leaving the Soviet Union on the fifth—I experienced massive self-doubt. If I'm a coward why has it taken me so long to discover it? Where does anxiety end and cowardice begin? Feelings get mixed, sure enough, but not all cowards are anxious men and not all anxious men are cowards. Many "sensitive" (Rose's word), tense, even frightened human beings did in fear what had to be done, the fear calling up effort when it's time to fight or jump off a rooftop into a river. There comes a time in a man's life when to get where he has to—if there are no doors or windows—he walks through a wall.

On the other hand, suppose one is courageous in a hopeless cause—you concentrate on courage but not enough on horse sense? To get to the point of the problem endlessly on my mind, how do I finally decide it's a sensible and worthwhile thing to smuggle out Levitansky's manuscript, given my reasonable doubts of the ultimate worth of the operation? Granted, as I now grant, he's trustworthy and his wife is that and more; still, does it pay a man like me to run the risk?

If six thousand Soviet writers can't do very much to squeeze out another drop of freedom as artists, who am I to fight their battle—H. Harvitz, knight-of-the-free-lance from Manhattan? How far do you go, granted all men, including Communists, are created free and equal and justice is for all? How far do you go for art, if you're for Yeats, Matisse, and Ludwig van Beethoven?

Not to mention Tolstoy and Dostoevsky. So far as to get yourself intentionally involved: the HH Ms. Smuggling Service? Will the President and State Department send up three cheers for my contribution to the cause of artistic social justice? And suppose it amounts to no more than a gaffe in the end?— What will I prove if I sneak out Levitansky's manuscript and all it turns out to be is just another passable book of stories?

That's how I argued with myself on more than one occasion, but soon I argued myself into solid indecision. What it boils down to, I'd say, is he expects me to help him because I'm an American. That's quite a nerve.

Two nights later—odd not to have the Fourth of July on July 4 (I was listening for firecrackers)—a quiet light-lemon summer's evening in Moscow, after two monotonously uneasy days, though I was still writing museum notes, for relief I took myself off to the Bolshoi to hear *Tosca*. It was sung in Russian by a busty lady and a handsome Slavic tenor, but the Italian plot was unchanged, and in the end Scarpia, who had promised "death" by fake bullets, gave in sneaky exchange a fusillade of hot lead; another artist bit the dust and Floria Tosca learned the hard way that love wasn't what she had thought.

Next to me sat another full-breasted woman, this one a lovely Russian of maybe thirty in a white dress that fitted a well-formed figure, her blond hair piled in a birdlike mass on her splendid head. Lillian could look like that though not Rose. This woman —sitting alone, it turned out—spoke flawless English in a mezzo-soprano with a slight accent.

During the first intermission she asked in friendly fashion, managing to seem detached but interested: "Are you American? Or perhaps Swedish?"

"Not Swedish. American is correct. How did you happen to guess?"

"I noticed, if it does not bother you that I say it," she remarked with a charming laugh, "a certain self-satisfaction."

"You got the wrong party."

When she opened her purse a fragrance of springtime burst forth—fresh flowers; the warmth of her body rose to my nostrils. I was moved by memories of the hungers of youth—dreams, longing.

During intermission she touched my arm and said in a low voice, "May I ask a favor? Do you depart soon from the Soviet Union?"

"In fact tomorrow."

"How fortunate for me. Would it offer too much difficulty to mail, wherever you are going, an airmail letter addressed to my husband, who is presently in Paris? Our airmail service takes two weeks to arrive in the West. I shall be grateful."

I glanced at the envelope addressed half in French, half in Cyrillic, and said I wouldn't mind. But during the next act sweat grew active on my body, and at the end of the opera, after Tosca's shriek of death, I handed the letter back to the not wholly surprised lady, saying I was sorry. I had the feeling I had heard her voice before. I hurried back to the hotel, determined not to leave my room for any reason other than breakfast; then out and into the wide blue sky.

I later fell asleep over a book and a bottle of sweetish warm beer a waiter had brought up, pretending to myself I was relaxed though I was concerned with worried thoughts of the departure and flight home; and when I awoke, three minutes on my wristwatch later, it seemed to me I had made the acquaintance of some new nightmares. I was momentarily panicked by the idea that someone had planted a letter on me, and I searched through the pockets of my two suits. Nyet. Then I recalled that in one of my dreams a drawer in a table I was sitting at had slowly come open, and Feliks Levitansky, a dwarf who lived in it along with a few friendly mice, managed to scale the wooden wall on the comb he used as a ladder, and to hop from the drawer ledge to the top of the table. He leered in my face, shook his Lilliputian fist, and shouted in high-pitched but (to me) understandable Russian, "Atombombnik! You massacred innocent Japanese people! Amerikansky bastards!"

"That's unfair," I cried out. "I was no more than a kid in college."

That's a sad dream, I thought.

Afterwards this occurred to me: Suppose what happened to Levitansky happens to me. Suppose America gets caught up in a war with China in some semi-reluctant stupid way, and to make fast hash of it—despite my frantic loud protestations: mostly I wave my arms and shout obscenities—we spatter them, before they can get going, with a few dozen H-bombs, boiling up a thick atomic soup of about two hundred million Orientals—blood, gristle, marrow, and lots of floating Chinese eyeballs. We win the war because the Soviets hadn't been able to make up their minds whom to shoot their missiles at first. And suppose after this unheard-of slaughter, about ten million Americans, in self-revulsion, head for the borders to flee the country. To stop the loss of wealth, the refugees are intercepted by the army in tanks and turned back. Harvitz hides in his room with shades drawn, writing in a fury of protest an epic poem condemning the mass butchery by America. What nation, Asiatic or other, is next? Nobody in the States wants to publish the poem because it might start riots and another flight of refugees to Canada and Mexico; then one day there's a knock on the door, and it isn't the F.B.I. but a bearded Levitansky, in better times a Soviet tourist, a modern, not medieval, Communist. He kindly offers to sneak the manuscript of the poem out for publication in the Soviet Union.

Why? Harvitz suspiciously asks.

Why not? To give the book its liberty.

I awoke after a restless night. I had been instructed by Intourist to be in the lobby with my baggage two hours before flight time, at 11 a.m. I was shaved and dressed by six, and at seven had breakfast—I was very hungry—of yogurt, sausage, and scrambled eggs in the twelfth-floor buffet. I went out to hunt for a taxi. They were hard to come by at this hour, but I finally located one near the American Embassy, not far from the hotel. Speaking my usual mixture of primitive German and French, I persuaded the driver by first suggesting, then slipping him an acceptable two rubles, to take me to Levitansky's house and wait a few minutes till I came out. Going hastily up the stairs, I knocked on his door, apologizing when he opened it, to the half-pajamaed, iron-faced writer, for waking him this early in the day. Without peace of mind or certainty of purpose I asked him whether he still wanted me to smuggle out his manuscript of stories. I got for my trouble the door slammed in my face.

A half hour later I had everything packed and was locking the suitcase. A knock on the door—half a rap, you might call it. For the suitcase, I thought. I was momentarily startled by the sight of a small man in a thick cap wearing a long trench coat. He winked, and against the will I winked back. I had recognized Levitansky's brother-in-law Dmitri, the taxi driver. He slid in, unbuttoned his coat, and brought forth the wrapped manuscript. Holding a finger to his lips, he handed it to me before I could say I was no longer interested.

"Levitansky changed his mind?"

"Not changed mind," he whispered. "Was afraid your voice to be heard by Kovalevsky."

"I'm sorry, I should have thought of that."

"Levitansky say not write to him," the brother-in-law said in a low tone. "When is published book, please to send to him copy of *Das Kapital*. He will understand message."

I reluctantly agreed.

The brother-in-law, a short shapeless figure with sad eyes,

winked again, shook hands with a steamy palm, and slipped out of my room.

I unlocked my suitcase and laid the manuscript on top of my shirts. Then I unpacked half the contents and slipped the manuscript into a folder containing my notes on literary museums and a few letters from Lillian. I then and there decided that if I got back to the States, the next time I saw her I would ask her to marry me. The phone was ringing as I left the room.

On my way to the airport, alone in a taxi—no Intourist girl accompanied me—I felt, on and off, nauseated. If it's not the sausage and yogurt it must just be ordinary fear. Still, if Levitansky has the courage to send these stories out, the least I can do is give him a hand. When one thinks of it it's little enough he does for human freedom during the course of his life. At the airport if I can dig up a Bromo or its Russian equivalent I know I'll feel better.

The driver was observing me in the mirror, a stern man with the head of a scholar, impassively smoking.

"Le jour fait beau," I said.

He pointed with an upraised finger to a sign in English at one side of the road to the airport:

"Long live peace in the world!"

"Peace with freedom." I smiled at the thought of somebody, not Howard Harvitz, painting that in red on the Soviet sign.

We drove on, I foreseeing my exit from the Soviet Union. I had made discreet inquiries from time to time and an Intourist girl in Leningrad had told me I had first to show my papers at the passport-control desk, turn in all my rubles—a serious offense to walk off with any—and then check luggage; no inspection, she swore. And that was that. Unless, of course, the official at the passport desk found my name on a list and said I had to go to the customs office for a package. In that case—if nobody said so I wouldn't remind him—I would go get my books. I figured I wouldn't open the package, just tear off a bit of the wrapping, if they were wrapped, as though to make sure they were the books I expected, and then saunter away with the package under my arm.

I had heard that a KGB man was stationed at the ramp as one boarded a plane. He asked for your passport, checked the picture, threw you a stare through dark lenses and, if there was no serious lack of resemblance, tore out your expired visa, pocketed it, and let you embark.

In ten minutes you were aloft, seat belts fastened in three languages, watching the plane banking west. Maybe if I looked hard I might see in the distance Feliks Levitansky on the roof waving his red-white-and-blue socks on a bamboo pole. Then the plane leveled off, and we were above the clouds, flying westward. And that's what I would be doing for five or six hours unless the pilot received radio instructions to turn back; or maybe land in Czechoslovakia or East Germany, where two big-hatted detectives boarded the plane. By an act of imagination and will I made it some other passenger they were arresting. I got the plane into the air again and we flew on without incident until we touched down in free London.

As the taxi approached the Moscow airport, fingering my ticket and gripping my suitcase handle, I wished for courage equal to Levitansky's when they discovered he was the author of a book of stories I had managed to get published, and his trial and suffering began.

:   :   :

Levitansky's first story, translated by his wife, Irina Filipovna, was about an old man, a widower of seventy-eight, who hoped to have matzos for Passover.

Last year he had got his quota. They had been baked in the State bakery and sold in the State stores; but this year the State bakeries were not permitted to bake them. The officials said the machines had broken down but who believed them?

The old man went to the rabbi, an older man with a tormented beard, and asked him where he could get matzos. He feared that he mightn't have them this year.

"So do I," confessed the old rabbi. He said he had been told to tell his congregants to buy flour and bake them at home. The State stores would sell them the flour.

"What good is that for me?" asked the widower. He reminded the rabbi that he had no home to speak of, a single small room with a one-burner electric stove. His wife had died two years ago. His only living child, a married daughter, was with her husband in Birobijan. His other relatives—the few who were left after the German invasion—two female cousins his age—lived in Odessa; and he himself, even if he could find an oven, did not know how to bake matzos. And if he couldn't what should he do?

The rabbi then promised he would try to get the widower a kilo or two of matzos, and the old man, rejoicing, blessed him.

He waited anxiously a month but the rabbi never mentioned the matzos. Maybe he had forgotten. After all he was an old man burdened with worries, and the widower did not want to press him. However, Passover was coming on wings, so he must do something. A week before the Holy Days he hurried to the rabbi's flat and spoke to him there.

"Rabbi," he begged, "you promised me a kilo or two of matzos. What happened to them?"

"I know I promised," said the rabbi, "but I'm no longer sure to whom. It's easy to promise." He dabbed at his face with a damp handkerchief. "I was warned I could be arrested on charges of profiteering in the production and sale of matzos. I was told it could happen even if I were to give them away for nothing. It's a new crime they've invented. Still, take them anyway. If they arrest me, I'm an old man, and how long can an old man live in Lubyanka? Not so long, thank God. Here, I'll give you a small pack but you must tell no one where you got the matzos."

"May the Lord eternally bless you, rabbi. As for dying in prison, rather let it happen to our enemies."

The rabbi went to his closet and got out a small pack of matzos, already wrapped and tied with knotted twine. When the widower offered in a whisper to pay him, at least the cost of the flour, the rabbi wouldn't hear of it. "God provides," he said, "although at times with difficulty." He said there was hardly enough for all who wanted matzos, so he must take what he got and be thankful.

"I will eat less," said the old man. "I will count mouthfuls. I will save the last matzo to look at and kiss if there isn't enough to last me. He will understand."

Overjoyed to have even a few matzos, he rode home on the trolley car and there met another Jew, a man with a withered hand. They conversed in Yiddish in low tones. The stranger had glanced at the almost square package, then at the widower, and had hoarsely whispered, "Matzos?" The widower, tears starting in his eyes, nodded. "With God's grace." "Where did you get them?" "God provides." "So if He provides let Him provide me," the stranger brooded. "I'm not so lucky. I was hoping for a package from relatives in Cleveland, America. They wrote they would send me a large pack of the finest matzos, but when I inquire of the authorities they say no matzos have arrived. You know when they will get here?" he muttered. "After Passover by a month or two, and what good will they be then?"

The widower nodded sadly. The stranger wiped his eyes with his good hand and after a short while left the trolley amid a number of people getting off. He had not bothered to say goodbye, and neither had the widower, not to remind him of his own good fortune. But when the time came for the old man to leave the trolley he glanced down between his feet where he had placed the package of matzos, and nothing was there. His feet were there. The old man felt harrowed, as though someone had ripped a large nail up his spine. He searched frantically throughout that car, going a long way past his stop, querying every passenger, the woman conductor, the motorman, but they all swore they had not seen his matzos.

Then it occurred to him that the stranger with the withered hand had stolen them.

The widower in his misery asked himself, Would a Jew have robbed another of his precious matzos? It didn't seem possible, but it was.

As for me I haven't even a matzo to look at now. If I could steal any, whether from Jew or Russian, I would steal them. He thought he would steal them even from the old rabbi.

The widower went home without his matzos and had none for Passover.

:   :   :

The story called "Tallith" concerned a youth of seventeen, beardless but for some stray hairs on his chin, who had come from Kirov to the steps of the synagogue on Arkhipova Street in Moscow. He had brought with him a capacious prayer shawl, a white garment of luminous beauty, which he offered for sale to a cluster of Jews of various sorts and sizes—curious, apprehensive, greedy at the sight of the shawl—for fifteen rubles. Most of them avoided the youth, particularly the older Jews, despite the fact that some of the more devout among them were worried about their prayer shawls, eroded on their shoulders after years of daily use, which they could not replace. "It's the informers among us who have put him up to this," they whispered among themselves, "so they will have someone to inform on."

Still, in spite of the warnings of their elders, several of the younger men examined the tallith and admired it. "Where did you get such a fine prayer shawl?" the youth was asked. "It was my father's who recently died," he said. "It was given to him by a rich Jew he had once befriended." "Then why don't you keep it for yourself, you're a Jew, aren't you?" "Yes," said the youth, not the least embarrassed, "but I am going to Bratsk as a komsomol volunteer and I need a few rubles to get married. Besides I'm a confirmed atheist."

One young man with fat unshaven cheeks, who admired the deeply white shawl, its white glowing in whiteness, with its long silk fringes, whispered to the youth he might consider buying it for five rubles. But he was overheard by the gabbai, the lay leader of the congregation, who raised his cane and shouted at the whisperer, "Hooligan, if you buy that shawl, beware it doesn't become your shroud." The Jew with the unshaven cheeks retreated.

"Don't strike him," cried the frightened rabbi, who had come out of the synagogue and saw the gabbai with his cane upraised. He urged the congregants to begin prayers at once. To the youth he said, "Please go away from here, we are burdened with enough trouble. It is forbidden for anyone to sell religious articles. Do you want us to be accused of criminal economic activity? Do you want the doors of the shul to be shut forever? So do us and yourself a mitzvah and go away."

The congregants moved inside. The youth was left standing alone on the steps; but then the gabbai came out of the door, a man with a deformed spine and a wad of cotton stuck in a leaking ear.

"Look here," he said. "I know you stole it. Still, after all is said and done, a tallith is a tallith and God asks no questions of His worshippers. I offer eight rubles for it, take it or leave it. Talk fast before the services end and the others come out."

"Make it ten and it's yours," said the youth. The gabbai gazed at him shrewdly. "Eight is all I have, but wait here and I'll borrow two rubles from my brother-in-law."

The youth waited patiently. Dusk was heavy. In a few minutes a black car drove up, stopped in front of the synagogue, and two policemen got out. The youth realized that the gabbai had informed on him. Not knowing what else to do he hastily draped the prayer shawl over his head and began loudly to pray. He prayed a passionate kaddish. The police hesitated to approach him while he was praying, and they stood at the bottom of the steps waiting for him to be done. The congregants came out and could not believe their ears. No one imagined the youth could pray so fervently. What moved them was the tone, the wail and passion of a man truly praying. Perhaps his father had indeed recently died. All listened attentively, and many wished he would pray forever, for they knew that as soon as he stopped he would be seized and thrown into prison.

It has grown dark. A moon hovers behind murky clouds over the synagogue steeple. The youth's voice is heard in prayer. The congregants are huddled in the dark street, listening. Both police agents are still there, although they cannot be seen. Neither can the youth. All that can be seen is the white shawl luminously praying.

:⠀⠀⠀⠀:⠀⠀⠀⠀:

The last of the stories translated by Irina Filipovna was about a writer of mixed parentage, a Russian father and Jewish mother, who had secretly been writing stories for years. He had from a young age wanted to write but had at first not had the courage —it seemed like such a merciless undertaking—so he had gone into translation instead; and then when he had, one day, started to write seriously and exultantly, after a while he found to his surprise that many of his stories—about half—were of Jews.

For a half-Jew that's a reasonable proportion, he thought. The others were about Russians who sometimes resembled members of his father's family. "It's good to have such different sources for ideas," he told his wife. "This way I can cover a varied range of experiences in life."

After several years of work he had submitted a selection of his stories to a trusted friend of university days, Viktor Zverkov, an editor of the Progress Publishing House; and the writer appeared at his office one morning after receiving a hastily scribbled cryptic note from his friend, to discuss his work with him. Zverkov, a troubled man to begin with—he told everyone his wife did not respect him—jumped up from his chair and turned the key in the door, his ear pressed a minute at the crack. He then went quickly to his desk and withdrew the manuscript from a drawer he first had to unlock with a key he kept in his pocket. He was a heavy-set man with a flushed complexion, stained teeth, and a hoarse voice; and he handled the writer's manuscript with unease, as if it might leap up and wound him in the face.

"Please, Tolya," he whispered breathily, bringing his head close to the writer's, "you must take these awful stories away at once."

"What's the matter with you? Why are you shaking so?" said the writer.

"Don't pretend to be naïve. I am frankly amazed that you are submitting such unorthodox material for publication. My opinion as an editor is that they are of doubtful literary merit—I won't say devoid of it, Tolya, I have to be honest—but as stories they are a frightful affront to our society. I can't understand why you should take it on yourself to write about Jews. What do you know about them? Your culture is not the least Jewish, it's Soviet Russian. The whole business smacks of hypocrisy—of anti-Semitism."

He got up to shut the window and peered into a closet before sitting down.

"Are you out of your mind, Viktor?" said the writer. "My stories are in no sense anti-Semitic. One would have to read them standing on his head to make that judgment."

"There can be only one logical interpretation," the editor argued. "According to my most lenient analysis, which is favorable to you as a person—of let's call it decent intent—the stories fly in the face of socialist realism and reveal a dangerous inclination—perhaps even a stronger word should be used—to anti-Soviet sentiment. Maybe you're not entirely aware of this—I know how a story can pull a writer by the nose. As an editor I have to be sensitive to such things. I know, Tolya, from our conversations that you are a sincere believer in socialism; I won't accuse you of being defamatory to the Soviet system, but others may. In fact, I know they will. If one of the editors of *Oktyabr* was to read your stories, believe me, your career would explode in a mess. You seem not to have a normal awareness of what self-preservation is, and what's appallingly worse, you're not above entangling innocent bystanders in your fate. If these stories were mine, I assure you I would never have brought them to you. I urge you to destroy them at once before they destroy you."

He drank thirstily from a glass of water on his desk.

"That's the last thing I would do," answered the writer in anger. "These stories, if not in tone or subject matter, are written in the spirit of our early Soviet writers—the joyous spirits of the years just after the Revolution."

"I think you know what happened to many of those 'joyous spirits.' "

The writer for a moment stared at him. "Well, then, what of those stories that are not about the experience of Jews? Some are pieces about homely aspects of Russian life. What I hoped is that you might personally recommend one or two such stories to *Novy Mir* or *Yunost*. They are innocuous sketches and well written."

"Not the one about the two prostitutes," said the editor. "That contains hidden social criticism, and is adversely naturalistic."

"A prostitute lives a social life."

"That may be but I can't recommend it for publication. I must advise you, Tolya, if you expect to receive further commissions for translations from us, you must immediately rid yourself of this whole manuscript so as to avoid the possibility of serious consequences both to yourself and family, and to the publishing house that has employed you so faithfully and generously in the past."

"Since you didn't write the stories yourself, you needn't be afraid, Viktor Alexandrovich," the writer said ironically.

"I am not a coward, if that's what you're hinting, Anatoly Borisovich, but if a wild locomotive is running loose on the rails, I know which way to jump."

The writer hastily gathered up his manuscript, stuffed the papers into his leather case, and returned home by bus. His wife was still away at work. He took out the stories and, after reading through one, burned it, page by page, in the kitchen sink.

His nine-year-old son, returning from school, said, "Papa, what are you burning in the sink? That's no place for a fire."

"I'm burning my talent," said the writer. He said, "And my integrity, and my heritage."

The Death of Me

MARCUS was a tailor, long ago before the war, a buoyant man with a bushy head of graying hair, fine fragile brows, and benevolent hands, who comparatively late in life had become a clothier. Because he had prospered, so to say, into ill health, he had to employ an assistant tailor in the rear room, who made alterations on garments but could not, when the work piled high, handle the pressing, so that it became necessary to put on a presser; therefore though the store did well, it did not do too well.

It might have done better but the presser, Josip Bruzak, a heavy, beery, perspiring Pole, who worked in undershirt and felt slippers, his pants loose on his beefy hips, the legs crumpling around his ankles, conceived a violent dislike for Emilio Vizo, the tailor—or it worked the other way, Marcus wasn't sure—a thin, dry, pigeon-chested Sicilian, who bore or returned the Pole a steely malice. Because of their quarrels the business suffered.

Why they should fight as they did, fluttering and snarling like angry cocks, and using, in the bargain, terrible language, loud coarse words that affronted the customers and sometimes made the embarrassed Marcus feel dizzy to the point of fainting, mystified the clothier, who knew their troubles and felt they were, as people, much alike. Bruzak, who lived in a half-ruined rooming house near the East River, constantly guzzled beer at work and kept a dozen bottles in a rusty pan full of ice. When Marcus, in the beginning, objected, Josip, always respectful to the clothier, locked away the pan and disappeared through the back door into the tavern down the block where he had his glass, in the process wasting so much precious time it paid Marcus to tell him to go back to the pan. Every day at lunch Josip pulled out of the drawer a small sharp knife and cut chunks of the hard garlic salami he ate with puffy lumps of white bread, washing it all down with beer and then black coffee brewed on the one-burner gas stove for the tailor's iron. Sometimes he cooked up a soupy mess of cabbage which stank up the store, but on the whole neither the salami nor the cabbage interested him, and for days he seemed weary and uneasy until the mailman brought him, about every third week, a letter from the other side. When the letters came, he more than once tore them in half with his bumbling fingers; he forgot his work, and sitting on a backless chair, fished out of the same drawer where he kept his salami a pair of cracked eyeglasses which he attached to his ears by means of looped cords he had tied on in place of the broken sidepieces. Then he read the tissue sheets he held in his fist, a crabbed Polish writing in faded brown ink whose every word he uttered aloud so that Marcus, who understood the language but preferred not to hear, heard. Before the presser had dipped two sentences into the letter, his face dissolved and he cried, tears smearing his cheeks and chin so that it looked as though he had been sprayed with something to kill flies. At the end he fell into a roar of sobbing, a terrible thing to behold, which incapacitated him for hours and wasted the morning.

Marcus had often thought of telling him to read his letters at home, but the news in them wrung his heart and he could not bring himself to scold Josip, who was, by the way, a master presser. Once he began on a pile of suits, the steaming machine hissed without letup, and every garment came out neat, without puff or excessive crease, and the arms, legs, and pleats were as sharp as knives. As for the news in the letters it was always the same, concerning the sad experiences of his tubercular wife and unfortunate fourteen-year-old son, whom Josip, except in pictures, had never seen, a boy who lived, literally, in the mud with the pigs, and was also sick, so that even if his father saved up money for his passage to America, and the boy could obtain a visa, he would never get past the immigration doctors. Marcus more than once gave the presser a suit of clothes to send to his son, and occasionally some cash, but he wondered if these things ever got to him. He had the uncomfortable thought that Josip, in the last fourteen years, might have brought the boy over had he wanted, his wife too, before she had contracted tuberculosis, but for some reason he preferred to weep over them where they were.

Emilio, the tailor, was another lone wolf. Every day he had a forty-cent lunch in the diner about three blocks away but returned early to read his *Corriere*. His strangeness was that he was always whispering to himself. No one could understand what he said, but it was sibilant and insistent, and wherever he stood, one could hear his hissing voice urging something, or moaning softly though he never wept. He whispered when he sewed a button on, or shortened a sleeve, or when he used the iron. Whispering when he hung up his coat in the morning, he was still whispering when he put on his black hat, wriggled his sparse shoulders into his coat, and left, in loneliness, the store at night. Only once did he hint what the whispering was about; when the clothier, noticing his pallor one morning, brought him a cup of coffee, in gratitude the tailor confided that his wife, who had returned last week, had left him again this, and he held up the outstretched fingers of one bony hand to show she had five times run out on him. Marcus offered the man his sympathy, and thereafter when he heard the tailor whispering in the rear of the store, could always picture the wife coming back to him from wherever she had been, saying she was this time—she swore—going to stay for good, but at night when they were in bed and he was whispering about her in the dark, she would think to herself she was sick of this and in the morning was gone. And so the man's ceaseless whisper irritated Marcus; he had to leave the store to hear silence, yet he kept Emilio on because he was a fine tailor, a demon with a needle, who could sew up a perfect cuff in less time than it takes an ordinary workman to take measurements, the kind of tailor who, when you were looking for one, was very rare.

For more than a year, despite the fact that they both made noises in the rear room, neither the presser nor the tailor seemed to notice one another; then one day, as though an invisible wall between them had fallen, they were at each other's throat. Marcus, it appeared, walked in at the very birth of their venom, when, leaving a customer in the store one afternoon, he went back to get a piece of marking chalk and came on a sight that froze him. There they were in the afternoon sunlight that flooded the rear of the shop, momentarily blinding the clothier so that he had time to think he couldn't possibly be seeing what he saw— the two at opposite corners staring stilly at one another—a live, almost hairy staring of intense hatred. The sneering Pole in one trembling hand squeezed a heavy wooden pressing block, while the livid tailor, his back like a cat's against the wall, held aloft in his rigid fingers a pair of cutter's shears.

"What is it?" Marcus shouted when he had recovered his voice, but neither of them would break the stone silence and remained as when he had discovered them, glaring across the shop at the other, the tailor's lips moving, and the presser breathing like a dog in heat, an eeriness about them that Marcus had never suspected.

"My God," he cried, his body drenched in cold creeping wetness, "tell me what happened here." But neither uttered a sound, so he shrieked through the constriction in his throat, which made the words grate awfully, "Go back to work—" hardly believing they would obey; and when they did, Bruzak turning like a lump back to the machine, and the tailor stiffly to his hot iron, Marcus was softened by their compliance and, speaking as if to children, said with tears in his eyes, "Boys, remember, don't fight."

Afterwards the clothier stood alone in the shade of the store, staring through the glass of the front door at nothing at all; lost, in thinking of them at his very back, in a horrid world of gray grass and mottled sunlight, of moaning and blood-smell. They had made him dizzy. He lowered himself into the leather chair, praying no customer would enter until he had sufficiently recovered from his nausea. So sighing, he shut his eyes and felt his skull liven with new terror to see them both engaged in round pursuit in his mind. One ran hot after the other, lumbering but in flight, who had stolen his box of broken buttons. Skirting the lit and smoking sands, they scrambled high up a craggy cliff, locked in two-handed struggle, teetering on the ledge, till one slipped in slime and pulled the other with him. Reaching forth empty hands, they clutched nothing in stiffened fingers, as Marcus, the watcher, shrieked without sound at their evanescence.

He sat dizzily until these thoughts had left him.

When he was again himself, remembrance made it a kind of dream. He denied any untoward incident had happened; yet knowing it had, called it a triviality—hadn't he, in the factory he had worked in on coming to America, often seen such fights among the men?—trivial things they all forgot, no matter how momentarily fierce.

However, on the very next day, and thereafter without skipping a day, the two in the back broke out of their hatred into thunderous quarreling that did damage to the business; in ugly voices they called each other dirty names, embarrassing the clothier so that he threw the measuring tape he wore like a garment on his shoulders once around his neck. Customer and clothier glanced nervously at each other, and Marcus quickly ran through the measurements; the customer, who as a rule liked to linger in talk of his new clothes, left hurriedly after paying cash, to escape the drone of disgusting names hurled about in the back yet clearly heard in front so that no one had privacy.

Not only would they curse and heap destruction on each other but they muttered in their respective tongues other dreadful things. The clothier understood Josip shouting he would tear off someone's genitals and rub the bloody mess in salt; so he guessed Emilio was shrieking the same things, and was saddened and maddened at once.

He went many times to the rear, pleading with them, and they listened to his every word with interest and tolerance, because the clothier, besides being a kind man—this showed in his eyes— was also eloquent, which they both enjoyed. Yet, whatever his words, they did no good, for the minute he had finished and turned his back on them they began again. Embittered, Marcus withdrew into the store and sat nursing his misery under the yellow-faced clock ticking away yellow minutes, till it was time to stop—it was amazing they got anything done—and go home.

His urge was to bounce them out on their behinds but he couldn't conceive where to find two others who were such skilled and, in essence, proficient workers, without having to pay a fortune in gold. Therefore, with reform uppermost in his mind, he caught Emilio one noon as he was leaving for lunch, whispered him into a corner and said, "Listen, Emilio, you're the smart one, tell me why do you fight? Why do you hate him and why does he hate you, and why do you use such bad words?"

Though he enjoyed the whispering and was soft in the clothier's palms, the tailor, who liked these little attentions, lowered his eyes and blushed darkly, but either would not or could not reply.

So Marcus sat under the clock all afternoon with his fingers in his ears. And he caught the presser on his way out that evening and said to him, "Please, Josip, tell me what he did to you? Josip, why do you fight, you have a sick wife and boy?" But Josip, who also felt an affection for the clothier—he was, despite Polish, no anti-Semite—merely caught him in his hammy arms, and though he had to clutch at his trousers which were falling and impeding his movements, hugged Marcus in a ponderous polka, then with a cackle pushed him aside, and in his beer jag, danced away.

When they began the same dirty hullabaloo the next morning and drove a customer out at once, the clothier stormed into the rear and they turned from their cursing—both fatigued and green-gray to the gills—and listened to Marcus begging, shaming, weeping, but especially paid heed when he, who found screeching unsuited to him, dropped it and gave advice and little preachments in a low becoming tone. He was a tall man, and because of his illness, quite thin. What flesh remained had wasted further in these troublesome months, and his hair was white now so that, as he stood before them, expostulating, exhorting, he was in appearance like an old hermit, if not a saint, and the workers showed respect and keen interest as he spoke.

It was a homily about his long-dead dear father, when they were all children living in a rutted village of small huts, a gaunt family of ten—nine boys and an undersized girl. Oh, they were marvelously poor: on occasion he had chewed bark and even grass, bloating his belly, and often the boys bit one another, including the sister, upon the arms and neck in rage at their hunger.

"So my poor father, who had a long beard down to here"—he

stooped reaching his hand to his knee and at once tears sprang up in Josip's eyes—"my father said, 'Children, we are poor people and strangers wherever we go, let us at least live in peace, or if not—' "

But the clothier was not able to finish because the presser, plumped down on the backless chair, where he read his letters, swaying a little, had begun to whimper and then bawl, and the tailor, who was making odd clicking noises in his throat, had to turn away.

"Promise," Marcus begged, "that you won't fight any more."

Josip wept his promise, and Emilio, with wet eyes, gravely nodded.

This, the clothier exulted, was fellowship, and with a blessing on both their heads, departed, but even before he was altogether gone the air behind him was greased with their fury.

Twenty-four hours later he fenced them in. A carpenter came and built a thick partition, halving the presser's and tailor's work space, and for once there was astonished quiet between them. They were, in fact, absolutely silent for a full week. Marcus, had he had the energy, would have jumped in joy, and kicked his heels together. He noticed, of course, that the presser occasionally stopped pressing and came befuddled to the new door to see if the tailor was still there, and though the tailor did the same, it went no further than that. Thereafter Emilio Vizo no longer whispered to himself and Josip Bruzak touched no beer; and when the emaciated letters arrived from the other side, he took them home to read by the dirty window of his dark room; when night came, though there was electricity, he preferred to read by candlelight.

One Monday morning he opened his table drawer to get at his garlic salami and found it had been roughly broken in two. With his pointed knife, he rushed at the tailor, who, at that very moment, because someone had battered his black hat, was coming at him with his burning iron. He caught the presser along the calf of the arm and opened a smelly purple wound, just as Josip stuck him in the groin, and the knife hung there for a minute.

Roaring, wailing, the clothier ran in, and, despite their wounds, sent them packing. When he left, they locked themselves together and choked necks.

Marcus rushed in again, shouting, "No, no, please, *please,*" flailing his withered arms, nauseated, enervated (all he could hear in the uproar was the thundering clock), and his heart, like a fragile pitcher, toppled from the shelf and bump-bumped down the stairs, cracking at the bottom, the shards flying everywhere.

Although the old Jew's eyes were glazed as he crumpled, the assassins could plainly read in them, What did I tell you? *You see?*

The Bill

THOUGH the street was somewhere near a river, it was landlocked and narrow, a crooked row of aged brick tenement buildings. A child throwing a ball straight up saw a bit of pale sky. On the corner, opposite the blackened tenement where Schlegel worked as janitor, stood another like it except that this included the only store on the street—going down five stone steps into the basement, a small, dark delicatessen owned by Mr. and Mrs. F. Panessa, really a hole in the wall.

They had just bought it with the last of their money, Mrs. Panessa told the janitor's wife, so as not to have to depend on either of their daughters, both of whom, Mrs. Schlegel understood, were married to selfish men who had badly affected their characters. To be completely independent of them, Panessa, a retired factory worker, withdrew his three thousand of savings and bought this little delicatessen store. When Mrs. Schlegel, looking around—though she knew the delicatessen quite well for the many years she and Willy had been janitors across the way—when she asked, "Why did you buy this one?" Mrs. Panessa cheerfully replied because it was a small place and they would not have to overwork; Panessa was sixty-three. They were not here to coin money but to support themselves without working too hard. After talking it over many nights and days, they had decided that the store would at least give them a living. She gazed into Etta Schlegel's gaunt eyes and Etta said she hoped so.

She told Willy about the new people across the street who had bought out the Jew, and said to buy there if there was a chance; she meant by that they would continue to shop at the self-service, but when they had forgotten to buy something, they could go to Panessa's. Willy did as he was told. He was tall and broad-backed, with a heavy face seamed dark from the coal and ashes he shoveled around all winter, and his hair often looked gray from the dust the wind whirled up at him out of the ashcans, when he was lining them up for the sanitation truck. Always in overalls—he complained he never stopped working—he would drift across the street and down the steps when something was needed, and lighting his pipe, would stand around talking to Mrs. Panessa as her husband, a small bent man with a fitful smile, stood behind the counter waiting for the janitor after a long interval of talk to ask, upon reflection, for a dime's worth of this or that, the whole business never amounting to more than half a dollar. Then one day Willy got to talking about how the tenants goaded him all the time, and what the cruel and stingy landlord could think up for him to do in that smelly five-floor dungeon. He was absorbed by what he was saying and before he knew it had run up a three-dollar order, though all he had on him was fifty cents. Willy looked like a dog that had just had a licking, but Mr. Panessa, after clearing his throat, chirped up it didn't matter, he could pay the rest whenever he wanted. He said that everything was run on credit, business and everything else, because after all what was credit but the fact that people were human beings, and if you were really a human being you gave credit to somebody else and he gave credit to you. That surprised Willy because he had never heard a storekeeper say it before. After a couple of days he paid the two-fifty, but when Panessa said he could trust whenever he felt like it, Willy sucked a flame into his pipe, then began to order all sorts of things.

When he brought home two large bagfuls of stuff, Etta shouted he must be crazy. Willy answered he had charged everything and paid no cash.

"But we have to pay sometime, don't we?" Etta shouted. "And we have to pay higher prices than in the self-service." She said then what she always said, "We're poor people, Willy. We can't afford too much."

Though Willy saw the justice of her remarks, despite her scolding he still went across the street and trusted. Once he had a crumpled ten-dollar bill in his pants pocket and the amount came to less than four, but he didn't offer to pay, and let Panessa write it in the book. Etta knew he had the money so she screamed when he admitted he had bought on credit.

"Why are you doing it for? Why don't you pay if you have the money?"

He didn't answer but after a time he said there were other things he had to buy once in a while. He went into the furnace room and came out with a wrapped package which he opened, and it contained a beaded black dress.

Etta cried over the dress and said she would never wear it because the only time he ever brought her anything was when he had done something wrong. Thereafter she let him do all the grocery shopping and she did not speak when he bought on trust.

:　　　　:　　　　:

Willy continued to buy at Panessa's. It seemed they were always waiting for him to come in. They lived in three tiny rooms on the floor above the store, and when Mrs. Panessa saw him out of her window, she ran down to the store. Willy came up from his basement, crossed the street, and went down the steps into the delicatessen, looming large as he opened the door. Every time he bought, it was never less than two dollars' worth, and sometimes it would go as high as five. Mrs. Panessa would pack everything into a deep double bag, after Panessa had called off each item and written the price with a smeary black pencil into his looseleaf notebook. Whenever Willy walked in, Panessa would open the book, wet his fingertip, and flip through a number of blank pages till he found Willy's account in the center of the book. After the order was packed and tied up, Panessa added the amount, touching each figure with his pencil, hissing to himself as he added, and Mrs. Panessa's bird eyes would follow the figuring until Panessa wrote down a sum, and the new total sum (after Panessa had glanced up at Willy and saw that Willy was looking) was twice underscored and then Panessa shut the book. Willy, with his loose unlit pipe in his mouth, did not move until the book was put away under the counter; then he roused himself and embracing the bundles—with which they offered to help him across the street though he always refused—plunged out of the store.

One day when the sum total came to eighty-three dollars and some cents, Panessa, lifting his head and smiling, asked Willy when he could pay something on the account. The very next day Willy stopped buying at Panessa's and after that Etta, with her cord market bag, began to shop again at the self-service, and neither of them went across the street for as much as a pound of prunes or a box of salt they had meant to buy but had forgotten.

Etta, when she returned from shopping at the self-service, scraped the wall on her side of the street to get as far away as possible from Panessa's.

Later she asked Willy if he had paid them anything.

He said no.

"When will you?"

He said he didn't know.

A month went by, then Etta met Mrs. Panessa around the corner, and though Mrs. Panessa, looking unhappy, said nothing about the bill, Etta came home and reminded Willy.

"Leave me alone," he said, "I got enough trouble of my own."

"What kind of trouble have you got, Willy?"

"The goddamn tenants and the goddamn landlord," he shouted and slammed the door.

When he returned he said, "What have I got that I can pay? Ain't I a poor man every day of my life?"

She was sitting at the table and lowered her arms and put her head down on them and wept.

"With what?" he shouted, his face lit dark and webbed. "With the meat off of my bones? With the ashes in my eyes. With the piss I mop up on the floors. With the cold in my lungs when I sleep."

He felt for Panessa and his wife a grating hatred and vowed never to pay because he hated them so much, especially the humpback behind the counter. If he ever smiled at him again with those goddamn eyes he would lift him off the floor and crack his bent bones.

That night he went out and got drunk and lay till morning in the gutter. When he returned, with filthy clothes and bloodied eyes, Etta held up to him the picture of their four-year-old son who had died of diphtheria, and Willy, weeping splashy tears, swore he would never touch another drop.

Each morning he went out to line up the ashcans he never looked the full way across the street.

"Give credit," he mimicked, "give credit."

Hard times set in. The landlord ordered cut down on heat, cut down on hot water. He cut down on Willy's expense money and wages. The tenants were angered. All day they pestered Willy like clusters of flies and he told them what the landlord had ordered. Then they cursed Willy and Willy cursed them. They telephoned the Board of Health, but when the inspectors arrived they said the temperature was within the legal minimum though the house was drafty. However, the tenants still complained they were cold and goaded Willy about it all day, but he said he was cold too. He said he was freezing but no one believed him.

One day he looked up from lining up four ashcans for the sanitation truck to remove and saw Mr. and Mrs. Panessa staring at him from the store. They were staring up through the glass front door and when he looked at them at first his eyes blurred, and they appeared to be two scrawny, loose-feathered birds.

He went down the block to get a wrench from another janitor, and when he got back they then reminded him of two skinny leafless bushes sprouting up through the wooden floor. He could see through the bushes to the empty shelves.

In the spring, when the grass shoots were sticking up in the cracks in the sidewalk, he told Etta, "I'm only waiting till I can pay it all."

"How, Willy?"

"We can save up."

"How?"

"How much do we save a month?"

"Nothing."

"How much have you got hid away?"

"Nothing any more."

"I'll pay them bit by bit. I will, by Jesus."

The trouble was there was no place they could get the money. Sometimes when he was trying to think of the different ways there were to get money his thoughts ran ahead and he saw what it would be like when he paid. He would wrap the wad of bills with a thick rubber band and then go up the stairs and cross the street and go down the five steps into the store. He would say to Panessa, "Here it is, little old man, and I bet you didn't think I would do it, and I don't suppose nobody else did and sometimes me myself, but here it is in bucks all held together by a fat rubber band." After hefting the wad a little, he placed it, like making a move on a checkerboard, squarely in the center of the counter, and the diminutive man and his wife both unpeeled it, squeaking and squealing over each blackened buck, and marveling that so many ones had been put together into such a small pack.

Such was the dream Willy dreamed but he could never make it come true.

He worked hard to. He got up early and scrubbed the stairs from cellar to roof with soap and a hard brush, then went over that with a wet mop. He cleaned the woodwork too and oiled the bannister till it shone the whole zigzag way down, and rubbed the mailboxes in the vestibule with metal polish and a soft rag until you could see your face in them. He saw his own heavy face with a surprising yellow mustache he had recently grown and the tan felt cap he wore that a tenant had left behind in a closetful of junk when he had moved. Etta helped him and they cleaned the whole cellar and the dark courtyard under the crisscrossed clotheslines, and they were quick to respond to any kind of request, even from tenants they didn't like, for sink or toilet repairs. Both worked themselves to exhaustion every day, but as they knew from the beginning, no extra money came in.

One morning when Willy was shining up the mailboxes, he found in his own a letter for him. Removing his cap, he opened the envelope and held the paper to the light as he read the trembling writing. It was from Mrs. Panessa, who wrote her husband was sick across the street, and she had no money in the house so could he pay her just ten dollars and the rest could wait for later.

He tore the letter to bits and hid all day in the cellar. That night, Etta, who had been searching for him in the streets, found him behind the furnace amid the pipes, and she asked him what he was doing there.

He explained about the letter.

"Hiding won't do you any good at all," she said hopelessly.

"What should I do then?"

"Go to sleep, I guess."

He went to sleep but the next morning burst out of his covers, pulled on his overalls, and ran out of the house with an overcoat flung over his shoulders. Around the corner he found a pawn-shop, where he got ten dollars for the coat and was gleeful.

But when he ran back, there was a hearse or something across the street and two men in black were carrying this small and narrow pine box out of the house.

"Who's dead, a child?" he asked one of the tenants.

"No, a man named Mr. Panessa."

Willy couldn't speak. His throat had turned to bone.

After the pine box was squeezed through the vestibule doors, Mrs. Panessa, grieved all over, tottered out alone. Willy turned his head away although he thought she wouldn't recognize him because of his new mustache and tan cap.

"What'd he die of?" he whispered to the tenant.

"I really couldn't say."

But Mrs. Panessa, walking behind the box, had heard.

"Old age," she shrilly called back.

He tried to say some sweet thing but his tongue hung in his mouth like dead fruit on a tree, and his heart was a black-painted window.

Mrs. Panessa moved away to live first with one stone-faced daughter, then with the other. And the bill was never paid.

God's Wrath

GLASSER, a retired sexton, a man with a short beard and rheumy eyes, lived with his daughter on the top floor of a narrow brick building on Second Avenue and Sixth Street. He stayed in most of the day, hated going up and hated going out. He felt old, tired, and irritable. He felt he had done something wrong with his life and didn't know what. The oak doors of the old synagogue in the neighborhood had been nailed shut, its windows boarded, and the white-bearded rabbi, whom the sexton disliked, had gone off to live with his son in Detroit.

The sexton retired on social security and continued to live with his youngest daughter, the only child of his recently deceased second wife. She was a heavy-breasted, restless girl of twenty-six who called herself Luci on the phone and worked as an assistant bookkeeper in a linoleum factory during the day. She was by nature a plain and lonely girl with thoughts that bothered her; as a child she had often been depressed. The telephone in the house rarely rang.

After his shul had closed its doors, the sexton rode on the subway twice a day to a synagogue on Canal Street. On the anniversary of his first wife's death he said kaddish for both wives and barely resisted saying it for his youngest daughter. He was at times irritated by her fate. Why is my luck with my daughters so bad?

Still in all, though twice a widower, Glasser got along, thanks to God. He asked for little and was the kind of man who functioned well alone. Nor did he see much of his daughters from his first marriage, Helen, forty, and Fay, thirty-seven. Helen's husband, a drinker, a bum, supported her badly and Glasser handed her a few dollars now and then; Fay had a goiter and five children. He visited each of them every six weeks or so. His daughters served him a glass of tea.

Lucille he had more affection for, and sometimes she seemed to have affection for him. More often not; this was his second wife's doing. She had been a dissatisfied woman, complained, bewailed her fate. Anyway, the girl did little for herself, had few friends—once in a while a salesman where she worked asked her out—and it was possible, more and more likely, that she would in the end be left unmarried. No young man with or without long hair had asked her to live with him. The sexton would have disliked such an arrangement but he resolved, if ever the time came, not to oppose it. If God in His mercy winks an eye, He doesn't care who sees with two. What God in His mystery won't allow in the present, He may permit in the future, possibly even marriage for Lucille. Glasser remembered friends from the old country, some were Orthodox Jews, who had lived for years with their wives before marrying them. It was, after all, a way of life. Sometimes this thought worried him. If you opened the door a crack too much the wind would invade the bedroom. The devil, they said, hid in a cold wind. The sexton was uneasy. Who could tell where an evil began? Still, better a cold bedroom than one without a double bed. Better a daughter ultimately married than an empty vessel all her life. Glasser had seen some

people, not many, come to better fates than had been expected
for them.

At night after Lucille returned from work she prepared supper, and then her father cleaned up the kitchen so she could
study or go to her classes. He also thoroughly cleaned the house
on Fridays; he washed the windows and mopped the floors.
Being twice a widower, used to looking out for himself, he was
not bothered by having to do domestic tasks. What most disappointed the retired sexton in his youngest daughter was her lack
of ambition. She had wanted to be a secretary after finishing high
school and was now, five years later, an assistant bookkeeper. A
year ago he had said to her, "You won't get better wages if you
don't have a college diploma." "None of my friends go to college
any more," she said. "So how many friends have you got?" "I'm
talking about the friends I know who started and stopped," Lucille said; but Glasser finally persuaded her to register at Hunter
College at night, where she took two courses a term. Although
she had done that reluctantly, now once in a while she talked of
becoming a teacher.

"Someday I will be dead," the sexton remarked, "and you'll be
better off with a profession."

Both of them knew he was reminding her she might be an old
maid. She seemed not to worry, but later he heard her, through
the door, crying in her room.

Once on a hot summer's day they went together on the subway
to Manhattan Beach for a dip in the ocean. Glasser, perspiring,
wore his summer caftan and a black felt hat of twenty years. He
had on white cotton socks, worn bulbous black shoes, and a
white shirt open at the collar. Part of his beard was faintly brown
and his complexion was flushed. On the train Lucille wore tight
bell-bottom ducks and a lacy blue blouse whose long sleeves
could be seen through up to her armpits; she wore clogs and had
braided her dark hair to about six inches of pony tail, which she

tied off with a green ribbon. Her father was uncomfortable at an inch of bare midriff, her heavy breasts, and the tightness of her pants, but said nothing. One of her troubles was that, however she dressed, she had little to say, and he hoped the college courses would help her. Lucille had gold-flecked grayish eyes, and in a bathing suit showed a plumpish but not bad figure. A Yeshiva bocher, dressed much like her father, stared at her from across the aisle of the train, and though Glasser sensed she was interested, her face self-consciously stiffened. He felt for her an affectionate contempt.

In September Lucille delayed, then would not go to reregister for night college. She had spent the summer mostly alone. The sexton argued kindly and furiously but she could not be moved. After he had shouted for an hour she locked herself in the bathroom and would not come out though he swore he had to urinate. The next day she returned very late from work and he had to boil an egg for supper. It ended the argument; she did not return to her night classes. As though to balance that, the telephone in her room began to ring more often, and she called herself Luci when she picked up the receiver. Luci bought herself new clothes—dresses, miniskirts, leotards, new sandals and shoes, and wore them in combinations and bright colors he had never seen on her before. So let her go, Glasser thought. He watched television and was usually asleep when she got home late from a date.

"So how was your evening?" he asked in the morning.

"That's my own business," Luci said.

When he dreamed of her, as he often did, he was upbraiding her for her short dresses; when she bent over he could see her behind. And for the disgusting costume she called hot pants. And the eyeliner and violet eye shadow she now used regularly. And for the way she looked at him when he complained about her.

One day when the sexton was praying in the shul on Canal Street Luci moved out of the house on Second Avenue. She had left a green-ink note on lined paper on the kitchen table, saying she wanted to live her own life but would phone him once in a while. He telephoned the linoleum office the next day and a man there said she had quit her job. Though shaken that she had left the house in this fashion, the sexton felt it might come to some good. If she was living with someone, all he asked was that it be an honest Jew.

Awful dreams invaded his sleep. He woke enraged at her. Sometimes he woke in fright. The old rabbi, the one who had gone to live with his son in Detroit, in one dream shook his fist at him.

On Fourteenth Street, one night on his way home from Helen's house, he passed a prostitute standing in the street. She was a heavily made-up woman of thirty or so, and at the sight of her he became, without cause, nauseated. The sexton felt a weight of sickness on his heart and was moved to cry out to God but could not. For five minutes, resting his swaying weight on his cane, he was unable to walk. The prostitute had taken a quick look at his face and had run off. If not for a stranger who had held him against a telephone pole until he had flagged down a police car that drove the sexton home, he would have collapsed in the street.

In the house he pounded clasped hands against the wall of Lucille's room, bare except for her bed and a chair. He wept, wailing. Glasser telephoned his eldest daughter and cried out his terrible fear.

"How can you be so positive about that?"

"I know in my heart. I wish I didn't know but I know it."

"So in that case she's true to her nature," Helen said. "She can't be otherwise than she is, I never trusted her."

He hung up on her and called Fay.

"All I can say," said Fay, "is I saw it coming, but what can you do about such things? Who could I tell it to?"

"What should I do?"

"Ask for God's help, what else can you do?"

The sexton hurried to the synagogue and prayed for God's intervention. When he returned to his flat he felt unrelieved, outraged, miserable. He beat his chest with his fists, blamed himself for not having been stricter with her. He was angered with her for being the kind she was and sought ways to punish her. Really, he wanted to beg her to return home, to be a good daughter, to ease the pain in his heart.

The next morning he woke in the dark and determined to find her. But where do you look for a daughter who has become a whore? He waited a few days for her to call, and when she didn't, on Helen's advice he dialed information and asked if there was a new telephone number in the name of Luci Glasser.

"Not for Luci Glasser but for Luci Glass," said the operator.

"Give me this number."

The operator, at his impassioned insistence, gave him an address as well, a place on midtown Ninth Avenue. Though it was still September and not cold, the sexton put on his winter coat and took his rubber-tipped heavy cane. He rode, whispering to himself, on the subway to West Fiftieth Street, and walked to Ninth, to a large new orange-brick apartment house.

All day, though it rained intermittently, he waited across the street from the apartment house until his daughter appeared late at night; then he followed her. She walked quickly, lightly, as though without a worry, down the avenue. As he hurried after her she hailed a cab. Glasser shouted at it but no one looked back.

In the morning he telephoned her and she did not answer, as though she knew her father was calling. That evening Glasser went once more to the apartment house and waited across the street. He had considered going in and asking the doorman for her apartment number but was ashamed to.

"Please, give me the number of my daughter, Luci Glasser, the prostitute."

At eleven that night Luci came out. From the way she was dressed and made up he was positive he had not been mistaken.

She turned on Forty-eighth Street and walked to Eighth Avenue. Luci sauntered calmly along the avenue. The sidewalks were crowded with silent men and showily dressed young women. Traffic was heavy and there were strong lights everywhere, yet the long street looked dark and evil. Some of the stores, in their spotlit windows, showed pictures of men and women in sexual embrace. The sexton groaned. Luci wore a purple silk sweater with red sequins, almost no skirt, and long black net stockings. She paused for a while on a street corner, apart from a group of girls farther up the block. She would speak to the men passing by, and one or two would stop to speak to her, then she waited again. One man spoke quietly for a while as she listened intently. Then Luci went into a drugstore to make a telephone call, and when she came out, her father, half dead, was waiting for her at the door. She walked past him.

Incensed, he called her name and she turned in frightened surprise. Under the makeup, false eyelashes, gaudy mouth, her face had turned ashen, eyes anguished.

"Papa, go home," she cried in fright.

"What did I do to you that you do this to me?"

"It's not as bad as people think," Luci said.

"It's worse, it's filthy."

"Not if you don't think so. I meet lots of people—some are Jewish."

"A black year on their heads."

"You live your life, let me live mine."

"God will curse you, He will rot your flesh."

"You're not God," Luci cried in sudden rage.

"Cocksucker," the sexton shouted, waving his cane.

A policeman approached. Luci ran off. The sexton, to the man's questions, was inarticulate.

When he sought her again Luci had disappeared. He went to the orange apartment house and the doorman said Miss Glass had moved out; he could not say where. Though Glasser returned several times the doorman always said the same thing. When he telephoned her number he got a tape recording of the operator saying the number had been disconnected.

The sexton walked the streets looking for her, though Fay and Helen begged him not to. He said he must. They asked him why. He wept aloud. He sought her among the streetwalkers on Eighth and Ninth Avenues and on Broadway. Sometimes he went into a small cockroachy hotel and uttered her name, but nobody knew her.

Late one October night he saw her on Third Avenue near Twenty-third Street. Luci was standing in midblock near the curb, and though it was a cold night she was not wearing a coat. She had on a heavy white sweater and a mirrored leather miniskirt. A round two-inch mirror in a metal holder was sewn onto the back of the skirt, above her plump thighs, and it bounced on her buttocks as she walked.

Glasser crossed the street and waited in silence through her alarm of recognition.

"Lucille," he begged her, "come home with your father. We won't tell anybody. Your room is waiting."

She laughed angrily. She had gained weight. When he attempted to follow her she called him dirty names. He hobbled across the street and waited in an unlit doorway.

Luci walked along the block and when a man approached she spoke to him. Sometimes the man stopped to speak to her. Then they would go together to a run-down, dark, squat hotel on a side street nearby, and a half hour later she returned to Third Avenue, standing between Twenty-third and -second, or higher up the avenue, near Twenty-sixth.

The sexton follows her and waits on the other side of the street by a bare-branched tree. She knows he is there. He waits. He counts the number of her performances. He punishes by his presence. He calls down God's wrath on the prostitute and her blind father.

Rembrandt's Hat

RUBIN, in careless white cloth hat, or visorless soft round cap, however one described it, wandered with unexpressed or inexpressive thoughts up the stairs from his studio in the basement of the New York art school where he made his sculpture, to a workshop on the second floor, where he taught. Arkin, the art historian, a hypertensive bachelor of thirty-four—a man often swept by strong feeling, he thought—about a dozen years younger than the sculptor, observed him through his open office door, wearing his cap amid a crowd of art students and teachers in the hall during a change of classes. In his white hat he stands out and apart, the art historian thought. It illumines a lonely inexpressiveness arrived at after years of experience. Though it was not entirely apt he imagined a lean white animal—hind, stag, goat?—staring steadfastly but despondently through trees of a dense wood. Their gazes momentarily interlocked and parted. Rubin hurried to his workshop class.

Arkin was friendly with Rubin though they were not really friends. Not his fault, he felt; the sculptor was a very private person. When they talked, he listened, looking away, as though guarding his impressions. Attentive, apparently, he seemed to be thinking of something else—his sad life no doubt, if saddened eyes, a faded green mistakable for gray, necessarily denote sad life. Sometimes he uttered an opinion, usually a flat statement about the nature of life, or art, never much about himself; and he said absolutely nothing about his work.

"Are you working, Rubin?" Arkin was reduced to.

"Of course I'm working."

"What are you doing if I may ask?"

"I have a thing going."

There Arkin let it lie.

Once, in the faculty cafeteria, listening to the art historian discourse on the work of Jackson Pollock, the sculptor's anger had flared.

"The world of art ain't necessarily in your eyes."

"I have to believe that what I see is there," Arkin had politely responded.

"Have you ever painted?"

"Painting is my life."

Rubin, with dignity, reverted to silence. That evening, leaving the building, they tipped hats to each other over small smiles.

In recent years, after his wife had left him and costume and headdress became a mode among students, Rubin had taken to wearing various odd hats from time to time, and this white one was the newest, resembling Nehru's Congress Party cap, but rounded—a cross between a cantor's hat and a bloated yarmulke; or perhaps like a French judge's in Rouault, or working doctor's in a Daumier print. Rubin wore it like a crown. Maybe it kept his head warm under the cold skylight of his large studio.

When the sculptor again passed along the crowded hall on his way down to his studio that day he had first appeared in his white cap, Arkin, who had been reading an article on Giacometti, put it down and went into the hall. He was in an ebullient mood he could not explain to himself, and told Rubin he very much admired his hat.

"I'll tell you why I like it so much. It looks like Rembrandt's hat that he wears in one of the middle-aged self-portraits, the really profound ones. May it bring you the best of luck."

Rubin, who had for a moment looked as though he was struggling to say something extraordinary, fixed Arkin in a strong stare and hurried downstairs. That ended the incident, though it did not diminish the art historian's pleasure in his observation.

Arkin later remembered that when he had come to the art school via an assistant curator's job in a museum in St. Louis, seven years ago, Rubin had been working in wood; he now welded triangular pieces of scrap iron to construct his sculptures. Working at one time with a hatchet, later a modified small meat cleaver, he had reshaped driftwood pieces, out of which he had created some arresting forms. Dr. Levis, the director of the art school, had talked the sculptor into giving an exhibition of his altered driftwood objects in one of the downtown galleries. Arkin, in his first term at the school, had gone on the subway to see the show one winter's day. This man is an original, he thought, maybe his work will be, too. Rubin had refused a gallery vernissage, and on the opening day the place was nearly deserted. The sculptor, as though escaping his hacked forms, had retreated into a storage room at the rear of the gallery and stayed there looking at pictures. Arkin, after reflecting whether he ought to, sought him out to say hello, but seeing Rubin seated on a crate with his back to him, examining a folio of somebody's prints, silently shut the door and departed. Although in time two notices of the show appeared, one bad, the other mildly favorable, the sculptor seemed unhappy about having exhibited his work, and after that didn't for years. Nor had there been any sales. Recently, when Arkin had suggested it might be a good idea to show what he was doing with his welded iron triangles,

Rubin, after a wildly inexpressive moment, had answered, "Don't bother playing around with that idea."

The day after the art historian's remarks in the hall about Rubin's white cap, it disappeared from sight—gone totally; for a while he wore on his head nothing but his heavy reddish hair. And a week or two later, though he could momentarily not believe it, it seemed to Arkin that the sculptor was avoiding him. He guessed the man was no longer using the staircase to the right of his office, but was coming up from the basement on the other side of the building, where his corner workshop room was anyway, so he wouldn't have to pass Arkin's open door. When he was certain of this Arkin felt uneasy, then experienced moments of anger.

Have I offended him in some way? he asked himself. If so, what did I say that's so offensive? All I did was remark on the hat in one of Rembrandt's self-portraits and say it looked like the cap he was wearing. How can that be offensive?

He then thought: no offense where none's intended. All I have is good will to him. He's shy and may have been embarrassed in some way—maybe my exuberant voice in the presence of students—if that's so it's no fault of mine. And if that's not it, I don't know what's the matter except his own nature. Maybe he hasn't been feeling well, or it's some momentary mishigas—nowadays there are more ways of insults without meaning to than ever before—so why raise up a sweat over it? I'll wait it out.

But as weeks, then months went by and Rubin continued to shun the art historian—he saw the sculptor only at faculty meetings when Rubin attended them; and once in a while glimpsed him going up or down the left staircase; or sitting in the Fine Arts secretary's office poring over inventory lists of supplies for sculpture—Arkin thought maybe the man is having a breakdown. He did not believe it. One day they met in the men's room and Rubin strode out without a word. Arkin felt for the sculptor surges of hatred. He didn't like people who didn't like him. Here I make a sociable, innocent remark to the son of a bitch—at worst it might be called innocuous—and to him it's an insult. I'll give him tit for tat. Two can play.

But when he had calmed down, Arkin continued to wonder and worry over what might have gone wrong. I've always thought I was fairly good in human relationships. Yet he had a worrisome nature and wore a thought ragged if in it lurked a fear the fault was his own. Arkin searched the past. He had always liked the sculptor, even though Rubin offered only his fingertip in friendship; yet Arkin had been friendly, courteous, interested in his work, and respectful of his dignity, almost visibly weighted with unspoken thoughts. Had it, he often wondered, something to do with his mentioning—suggesting—not long ago, the possibility of a new exhibition of his sculpture, to which Rubin had reacted as though his life was threatened?

It was then he recalled he had never told Rubin how he had felt about his hacked-driftwood show—never once commented on it, although he had signed the guest book. Arkin hadn't liked the show, yet he wanted to seek Rubin out to name one or two interesting pieces. But when he had located him in the storage room, intently involved with a folio of prints, lost in hangdog introspection so deeply he had been unwilling, or unable, to greet whoever was standing at his back—Arkin had said to himself, better let it be. He had ducked out of the gallery. Nor had he mentioned the driftwood exhibition thereafter. Was this kindness cruel?

Still it's not very likely he's been avoiding me so long for that alone, Arkin reflected. If he was disappointed, or irritated, by my not mentioning his driftwood show, he would then and there have stopped talking to me, if he was going to stop. But he didn't. He seemed as friendly as ever, according to his measure, and he isn't a dissembler. And when I afterwards suggested the

possibility of a new show he obviously wasn't eager to have—
which touched him to torment on the spot—he wasn't at all
impatient with me but only started staying out of my sight after
the business of his white cap, whatever that meant to him. Maybe
it wasn't my mention of the cap itself that's annoyed him.
Maybe it's a cumulative thing—three minuses for me? Arkin felt
it was probably cumulative; still it seemed that the cap remark
had mysteriously wounded Rubin most, because nothing that had
happened before had threatened their relationship, such as it
was, and it was then at least amicable. Having thought it through
to this point, Arkin had to admit he did not know why Rubin
acted as strangely as he was now acting.

Off and on, the art historian considered going down to the
sculptor's studio and there apologizing to him if he had said
something inept, which he certainly hadn't meant to do. He
would ask Rubin if he'd mind telling him what bothered him; if it
was something *else* he had inadvertently said or done, he would
apologize and clear things up. It would be mutually beneficial.

One early spring day he made up his mind to visit Rubin after
his seminar that afternoon, but one of his students, a bearded
printmaker, had found out it was Arkin's thirty-fifth birthday
and presented the art historian with a white ten-gallon Stetson
that the student's father, a traveling salesman, had brought back
from Waco, Texas.

"Wear it in good health, Mr. Arkin," said the student. "Now
you're one of the good guys."

Arkin was wearing the hat, going up the stairs to his office
accompanied by the student who had given it to him, when they
encountered the sculptor, who grimaced in disgust.

Arkin was upset, though he felt at once that the force of this
uncalled-for reaction indicated that, indeed, the hat remark had
been taken by Rubin as an insult. After the bearded student left
Arkin he placed the Stetson on his worktable—it had seemed to

him—before going to the men's room; and when he returned the cowboy hat was gone. The art historian searched for it in his office and even hurried back to his seminar room to see whether it could possibly have landed up there, someone having snatched it as a joke. It was not in the seminar room. Arkin thought of rushing down and confronting Rubin nose to nose in his studio, but could not bear the thought. What if he hadn't taken it?

Now both evaded each other. But after a period of rarely meeting they began, ironically, Arkin thought, to encounter one another everywhere—even in the streets, especially near galleries on Madison, or Fifty-seventh, or in SoHo; or on entering or leaving movie houses. Each then hastily crossed the street to skirt the other. In the art school both refused to serve together on committees. One, if he entered the lavatory and saw the other, stepped outside and remained a distance away till he had left. Each hurried to be first into the basement cafeteria at lunchtime because when one followed the other in and observed him standing on line, or already eating at a table, alone or in the company of colleagues, invariably he left and had his meal elsewhere.

Once, when they came in together they hurriedly departed together. After often losing out to Rubin, who could get to the cafeteria easily from his studio, Arkin began to eat sandwiches in his office. Each had become a greater burden to the other, Arkin felt, than he would have been if only one was doing the shunning. Each was in the other's mind to a degree and extent that bored him. When they met unexpectedly in the building after turning a corner or opening a door, or had come face-to-face on the stairs, one glanced at the other's head to see what, if anything, adorned it; they then hurried away in opposite directions. Arkin as a rule wore no hat unless he had a cold; and Rubin lately affected a railroad engineer's cap. The art historian hated Rubin for hating him and beheld repugnance in Rubin's eyes.

"It's your doing," he heard himself mutter. "You brought me to this, it's on your head."

After that came coldness. Each froze the other out of his life; or froze him in.

One early morning, neither looking where he was going as he rushed into the building to his first class, they bumped into each other in front of the arched art school entrance. Both started shouting. Rubin, his face flushed, called Arkin "murderer," and the art historian retaliated by calling the sculptor "hat thief." Rubin smiled in scorn, Arkin in pity; they then fled.

Afterwards Arkin felt faint and had to cancel his class. His weakness became nausea, so he went home and lay in bed, nursing a severe occipital headache. For a week he slept badly, felt tremors in his sleep, ate next to nothing. "What has this bastard done to me?" Later he asked, "What have I done to myself?" I'm in this against my will, he thought. It had occurred to him that he found it easier to judge paintings than to judge people. A woman had said this to him once but he denied it indignantly. Arkin answered neither question and fought off remorse. Then it went through him again that he ought to apologize, if only because if the other couldn't he could. Yet he feared an apology would cripple his craw.

Half a year later, on his thirty-sixth birthday, Arkin, thinking of his lost cowboy hat and having heard from the Fine Arts secretary that Rubin was home sitting shiva for his dead mother, was drawn to the sculptor's studio—a jungle of stone and iron figures—to look around for the hat. He found a discarded welder's helmet but nothing he could call a cowboy hat. Arkin spent hours in the large skylighted studio, minutely inspecting the sculptor's work in welded triangular iron pieces, set amid broken stone statuary he had been collecting for years—decorative garden figures placed charmingly among iron flowers seeking daylight. Flowers were what Rubin was mostly into now, on long stalks with small corollas, on short stalks with petaled blooms. Some of the flowers were mosaics of triangles fixing white stones and broken pieces of thick colored glass in jeweled forms. Rubin had in the last several years come from abstract driftwood sculptures to figurative objects—the flowers, and some uncompleted, possibly abandoned, busts of men and women colleagues, including one that vaguely resembled Rubin in a cowboy hat. He had also done a lovely sculpture of a dwarf tree. In the far corner of the studio was a place for his welding torch and gas tanks as well as arc-welding apparatus, crowded by open heavy wooden boxes of iron triangles of assorted size and thickness. The art historian studied each sculpture and after a while thought he understood why talk of a new exhibition had threatened Rubin. There was perhaps one fine piece, the dwarf tree, in the iron jungle. Was this what he was afraid he might confess if he fully expressed himself?

Several days later, while preparing a lecture on Rembrandt's self-portraits, Arkin, examining the slides, observed that the portrait of the painter which he had remembered as the one he had seen in the Rijksmuseum in Amsterdam was probably hanging in Kenwood House in London. And neither hat the painter wore in either gallery, though both were white, was that much like Rubin's cap. The observation startled Arkin. The Amsterdam portrait was of Rembrandt in a white turban he had wound around his head; the London portrait was him in a studio cap or beret worn slightly cocked. Rubin's white thing, on the other hand, looked more like an assistant cook's cap in Sam's Diner than like either of Rembrandt's hats in the large oils, or in the other self-portraits Arkin was showing himself on slides. What those had in common was the unillusioned honesty of his gaze. In his self-created mirror the painter beheld distance, objectivity painted to stare out of his right eye; but the left looked out of bedrock, beyond quality. Yet the expression of each of the portraits seemed magisterially sad; or was this what life was if when Rembrandt painted he did not paint the sadness?

After studying the pictures projected on the small screen in his dark office, Arkin felt he had, in truth, made a referential error, confusing the two hats. Even so, what had Rubin, who no doubt was acquainted with the self-portraits, or may have had a recent look at them—at *what* had he taken offense?

Whether I was right or wrong, so what if his white cap made me think of Rembrandt's hat and I told him so? That's not throwing rocks at his head, so what bothered him? Arkin felt he ought to be able to figure it out. Therefore suppose Rubin was Arkin and Arkin Rubin— Suppose it was me in his hat: "Here I am, an aging sculptor with only one show, which I never had confidence in and nobody saw. And standing close by, making critical pronouncements one way or another, is this art historian Arkin, a big-nosed, gawky, overcurious gent, friendly but no friend of mine because he doesn't know how to be. That's not his talent. An interest in art we have in common, but not much more. Anyway, Arkin, maybe not because it means anything in particular—who says he knows what he means?—mentions Rembrandt's hat on my head and wishes me good luck in my work. So say he meant well—but it's still more than I can take. In plain words it irritates me. The mention of Rembrandt, considering the quality of my own work, and what I am generally feeling about life, is a fat burden on my soul because it makes me ask myself once too often—why am I going on if this is the kind of sculptor I am going to be for the rest of my life? And since Arkin makes me think the same unhappy thing no matter what he says—or even what he doesn't say, as for instance about my driftwood show—who wants to hear more? From then on I avoid the guy —like forever."

After staring in the mirror in the men's room, Arkin wandered on every floor of the building, and then wandered down to Rubin's studio. He knocked on the door. No one answered. When he tested the knob it gave, and he thrust his head into the room and called Rubin's name.

Night lay on the skylight. The studio was lit with many dusty bulbs but Rubin was not present. The forest of sculptures was. Arkin went among the iron flowers and broken stone garden pieces to see if he had been wrong in his judgment. After a while he felt he hadn't been.

He was staring at the dwarf tree when the door opened and Rubin, wearing his railroad engineer's cap, in astonishment entered.

"It's a beautiful sculpture," Arkin got out, "the best in the room I'd say."

Rubin stared at him in flushed anger, his face lean; he had grown reddish sideburns. His eyes were for once green rather than gray. His mouth worked nervously, but he said nothing.

"Excuse me, Rubin, I came in to tell you I got those hats I mentioned to you some time ago mixed up."

"Damn right you did."

"Sorry it happened. Also for letting things get out of hand for a while."

"Damn right."

Rubin, though he tried not to, then began to cry. He wept silently, his shoulders shaking, tears seeping through his coarse fingers on his face.

Arkin had taken off.

They stopped avoiding each other and spoke pleasantly when they met, which wasn't often. One day Arkin, when he went into the men's room, saw Rubin regarding himself in the mirror in his white cap, the one that seemed to resemble Rembrandt's hat. He wore it like a crown of failure and hope.

Angel Levine

Manischevitz, a tailor, in his fifty-first year suffered many reverses and indignities. Previously a man of comfortable means, he overnight lost all he had, when his establishment caught fire, after a metal container of cleaning fluid exploded, and burned to the ground. Although Manischevitz was insured against fire, damage suits by two customers who had been hurt in the flames deprived him of every penny he had saved. At almost the same time, his son, of much promise, was killed in the war, and his daughter, without so much as a word of warning, married a lout and disappeared with him as off the face of the earth. Thereafter Manischevitz was victimized by excruciating backaches and found himself unable to work even as a presser—the only kind of work available to him—for more than an hour or two daily, because beyond that the pain from standing was maddening. His Fanny, a good wife and mother, who had taken in washing and sewing, began before his eyes to waste away. Suffering shortness of breath, she at last became seriously ill and took to her bed. The doctor, a former customer of Manischevitz, who out of pity treated them, at first had difficulty diagnosing her ailment, but later put it down as hardening of the arteries at an advanced stage. He took Manischevitz aside, prescribed complete rest for her, and in whispers gave him to know there was little hope.

Throughout his trials Manischevitz had remained somewhat stoic, almost unbelieving that all this had descended on his head, as if it were happening, let us say, to an acquaintance or some distant relative; it was in sheer quantity of woe, incomprehensible. It was also ridiculous, unjust, and because he had always been a religious man, an affront to God. Manischevitz believed this in all his suffering. When his burden had grown too crushingly heavy to be borne he prayed in his chair with shut hollow eyes: "My dear God, sweetheart, did I deserve that this should happen to me?" Then recognizing the worthlessness of it, he set aside the complaint and prayed humbly for assistance: "Give Fanny back her health, and to me for myself that I shouldn't feel pain in every step. Help now or tomorrow is too late." And Manischevitz wept.

:   :   :

Manischevitz's flat, which he had moved into after the disastrous fire, was a meager one, furnished with a few sticks of chairs, a table, and bed, in one of the poorer sections of the city. There were three rooms: a small, poorly papered living room; an apology for a kitchen with a wooden icebox; and the comparatively large bedroom where Fanny lay in a sagging secondhand bed, gasping for breath. The bedroom was the warmest room in the house and it was here, after his outburst to God, that Manischevitz, by the light of two small bulbs overhead, sat reading his Jewish newspaper. He was not truly reading because his thoughts were everywhere; however the print offered a convenient resting place for his eyes, and a word or two, when he permitted himself to comprehend them, had the momentary effect of helping him forget his troubles. After a short while he discovered, to his surprise, that he was actively scanning the news, searching for an item of great interest to him. Exactly what he thought he would read he couldn't say—until he realized, with some astonishment, that he was expecting to discover something about himself. Manischevitz put his paper down and looked up with the distinct impression that someone had come into the apartment, though he could not remember having heard the sound of the door opening. He looked around: the room was very still, Fanny sleeping, for once, quietly. Half frightened, he watched her until he was satisfied she wasn't dead; then, still disturbed by the thought of an unannounced visitor, he stumbled into the living room and there had the shock of his life, for at the table sat a black man reading a newspaper he had folded up to fit into one hand.

"What do you want here?" Manischevitz asked in fright.

The Negro put down the paper and glanced up with a gentle expression. "Good evening." He seemed not to be sure of himself, as if he had got into the wrong house. He was a large man, bonily built, with a heavy head covered by a hard derby, which he made no attempt to remove. His eyes seemed sad, but his lips, above which he wore a slight mustache, sought to smile; he was not otherwise prepossessing. The cuffs of his sleeves, Manischevitz noted, were frayed to the lining, and the dark suit was badly fitted. He had very large feet. Recovering from his fright, Manischevitz guessed he had left the door open and was being visited by a case worker from the Welfare Department—some came at night—for he had recently applied for welfare. Therefore he lowered himself into a chair opposite the Negro, trying, before the man's uncertain smile, to feel comfortable. The former tailor sat stiffly but patiently at the table, waiting for the investigator to take out his pad and pencil and begin asking questions; but before long he became convinced the man intended to do nothing of the sort.

"Who are you?" Manischevitz at last asked uneasily.

"If I may, insofar as one is able to, identify myself, I bear the name of Alexander Levine."

In spite of his troubles Manischevitz felt a smile growing on his lips. "You said Levine?" he politely inquired.

The Negro nodded. "That is exactly right."

Carrying the jest further, Manischevitz asked, "You are maybe Jewish?"

"All my life I was, willingly."

The tailor hesitated. He had heard of black Jews but had never met one. It gave an unusual sensation.

Recognizing in afterthought something odd about the tense of Levine's remark, he said doubtfully, "You ain't Jewish any more?"

Levine at this point removed his hat, revealing a very white part in his black hair, but quickly replaced it. He replied, "I have recently been disincarnated into an angel. As such, I offer you my humble assistance, if to offer is within my province and power—in the best sense." He lowered his eyes in apology. "Which calls for added explanation: I am what I am granted to be, and at present the completion is in the future."

"What kind of angel is this?" Manischevitz gravely asked.

"A bona fide angel of God, within prescribed limitations," answered Levine, "not to be confused with the members of any particular sect, order, or organization here on earth operating under a similar name."

Manischevitz was thoroughly disturbed. He had been expecting something, but not this. What sort of mockery was it—provided that Levine was an angel—of a faithful servant who had from childhood lived in the synagogues, concerned with the word of God?

To test Levine he asked, "Then where are your wings?"

The Negro blushed as well as he could. Manischevitz understood this from his altered expression. "Under certain circumstances we lose privileges and prerogatives upon returning to earth, no matter for what purpose or endeavoring to assist whomsoever."

"So tell me," Manischevitz said triumphantly, "how did you get here?"

"I was translated."

Still troubled, the tailor said, "If you are a Jew, say the blessing for bread."

Levine recited it in sonorous Hebrew.

Although moved by the familiar words Manischevitz still felt doubt he was dealing with an angel.

"If you are an angel," he demanded somewhat angrily, "give me the proof."

Levine wet his lips. "Frankly, I cannot perform either miracles or near-miracles, due to the fact that I am in a condition of probation. How long that will persist or even consist depends on the outcome."

Manischevitz racked his brains for some means of causing Levine positively to reveal his true identity, when the Negro spoke again:

"It was given me to understand that both your wife and you require assistance of a salubrious nature?"

The tailor could not rid himself of the feeling that he was the butt of a jokester. Is this what a Jewish angel looks like? he asked himself. This I am not convinced.

He asked a last question. "So if God sends to me an angel, why a black? Why not a white that there are so many of them?"

"It was my turn to go next," Levine explained.

Manischevitz could not be persuaded. "I think you are a faker."

Levine slowly rose. His eyes indicated disappointment and worry. "Mr. Manischevitz," he said tonelessly, "if you should desire me to be of assistance to you any time in the near future, or possibly before, I can be found"—he glanced at his fingernails —"in Harlem."

He was by then gone.

:   :   :

The next day Manischevitz felt some relief from his backache and was able to work four hours at pressing. The day after, he put in six hours; and the third day four again. Fanny sat up a little and asked for some halvah to suck. But after the fourth day the stabbing, breaking ache afflicted his back, and Fanny again lay supine, breathing with blue-lipped difficulty.

Manischevitz was profoundly disappointed at the return of his active pain and suffering. He had hoped for a longer interval of easement, long enough to have a thought other than of himself and his troubles. Day by day, minute after minute, he lived in pain, pain his only memory, questioning the necessity of it, inveighing, though with affection, against God. Why *so much,* Gottenyu? If He wanted to teach His servant a lesson for some reason, some cause—the nature of His nature—to teach him, say, for reasons of his weakness, his pride, perhaps, during his years of prosperity, his frequent neglect of God—to give him a little lesson, why then any of the tragedies that had happened to him, any *one* would have sufficed to chasten him. But *all together*—the loss of both his children, his means of livelihood, Fanny's health and his—that was too much to ask one frail-boned man to endure. Who, after all, was Manischevitz that he had been given so much to suffer? A tailor. Certainly not a man of talent. Upon him suffering was largely wasted. It went nowhere, into nothing: into more suffering. His pain did not earn him bread, nor fill the cracks in the wall, nor lift, in the middle of the night, the kitchen table; only lay upon him, sleepless, so sharply oppressive that he could many times have cried out yet not heard himself this misery.

In this mood he gave no thought to Mr. Alexander Levine, but at moments when the pain wavered, slightly diminishing, he sometimes wondered if he had been mistaken to dismiss him. A black Jew and angel to boot—very hard to believe, but suppose he *had* been sent to succor him, and he, Manischevitz, was in his blindness too blind to understand? It was this thought that put him on the knife-point of agony.

Therefore the tailor, after much self-questioning and continuing doubt, decided he would seek the self-styled angel in Harlem. Of course he had great difficulty because he had not asked for specific directions, and movement was tedious to him. The subway took him to 116th Street, and from there he wandered in the open dark world. It was vast and its lights lit nothing. Everywhere were shadows, often moving. Manischevitz hobbled along with the aid of a cane, and not knowing where to seek in the blackened tenement buildings, would look fruitlessly through store windows. In the stores he saw people and everybody was black. It was an amazing thing to observe. When he was too tired, too unhappy to go farther, Manischevitz stopped in front of a tailor's shop. Out of familiarity with the appearance of it, with some sadness he entered. The tailor, an old skinny man with a mop of woolly gray hair, was sitting cross-legged on his workbench, sewing a pair of tuxedo pants that had a razor slit all the way down the seat.

"You'll excuse me, please, gentleman," said Manischevitz, admiring the tailor's deft thimbled fingerwork, "but you know maybe somebody by the name Alexander Levine?"

The tailor, who, Manischevitz thought, seemed a little antagonistic to him, scratched his scalp.

"Cain't say I ever heared dat name."

"Alex-ander Lev-ine," Manischevitz repeated it.

The man shook his head. "Cain't say I heared."

Manischevitz remembered to say: "He is an angel, maybe."

"Oh *him*," said the tailor, clucking. "He hang out in dat honky-tonk down here a ways." He pointed with his skinny finger and returned to sewing the pants.

Manischevitz crossed the street against a red light and was almost run down by a taxi. On the block after the next, the sixth store from the corner was a cabaret, and the name in sparkling lights was Bella's. Ashamed to go in, Manischevitz gazed through the neon-lit window, and when the dancing couples had parted and drifted away, he discovered at a table on the side, toward the rear, Alexander Levine.

He was sitting alone, a cigarette butt hanging from the corner of his mouth, playing solitaire with a dirty pack of cards, and Manischevitz felt a touch of pity for him, because Levine had deteriorated in appearance. His derby hat was dented and had a gray smudge. His ill-fitting suit was shabbier, as if he had been sleeping in it. His shoes and trouser cuffs were muddy, and his face covered with an impenetrable stubble the color of licorice. Manischevitz, though deeply disappointed, was about to enter, when a big-breasted Negress in a purple evening gown appeared before Levine's table, and with much laughter through many white teeth, broke into a vigorous shimmy. Levine looked at Manischevitz with a haunted expression, but the tailor was too paralyzed to move or acknowledge it. As Bella's gyrations continued Levine rose, his eyes lit in excitement. She embraced him with vigor, both his hands clasped around her restless buttocks, and they tangoed together across the floor, loudly applauded by the customers. She seemed to have lifted Levine off his feet and his large shoes hung limp as they danced. They slid past the windows where Manischevitz, white-faced, stood staring in. Levine winked slyly and the tailor left for home.

:   :   :

Fanny lay at death's door. Through shrunken lips she muttered concerning her childhood, the sorrows of the marriage bed,

the loss of her children; yet wept to live. Manischevitz tried not
to listen, but even without ears he would have heard. It was not a
gift. The doctor panted up the stairs, a broad but bland, unshaven man (it was Sunday), and soon shook his head. A day at
most, or two. He left at once to spare himself Manischevitz's
multiplied sorrow; the man who never stopped hurting. He
would someday get him into a public home.

Manischevitz visited a synagogue and there spoke to God, but
God had absented himself. The tailor searched his heart and
found no hope. When she died, he would live dead. He considered taking his life although he knew he wouldn't. Yet it was
something to consider. Considering, you existed. He railed
against God— Can you love a rock, a broom, an emptiness?
Baring his chest, he smote the naked bones, cursing himself for
having, beyond belief, believed.

Asleep in a chair that afternoon, he dreamed of Levine. He
was standing before a faded mirror, preening small decaying
opalescent wings. "This means," mumbled Manischevitz, as he
broke out of sleep, "that it is possible he could be an angel."
Begging a neighbor lady to look in on Fanny and occasionally
wet her lips with water, he drew on his thin coat, gripped his
walking stick, exchanged some pennies for a subway token, and
rode to Harlem. He knew this act was the last desperate one of
his woe: to go seeking a black magician to restore his wife to
invalidism. Yet if there was no choice, he did at least what was
chosen.

He hobbled to Bella's, but the place seemed to have changed
hands. It was now, as he breathed, a synagogue in a store. In the
front, toward him, were several rows of empty wooden benches.
In the rear stood the Ark, its portals of rough wood covered with
rainbows of sequins; under it a long table on which lay the sacred
scroll unrolled, illuminated by the dim light from a bulb on a
chain overhead. Around the table, as if frozen to it and the

scroll, which they all touched with their fingers, sat four Negroes wearing skullcaps. Now as they read the Holy Word, Manischevitz could, through the plate-glass window, hear the singsong chant of their voices. One of them was old, with a gray beard. One was bubble-eyed. One was humpbacked. The fourth was a boy, no older than thirteen. Their heads moved in rhythmic swaying. Touched by this sight from his childhood and youth, Manischevitz entered and stood silent in the rear.

"Neshoma," said bubble eyes, pointing to the word with a stubby finger. "Now what dat mean?"

"That's the word that means soul," said the boy. He wore eyeglasses.

"Let's git on wid de commentary," said the old man.

"Ain't necessary," said the humpback. "Souls is immaterial substance. That's all. The soul is derived in that manner. The immateriality is derived from the substance, and they both, causally an' otherwise, derived from the soul. There can be no higher."

"That's the highest."

"Over de top."

"Wait a minute," said bubble eyes. "I don't see what is dat immaterial substance. How come de one gits hitched up to de odder?" He addressed the humpback.

"Ask me somethin' hard. Because it is substanceless immateriality. It couldn't be closer together, like all the parts of the body under one skin—closer."

"Hear now," said the old man.

"All you done is switched de words."

"It's the primum mobile, the substanceless substance from which comes all things that were incepted in the idea—you, me, and everything and -body else."

"Now how did all dat happen? Make it sound simple."

"It de speerit," said the old man. "On de face of de water

moved de speerit. An' dat was good. It say so in de Book. From de speerit ariz de man."

"But now listen here. How come it become substance if it all de time a spirit?"

"God alone done dat."

"Holy! Holy! Praise His Name."

"But has dis spirit got some kind of a shade or color?" asked bubble eyes, deadpan.

"Man, of course not. A spirit is a spirit."

"Then how come we is colored?" he said with a triumphant glare.

"Ain't got nothing to do wid dat."

"I still like to know."

"God put the spirit in all things," answered the boy. "He put it in the green leaves and the yellow flowers. He put it with the gold in the fishes and the blue in the sky. That's how come it came to us."

"Amen."

"Praise Lawd and utter loud His speechless Name."

"Blow de bugle till it bust de sky."

They fell silent, intent upon the next word. Manischevitz, with doubt, approached them.

"You'll excuse me," he said. "I am looking for Alexander Levine. You know him maybe?"

"That's the angel," said the boy.

"Oh *him*," snuffed bubble eyes.

"You'll find him at Bella's. It's the establishment right down the street," the humpback said.

Manischevitz said he was sorry that he could not stay, thanked them, and limped across the street. It was already night. The city was dark and he could barely find his way.

But Bella's was bursting with jazz and the blues. Through the window Manischevitz recognized the dancing crowd and among them sought Levine. He was sitting loose-lipped at Bella's side table. They were tippling from an almost empty whiskey fifth. Levine had shed his old clothes, wore a shiny new checkered suit, pearl-gray derby hat, cigar, and big, two-tone, button shoes. To the tailor's dismay, a drunken look had settled upon his formerly dignified face. He leaned toward Bella, tickled her earlobe with his pinky while whispering words that sent her into gales of raucous laughter. She fondled his knee.

Manischevitz, girding himself, pushed open the door and was not welcomed.

"This place reserved."

"Beat it, pale puss."

"Exit, Yankel, semitic trash."

But he moved toward the table where Levine sat, the crowd breaking before him as he hobbled forward.

"Mr. Levine," he spoke in a trembly voice. "Is here Manischevitz."

Levine glared blearily. "Speak yo' piece, son."

Manischevitz shivered. His back plagued him. Tremors tormented his legs. He looked around, everybody was all ears.

"You'll excuse me. I would like to talk to you in a private place."

"Speak, Ah is a private pusson."

Bella laughed piercingly. "Stop it, boy, you killin' me."

Manischevitz, no end disturbed, considered fleeing but Levine addressed him:

"Kindly state the pu'pose of yo' communication with yo's truly."

The tailor wet cracked lips. "You are Jewish. This I am sure."

Levine rose, nostrils flaring. "Anythin' else yo' got to say?"

Manischevitz's tongue lay like a slab of stone.

"Speak now or fo'ever hold off."

Tears blinded the tailor's eyes. Was ever man so tried? Should he say he believed a half-drunk Negro was an angel?

The silence slowly petrified.

Manischevitz was recalling scenes of his youth as a wheel in his mind whirred: believe, do not, yes, no, yes, no. The pointer pointed to yes, to between yes and no, to no, no it was yes. He sighed. It moved but one still had to make a choice.

"I think you are an angel from God." He said it in a broken voice, thinking, If you said it it was said. If you believed it you must say it. If you believed, you believed.

The hush broke. Everybody talked but the music began and they went on dancing. Bella, grown bored, picked up the cards and dealt herself a hand.

Levine burst into tears. "How you have humiliated me."

Manischevitz apologized.

"Wait'll I freshen up." Levine went to the men's room and returned in his old suit.

No one said goodbye as they left.

They rode to the flat via subway. As they walked up the stairs Manischevitz pointed with his cane at his door.

"That's all been taken care of," Levine said. "You go in while I take off."

Disappointed that it was so soon over, but torn by curiosity, Manischevitz followed the angel up three flights to the roof. When he got there the door was already padlocked.

Luckily he could see through a small broken window. He heard an odd noise, as though of a whirring of wings, and when he strained for a wider view, could have sworn he saw a dark figure borne aloft on a pair of strong black wings.

A feather drifted down. Manischevitz gasped as it turned white, but it was only snowing.

He rushed downstairs. In the flat Fanny wielded a dust mop under the bed, and then upon the cobwebs on the wall.

"A wonderful thing, Fanny," Manischevitz said. "Believe me, there are Jews everywhere."

Life Is Better

Than Death

SHE SEEMED to remember the man from the same day last year. He was standing at a nearby grave, occasionally turning to look around, while Etta, a rosary in her hand, prayed for the repose of the soul of her husband, Armando. Sometimes she prayed he would move over and let her lie down with him so her heart might be eased. It was the second of November, All Souls' Day in the cimitero Campo Verano, in Rome, and it had begun to drizzle after she had laid down the bouquet of yellow chrysanthemums on the grave Armando wouldn't have had if it wasn't for a generous uncle, a doctor in Perugia. Without this uncle Etta had no idea where Armando would be buried, certainly in a much less attractive grave, though she would have resisted his often expressed desire to be cremated.

Etta worked for meager wages in a draper's shop and Armando had left no insurance. The bright large yellow flowers, glowing in November gloom on the faded grass, moved her and tears gushed forth. Although she felt uncomfortably feverish when she cried like that, Etta was glad she had, because crying seemed to be the only thing that relieved her. She was thirty, dressed in full mourning. Her figure was slim, her moist brown eyes red-rimmed and darkly ringed, the skin pale and her features grown thin. Since the accidental death of Armando, a few months more than a year ago, she came almost daily during the long Roman afternoon to pray at his grave. She was devoted to his memory, ravaged within. Etta went to confession twice a week and took communion every Sunday. She lit candles for Armando at La Madonna Addolorata, and had a mass offered once a month, more often when she had a little extra money. Whenever she returned to the cold flat she still lived in and could not give up because it had once also been his, Etta thought of Armando, recalling him as he had looked ten years ago, not as when he had died. Invariably she felt an oppressive pang and ate very little.

It was raining quietly when she finished her rosary. Etta dropped the beads into her purse and opened a black umbrella. The man from the other grave, wearing a darkish green hat and a tight black overcoat, had stopped a few feet behind her, cupping his small hands over a cigarette as he lit it. Seeing her turn from the grave he touched his hat. He was a short man with dark eyes and a barely visible mustache. He had meaty ears but was handsome.

"Your husband?" he asked respectfully, letting the smoke flow as he spoke, holding his cigarette cupped in his palm to keep it from getting wet.

She said it was.

He nodded in the direction of the grave where he had stood. "My wife. One day while I was on my job she was hurrying to meet a lover and was killed at once by a taxi in the Piazza Bologna." He spoke without bitterness, without apparent emotion, but his eyes were restless.

She noticed that he had put up his coat collar and was getting wet. Hesitantly she offered to share her umbrella with him on the way to the bus stop.

"Cesare Montaldo," he murmured, gravely accepting the umbrella and holding it high enough for both of them.

"Etta Oliva." She was in her high heels almost half a head taller than he.

They walked slowly along an avenue of damp cypresses to the gates of the cemetery, Etta keeping from him that she had been so deeply stricken by his story she could not get out even a sympathetic comment.

"Mourning is a hard business," Cesare said. "If people knew there'd be less death."

She sighed a slight smile.

Across the street from the bus stop was a bar with tables under a drawn awning. Cesare suggested coffee or perhaps an ice.

She thanked him and was about to refuse but his sad serious expression changed her mind and she went with him across the street. He guided her gently by the elbow, the other hand firmly holding the umbrella over them. She said she felt cold and they went inside.

He ordered an espresso but Etta settled for a piece of pastry which she politely picked at with her fork. Between puffs of a cigarette he talked about himself. His voice was low and he spoke well. He was a free-lance journalist, he said. Formerly he had worked in a government office but the work was boring so he had quit in disgust although he was in line for the directorship. "I would have directed the boredom." Now he was toying with the idea of going to America. He had a brother in Boston who wanted him to visit for several months and then decide whether he would emigrate permanently. The brother thought they could arrange that Cesare might come in through Canada. He had considered the idea but could not bring himself to break his ties with this kind of life for that. He seemed also to think that he would find it hard not to be able to go to his dead wife's grave when he was moved to do so. "You know how it is," he said, "with somebody you have once loved."

Etta felt for her handkerchief in her purse and touched her eyes.

"And you?" he asked sympathetically.

To her surprise she began to tell him her story. Though she had often related it to priests, she never had to anyone else, not even a friend. But she was telling it to a stranger because he seemed to be a man who would understand. And if later she regretted telling him, what difference would it make once he was gone?

She confessed she had prayed for her husband's death, and Cesare put down his coffee cup and sat with his cigarette between his lips, not puffing as she talked.

Armando, Etta said, had fallen in love with a cousin who had come during the summer from Perugia for a job in Rome. Her father had suggested that she live with them, and Armando and Etta, after talking it over, decided to let her stay for a while. They would save her rent to buy a secondhand television set so they could watch "Lascia o Raddoppia," the quiz program that everyone in Rome watched on Thursday nights, and that way save themselves the embarrassment of waiting for invitations and having to accept them from neighbors they didn't like. The cousin came, Laura Ansaldo, a big-boned pretty girl of eighteen with thick brown hair and large eyes. She slept on the sofa in the living room, was easy to get along with, and made herself helpful in the kitchen before and after supper. Etta had liked her until she noticed that Armando had gone mad over the girl. She then tried to get rid of Laura but Armando threatened he would leave if she bothered her. One day Etta had come home from work and found them naked in the marriage bed. She had screamed and wept. She called Laura a stinking whore and swore she would kill her if she didn't leave the house that minute. Armando was contrite. He promised he would send the girl back to Perugia, and the next day in the Stazione Termini had put her on the train. But the separation from her was more than he could bear. He grew nervous and miserable. Armando confessed himself one Saturday night, and for the first time in ten years took communion, but instead of calming down he desired the girl ever so much more strongly. After a week he told Etta that he was going to get his cousin and bring her back to Rome.

"If you bring that whore here," Etta shouted, "I'll pray to Christ that you drop dead before you get back."

"In that case," Armando said, "start praying."

When he left the house she fell on her knees and prayed for his death.

That night Armando went with a friend to get Laura. The friend had a truck and was going to Assisi. On the way back he would pick them up in Perugia and drive to Rome. They started out when it was still twilight but it soon grew dark. Armando drove for a while, then felt sleepy and crawled into the back of the truck. The Perugian hills were foggy after a hot September day and the truck hit a rock in the road with a hard bump. Armando, in deep sleep, rolled out of the open tailgate of the truck, hitting the road with head and shoulders, then rolling down the hill. He was dead before he stopped rolling. When she heard of this Etta fainted away and it was two days before she could speak. After that she had prayed for her own death, and often did.

Etta turned her back to the other tables, though they were empty, and wept openly and quietly.

After a while Cesare squashed his butt. "Calma, signora. If God had wanted your husband to live he would still be living. Prayers have little relevance to the situation. To my way of thinking the whole thing was no more than a coincidence. It's best not to go too far with religion or it becomes troublesome."

"A prayer is a prayer," she said. "I suffer for mine."

Cesare pursed his lips. "But who can judge these things? They're much more complicated than most of us know. In the case of my wife I didn't pray for her death but I confess I might have wished it. Am I in a better position than you?"

"My prayer was a sin. You don't have that on your mind. It's worse than what you just might have thought."

"That's only a technical thing, signora."

"If Armando had lived," she said after a minute, "he would have been twenty-nine next month. I am a year older. But my life is useless now. I wait to join him."

He shook his head, seemed moved, and ordered an espresso for her.

Though Etta had stopped crying, for the first time in months she felt substantially disburdened.

Cesare would put her on the bus; as they were crossing the street he suggested they might meet now and then since they had so much in common.

"I live like a nun," she said.

He lifted his hat. "Coraggio," and she smiled at him for his kindness.

When she returned home that night the anguish of life without Armando recommenced. She remembered him as he had been when he was courting her and felt uneasy for having talked about him to Cesare. And she vowed for herself continued prayers, rosaries, her own penitence to win him further indulgences in Purgatory.

Etta saw Cesare on a Sunday afternoon a week later. He had written her name in his little book and was able to locate her apartment in a house on the Via Nomentana through the help of a friend in the electric company.

When he knocked on her door she was surprised to see him, turned rather pale, though he hung back doubtfully. He said he had found out by accident where she lived and she asked for no details. Cesare had brought a small bunch of violets which she embarrassedly accepted and put in water.

"You're looking better, signora," he said.

"My mourning for Armando goes on," she answered with a sad smile.

"Moderazione," he counseled, flicking his meaty ear with his finger. "You're still a young woman, and at that not bad-looking. You ought to acknowledge it to yourself. There are certain advantages to self-belief."

Etta made coffee and Cesare insisted on going out for a half dozen pastries.

He said as they were eating that he was considering emigrating if nothing better turned up soon. After a pause he said he had decided he had given more than his share to the dead. "I've been faithful to her memory but I have to think of myself once in a while. There comes a time when one has to return to life. It's only natural. Where there's life there's life."

She lowered her eyes and sipped her coffee.

Cesare set down his cup and got up. He put on his coat and thanked her. As he was buttoning his overcoat he said he would drop by again when he was in the neighborhood. He had a journalist friend who lived close by.

"Don't forget I'm still in mourning," Etta said.

He looked up at her respectfully. "Who can forget that, signora? Who would want to so long as you mourn?"

She then felt uneasy.

"You know my story." She spoke as though she was explaining again.

"I know," he said, "that we were both betrayed. They died and we suffer. My wife ate flowers and I belch."

"They suffer too. If Armando must suffer, I don't want it to be about me. I want him to feel that I'm still married to him." Her eyes were moist again.

"He's dead, signora. The marriage is over," Cesare said. "There's no marriage without his presence unless you expect the Holy Ghost." He spoke dryly, adding quietly, "Your needs are different from a dead man's, you're a healthy woman. Let's face the facts."

"Not spiritually," she said quickly.

"Spiritually and physically, there's no love in death."

She blushed and spoke in excitement. "There's love for the dead. Let him feel that I'm paying for my sin at the same time he is for his. To help him into heaven I keep myself pure. Let him feel that."

Cesare nodded and left, but Etta, after he had gone, continued to be troubled. She felt uneasy, could not define her mood, and stayed longer than usual at Armando's grave when she went the next day. She promised herself not to see Cesare again. In the next weeks she became a little miserly.

The journalist returned one evening almost a month later and Etta stood at the door in a way that indicated he would not be asked in. She had seen herself doing this if he appeared. But Cesare, with his hat in his hand, suggested a short stroll. The suggestion seemed so modest that she agreed. They walked down the Via Nomentana, Etta wearing her highest heels, Cesare un-self-consciously talking. He wore small patent-leather shoes and smoked as they strolled.

It was already early December, still late autumn rather than winter. A few leaves clung to a few trees and a warmish mist hung in the air. For a while Cesare talked of the political situation, but after an espresso in a bar on the Via Venti Settembre, as they were walking back he brought up the subject she had hoped to avoid. Cesare seemed suddenly to have lost his calm, unable to restrain what he had been planning to say. His voice was intense, his gestures impatient, his dark eyes restless. Although his outburst frightened her she could do nothing to prevent it.

"Signora," he said, "wherever your husband is you're not helping him by putting this penance on yourself. To help him, the best thing you can do is take up your normal life. Otherwise he will continue to suffer doubly, once for something he was guilty of, and the second time for the unfair burden your denial of life imposes on him."

"I am repenting my sins, not punishing him." She was too disturbed to say more, considered walking home wordless, then slamming the front door in his face; but she heard herself hastily saying, "If we became intimate it would be like adultery. We would be betraying the dead."

"Why is it you see everything in reverse?"

Cesare had stopped under a tree and almost jumped as he spoke. "They—*they* betrayed us. If you'll pardon me, signora, the truth is my wife was a pig. Your husband was a pig. We mourn because we hate them. Let's have the dignity to face the facts."

"No more," she moaned, hastily walking on. "Don't say anything else, I don't want to hear it."

"Etta," said Cesare passionately, walking after her, "this is my last word and then I'll nail my tongue to my jaw. Just remember this. If Our Lord Himself, this minute, let Armando rise from the dead to take up his life on earth, tonight—he would be lying in his cousin's bed."

She began to cry. Etta walked on, crying, realizing the truth of his remark. Cesare seemed to have said all he had wanted to, gently held her arm, breathing heavily as he escorted her back to her apartment. At the outer door, as she was trying to think how to get rid of him, how to end this, without waiting a minute he tipped his hat and walked off.

For more than a week Etta went through many torments. She felt a passionate desire to sleep with Cesare. Overnight her body became a torch. Her dreams were erotic. She saw Armando naked in bed with Laura, and in the same bed she saw herself with Cesare, clasping his body to hers. But she resisted—prayed, confessed her most lustful thoughts, and stayed for hours at Armando's grave to calm her mind.

Cesare knocked at her door one night, and because she was repelled when he suggested the marriage bed, went with him to his rooms. Though she felt guilty afterwards she continued to visit Armando's grave, though less frequently, and she didn't tell Cesare that she had been to the cemetery when she went to his flat afterwards. Nor did he ask her, nor talk about his wife or Armando.

At first her uneasiness was intense. Etta felt as though she had committed adultery against the memory of her husband, but when she told herself over and over—there was no husband, he was dead; there was no husband, she was alone—she began to believe it. There was no husband, there was only his memory. She was not committing adultery. She was a lonely woman and had a lover, a widower, a gentle and affectionate man.

One night as they were lying in bed she asked Cesare about the possibility of marriage and he said that love was more important. They both knew how marriage destroyed love.

And when, two months later, she found she was pregnant and hurried that morning to Cesare's rooms to tell him, the journalist, in his pajamas, calmed her. "Let's not regret human life."

"It's your child," said Etta.

"I'll acknowledge it as mine," Cesare said, and Etta went home disturbed but happy.

The next day, when she returned at her usual hour, after having told Armando at his grave that she was at last going to have a baby, Cesare was gone.

"Moved," the landlady said, with a poof of her hand, and she didn't know where.

Though Etta's heart hurt and she mourned the loss of Cesare, try as she would she could not, even with the life in her womb, escape thinking of herself as a confirmed sinner; and she never returned to the cemetery to stand again at Armando's grave.

The Model

Early one morning Ephraim Elihu rang up the Art Students League and asked them how he could locate an experienced female model he could paint nude. He told the woman speaking to him on the phone that he wanted someone of about thirty. "Could you possibly help me?"

"I don't recognize your name," said the woman on the telephone. "Have you ever dealt with us before? Some of our students will work as models but usually only for painters we know." Mr. Elihu said he hadn't. He wanted it understood he was an amateur painter who had once studied at the League.

"Do you have a studio?"

"It's a large living room with lots of light.

"I'm no youngster," he went on, "but after many years I've begun painting again and I'd like to do some nude studies to get back my feeling for form. I'm not a professional painter you understand but I'm serious about painting. If you want any references as to my character, I can supply them." He asked her what the going rate for models was, and the woman, after a pause, said, "Six-fifty the hour." Mr. Elihu said that was satisfactory.

He seemed to want to talk longer but she did not encourage him. She wrote down his name and address and said she thought she could have someone for him the day after tomorrow. He thanked her for her consideration.

That was on Wednesday. The model appeared on Friday morning. She had telephoned the night before and they settled on a time for her to come. She rang his bell shortly after 9 a.m. and Mr. Elihu went at once to the door. He was a gray-haired man of seventy who lived in a brownstone house near Ninth Avenue, and he was excited by the prospect of painting this young woman.

The model was a plain-looking woman of twenty-seven or so, and the old painter decided her best feature was her eyes. She was wearing a blue raincoat on a clear spring day. The old painter liked her face but kept that to himself. She barely glanced at him as she walked firmly into the room.

"Good day," he said, and she answered, "Good day."

"It's like spring," said the old man. "The foliage is starting up again."

"Where do you want me to change?" asked the model.

Mr. Elihu asked her name and she responded, "Ms. Perry."

"You can change in the bathroom, I would say, Miss Perry, or if you like, my own room—down the hall—is empty and you can change there also. It's warmer than the bathroom."

The model said it made no difference to her but she thought she would rather change in the bathroom.

"That is as you wish," said the elderly man.

"Is your wife around?" she then asked, glancing into the room.

"I happen to be a widower."

He said he had had a daughter once but she had died in an accident.

The model said she was sorry. "I'll change and be out in a few fast minutes."

"No hurry at all," said Mr. Elihu, glad he was about to paint her.

Ms. Perry entered the bathroom, undressed there, and returned quickly. She slipped off her terry cloth robe. Her head and shoulders were slender and well formed. She asked the old man how he would like her to pose. He was standing by an enamel-top kitchen table in a living room with a large window. On the tabletop he had squeezed out, and was mixing together, the contents of two small tubes of paint. There were three other tubes he did not touch. The model, taking a last drag of a cigarette, pressed it out against a coffee can lid on the kitchen table.

"I hope you don't mind if I take a puff once in a while?"

"I don't mind, if you do it when we take a break."

"That's all I meant."

She was watching him as he slowly mixed his colors.

Mr. Elihu did not immediately look at her nude body but said he would like her to sit in the chair by the window. They were facing a back yard with an ailanthus tree whose leaves had just come out.

"How would you like me to sit, legs crossed or not crossed?"

"However you prefer that. Crossed or uncrossed doesn't make much of a difference to me. Whatever makes you feel comfortable."

The model seemed surprised at that, but she sat down in the yellow chair by the window and crossed one leg over the other. Her figure was good.

"Is this O.K. for you?"

Mr. Elihu nodded. "Fine," he said. "Very fine."

He dipped the brush into the paint he had mixed on the tabletop, and after glancing at the model's nude body, began to paint. He would look at her, then look quickly away, as if he was afraid of affronting her. But his expression was objective. He painted apparently casually, from time to time gazing up at the model. He did not often look at her. She seemed not to be aware of him.

Once, she turned to observe the ailanthus tree and he studied her momentarily to see what she might have seen in it.

Then she began to watch the painter with interest. She watched his eyes and she watched his hands. He wondered if he was doing something wrong. At the end of about an hour she rose impatiently from the yellow chair.

"Tired?" he asked.

"It isn't that," she said, "but I would like to know what in the name of Christ you think you are doing? I frankly don't think you know the first thing about painting."

She had astonished him. He quickly covered the canvas with a towel.

After a long moment, Mr. Elihu, breathing shallowly, wet his dry lips and said he was making no claims for himself as a painter. He said he had tried to make that absolutely clear to the woman he had talked to at the art school when he had called.

Then he said, "I might have made a mistake in asking you to come to this house today. I think I should have tested myself a while longer, just so I wouldn't be wasting anybody's time. I guess I am not ready to do what I would like to do."

"I don't care how long you have tested yourself," said Ms. Perry. "I honestly don't think you have painted me at all. In fact, I felt you weren't interested in painting me. I think you're interested in letting your eyes go over my naked body for certain reasons of your own. I don't know what your personal needs are but I'm damn well sure that most of them are not about painting."

"I guess I have made a mistake."

"I guess you have," said the model. She had her robe on now, the belt pulled tight.

"I'm a painter," she said, "and I model because I am broke but I know a fake when I see one."

"I wouldn't feel so bad," said Mr. Elihu, "if I hadn't gone

out of my way to explain the situation to that lady at the Art Students League.

"I'm sorry this happened," Mr. Elihu said hoarsely. "I should have thought it through but didn't. I'm seventy years of age. I have always loved women and felt a sad loss that I have no particular women friends at this time of my life. That's one of the reasons I wanted to paint again, though I make no claims that I was ever greatly talented. Also, I guess I didn't realize how much about painting I have forgotten. Not only that, but about the female body. I didn't realize I would be so moved by yours, and, on reflection, about the way my life has gone. I hoped painting again would refresh my feeling for life. I regret that I have inconvenienced and disturbed you."

"I'll be paid for my inconvenience," Ms. Perry said, "but what you can't pay me for is the insult of coming here and submitting myself to your eyes crawling on my body."

"I didn't mean it as an insult."

"That's what it feels like to me."

She then asked Mr. Elihu to disrobe.

"I?" he said, surprised. "What for?"

"I want to sketch you. Take your pants and shirt off."

He said he had barely got rid of his winter underwear but she did not smile.

Mr. Elihu disrobed, ashamed of how he must look to her.

With quick strokes she sketched his form. He was not a bad-looking man but felt bad. When she had the sketch she dipped his brush into a blob of black pigment she had squeezed out of a tube and smeared his features, leaving a black mess.

He watched her hating him but said nothing.

Ms. Perry tossed the brush into a wastebasket and returned to the bathroom for her clothing.

The old man wrote out a check for her for the sum they had agreed on. He was ashamed to sign his name but he signed it and handed it to her. Ms. Perry slipped the check into her large purse and left.

He thought that in her way she was not a bad-looking woman though she lacked grace. The old man then asked himself, "Is there nothing more to my life than it is now? Is this all that is left to me?"

The answer seemed yes and he wept at how old he had so quickly become.

Afterwards he removed the towel over his canvas and tried to fill in her face, but he had already forgotten it.

The Silver Crown

GANS, the father, lay dying in a hospital bed. Different doctors said different things, held different theories. There was talk of an exploratory operation but they thought it might kill him. One doctor said cancer.

"Of the heart," the old man said bitterly.

"It wouldn't be impossible."

The young Gans, Albert, a high school biology teacher, in the afternoons walked the streets in sorrow. What can anybody do about cancer? His soles wore thin with walking. He was easily irritated; angered by the war, atom bomb, pollution, death, obviously the strain of worrying about his father's illness. To be able to do nothing for him made him frantic. He had done nothing for him all his life.

A female colleague, an English teacher he had slept with once, a girl who was visibly aging, advised, "If the doctors don't know, Albert, try a faith healer. Different people know different things; nobody knows everything. You can't tell about the human body."

Albert laughed mirthlessly but listened. If specialists disagree, who do you agree with? If you've tried everything, what else can you try?

One afternoon after a long walk alone, as he was about to descend the subway stairs somewhere in the Bronx, still burdened by his worries, uneasy that nothing had changed, he was accosted by a fat girl with bare meaty arms who thrust a soiled card at him that he tried to avoid. She was a stupefying sight, retarded at the very least. Fifteen, he'd say, though she looks thirty and probably has the mentality of age ten. Her skin glowed, face wet, fleshy, a small mouth open and would be forever; eyes set wide apart on the broad unfocused face, either watery green or brown, or one of each—he wasn't sure. She seemed not to mind his appraisal, gurgled faintly. Her thick hair was braided in two ropelike strands; she wore bulging cloth slippers bursting at seams and soles; a faded red skirt down to massive ankles, and a heavy brown sweater vest buttoned over blown breasts, though the weather was still hot September.

The teacher's impulse was to pass by her outthrust plump baby hand. Instead he took the card from her. Simple curiosity—once you had learned to read you read anything? Charitable impulse?

Albert recognized Yiddish and Hebrew but read in English: "Heal The Sick. Save The Dying. Make A Silver Crown."

"What kind of silver crown would that be?"

She uttered impossible noises. Depressed, he looked away. When his eyes turned to hers she ran off.

He studied the card. "Make A Silver Crown." It gave a rabbi's name and address no less: Jonas Lifschitz, close by in the neighborhood. The silver crown mystified him. He had no idea what it had to do with saving the dying but felt he ought to know. Although at first repelled by the thought, he made up his mind to visit the rabbi and felt, in a way, relieved.

The teacher hastened along the street a few blocks until he came to the address on the card, a battered synagogue in a store, Congregation Theodor Herzl, painted in large uneven white letters on the plate-glass window. The rabbi's name, in smaller, gold letters, was A. Marcus. In the doorway to the left of the store the number of the house was repeated in tin numerals, and on a card under the vacant name plate under the mezuzah appeared in pencil, "Rabbi J. Lifschitz. Retired. Consultations. Ring The Bell." The bell, when he decided to chance it, did not work—seemed dead to the touch—so Albert, his heartbeat erratic, turned the knob. The door gave easily enough and he hesitantly walked up a dark flight of narrow wooden stairs. Ascending, assailed by doubts, peering up through the gloom, he thought of turning back but at the first-floor landing compelled himself to knock loudly on the door.

"Anybody home here?"

He rapped harder, annoyed with himself for being there, engaging in the act of entrance—who would have predicted it an hour ago? The door opened a crack and that broad, badly formed face appeared. The retarded girl, squinting one bulbous eye, made noises like two eggs frying, and ducked back, slamming the door. The teacher, after momentary reflection, thrust it open in time to see her, bulky as she was, running along the long tight corridor, her body bumping the walls as she disappeared into a room at the rear.

Albert entered cautiously, with a sense of embarrassment, if not danger, warning himself to depart at once; yet stayed to peek curiously into a front room off the hallway, darkened by lowered green shades through which threadlike rivulets of light streamed. The shades resembled faded maps of ancient lands. An old gray-bearded man with thickened left eyelid, wearing a yarmulke, sat heavily asleep, a book in his lap, on a sagging armchair. Someone in the room gave off a stale odor, unless it was the armchair. As Albert stared, the old man awoke in a hurry. The small thick book on his lap fell with a thump to the floor, but instead of picking it up, he shoved it with a kick of his heel under the chair.

"So where were we?" he inquired pleasantly, a bit breathless.

The teacher removed his hat, remembered whose house he was in, and put it back on his head.

He introduced himself. "I was looking for Rabbi J. Lifschitz. Your—ah—girl let me in."

"Rabbi Lifschitz—this was my daughter Rifkele. She's not perfect, though God, who made her in His image, is Himself perfection. What this means I don't have to tell you."

His heavy eyelid went down in a wink, apparently involuntarily.

"What does it mean?" Albert asked.

"In her way she is also perfect."

"Anyway, she let me in and here I am."

"So what did you decide?"

"About what?"

"What did you decide about what we were talking about—the silver crown?"

His eyes roved as he spoke; he rubbed a nervous thumb and forefinger. Crafty type, the teacher decided. Him I have to watch myself with.

"I came here to find out about this crown you advertised," he said, "but actually we haven't talked about it or anything else. When I entered here you were sound asleep."

"At my age—" the rabbi explained with a little laugh.

"I don't mean any criticism. All I'm saying is I am a stranger to you."

"How can we be strangers if we both believe in God?"

Albert made no argument of it.

The rabbi raised the two shades and the last of daylight fell into the spacious high-ceilinged room, crowded with at least a dozen stiff-back and folding chairs, plus a broken sofa. What kind of operation is he running here? Group consultations? He dispensed rabbinic therapy? The teacher felt renewed distaste for himself for having come. On the wall hung a single oval mirror, framed in gold-plated groupings of joined metal circles, large and small; but no pictures. Despite the empty chairs, or perhaps because of them, the room seemed barren.

The teacher observed that the rabbi's trousers were a week from ragged. He was wearing an unpressed worn black suit-coat and a yellowed white shirt without a tie. His wet grayish-blue eyes were restless. Rabbi Lifschitz was a dark-faced man with brown eye pouches and smelled of old age. This was the odor. It was hard to say whether he resembled his daughter; Rifkele resembled her species.

"So sit," said the old rabbi with a light sigh. "Not on the couch, sit on a chair."

"Which in particular?"

"You have a first-class humor." Smiling absently, he pointed to two kitchen chairs and seated himself in one.

He offered a thin cigarette.

"I'm off them," the teacher explained.

"I also." The old man put the pack away. "So who is sick?" he inquired.

Albert tightened at the question, as he recalled the card he had taken from the girl: "Heal The Sick, Save The Dying."

"To come to the point, my father's in the hospital with a serious ailment. In fact he's dying."

The rabbi, nodding gravely, dug into his pants pocket for a pair of glasses, wiped them with a large soiled handkerchief, and put them on, lifting the wire earpieces over each fleshy ear.

"So we will make then a crown for him?"

"That depends. The crown is what I came here to find out about."

"What do you wish to find out?"

"I'll be frank with you." The teacher blew his nose and slowly wiped it. "My cast of mind is naturally empiric and objective—

you might say non-mystical. I'm suspicious of faith healing, but I've come here, frankly, because I want to do anything possible to help my father recover his former health. To put it otherwise, I don't want anything to go untried."

"You love your father?" the rabbi clucked, a glaze of sentiment veiling his eyes.

"What I feel is obvious. My real concern right now mainly is how does the crown work. Could you be explicit about the mechanism of it all? Who wears it, for instance? Does he? Do you? Or do I have to? In other words, how does it function? And if you wouldn't mind saying, what's the principle, or rationale, behind it? This is terra incognita for me, but I think I might be willing to take a chance if I could justify it to myself. Could I see a sample of the crown, for instance, if you have one on hand?"

The rabbi, with an absentminded start, seemed to interrupt himself about to pick his nose.

"What is the crown?" he asked, at first haughtily, then again, gently. "It's a crown, nothing else. There are crowns in Mishna, Proverbs, Kabbalah; the holy scrolls of the Torah are often protected by crowns. But this one is different, this you will understand when it does the work. It's a miracle. A sample doesn't exist. The crown has to be made individual for your father. Then his health will be restored. There are two prices—"

"Kindly explain what's supposed to cure the sickness," Albert said. "Does it work like sympathetic magic? I'm not nay-saying, you understand. I just happen to be interested in all kinds of phenomena. Is the crown supposed to draw off the illness like some kind of poultice, or what?"

"The crown is not a medicine, it is the health of your father. We offer the crown to God and God returns to your father his health. But first we got to make it the way it must be made—this I will do with my assistant, a retired jeweler. He has helped me to make a thousand crowns. Believe me, he knows silver—the right amount to the ounce according to the size you wish. Then I will say the blessings. Without the right blessings, exact to each word, the crown don't work. I don't have to tell you why. When the crown is finished your father will get better. This I will guarantee you. Let me read you some words from the mystic book."

"The Kabbalah?" the teacher asked respectfully.

"Like the Kabbalah."

The rabbi rose, went to his armchair, got slowly down on his hands and knees and withdrew the book he had shoved under the misshapen chair, a thick small volume with faded purple covers, not a word imprinted on it. The rabbi kissed the book and murmured a prayer.

"I hid it for a minute," he explained, "when you came in the room. It's a terrible thing nowadays, goyim come in your house in the middle of the day and take away that which belongs to you, if not your life itself."

"I told you right away that your daughter had let me in," Albert said in embarrassment.

"Once you mentioned I knew."

The teacher then asked, "Suppose I am a non-believer? Will the crown work if it's ordered by a person who has his doubts?"

"Doubts we all got. We doubt God and God doubts us. This is natural on account of the nature of existence. Of this kind doubts I am not afraid so long as you love your father."

"You're putting it as sort of a paradox."

"So what's so bad about a paradox?"

"My father wasn't the easiest man in the world to get along with, and neither am I for that matter, but he has been generous to me and I'd like to repay him in some way."

"God respects a grateful son. If you love your father this will go in the crown and help him to recover his health. Do you understand Hebrew?"

"Unfortunately not."

The rabbi flipped a few pages of his thick tome, peered at one closely and read aloud in Hebrew, which he then translated into English. " 'The crown is the fruit of God's grace. His grace is love of creation.' These words I will read seven times over the silver crown. This is the most important blessing."

"Fine. But what about those two prices you quoted me a minute ago?"

"This depends how quick you wish the cure."

"I want the cure to be immediate, otherwise there's no sense to the whole deal," Albert said, controlling anger. "If you're questioning my sincerity, I've already told you I'm considering this recourse even though it goes against the grain of some of my strongest convictions. I've gone out of my way to make my pros and cons absolutely clear."

"Who says no?"

The teacher became aware of Rifkele standing at the door, eating a slice of bread with lumps of butter on it. She beheld him in mild stupefaction, as though seeing him for the first time.

"Shpeter, Rifkele," the rabbi said patiently.

The girl shoved the bread into her mouth and ran ponderously down the passageway.

"Anyway, what about those two prices?" Albert asked, annoyed by the interruption. Every time Rifkele appeared his doubts of the enterprise rose before him like warriors with spears.

"We got two kinds crowns," said the rabbi. "One is for 401 and the other is 986."

"Dollars, you mean, for God's sake?—that's fantastic."

"The crown is pure silver. The client pays in silver dollars. So the silver dollars we melt—more for the large-size crown, less for the medium."

"What about the small?"

"There is no small. What good is a small crown?"

"I wouldn't know, but the assumption seems to be the bigger the better. Tell me, please, what can a 986 crown do that a 401 can't? Does the patient get better faster with the larger one? It hastens the reaction?"

The rabbi, five fingers hidden in his limp beard, assented.

"Are there any other costs?"

"Costs?"

"Over and above the quoted prices?"

"The price is the price, there is no extra. The price is for the silver and for the work and for the blessings."

"Now would you kindly tell me, assuming I decide to get involved in this deal, where I am supposed to lay my hands on 401 silver dollars? Or if I should opt for the 986 job, where can I get a pile of cartwheels of that amount? I don't suppose that any bank in the whole Bronx would keep that many silver dollars on hand nowadays. The Bronx is no longer the Wild West, Rabbi Lifschitz. But what's more to the point, isn't it true the mint isn't making silver dollars all silver any more?"

"So if they are not making we will get wholesale. If you will leave with me the cash, I will order the silver from a wholesaler, and we will save you the trouble to go to the bank. It will be the same amount of silver, only in small bars, I will weigh them on a scale in front of your eyes."

"One other question. Would you take my personal check in payment? I could give it to you right away once I've made my final decision."

"I wish I could, Mr. Gans," said the rabbi, his veined hand still nervously exploring his beard, "but it's better cash when the patient is so sick, so I can start to work right away. A check sometimes comes back, or gets lost in the bank, and this interferes with the crown."

Albert did not ask how, suspecting that a bounced check, or a lost one, wasn't the problem. No doubt some customers for crowns had stopped their checks on afterthought.

As the teacher reflected concerning his next move—should he, shouldn't he?—weighing a rational thought against a sentimental, the old rabbi sat in his chair, reading quickly in his small mystic book, his lips hastening along silently.

Albert at last got up.

"I'll decide the question once and for all tonight. If I go ahead and commit myself on the crown I'll bring you the cash after work tomorrow."

"Go in good health," said the rabbi. Removing his glasses he wiped both eyes with his handkerchief.

Wet or dry? thought the teacher.

As he let himself out of the downstairs door, more inclined than not toward trying the crown, he felt relieved, almost euphoric.

But by the next morning, after a difficult night, Albert's mood had about-faced. He fought gloom, irritation, felt flashes of hot and cold anger. It's throwing money away, pure and simple. I'm dealing with a clever confidence man, that's plain to me, but for some reason I am not resisting strongly. Maybe my subconscious is telling me to go along with a blowing wind and have the crown made. After that we'll see what happens—whether it rains, snows, or spring comes. Not much will happen, I suppose, but whatever does, my conscience will be in the clear.

But when he visited Rabbi Lifschitz that afternoon in the same roomful of empty chairs, though the teacher carried the required cash in his wallet, he was still uncomfortable about parting with it.

"Where do the crowns go after they are used and the patient recovers his health?" he cleverly asked the rabbi.

"I'm glad you asked me this question," said the rabbi alertly, his thick lid drooping. "They are melted, and the silver we give to the poor. A mitzvah for one makes a mitzvah for another."

"To the poor you say?"

"There are plenty poor people, Mr. Gans. Sometimes they need a crown for a sick wife or a sick child. Where will they get the silver?"

"I see what you mean—recycled, sort of, but can't a crown be reused as it is? I mean, do you permit a period of time to go by before you melt them down? Suppose a dying man who recovers gets seriously ill again at a future date?"

"For a new sickness you will need a new crown. Tomorrow the world is not the same as today, though God listens with the same ear."

"Look, Rabbi Lifschitz," Albert said impatiently, "I'll tell you frankly that I am inching toward ordering the crown, but it would make my decision a whole lot easier all around if you would let me have a quick look at one of them—it wouldn't have to be for more than five seconds—at a crown-in-progress for some other client."

"What will you see in five seconds?"

"Enough—whether the object is believable, worth the fuss and not inconsequential investment."

"Mr. Gans," replied the rabbi, "this is not a showcase business. You are not buying from me a new Chevrolet automobile. Your father lays now dying in the hospital. Do you love him? Do you wish me to make a crown that will cure him?"

The teacher's anger flared. "Don't be stupid, rabbi, I've answered that. Please don't sidetrack the real issue. You're working on my guilt so I'll suspend my perfectly reasonable doubts of the whole freaking enterprise. I won't fall for that."

They glared at each other. The rabbi's beard quivered. Albert ground his teeth.

Rifkele, in a nearby room, moaned.

The rabbi, breathing emotionally, after a moment relented.

"I will show you the crown," he sighed.

"Accept my apologies for losing my temper."

The rabbi accepted. "Now tell me please what kind of sickness your father has got."

"Ah," said Albert, "nobody is certain for sure. One day he got into bed, turned to the wall and said, 'I'm sick.' They suspected leukemia at first but the lab tests didn't confirm it."

"You talked to the doctors?"

"In droves. Till I was blue in the face. A bunch of ignoramuses," said the teacher hoarsely. "Anyway, nobody knows exactly what he has wrong with him. The theories include rare blood diseases, also a possible carcinoma of certain endocrine glands. You name it, I've heard it, with complications suggested, like Parkinson's or Addison's disease, multiple sclerosis, or something similar, alone or in combination with other sicknesses. It's a mysterious case, all in all."

"This means you will need a special crown," said the rabbi.

The teacher bridled. "What do you mean special? What will it cost?"

"The cost will be the same," the rabbi answered dryly, "but the design and the kind of blessings will be different. When you are dealing with such a mystery you got to make another one but it must be bigger."

"How would that work?"

"Like two winds that they meet in the sky. A white and a blue. The blue says, 'Not only I am blue but inside I am also purple and orange.' So the white goes away."

"If you can work it up for the same price, that's up to you."

Rabbi Lifschitz then drew down the two green window shades and shut the door, darkening the room.

"Sit," he said in the heavy dark, "I will show you the crown."

"I'm sitting."

"So sit where you are, but turn your head to the wall where is the mirror."

"But why so dark?"

"You will see light."

He heard the rabbi strike a match and it flared momentarily, casting shadows of candles and chairs amid the empty chairs in the room.

"Look now in the mirror."

"I'm looking."

"What do you see?"

"Nothing."

"Look with your eyes."

A silver candelabrum, first with three, then five, then seven burning bony candlesticks, appeared like ghostly hands with flaming fingertips in the oval mirror. The heat of it hit Albert in the face and for a moment he was stunned.

But recalling the games of his childhood, he thought, who's kidding who? It's one of those illusion things I remember from when I was a kid. In that case I'm getting the hell out of here. I can stand maybe mystery but not magic tricks or dealing with a rabbinical magician.

The candelabrum had vanished, although not its light, and he now saw the rabbi's somber face in the glass, his gaze addressing him. Albert glanced quickly around to see if anyone was standing at his shoulder, but nobody was. Where the rabbi was hiding at the moment the teacher did not know; but in the lit glass appeared his old man's lined and shrunken face, his sad eyes, compelling, inquisitive, weary, perhaps even frightened, as though they had seen more than they had cared to but were still looking.

What's this, slides or home movies? Albert sought some source of projection but saw no ray of light from wall or ceiling, nor object or image that might be reflected by the mirror.

The rabbi's eyes glowed like sun-filled clouds. A moon rose in the blue sky. The teacher dared not move, afraid to discover he was unable to. He then beheld a shining crown on the rabbi's head.

It had appeared at first like a braided mother-of-pearl turban, then had luminously become—like an intricate star in the night sky—a silver crown, constructed of bars, triangles, half-moons and crescents, spires, turrets, trees, points of spears; as though a wild storm had swept them up from the earth and flung them together in its vortex, twisted into a single glowing interlocked sculpture, a forest of disparate objects.

The sight in the ghostly mirror, a crown of rare beauty—very impressive, Albert thought—lasted no longer than five short seconds, then the reflecting glass by degrees turned dark and empty.

The shades were up. The single bulb in a frosted lily fixture on the ceiling shone harshly in the room. It was night.

The old rabbi sat, exhausted, on the broken sofa.

"So you saw it?"

"I saw something."

"You believe what you saw—the crown?"

"I believe I saw. Anyway, I'll take it."

The rabbi gazed at him blankly.

"I mean I agree to have the crown made," Albert said, having to clear his throat.

"Which size?"

"Which size was the one I saw?"

"Both sizes. This is the same design for both sizes, but there is more silver and also more blessings for the $986 size."

"But didn't you say that the design for my father's crown, because of the special nature of his illness, would have a different style, plus some special blessings?"

The rabbi nodded. "This comes also in two sizes—the $401 and $986."

The teacher hesitated a split second. "Make it the big one," he said decisively.

He had his wallet in his hand and counted out fifteen new bills—nine one hundreds, four twenties, a five, and a single—adding to $986.

Putting on his glasses, the rabbi hastily counted the money, snapping with thumb and forefinger each crisp bill as though to be sure none had stuck together. He folded the stiff paper and thrust the wad into his pants pocket.

"Could I have a receipt?"

"I would like to give you a receipt," said Rabbi Lifschitz earnestly, "but for the crowns there are no receipts. Some things are not a business."

"If money is exchanged, why not?"

"God will not allow. My father did not give receipts and also my grandfather."

"How can I prove I paid you if something goes wrong?"

"You have my word, nothing will go wrong."

"Yes, but suppose something unforeseen did," Albert insisted, "would you return the cash?"

"Here is your cash," said the rabbi, handing the teacher the packet of folded bills.

"Never mind," said Albert hastily. "Could you tell me when the crown will be ready?"

"Tomorrow night before Shabbos, the latest."

"So soon?"

"Your father is dying."

"That's right, but the crown looks like a pretty intricate piece of work to put together out of all those odd pieces."

"We will hurry."

"I wouldn't want you to rush the job in any way that would— let's say—prejudice the potency of the crown, or for that matter, in any way impair the quality of it as I saw it in the mirror—or however I saw it."

Down came the rabbi's eyelid, quickly raised without a sign of self-consciousness. "Mr. Gans, all my crowns are first-class jobs. About this you got nothing to worry about."

They then shook hands. Albert, still assailed by doubts,

stepped into the corridor. He felt he did not, in essence, trust the rabbi; and suspected that Rabbi Lifschitz knew it and did not, in essence, trust him.

Rifkele, panting like a cow for a bull, let him out the front door, perfectly.

In the subway, Albert figured he would call it an investment in experience and see what came of it. Education costs money, but how else can you get it? He pictured the crown, as he had seen it, established on the rabbi's head, and then seemed to remember that as he had stared at the man's shifty face in the mirror the thickened lid of his right eye had slowly dropped into a full wink. Did he recall this in truth, or was he seeing in his mind's eye and transposing into the past something that had happened just before he left the house? What does he mean by his wink?—not only is he a fake but he kids you? Uneasy once more, the teacher clearly remembered, when he was staring into the rabbi's fish eyes in the glass, after which they had lit in visionary light, that he had fought a hunger to sleep; and the next thing there's the sight of the old boy, as though on the television screen, wearing this high-hat magic crown.

Albert, rising, cried, "Hypnosis! The bastard magician hypnotized me! He never did produce a silver crown, it's out of my imagination—I've been suckered!"

He was outraged by the knavery, hypocrisy, fat nerve of Rabbi Jonas Lifschitz. The concept of a curative crown, if he had ever for a moment believed in it, crumbled in his brain and all he could think of were 986 blackbirds flying in the sky. As three curious passengers watched, Albert bolted out of the car at the next stop, rushed up the stairs, hurried across the street, then cooled his impatient heels for twenty-two minutes till the next train clattered into the station, and he rode back to the stop near the rabbi's house. Though he banged with both fists on the door, kicked at it, "rang" the useless bell until his thumb was blistered, the boxlike wooden house, including dilapidated synagogue store, was dark, monumentally starkly still, like a gigantic, slightly tilted tombstone in a vast graveyard; and in the end unable to arouse a soul, the teacher, long past midnight, had to head home.

He awoke next morning cursing the rabbi and his own stupidity for having got involved with a faith healer. This is what happens when a man—even for a minute—surrenders his true beliefs. There are less punishing ways to help the dying. Albert considered calling the cops but had no receipt and did not want to appear that much a fool. He was tempted, for the first time in six years of teaching, to phone in sick; then take a cab to the rabbi's house and demand the return of his cash. The thought agitated him. On the other hand, suppose Rabbi Lifschitz was seriously at work assembling the crown with his helper; on which, let's say, after he had bought the silver and paid the retired jeweler for his work, he made, let's say, a hundred bucks clear profit—not so very much; and there really *was* a silver crown, and the rabbi sincerely and religiously believed it would reverse the course of his father's illness? Although nervously disturbed by his suspicions, Albert felt he had better not get the police into the act too soon, because the crown wasn't promised—didn't the old gent say—until before the Sabbath, which gave him till sunset tonight.

If he produces the thing by then, I have no case against him even if it's a piece of junk. So I better wait. But what a dope I was to order the $986 job instead of the $401. On that decision alone I lost $585.

After a distracted day's work Albert taxied to the rabbi's house and tried to rouse him, even hallooing at the blank windows facing the street; but either nobody was home or they were both hiding, the rabbi under the broken sofa, Rifkele trying to shove her bulk under a bathtub. Albert decided to wait them out.

Soon the old boy would have to leave the house to step into the shul on Friday night. He would speak to him, warn him to come clean. But the sun set; dusk settled on the earth; and though the autumn stars and a sliver of moon gleamed in the sky, the house was dark, shades drawn; and no Rabbi Lifschitz emerged. Lights had gone on in the little shul, candles were lit. It occurred to Albert, with chagrin, that the rabbi might be already worshipping; he might all this time have been in the synagogue.

The teacher entered the long, brightly lit store. On yellow folding chairs scattered around the room sat a dozen men holding worn prayer books, praying. The Rabbi A. Marcus, a middle-aged man with a high voice and a short reddish beard, was dovening at the Ark, his back to the congregation.

As Albert entered and embarrassedly searched from face to face, the congregants stared at him. The old rabbi was not among them. Disappointed, the teacher withdrew.

A man sitting by the door touched his sleeve.

"Stay awhile and read with us."

"Excuse me, I'd like to but I'm looking for a friend."

"Look," said the man, "maybe you'll find him."

Albert waited across the street under a chestnut tree losing its leaves. He waited patiently—till tomorrow if he had to.

Shortly after nine the lights went out in the synagogue and the last of the worshippers left for home. The red-bearded rabbi then emerged with his key in his hand to lock the store door.

"Excuse me, rabbi," said Albert, approaching. "Are you acquainted with Rabbi Jonas Lifschitz, who lives upstairs with his daughter Rifkele—if she is his daughter?"

"He used to come here," said the rabbi with a small smile, "but since he retired he prefers a big synagogue on Mosholu Parkway, a palace."

"Will he be home soon, do you think?"

"Maybe in an hour. It's Shabbat, he must walk."

"Do you—ah—happen to know anything about his work on silver crowns?"

"What kind of silver crowns?"

"To assist the sick, the dying?"

"No," said the rabbi, locking the shul door, pocketing the key, and hurrying away.

The teacher, eating his heart, waited under the chestnut tree till past midnight, all the while urging himself to give up and go home, but unable to unstick the glue of his frustration and rage. Then shortly before 1 a.m. he saw some shadows moving and two people drifting up the shadow-encrusted street. One was the old rabbi, in a new caftan and snappy black Homburg, walking tiredly. Rifkele, in sexy yellow mini, exposing to above the big-bone knees her legs like poles, walked lightly behind him, stopping to strike her ears with her hands. A long white shawl, pulled short on the right shoulder, hung down to her left shoe.

"On my income their glad rags."

Rifkele chanted a long "Boooo" and slapped both ears with her pudgy hands to keep from hearing it.

They toiled up the ill-lit narrow staircase, the teacher trailing them.

"I came to see my crown," he told the pale, astonished rabbi, in the front room.

"The crown," the rabbi said haughtily, "is already finished. Go home and wait, your father will soon get better."

"I called the hospital before leaving my apartment, there's been no improvement."

"How can you expect so soon improvement if the doctors themselves don't know what is the sickness? You must give the crown a little more time. God Himself has trouble to understand human sickness."

"I came to see the thing I paid for."

"I showed you already, you saw before you ordered."

"That was an image of a facsimile, maybe, or something of the sort. I insist on seeing the real thing, for which I paid close to one thousand smackers."

"Listen, Mr. Gans," said the rabbi patiently, "there are some things we are allowed to see which He lets us see them. Sometimes I wish He didn't let us. There are other things we are not allowed to see—Moses knew this—and one is God's face, and another is the real crown that He makes and blesses it. A miracle is a miracle, this is God's business."

"Don't you see it?"

"Not with my eyes."

"I don't believe a word of it, you faker, two-bit magician."

"The crown is a real crown. If you think there is magic, it is on account those people that they insist to see it—we try to give them an idea. For those who believe, there is no magic."

"Rifkele," the rabbi said hurriedly, "bring to Papa my book of letters."

She left the room, after a while, a little in fright, her eyes evasive; and returned in ten minutes, after flushing the toilet, in a shapeless long flannel nightgown, carrying a large yellowed notebook whose loose pages were thickly interleaved with old correspondence.

"Testimonials," said the rabbi.

Turning several loose pages, with trembling hand he extracted a letter and read it aloud, his voice husky with emotion.

" 'Dear Rabbi Lifschitz: Since the miraculous recovery of my mother, Mrs. Max Cohen, from her recent illness, my impulse is to cover your bare feet with kisses. Your crown worked wonders and I am recommending it to all my friends. Yours truly and sincerely, (Mrs.) Esther Polatnik.'

"This is a college teacher."

He read another. " 'Dear Rabbi Lifschitz, Your $986 crown totally and completely cured my father of cancer of the pancreas, with serious complications of the lungs, after nothing else had worked. Never before have I believed in miraculous occurrences, but from now on I will have less doubts. My thanks to you and God. Most sincerely, Daniel Schwartz.'

"A lawyer," said the rabbi.

He offered the book to Albert. "Look yourself, Mr. Gans, hundreds of letters."

Albert wouldn't touch it.

"There's only one thing I want to look at, Rabbi Lifschitz, and it's not a book of useless testimonials. I want to see my father's silver crown."

"This is impossible. I already explained to you why I can't do this. God's word is God's law."

"So if it's the law you're citing, either I see the crown in the next five minutes, or the first thing tomorrow morning I'm reporting you and your activities to the Bronx County District Attorney."

"Boooo-ooo," sang Rifkele, banging her ears.

"Shut up!" Albert said.

"Have respect," cried the rabbi. "Grubber yung!"

"I will swear out a complaint and the D.A. will shut you down, the whole freaking plant, if you don't at once return the $986 you swindled me out of."

The rabbi wavered in his tracks. "Is this the way to talk to a rabbi of God?"

"A thief is a thief."

Rifkele blubbered, squealed.

"Sha," the rabbi thickly whispered to Albert, clasping and unclasping his gray hands. "You'll frighten the neighbors. Listen to me, Mr. Gans, you saw with your eyes what it looks like the real crown. I give you my word that nobody of my whole clientele ever saw this before. I showed you for your father's sake so you would tell me to make the crown which will save him. Don't spoil now the miracle."

"Miracle," Albert bellowed, "it's a freaking fake magic, with an idiot girl for a come-on and hypnotic mirrors. I was mesmerized, suckered by you."

"Be kind," begged the rabbi, tottering as he wandered amid empty chairs. "Be merciful to an old man. Think of my poor child. Think of your father who loves you."

"He hates me, the son of a bitch, I hope he croaks."

In an explosion of silence the girl slobbered in fright.

"Aha," cried the wild-eyed rabbi, pointing a finger at God in heaven. "Murderer," he cried, aghast.

Moaning, father and daughter rushed into each other's arms, as Albert, wearing a massive, spike-laden headache, rushed down the booming stairs.

An hour later the elder Gans shut his eyes and expired.

Talking Horse

Q. Am I a man in a horse or a horse that talks like a man? Suppose they took an X-ray, what would they see?—a man's luminous skeleton prostrate inside a horse, or just a horse with a complicated voice box? If the first, then Jonah had it better in the whale—more room all around; also he knew who he was and how he had got there. About myself I have to make guesses. Anyway, after three days and nights the big fish stopped at Nineveh and Jonah took his valise and got off. But not Abramowitz, still on board, or at hand, after years; he's no prophet. On the contrary, he works in a sideshow full of freaks— though recently advanced, on Goldberg's insistence, to the center ring inside the big tent in an act with his deaf-mute master —Goldberg himself, may the Almighty forgive him. All I know is I've been here for years and still don't understand the nature of my fate; in short if I'm Abramowitz, a horse; or a horse *including* Abramowitz. Why is anybody's guess. Understanding goes so far and no further, especially if Goldberg blocks the way. It might be because of something I said, or thought, or did, or didn't do in my life. It's easy to make mistakes and easy not to know who made them. I have my theories, glimmers, guesses, but can't prove a thing.

When Abramowitz stands in his stall, his hooves nervously booming on the battered wooden boards as he chews in his bag of hard yellow oats, sometimes he has thoughts, far-off remembrances they seem to be, of young horses racing, playing, nipping at each other's flanks in green fields; and other disquieting images that might be memories; so who's to say what's really the truth?

I've tried asking Goldberg, but save yourself the trouble. He goes black-and-blue in the face at questions, really uptight. I can understand—he's a deaf-mute from way back; he doesn't like interference with his thoughts or plans, or the way he lives, and no surprises except those he invents. In other words questions disturb him. Ask him a question and he's off his track. He talks to me only when he feels like it, which isn't so often—his little patience wears thin. Lately his mood is awful, he reaches too often for his bamboo cane—whoosh across the rump! There's usually plenty of oats and straw and water, and once in a while even a joke to relax me when I'm tensed up, but otherwise it's one threat or another, followed by a flash of pain if I don't get something or other right, or something I say hits him on his nerves. It's not only that cane that slashes like a whip; his threats have the same effect—like a zing-zong of lightning through the flesh; in fact the blow hurts less than the threat—the blow's momentary, the threat you worry about. But the true pain, at least to me, is when you don't know what you have to know.

Which doesn't mean we don't communicate to each other. Goldberg taps out Morse code messages on my head with his big knuckle—crack crack crack; I feel the vibrations run through my bones to the tip of my tail—when he orders me what to do next or he threatens how many lashes for the last offense. His first message, I remember, was NO QUESTIONS. UNDER-

STOOD? I shook my head yes and a little bell jingled on a strap under the forelock. That was the first I knew it was there.

TALK, he rapped on my head after he told me about the act. "You're a talking horse."

"Yes, master." What else can you say?

My voice surprised me when it came out high through the tunnel of a horse's neck. I can't exactly remember the occasion —go remember beginnings. My memory I have to fight to get an early remembrance out of. Don't ask me why unless I happened to fall and hurt my head, or was otherwise stunted. Goldberg is my deaf-mute owner; he reads my lips. Once when he was drunk and looking for company he tapped me that I used to carry goods on my back to fairs and markets in the old days before we joined the circus.

I used to think I was born here.

"On a rainy, snowy, crappy night," Goldberg Morse-coded me on my bony skull.

"What happened then?"

He stopped talking altogether. I should know better but don't.

I try to remember what night we're talking about and certain hazy thoughts flicker in my mind, which could be some sort of story I dream up when I have nothing to do but chew oats. It's easier than remembering. The one that comes to me most is about two men, or horses, or men on horses, though which was me I can't say. Anyway two strangers meet, somebody asks the other a question, and the next thing they're locked in battle, either hacking at one another's head with swords, or braying wildly as they tear flesh with their teeth; or both at the same time. If riders, or horses, one is thin and poetic, the other a fat stranger wearing a huge black crown. They meet in a stone pit on a rainy, snowy, crappy night, one wearing his cracked metal crown that weighs a ton on his head and makes his movements slow though nonetheless accurate, and the other on his head wears a ragged colored cap. All night they wrestle by weird light in the slippery stone pit.

Q. "What's to be done?"

A. "None of those accursed bloody questions."

The next morning one of us wakes with a terrible pain which feels like a wound in the neck but also a headache. He remembers a blow he can't swear to and a strange dialogue where the answers come first and the questions follow:

I descended a ladder.

How did you get here?

The up and the down.

Which is which?

Abramowitz, in his dream story, suspects Goldberg had walloped him over the head and stuffed him into a horse because he needed a talking one for his act and there was no such thing.

I wish I knew for sure.

DON'T DARE ASK.

That's his nature; he's a lout though not without a little consideration when he's depressed and tippling his bottle. That's when he taps me out a teasing anecdote or two. He has no visible friends. Family neither of us talks about. When he laughs he cries.

It must frustrate Goldberg that all he can say aloud is four-letter words like geee, gooo, gaaa, gaaw; and the circus manager who doubles as ringmaster, in for a snifter, looks embarrassed at the floor. At those who don't know the Morse code Goldberg grimaces, glares, and grinds his teeth. He has his mysteries. He keeps a mildewed three-prong spear hanging on the wall over a stuffed pony's head. Sometimes he goes down the cellar with an old candle and comes up with a new one lit though we have electric lights. Although he doesn't complain about his life, he worries and cracks his knuckles. He doesn't seem interested in women but sees to it that Abramowitz gets his chance at a mare in heat, if available. Abramowitz engages to satisfy his physical nature, a fact is a fact, otherwise it's no big deal; the mare has no interest in a talking courtship. Furthermore, Goldberg applauds when Abramowitz mounts her, which is humiliating.

And when they're in their winter quarters the owner once a week or so dresses up and goes out on the town. When he puts on his broadcloth suit, diamond stickpin, and yellow gloves, he preens before the full-length mirror. He pretends to fence, jabs the bamboo cane at the figure in the glass, twirls it around one finger. Where he goes when he goes he never informs Abramowitz. But when he returns he's usually melancholic, sometimes anguished, didn't have much of a good time; and in this mood may mete out a few loving lashes with that bastard cane. Or worse—make threats. Nothing serious but who needs it? Usually he prefers to stay home and watch television. He is fascinated by astronomy, and when they have those programs on the educational channel he's there night after night, staring at pictures of stars, quasars, infinite space. He also likes to read the *Daily News*, which he tears up when he's done. Sometimes he reads this book he hides on a shelf in the closet under some old hats. If the book doesn't make him laugh outright it makes him cry. When he gets excited over something he's reading in his fat book, his eyes roll, his mouth gets wet, and he tries to talk through his thick tongue, though all Abramowitz hears is geee, gooo, gaaa, gaaw. Always these words, whatever they mean, and sometimes gool goon geek gonk, in various combinations, usually gool with gonk, which Abramowitz thinks means Goldberg. And in such states he has been known to kick Abramowitz in the belly with his heavy boot. Ooof.

When he laughs he sounds like a horse, or maybe it's the way I hear him with these ears. And though he laughs once in a while, it doesn't make my life easier, because of my condition. I mean I think, Here I am in this horse. This is my theory though I have my doubts. Otherwise, Goldberg is a small stocky figure with a thick neck, heavy black brows, each like a small mustache, and big feet that swell in his shapeless boots. He washes his feet in the kitchen sink and hangs up his yellowed socks to dry on the white-washed walls of my stall. Phoo.

He likes to do card tricks.

In winter they live in the South in a small, messy, one-floor house with a horse's stall attached that Goldberg can approach, down a few steps, from the kitchen of the house. To get Abramowitz into the stall he is led up a plank from the outside and the door shuts on his rear end. To keep him from wandering all over the house there's a slatted gate to just under his head. Furthermore, the stall is next to the toilet and the broken water closet runs all night. It's a boring life with a deaf-mute except when Goldberg changes the act a little. Abramowitz enjoys it when they rehearse a new routine, although Goldberg hardly ever alters the lines, only the order of answer and question. That's better than nothing. Sometimes when Abramowitz gets tired of talking to himself, asking unanswered questions, he complains, shouts, calls the owner dirty names. He snorts, brays, whinnies shrilly. In his frustration he rears, rocks, gallops in his stall; but what good is a gallop if there's no place to go and Goldberg can't, or won't, hear complaints, pleas, protest?

Q. "Answer me this: If it's a sentence I'm serving, how long?"
A.

Once in a while Goldberg seems to sense somebody else's needs and is momentarily considerate of Abramowitz—combs and curries him, even rubs his bushy head against the horse's. He also shows interest in his diet and whether his bowel movements are regular and sufficient; but if Abramowitz gets sentimentally careless when the owner is close by and forms a question he can see on his lips, Goldberg punches him on the nose. Or threatens to. It doesn't hurt any the less.

All I know is he's a former vaudeville comic and acrobat. He did a solo act telling jokes with the help of a blind assistant before he went sad. That's about all he's ever tapped to me about himself. When I forgot myself and asked what happened then, he punched me in the nose.

Only once, when he was half drunk and giving me my bucket of water, I sneaked in a fast one which he answered before he knew it.

"Where did you get me, master? Did you buy me from somebody else? Maybe in some kind of auction?"

I FOUND YOU IN A CABBAGE PATCH.

Once he tapped my skull: "In the beginning was the word."

"Which word was that?"

Bong on the nose.

NO MORE QUESTIONS.

"Watch out for the wound on my head or whatever it is."

"Keep your trap shut or you'll lose your teeth."

Goldberg should read that story I once heard on his transistor radio, I thought to myself. It's about a poor cab driver driving his sledge in the Russian snow. His son, a fine promising lad, got sick with pneumonia and soon died, and the poor cabby can't find anybody to talk to so as to relieve his grief. Nobody wants to listen to his troubles, because that's the way it is in the world. When he opens his mouth to say a word, the customers insult him. So he finally tells the story to his bony nag in the stable, and the horse, munching oats, listens as the weeping old man tells him about his boy that he has just buried.

Something like that could happen to you, Goldberg, and you'd be a lot kinder to whoever I am.

"Will you ever free me out of here, master?"

I'LL FLAY YOU ALIVE, YOU BASTARD HORSE.

We have this act we do together. Goldberg calls it "Ask Me Another," an ironic title where I am concerned.

In the sideshow days people used to stand among the bearded ladies, the blobby fat men, Joey the snake boy, and other freaks, laughing beyond belief at Abramowitz talking. He remembers one man staring into his mouth to see who's hiding there. Homunculus? Others suggested it was a ventriloquist's act even though the horse told them Goldberg was a deaf-mute. But in the main tent the act got thunderous storms of applause. Reporters pleaded for permission to interview Abramowitz and he had plans to spill all, but Goldberg wouldn't allow it. "His head will swell up too big," Abramowitz said for him. "He will never be able to wear the same size hat he wore last summer."

For the performance the owner dresses up in a balloony red-and-white polka-dot clown's suit with a pointed clown's cap and has borrowed a ringmaster's snaky whip, an item Abramowitz is skittish of though Goldberg says it's nothing to worry about, little more than decoration in a circus act. No animal act is without one. People like to hear the snap. He also ties an upside-down feather duster on Abramowitz's head that makes him look like a wilted unicorn. The five-piece circus band ends its brassy "Overture to *William Tell*"; there's a flourish of trumpets, and Goldberg cracks the whip as Abramowitz, with his loose-feathered, upside-down duster, trots once around the spotlit ring and stops at attention, facing clown-Goldberg, his left foreleg pawing the sawdust-covered earth. They then begin the act; Goldberg's ruddy face, as he opens his painted mouth to express himself, flushes dark red, and his melancholy eyes under black brows protrude as he painfully squeezes out the abominable sounds, his only eloquence:

"Geee gooo gaaa gaaw?"

Abramowitz's resonant, beautifully timed response is:

A. "To get to the other side."

There's a gasp from the spectators, a murmur, perhaps of puzzlement, and a moment of intense expectant silence. Then at a roll of the drums Goldberg snaps his long whip and Abramowitz translates the owner's idiocy into something that makes sense and somehow fulfills expectations; though in truth it's no more than a question following a response already given.

Q. "Why does a chicken cross the road?"

Then they laugh. And do they laugh! They pound each other in merriment. You'd think this trite riddle, this sad excuse for a joke, was the first they had heard in their lives. And they're laughing at the translated question, of course, not at the answer, which is the way Goldberg has set it up. That's his nature for you. It's the only way he works.

Abramowitz used to sink into the dumps after that, knowing what really amuses everybody is not the old-fashioned tired conundrum but the fact it's put to them by a talking horse. That's what splits the gut.

"It's a stupid little question."

"There are no better," Goldberg said.

"You could try letting me ask one or two of my own."

YOU KNOW WHAT A GELDING IS?

I gave him no reply. Two can play at that game.

After the first applause both performers take a low bow. Abramowitz trots around the ring, his head with panache held high. And when Goldberg again cracks the pudgy whip, he moves nervously to the center of the ring and they go through the routine of the other infantile answers and questions in the same silly ass-backwards order. After each question Abramowitz runs around the ring as the spectators cheer.

A. "To hold up his pants."

Q. "Why does a fireman wear red suspenders?"

A. "Columbus."

Q. "What was the first bus to cross the Atlantic?"

A. "A newspaper."

Q. "What's black and white and red all over?"

We did a dozen like that, and when we finished up, Goldberg cracked the foolish whip, I galloped a couple more times around the ring, then we took our last bows.

Goldberg pats my steaming flank and in the ocean-roar of everyone in the tent applauding and shouting bravo, we leave the ring, running down the ramp to our quarters, Goldberg's personal wagon van and attached stall; after that we're private parties till tomorrow's show. Many customers used to come night after night to watch the performance, and they laughed at the riddles though they had known them from childhood. That's how the season goes, and nothing much has changed one way or the other except that recently Goldberg added a couple of silly elephant riddles to modernize the act.

A. "From playing marbles."
Q. "Why do elephants have wrinkled knees?"
A. "To pack their dirty laundry in."
Q. "Why do elephants have long trunks?"

Neither Goldberg nor I think much of the new jokes but they're the latest style. I reflect that we could do the act without jokes. All you need is a free talking horse.

One day Abramowitz thought he would make up a question-response of his own—it's not that hard to do. So that night after they had finished the routine, he slipped in his new riddle.

A. "To greet his friend the chicken."
Q. "Why does a yellow duck cross the road?"

After a moment of confused silence everybody cracked up; they beat themselves silly with their fists—broken straw boaters flew all over the place; but Goldberg in unbelieving astonishment glowered murderously at the horse. His ruddy face turned purple. When he cracked the whip it sounded like a river of ice breaking. Realizing in fright that he had gone too far, Abramowitz, baring his big teeth, reared up on his hind legs and took several steps forward against his will. But the spectators, thinking this was an extra flourish at the end of the act, applauded wildly. Goldberg's anger eased, and lowering his whip, he pretended to chuckle. Amid continuing applause he beamed at Abramowitz as if he were his only child and could do no wrong, though Abramowitz, in his heart of hearts, knew the owner was furious.

"Don't forget WHO'S WHO, you insane horse," Goldberg, his back to the audience, tapped out on Abramowitz's nose.

He made him gallop once more around the ring, mounted him in an acrobatic leap onto his bare back, and drove him madly to the exit.

Afterwards he Morse-coded with his hard knuckle on the horse's bony head that if he pulled anything like that again he would personally deliver him to the glue factory.

WHERE THEY WILL MELT YOU DOWN TO SIZE. "What's left over goes into dog food."

"It was just a joke, master," Abramowitz explained.

"To say the answer was O.K., but not to ask the question by yourself."

Out of stored-up bitterness the talking horse replied, "I did it on account of it made me feel free."

At that Goldberg whacked him hard across the neck with his murderous cane. Abramowitz, choking, staggered but did not bleed.

"Don't, master," he gasped, "not on my old wound."

Goldberg went into slow motion, still waving the cane.

"Try it again, you tub of guts, and I'll be wearing a horsehide coat with fur collar, gool, goon, geek, gonk." Spit crackled in the corners of his mouth.

Understood.

Sometimes I think of myself as an idea, yet here I stand in this filthy stall, my hooves sunk in my yellow balls of dreck. I feel old, disgusted with myself, smelling the odor of my bad breath as my teeth in the feedbag grind the hard oats into a foaming lump, while Goldberg smokes his panatela as he watches TV. He feeds me well enough, if oats are your dish, but hasn't had my stall cleaned for a week. It's easy to get even on a horse if that's the type you are.

So the act goes on every matinee and night, keeping Goldberg in good spirits and thousands in stitches, but Abramowitz had dreams of being in the open. They were strange dreams—if dreams; he isn't sure what they are or come from—hidden thoughts, maybe, of freedom, or some sort of self-mockery? You let yourself conceive what can't be? Anyhow, whoever heard of a talking horse's dreams? Goldberg hasn't said he knows what's going on but Abramowitz suspects he understands more than he seems to, because when the horse, lying in his dung and soiled straw, awakens from a dangerous reverie, he hears the owner muttering in his sleep in deaf-mute talk.

Abramowitz dreams, or something of the sort, of other lives he might live, let's say of a horse that can't talk, couldn't conceive the idea; is perfectly content to be simply a horse without speech. He sees himself, for instance, pulling a wagonload of yellow apples along a rural road. There are leafy beech trees on both sides and beyond them broad green fields full of wild flowers. If he were that kind of horse, maybe he might retire to graze in such fields. More adventurously, he sees himself a racehorse in goggles, thundering down the last stretch of muddy track, slicing through a wedge of other galloping horses to win by a nose at the finish; and the jockey is definitely not Goldberg. There is no jockey; he fell off.

Or if not a racehorse, if he has to be practical about it, Abramowitz continues on as a talking horse but not in circus work any longer; and every night on the stage he recites poetry. The theater is packed and people cry out oooh and aaah, what beautiful things that horse is saying.

Sometimes he thinks of himself as altogether a free "man,"

someone of indeterminate appearance and characteristics, who is maybe a doctor or lawyer helping poor people. Not a bad idea for a useful life.

But even if I am dreaming or whatever it is, I hear Goldberg talking in *my* sleep. He talks something like me:

As for number one, you are first and last a talking horse, not any nag that can't talk; and believe me I have got nothing against you that you *can* talk, Abramowitz, but on account of what you say when you open your mouth and break the rules.

As for a racehorse, if you take a good look at the broken-down type you are—overweight, with big sagging belly and a thick uneven dark coat that won't shine up no matter how much I comb or brush you, and four hairy, thick, bent legs, plus a pair of slight cross-eyes, you would give up that foolish idea you can be a racehorse before you do something very ridiculous.

As for reciting poetry, who wants to hear a horse recite poetry? That's for the birds.

As for the last dream, or whatever it is that's bothering you, that you can be a doctor or lawyer, you better forget it, it's not that kind of a world. A horse is a horse even if he's a talking horse; don't mix yourself up with human beings if you know what I mean. If you're a talking horse that's your fate. I warn you, don't try to be a wise guy, Abramowitz. Don't try to know everything, you might go mad. Nobody can know everything; it's not that kind of world. Follow the rules of the game. Don't rock the boat. Don't try to make a monkey out of me; I know more than you. It's my nature. We have to be who we are, although this is rough on both of us. But that's the logic of the situation. It goes by certain laws even though that's a hard proposition for some to understand. The law is the law, you can't change the order. That's the way things stay put together. We are mutually related, Abramowitz, and that's all there is to it. If it makes you feel any better, I will admit to you I can't live without you, and I won't let you live without me. I have my living to make and you are my talking horse I use in my act to earn my living, plus so I can take care of your needs. The true freedom, like I have always told you, though you never want to believe me, is to understand that and don't waste your energy resisting the rules; if so you waste your life. All you are is a horse who talks, and believe me, there are very few horses that can do that; so if you are smart, Abramowitz, it should make you happy instead of always and continually dissatisfied. Don't break up the act if you know what's good for you.

As for those yellow balls of your dreck, if you will behave yourself like a gentleman and watch out what you say, tomorrow the shovelers will come and after I will hose you down personally with warm water. Believe me, there's nothing like cleanliness.

Thus he mocks me in my sleep though I have my doubts that I sleep much nowadays.

In short hops between towns and small cities the circus moves in wagon vans. The other horses pull them, but Goldberg won't let me, which again wakes disturbing ideas in my head. For longer hauls, from one big city to another, we ride in red-and-white-striped circus trains. I have a stall in a freight car with some non-talking horses with fancy braided manes and sculptured tails from the bareback rider's act. None of us are much interested in each other. If they think at all they think a talking horse is a show-off. All they do is eat and drink, piss and crap. Not a single word goes back or forth among them. Nobody has a good or bad idea.

The long train rides generally give us a day off without a show, and Goldberg gets depressed and surly when we're not working the matinee or evening performance. Early in the morning of a long train-ride day he starts loving his bottle and Morse-coding me nasty remarks and threats.

"Abramowitz, you think too much, why do you bother? In the

first place your thoughts come out of you and you don't know that much, so your thoughts don't either. In other words don't get too ambitious. For instance, what's on your mind right now, tell me?"

"Answers and questions, master—some new ones to modernize the act."

"Feh, we don't need any new ones, the act is already too long."

He should know the questions I am really asking myself, though better not.

Once you start asking questions one leads to the next and in the end it's endless. And what if it turns out I'm always asking myself the same question in different words? I keep on wanting to know why I can't ask this coarse lout a simple question about *anything.* By now I have it figured out Goldberg is afraid of questions because a question could show he's afraid people will find out who he is. Somebody who all he does is repeat his fate. Anyway, Goldberg has some kind of past he is afraid to tell me about, though sometimes he hints. And when I mention my own past he says forget it. Concentrate on the future. What future? On the other hand, what does he think he can hide from Abramowitz, a student by nature, who spends most of his time asking himself questions Goldberg won't permit him to ask, putting one and one together, and finally making up his mind— miraculous thought—that he knows more than a horse should, even a talking horse, so therefore, given all the built-up evidence, he is positively not a horse. Not in origin anyway.

So I came once more to the conclusion that I am a man in a horse and not just a horse that happens to be able to talk. I had figured this out in my mind before; then I said, no it can't be. I feel more like a horse bodywise; on the other hand I talk, I think, I wish to ask questions. So I am what I am. Something tells me there is no such thing as a talking horse, even though Goldberg, pointing his fat finger at me, says the opposite. He lives on his lies, it's his nature.

After long days of traveling, when they were in their new quarters one night, finding the rear door to his stall unlocked— Goldberg grew careless when depressed—acting on belief as well as impulse, Abramowitz cautiously backed out. Avoiding the front of Goldberg's wagon van he trotted across the fairgrounds on which the circus was situated. Two of the circus hands who saw him trot by, perhaps because Abramowitz greeted them, "Hello, boys, marvelous evening," did not attempt to stop him. Outside the grounds, though exhilarated to be in the open, Abramowitz began to wonder if he was doing a foolish thing. He had hoped to find a wooded spot to hide in for the time being, surrounded by fields in which he could peacefully graze; but this was the industrial edge of the city, and though he clop-clopped from street to street there were no woods nearby, not even a small park.

Where can somebody who looks like a horse go by himself?

Abramowitz tried to hide in an old riding-school stable but was driven out by an irate woman. In the end they caught up with him on a station platform where he had been waiting for a train. Quite foolishly, he knew. The conductor wouldn't let him get on though Abramowitz had explained his predicament. The stationmaster ran out and pointed a pistol at his head. He held the horse there, deaf to his blandishments, until Goldberg arrived with his bamboo cane. The owner threatened to whip Abramowitz to the quick, and his description of the effects was so painfully lurid that Abramowitz felt as though he had been slashed into a bleeding pulp. A half hour later he found himself back in his locked stall, his throbbing head encrusted with dried horse blood. Goldberg ranted in deaf-mute talk, but Abramowitz, who with lowered head pretended contrition, felt none. To escape Goldberg he must first get out of the horse he was in.

But to exit a horse as a man takes some doing. Abramowitz planned to proceed slowly and appeal to public opinion. It might take months, possibly years, to do what he must. Protest! Sabotage if necessary! Revolt! One night after they had taken their bows and the applause was subsiding, Abramowitz, raising his head as though to whinny his appreciation of the plaudits, cried out to all assembled in the circus tent, "Help! Get me out of here, somebody! I am a prisoner in this horse! Free a fellow man!"

After a silence that grew like a dense forest, Goldberg, who was standing to the side, unaware of Abramowitz's passionate outcry—he picked up the news later from another ringmaster—saw at once from everybody's surprised and startled expression, not to mention Abramowitz's undisguised look of triumph, that something had gone seriously amiss. The owner at once began to laugh heartily, as though whatever was going on was more of the same, part of the act, a bit of personal encore by the horse. The spectators laughed too, again warmly applauding.

"It won't do you any good," the owner Morse-coded Abramowitz afterwards. "Because nobody is going to believe you."

"Then please let me out of here on your own account, master. Have some mercy."

"About that matter," Goldberg rapped out sternly, "I am already on record. Our lives and livings are dependent each on the other. You got nothing substantial to complain about, Abramowitz. I'm taking care on you better than you could take care on yourself."

"Maybe that's so, Mr. Goldberg, but what good is it if in my heart I am a man and not a talking horse?"

Goldberg's ruddy face blanched as he Morse-coded the usual NO QUESTIONS.

"I'm not asking, I'm trying to tell you something very serious."

"Watch out for your hubris, Abramowitz."

That night the owner went out on the town, came back dreadfully drunk, as though he had been lying with his mouth open under a spigot pouring brandy; and he threatened Abramowitz with the trident spear he kept in his trunk when they traveled. This is a new torment.

Anyway, the act goes on but definitely altered, not as before. Abramowitz, despite numerous warnings and various other painful threats, daily disturbs the routine. After Goldberg makes his idiot noises, his geee gooo gaaa gaaw, Abramowitz purposely mixes up the responses to the usual ridiculous riddles.

A. "To get to the other side."

Q. "Why does a fireman wear red suspenders?"

A. "From playing marbles."

Q. "Why do elephants have long trunks?"

And he adds dangerous A.'s and Q.'s without permission despite the inevitability of punishment.

A. "A talking horse."

Q. "What has four legs and wishes to be free?"

At that nobody laughed.

He also mocked Goldberg when the owner wasn't attentively reading his lips; called him "deaf-mute," "stupid ears," "lock mouth"; and whenever possible addressed the public, requesting, urging, begging their assistance.

"Gevalt! Get me out of here! I am one of you! This is slavery! I wish to be free!"

Now and then when Goldberg's back was turned, or when he was too lethargic with melancholy to be much attentive, Abramowitz clowned around and in other ways ridiculed the owner. He heehawed at his appearance, brayed at his "talk," stupidity, arrogance. Sometimes he made up little songs of freedom as he jigged on his hind legs, exposing his private parts. And at times Goldberg, to mock the mocker, danced gracelessly with him—a clown with a glum-painted smile, waltzing with a horse. Those who had seen the act last season were astounded, stunned by the change, uneasy, as though the future threatened.

"Help! Help, somebody help me!" Abramowitz pleaded. Nobody moved.

Sensing the tension in and around the ring, the audience sometimes booed the performers, causing Goldberg, in his red-and-white polka-dot suit and white clown's cap, great embarrassment, though on the whole he kept his cool during the act and never used the ringmaster's whip. In fact he smiled as he was insulted, whether he "listened" or not. He heard what he saw. A sly smile was fixed on his face and his lips twitched. And though his fleshy ears flared like torches at the gibes and mockeries he endured, Goldberg laughed to the verge of tears at Abramowitz's sallies and shenanigans; many in the big tent laughed along with him. Abramowitz was furious.

Afterwards Goldberg, once he had stepped out of his clown suit, threatened him to the point of collapse, or flayed him viciously with his cane; and the next day fed him pep pills and painted his hide black before the performance so that people wouldn't see his wounds.

"You bastard horse, you'll lose us our living."

"I wish to be free."

"To be free you got to know when you are free. Considering your type, Abramowitz, you'll be free in the glue factory."

One night when Goldberg, after a day of profound depression, was listless and logy in the ring, could not evoke so much as a limp snap out of his whip, Abramowitz, thinking that where the future was concerned, glue factory or his present condition of life made little difference, determined to escape either fate; he gave a solo performance for freedom, the best of his career. Though desperate, he entertained, made up hilarious riddles: A. "By jumping through the window." Q. "How do you end the pane?"; he recited poems he had heard on Goldberg's radio, which sometimes stayed on all night after the owner had fallen asleep; he also told stories and ended the evening with a moving speech.

He told sad stories of the lot of horses, one, for instance, beaten to death by his cruel owner, his brains battered with a log because he was too weakened by hunger to pull a wagonload of wood. Another concerned a racehorse of fabulous speed, a sure winner in the Kentucky Derby, had he not in his very first race been doped by his avaricious master, who had placed a fortune in bets on the next best horse. A third was about a fabulous flying horse shot down by a hunter who couldn't believe his eyes. And then Abramowitz told a story of a youth of great promise who, out for a stroll one spring day, came upon a goddess bathing naked in a stream. As he gazed at her beauty in amazement and longing, she let out a piercing scream to the sky. The youth took off at a fast gallop, realizing from the snorting, and sound of pounding hoofs as he ran, that he was no longer a youth of great promise, but a horse running.

Abramowitz then cried out to the faces that surrounded him, "I also am a man in a horse. Is there a doctor in the house?"

Dead silence.

"Maybe a magician?"

No response but nervous tittering.

He then delivered an impassioned speech on freedom for all. Abramowitz talked his brains blue, ending once more with a personal appeal. "Help me to recover my original form. It's not what I am but what I wish to be. I wish to be what I really am, which is a man."

At the end of the act many people in the tent were standing wet-eyed and the band played "The Star-Spangled Banner."

Goldberg, who had been dozing in a sawdust pile for a good part of Abramowitz's solo act, roused himself in time to join the horse in a bow. Afterwards, on the enthusiastic advice of the new circus manager, he changed the name of the act from "Ask Me Another" to "Goldberg's Varieties." And wept himself for unknown reasons.

Back in the stall after the failure of his most passionate, most inspired, pleas for assistance, Abramowitz butted his head in frustration against the stall gate until his nostrils bled into the feedbag. He thought he would drown in the blood and didn't much care. Goldberg found him lying on the floor in the dirty straw, in a deep faint, and revived him with aromatic spirits of ammonia. He bandaged his nose and spoke to him in a fatherly fashion.

"That's how the mop flops," he Morse-coded with his blunt fingertip, "but things could be worse. Take my advice and settle for a talking horse, it's not without distinction."

"Make me either into a man or make me into a horse," Abramowitz pleaded. "It's in your power, Goldberg."

"You got the wrong party, my friend."

"Why do you always say lies?"

"Why do you always ask questions you can't ask?"

"I ask because I am. Because I wish to be free."

"So who's free, tell me?" Goldberg mocked.

"If so," said Abramowitz, "what's to be done?"

DON'T ASK, I WARNED YOU.

He warned he would punch his nose; it bled again.

Abramowitz later that day began a hunger strike which he carried on for the better part of a week; but Goldberg threatened force-feeding with thick rubber tubes in both nostrils, and that ended that. Abramowitz almost choked to death at the thought of it. The act went on as before, and the owner changed its name back to "Ask Me Another." When the season was over the circus headed south, Abramowitz trotting along in a cloud of dust with the other horses.

Anyway I got my own thoughts.

One fine autumn, after a long hard summer, Goldberg washed his big feet in the kitchen sink and hung his smelly socks to dry on the gate of Abramowitz's stall before sitting down to watch astronomy on ETV. To see better he placed a lit candle on top of the color set. But he had carelessly left the stall gate open, and Abramowitz hopped up three steps and trotted through the messy kitchen, his eyes flaring. Confronting Goldberg staring in awe at the universe on the screen, he reared with a bray of rage, to bring his hoofs down on the owner's head. Goldberg, seeing him out of the corner of his eye, rose to protect himself. Instantly jumping up on the chair, he managed with a grunt to grab Abramowitz by both big ears as though to lift him by them, and the horse's head and neck, up to an old wound, came off in his hands. Amid the stench of blood and bowel a man's pale head popped out of the hole in the horse. He was in his early forties, with fogged pince-nez, intense dark eyes, and a black mustache. Pulling his arms free, he grabbed Goldberg around his thick neck with both bare arms and held on for dear life. As they tugged and struggled, Abramowitz, straining to the point of madness, slowly pulled himself out of the horse up to his navel. At that moment Goldberg broke his frantic grip and, though the astronomy lesson was still going on in a blaze of light, disappeared. Abramowitz later made a few discreet inquiries, but no one could say where.

Departing the circus grounds, he cantered across a grassy soft field into a dark wood, a free centaur.